PENGUIN MODERN CLASSICS

THE COUNTERFEITERS

André Paul Guillaume Gide was born in Paris on 22 November 1869. His father, who died when he was eleven, was Professor of Law at the Sorbonne. An only child, Gide had an irregular and lonely upbringing and was educated in a Protestant secondary school in Paris and privately. He became devoted to literature and music, and began his literary career as an essayist, and then went on to poetry, biography, fiction, drama, criticism, reminiscence, and translation. By 1917 he had emerged as a prophet to French youth and his unorthodox views were a source of endless debate and attack. In 1947 he was awarded the Nobel Prize for Literature and in 1948, as a distinguished foreigner, was given an honorary degree at Oxford. He married his cousin in 1892; he died in Paris in 1951 at the age of eighty-one.

Gide's best-known works in England are *Strait is the Gate* (*La Porte étroite*), the first novel he wrote, which was published in France in 1909; *The Immoralist* (*L'Immoraliste*), 1902; *The Counterfeiters* (*Les Faux-Monnayeurs*), 1925; and the famous *Journals* covering his life from 1889 to 1949 and published in four volumes.

ANDRÉ GIDE

The Counterfeiters

TRANSLATED FROM THE FRENCH BY

DOROTHY BUSSY

PENGUIN BOOKS

Penguin Books Ltd, Harmondsworth, Middlesex, England
Viking Penguin Inc., 40 West 23rd Street, New York, New York 10010, U.S.A.
Penguin Books Australia Ltd, Ringwood, Victoria, Australia
Penguin Books Canada Limited, 2801 John Street, Markham, Ontario, Canada L3R 1B4
Penguin Books (N.Z.) Ltd, 182–190 Wairau Road, Auckland 10, New Zealand

—

Les Faux-Monnayeurs first published in France 1925
This translation first published by Cassell 1931
Published in Penguin Books 1966
Reprinted 1971, 1973, 1975, 1978, 1982, 1985, 1987

—

—

Set, printed and bound in Great Britain by
Cox & Wyman Ltd, Reading
Set in Monotype Garamond

CONTENTS

FIRST PART: PARIS

SECOND PART: SAAS-FÉE

CONTENTS

I DEDICATE

THIS, MY FIRST NOVEL,

TO

ROGER MARTIN DU GARD

IN TOKEN OF PROFOUND

FRIENDSHIP

A.G.

FIRST PART

PARIS

I

THE LUXEMBOURG GARDENS

'THE time has now come for me to hear a step in the passage,' said Bernard to himself. He raised his head and listened. Nothing! His father and elder brother were away at the law-courts; his mother paying visits; his sister at a concert; as for his small brother Caloub – the youngest – he was safely shut up for the whole afternoon in his day-school. Bernard Profitendieu had stayed at home to cram for his *bachot**; he had only three more weeks before him. His family respected his solitude – not so the demon! Although Bernard had stripped off his coat, he was stifling. The window that looked on to the street stood open, but it let in nothing but heat. His forehead was streaming. A drop of perspiration came dripping from his nose and fell on to the letter he was holding in his hand.

'Pretending to be a tear!' thought he. 'But it's better to sweat than to weep.'

Yes; the date was conclusive. No one could be in question but him, Bernard himself. Impossible to doubt it. The letter was addressed to his mother – a love-letter – seventeen years old, unsigned.

'What can this initial stand for? A "V"? It might just as well be an "N" . . . Would it be becoming to question my mother? . . . We must give her credit for good taste. I'm free to imagine he's a prince. It wouldn't advance matters much to know that I was the son of a rapscallion. There's no better cure for the fear of taking after one's father, than not to know who he is. The mere fact of inquiry binds one. The only thing to do is to welcome deliverance and not attempt to go any deeper. Besides which, I've had sufficient for the day.'

Bernard folded the letter up again. It was on paper of the same size and shape as the other twelve in the packet. They were tied up with pink ribbon which there had been no need for him to untie, and which he was easily able to slip round the bundle

* Schoolboy's slang for the *baccalauréat* examination.

again to keep it tight. He put the bundle back into the casket and the casket back into the drawer of the console table. The drawer was not open. It had yielded its secret from above. Bernard fitted together the pieces of wood which formed its top, and which were made to support a heavy slab of onyx, readjusted the slab carefully and gently, and put back in their places on the top, a pair of glass candelabra and a cumbersome clock, which he had been amusing himself by repairing.

The clock struck four. He had set it to the right time.

'His Honour the judge and his learned son the barrister will not be back before six. I shall have time. When His Honour comes in he must find a letter from me on his writing table, informing him in eloquent terms of my departure. But before I write it, I feel that it's absolutely essential to air my mind a little. I must talk to my dear Olivier, and make certain of a perch – at any rate a temporary one. Olivier, my friend, the time has come for *me* to put your good-fellowship to the test, and for *you* to show your mettle. The fine thing about our friendship so far has been that we have never made any use of one another. Pooh! it can't be unpleasant to ask a favour that's amusing to grant. The tiresome thing is that Olivier won't be alone. Never mind! I shall have to take him aside. I want to appal him by my calm. It's when things are most extraordinary that I feel most at home.'

The street where Bernard Profitendieu had lived until then was quite close to the Luxembourg Gardens. There, in the path that overlooks the Medici fountains, some of his schoolfellows were in the habit of meeting every Wednesday afternoon, between four and six. The talk was of art, philosophy, sport, politics and literature. Bernard walked to the gardens quickly, but as soon as he caught sight of Olivier Molinier through the railings, he slackened his pace. The gathering that day was more numerous than usual – because of the fine weather, no doubt. Some of the boys who were there were newcomers, whom Bernard had never seen before. Every one of them, as soon as he was in company with the others, lost his naturalness and began to act a part.

Olivier blushed when he saw Bernard coming up. He left the side of a young woman to whom he had been talking and walked away a little abruptly. Bernard was his most intimate friend, so that he took great pains not to show that he liked being with him; sometimes he would even pretend not to see him.

Before joining him, Bernard had to run the gauntlet of several groups and, as he himself affected not to be looking for Olivier, he lingered among the others.

Four of his schoolfellows were surrounding a little fellow with a beard and a pince-nez, who was perceptibly older than the rest. This was Dhurmer. He was holding a book and addressing one boy in particular, though at the same time he was obviously delighted that the others were listening.

'I can't help it,' he was saying, 'I've got as far as page thirty without coming across a single colour or a single word that makes a picture. He speaks of a woman and I don't know whether her dress was red or blue. As far as I'm concerned, if there are no colours, it's useless, I can see nothing.' And feeling that the less he was taken in earnest, the more he must exaggerate, he repeated: '– absolutely nothing!'

Bernard stopped attending; he thought it would be ill-mannered to walk away too quickly, but he began to listen to some others who were quarrelling behind him and who had been joined by Olivier after he had left the young woman; one of them was sitting on a bench, reading *L'Action Française*.

Amongst all these youths how grave Olivier Molinier looks! And yet he was one of the youngest. His face, his expression, which are still almost a child's, reveal a mind older than his years. He blushes easily. There is something tender about him. But however gracious his manners, some kind of secret reserve, some kind of sensitive delicacy, keeps his schoolfellows at a distance. This is a grief to him. But for Bernard, it would be a greater grief still.

Molinier, like Bernard, had stayed a minute or two with each of the groups – out of a wish to be agreeable, not that anything he heard interested him. He leant over the reader's shoulder, and Bernard, without turning round, heard him say:

'You shouldn't read the papers – they'll give you apoplexy.'

The other replied tartly: 'As for you, the very name of Maurras makes you turn green.'

A third boy asked, deridingly: 'Do Maurras' articles amuse you?'

And the first answered: 'They bore me bloody well stiff, but I think he's right.'

Then a fourth, whose voice Bernard didn't recognize: 'Unless a thing bores you, you think there's no depth in it.'

'*You* seem to think that one's only got to be stupid to be funny.'

'Come along,' whispered Bernard, suddenly seizing Olivier by the arm and drawing him aside. 'Answer quickly. I'm in a hurry. You told me you didn't sleep on the same floor as your parents?'

'I've shown you the door of my room. It opens straight on to the staircase, half a floor below our flat.'

'Didn't you say your brother slept with you?'

'George. Yes.'

'Are you two alone?'

'Yes.'

'Can the youngster hold his tongue?'

'If necessary.'

'Listen. I've left home – or at any rate I'm going to this evening. I don't know where to go yet. Can you take me in for one night?'

Olivier turned very pale. His emotion was so great that he was hardly able to look at Bernard.

'Yes,' said he, 'but don't come before eleven. Mamma comes down to say good night to us and lock the door every evening.'

'But then...?'

Olivier smiled. 'I've got another key. You must knock softly, so as not to wake George if he's asleep.'

'Will the concierge let me in?'

'I'll warn him. Oh, I'm on very good terms with him. It's he who gives me the key. Good-bye! Till tonight!'

They parted without shaking hands. While Bernard was walking away, reflecting on the letter he meant to write for the magistrate to find when he came in, Olivier, not wishing it to be thought that Bernard was the only person he liked talking to in private, went up to Lucien Bercail, who was sitting by himself as usual, for he was generally left a little out of it by the others. Olivier would be very fond of him, if he didn't prefer Bernard. Lucien is as timid as Bernard is spirited. He cannot hide his weakness; he seems to live only with his head and his heart. He hardly ever dares to make advances, but when he sees Olivier coming towards him, he is beside himself with joy; Lucien writes poetry – everyone suspects as much; but I am pretty sure that Olivier is the only person to whom Lucien talks of his ideas. They walked together to the edge of the terrace.

'What I should like,' said Lucien, 'would be to tell the story – no, not of a person, but of a place – well, for instance, of a garden path, like this – just tell what happens in it from morning to evening. First of all, come the children's nurses and the children, and the babies' nurses with ribbons in their caps.... No, no ... first of all, people who are grey all over and ageless and sexless and who come to sweep the path, and water the grass, and change the flowers – in fact, to set the stage and get ready the scenery before the opening of the gates. D'you see? *Then* the nurses come in ... the kids make mud-pies and squabble; the nurses smack them. Then the little boys come out of school; then there are the workgirls; then the poor people who eat their scrap upon a bench, and later people come to meet each other, and others avoid each other, and others go by themselves – dreamers. And then when the band plays and the shops close, there's the crowd.... Students, like us; in the evening, lovers who embrace – others who cry at parting. And at the end, when the day is over, there's an old couple ... And suddenly the drum beats. Closing time! Everyone goes off. The play is ended. Do you understand? Something which gives the impression of the end of everything – of death ... but without mentioning death, of course.'

'Yes, I see it all perfectly,' said Olivier, who was thinking of Bernard and had not listened to a word.

'And that's not all,' went on Lucien, enthusiastically; 'I should like to have a kind of epilogue and show the same garden path at night, after everyone has gone, deserted and much more beautiful than in the daytime. In the deep silence; all the natural sounds intensified – the sound of the fountain, and the wind in the trees, and the song of a night-bird. First of all, I thought that I'd bring in some ghosts to wander about – or perhaps some statues – but I think that would be more common-place. What do you say?'

'No, no! No statues, no statues!' said Olivier absent-mindedly; and then, seeing the other's disappointed face: 'Well, old fellow, if you bring it off, it'll be splendid!' he exclaimed warmly.

2

THE PROFITENDIEUS

There is no trace in Poussin's letters of any feeling of obligation towards his parents.

He never in later days showed any regret at having left them; transplanted to Rome of his own free will, he lost all desire to return to his home – and even, it would seem, all recollection of it.

PAUL DESJARDINS: *Poussin*

MONSIEUR PROFITENDIEU was in a hurry to get home and wished that his colleague Molinier, who was keeping him company up the Boulevard St Germain, would walk a little faster. Albéric Profitendieu had just had an unusually heavy day at the law-courts; an uncomfortable sensation in his right side was causing him some uneasiness; fatigue in his case usually went to his liver, which was his weak point. He was thinking of his bath; nothing rested him better after the cares of the day than a good bath – with an eye to which he had taken no tea that afternoon, esteeming it imprudent to get into any sort of water – even warm – with a loaded stomach. Merely a prejudice perhaps; but prejudices are the props of civilization. Oscar Molinier walked as quickly as he could and made every effort to keep up with his companion; but he was much shorter than Profitendieu and his crural development was slighter; besides which there was a little fatty accumulation round his heart and he easily became short-winded. Profitendieu, who was still sound at the age of fifty-five, with a well-developed chest and a brisk gait, would have gladly given him the slip; but he was very particular as to the proprieties; his colleague was older than he and higher up in the career; respect was due to him. And besides, since the death of his wife's parents, Profitendieu had a very considerable fortune to be forgiven him, whereas Monsieur Molinier – who was *Président de chambre*, had nothing but his salary – a derisory salary, utterly disproportionate to the high situation he filled with dignity, which was all the more imposing because of the mediocrity it cloaked. Profitendieu concealed his impatience; he turned to Molinier and looked at him mopping himself; for that matter, he was exceedingly interested by what Molinier was saying; but their point of view was not the same and the discussion was beginning to get warm.

'Have the house watched, by all means,' said Molinier. 'Get the reports of the concierge and the sham maidservant – very good! But mind, if you push the inquiry too far, the affair will be taken out of your hands. . . . I mean there's a risk of your being led on much further than you bargained for.'

'Justice should have no such considerations.'

'Tut, tut, my dear sir; you and I know very well what justice ought to be and what it is. We're all agreed that we act for the best, but, however we act, we never get nearer than an approximation. The case before us now is a particularly delicate one. Out of the fifteen accused persons – or persons who at a word from you will be accused tomorrow – nine are minors. And some of these boys, as you know, come of very honourable families. In such circumstances, I consider that to issue a warrant at all would be the greatest mistake. The newspapers will get hold of the affair and you open the door to every sort of blackmail and calumny. In spite of all your efforts you'll not prevent names from coming out. . . . It's no business of mine to give you advice – on the contrary – it's much more my place to receive it. You're well aware how highly I've always rated your lucidity and your fair-mindedness. . . . But if I were you, this is what I should do: I should try to put an end to this abominable scandal by laying hold of the four or five instigators. . . . Yes! I know they're difficult to catch; but what the deuce, that's part of our trade. I should have the flat – the scene of the orgies – closed, and I should take steps for the brazen young rascals' parents to be informed of the affair – quietly and secretly; and merely in order to avoid any repetition of the scandal. Oh! as to the women, collar *them* by all means. I'm entirely with you there. We seem to be up against a set of creatures of unspeakable perversity, and society should be cleansed of them at all costs. But, let me repeat, leave the boys alone; content yourself with giving them a fright, and then hush the matter up with some vague term like "youthful indiscretion". Their astonishment at having got off so cheaply will last them for a long time to come. Remember that three of them are not fourteen years old and that their parents no doubt consider them angels of purity and innocence. But really, my dear fellow, between ourselves, come now, did *we* think of women when we were that age?'

He came to a stop, breathless rather with talking than with walking, and forced Profitendieu, whose sleeve he was holding, to stop too.

'Or if we thought of them,' he went on, 'it was ideally – mystically – religiously, if I may say so. The boys of today, don't you think, have no ideals – no! no ideals. . . . Apropos, how are yours? Of course, I'm not alluding to them when I speak so. I know that with your careful bringing-up – with the education you've given them, there's no fear of any such reprehensible follies.'

And indeed, up to that time, Profitendieu had had every reason to be satisfied with his sons. But he was without illusions – the best education in the world was of no avail against bad instincts. God be praised, *his* children had no bad instincts – nor Molinier's either, no doubt; they were their own protectors against bad companions and bad books. For of what use is it to forbid what we can't prevent? If books are forbidden, children read them on the sly. His own plan was perfectly simple – he didn't forbid bad books, but he so managed that his children had no desire to read them. As for the matter in question, he would think it over again, and in any case, he promised Molinier to do nothing without consulting him. He would simply give orders for a discreet watch to be kept, and as the thing had been going on for three months, it might just as well go on for another few days or weeks. Besides, the summer holidays were upon them and would necessarily disperse the delinquents. *Au revoir!*

At last Profitendieu was able to quicken his pace.

As soon as he got in, he hurried to his dressing-room and turned on the water for his bath. Antoine had been looking out for his master's return and managed to come across him in the passage.

This faithful manservant had been in the family for the last fifteen years; he had seen the children grow up. He had seen a great many things – and suspected a great many more; but he pretended not to notice anything his master wished to keep hidden.

Bernard was not without affection for Antoine; he had not wanted to leave the house without saying good-bye to him. Perhaps it was out of irritation against his family that he made a point of confiding to a servant that he was going away, when none of his own people knew it; but, in excuse for Bernard, it must be pointed out that none of his own people were at that time in the house. And besides, Bernard could not have said good-bye to them without the risk of being detained. Whereas to Antoine, he could simply say: 'I'm going away.' But as he said it, he put out his hand with such a solemn air that the old servant was astonished.

'Not coming back to dinner, Master Bernard?'

'Nor to sleep, Antoine.' And as Antoine hesitated, not knowing what he was expected to understand, nor whether he ought to ask any further questions, Bernard repeated still more meaningly: 'I'm going away'; then he added: 'I've left a letter for . . .' He couldn't bring himself to say 'Papa,' so he corrected his sentence to 'on the study writing-table. Good-bye.'

As he squeezed Antoine's hand, he felt as moved as if he were then and there saying good-bye to all his past life. He repeated 'good-bye' very quickly and then hurried off before the sob that was rising in his throat burst from him.

Antoine wondered whether it were not a heavy responsibility to let him go in this way – but how could he have prevented him?

That this departure of Bernard's would be a blow to the whole family – an unexpected – a monstrous blow – Antoine indeed was well aware; but his business as a perfect servant was to pretend to take it as a matter of course. It was not for him to know what Monsieur Profitendieu was ignorant of. No doubt, he might simply have said to him: 'Do you know, sir, that Master Bernard has gone away?' But by so saying, he would lose his advantage, and that was highly undesirable. If he awaited his master so impatiently, it was to drop out in a noncommittal, deferential voice, and as if it were a simple message left by Bernard, this sentence, which he had elaborately prepared beforehand:

'Before going away, sir, Master Bernard left a letter for you in the study' – a sentence so simple that there was a risk of its passing unperceived; he had racked his brains in vain for something which would be more striking, and had found nothing which would be at the same time natural. But as Bernard never left home, Profitendieu, whom Antoine was watching out of the corner of his eye, could not repress a start.

'Before going...'

He pulled himself up at once; it was not for him to show his astonishment before a subordinate; the consciousness of his superiority never left him. His tone as he continued was very calm – really magisterial.

'Thank you.' And as he went towards his study: 'Where did you say the letter was?'

'On the writing-table, sir.'

And in fact, as Profitendieu entered the room, he saw an envelope placed conspicuously opposite the chair in which he usually sat when writing; but Antoine was not to be choked off so easily, and Monsieur Profitendieu had not read two lines of the letter, when he heard a knock at the door.

'I forgot to tell you, sir, that there are two persons waiting to see you in the back drawing-room.'

'Who are they?'

'I don't know, sir.'

'Are they together?'

'They don't seem to be, sir.'

'What do they want?'

'I don't know. They want to see you, sir.'

Profitendieu felt his patience giving way.

'I have already said and repeated that I don't want to be disturbed when I'm at home – especially at this time of day; I have my consulting-room at the law-courts. Why did you let them in?'

'They both said they had something very urgent to say to you, sir.'

'Have they been here long?'

'Nearly an hour.'

Profitendieu took a few steps up and down the room, and passed one hand over his forehead; with the other he held Bernard's letter. Antoine stood at the door, dignified and impassive. At last, he had the joy of seeing the judge lose his temper and of hearing him for the first time in his life stamp his foot and scold angrily.

'Deuce take it all! Can't you leave me alone? Can't you leave me alone? Tell them I'm busy. Tell them to come another day.'

Antoine had no sooner left the room than Profitendieu ran to the door.

'Antoine! Antoine! And then go and turn off my bath.'

Much inclined for a bath, truly! He went up to the window and read:

SIR, – Owing to an accidental discovery I happened to make this afternoon, I have become aware that I must cease to regard you as my father. This is an immense relief to me. Realizing as I do how little affection I feel for you, I have for a long time past been thinking myself an unnatural son: I prefer knowing I am not your son at all. You will perhaps consider that I ought to be grateful to you for having treated me as if I were one of your own children; but, in the first place, I have always felt the difference between your behaviour to them and to me, and, secondly, I know you well enough to feel certain that you acted as you did because you were afraid of the scandal and because you wished to conceal a situation which did you no great honour – and, finally, because you could not have acted otherwise. I prefer to leave without seeing my mother again, because I am afraid that the emotion of bidding her a final good-bye might affect me too much and also because she might feel herself in a false position in my presence – which I should dislike. I doubt whether she has any very lively affection for me; as I was almost always away at school, she never had time to know much of me, and as the sight of me must have continually reminded her of an episode in her life which she would have liked to efface, I think my departure will be a relief and a pleasure to her. Tell her, if you have the courage to, that I bear her no grudge for having made a bastard of me; on the contrary, I prefer that to knowing I am your son. (Pray excuse me for writing in this way; it is not my object to insult you; but my words will give you an excuse for despising me and that will be a relief to you.)

If you wish me to keep silent as to the secret reasons which have induced me to leave your roof, I must beg you not to attempt to make me return to it. The decision I have taken is irrevocable. I do not know how much you may have spent on supporting me up till now; as long as I was ignorant of the truth I could accept living at your expense, but it is needless to say that I prefer to receive nothing from you for the future. The idea of owing you anything is intolerable to me and I think I had rather die of hunger than sit at your table again. Fortunately I seem to remember having heard that my mother was richer than you when she married you. I am free to think, therefore, that the burden of supporting me fell only on her. I thank her – consider her quit of anything else she may owe me – and beg her to forget me. You will have no difficulty in explaining my departure to those it may surprise. I give you free leave to put what blame you choose on me (though I know well enough that you will not wait for my leave to do this).

I sign this letter with that ridiculous name of yours, which I should like to fling back in your face, and which I am longing and hoping soon to dishonour.

BERNARD PROFITENDIEU

P.S.—I am leaving all my things behind me. They belong more legitimately to Caloub – at any rate I hope so, for your sake.

Monsieur Profitendieu totters to an arm-chair. He wants to reflect, but his mind is in a confused whirl. Moreover, he feels a little stabbing pain in his right side, just below his ribs. There can be no question about it. It is a liver attack. Would there be any Vichy water in the house? If only his wife had not gone out! How is he to break the news of Bernard's flight to her? Ought he to show her the letter? It is an unjust letter – abominably unjust. He ought to be angry. But it is not anger he feels – he wishes it were – it is sorrow. He breathes deeply and at each breath exhales an 'Oh, dear! Oh, dear!' as swift and low as a sigh. The pain in his side becomes one with his other pain – proves it – localizes it. He feels as if his grief were in his liver. He drops into an arm-chair and re-reads Bernard's letter. He shrugs his shoulders sadly. Yes, it is a cruel letter – but there is wounded vanity, defiance – bravado in it, too. Not one of his other children – his real children – would have been capable – any more than he would have been capable himself – of writing it.

He knows this, for there is nothing in them which he does not recognize only too well in himself. It is true that he has always thought it his duty to blame Bernard for his rawness, his roughness, his unbroken temper, but he realizes that it is for those very things that he loved him as he had never loved any of the others.

In the next room, Cécile, who had come in from her concert, had begun to practise the piano and was obstinately going over and over again the same phrase in a barcarole. At last Albéric Profitendieu could bear it no longer. He opened the drawing-room door a little way and in a plaintive, half supplicating voice, for his liver was beginning to hurt him cruelly (and besides he had always been a little frightened of her):

'Cécile, my dear,' he asked, 'would you mind seeing whether there's any Vichy water in the house and if there isn't, sending out to get some? And, it would be very nice of you to stop playing for a little.'

'Are you ill?'

'No, no, not at all. I've just got something that needs thinking over a little before dinner, and your music disturbs me.'

And then a kindly feeling – for he was softened by suffering – made him add:

'That's a very pretty thing you're playing. What is it?'

But he went away without waiting for the answer. For that matter, his daughter, who was aware that he knew nothing whatever about music and could not distinguish between '*Viens Poupoule*' and the *March* in *Tannhäuser* (at least, so she used to say), had no intention of answering.

But there he was at the door again!

'Has your mother come in?'

'No, not yet.'

Absurd! she would be coming in so late that he would have no time to speak to her before dinner. What could he invent to explain Bernard's absence? He really couldn't tell the truth – let the children into the secret of their mother's temporary lapse. Ah! all had been forgotten, forgiven, made up. The birth of their last son had cemented their reconciliation. And now, suddenly this avenging spectre had re-risen from the past – this corpse had been washed up again by the tide.

Good! Another interruption! As the study door noiselessly opens, he slips the letter into the inside pocket of his coat; the *portiere* is gently raised – Caloub!

'Oh, Papa, please tell me what this Latin sentence means. I can't make head or tail of it. . . .'

'I've already told you not to come in here without knocking. You mustn't disturb me like this for anything and everything. You are getting too much into the habit of relying on other people instead of making an effort yourself. Yesterday it was your geometry problem, and now today it's . . . by whom is your sentence?'

Caloub holds out his copy-book.

'He didn't tell us; but just look at it; *you'll* know all right. He dictated it to us. But perhaps I took it down wrong. You might at any rate tell me if it's correct!'

Monsieur Profitendieu took the copy-book, but he was in too much pain. He gently pushed the child away.

'Later on. It's just dinner-time. Has Charles come in?'

'He went down to his consulting-room.' (The barrister receives his clients in a room on the ground floor.)

'Go and tell him I want to speak to him. Quick!'

A ring at the door bell! Madame Profitendieu at last! She apologizes for being late. She had a great many visits to pay. She is sorry to see her husband so poorly. What can be done for him? He certainly looks very unwell. He won't be able to eat anything. They must sit down without him, but after dinner, will she come to his study with the children? – Bernard? – Oh, yes; his friend . . . you know – the one he is reading mathematics with – came and took him out to dinner.

Profitendieu felt better. He had at first been afraid he would be too ill to speak. And yet it was necessary to give an explanation of Bernard's disappearance. He knew now what he must say – however painful it might be. He felt firm and determined. His only fear was that his wife might interrupt him by crying – that she might exclaim – that she might faint. . . .

An hour later she comes into the room with the three children. He makes her sit down beside him, close against his arm-chair.

'Try to control yourself,' he whispers, but in a tone of

command; 'and don't speak a word. We will talk together afterwards.'

And all the time he is speaking, he holds one of her hands in both his.

'Come, my children, sit down. I don't like to see you standing there as if you were in front of an examiner. I have something very sad to say to you. Bernard has left us and we shall not see him again . . . for some time to come. I must now tell you what I at first concealed from you, because I wanted you to love Bernard like a brother; your mother and I loved him like our own child. But he was not our child . . . and one of his uncles – a brother of his real mother, who confided him to us on her death-bed – came and fetched him away this evening.'

A painful silence follows these words and Caloub sniffles. They all wait, expecting him to go on. But he dismisses them with a wave of his hand.

'You can go now, my dears. I must speak to your mother.'

After they have left the room, Monsieur Profitendieu remains silent for a long time. The hand which Madame Profitendieu had left in his seems like a dead thing; with the other she presses a handkerchief to her eyes. Leaning on the writing-table, she turns her head away to cry. Through the sobs which shake her, Monsieur Profitendieu hears her murmur:

'Oh, how cruel of you! . . . Oh! You have turned him out. . . .'

A moment ago, he had resolved to speak to her without showing her Bernard's letter; but at this unjust accusation, he holds it out:

'Here! Read this.'

'I can't.'

'You *must* read it.'

He has forgotten his pain. He follows her with his eyes all through the letter, line by line. Just now when he was speaking, he could hardly keep back his tears; but now all emotion has left him; he watches his wife. What is she thinking? In the same plaintive voice, broken by the same sobs, she murmurs again:

'Oh! why did you tell him? . . . You shouldn't have told him.'

'But you can see for yourself that I never told him anything. Read his letter more carefully.'

'I did read it. . . . But how did he find out? Who told him then?'

So *that* is what she is thinking! *Those* are the accents of her grief!

This sorrow should bring them together, but, alas! Profitendieu feels obscurely that their thoughts are travelling by divergent ways. And while she laments and accuses and recriminates, he endeavours to bend her unruly spirit and to bring her to a more pious frame of mind.

'This is the expiation,' he says.

He has risen, from an instinctive desire to dominate; he stands there before her upright – forgetful or regardless of his physical pain – and lays his hand gravely, tenderly, authoritatively on Marguerite's shoulder. He is well aware that her repentance for what he chooses to consider a passing weakness, has never been more than half-hearted; he would like to tell her now that this sorrow, this trial may serve to redeem her; but he can find no formula to satisfy him – none that he can hope she will listen to. Marguerite's shoulder resists the gentle pressure of his hand. She knows so well that from every event of life – even the smallest – he invariably, intolerably, extracts as with a forceps, some moral teaching – he interprets and twists everything to suit his own dogmas. He bends over her. This is what he would like to say:

'You see, my dear, no good thing can be born of sin. It was no use covering up your fault. Alas! I did what I could for the child. I treated him as my own. God shows us today that it was an error to try . . .'

But at the first sentence he stops.

No doubt she understands these words, heavy with meaning as they are; they have struck home to her heart, for though she had stopped crying some moments before, her sobs break out afresh, more violently than ever: then she bows herself, as though she were going to kneel before him, but he stoops over her and holds her up. What is it she is saying through her tears? He stoops his ear almost to her lips and hears:

'You see . . . You . . . Oh! why did you forgive me? Oh! I shouldn't have come back.'

He is almost obliged to divine her words. Then she stops. She too can say no more. How can she tell him that she feels imprisoned in this virtue which he exacts from her... that she is stifling . . . that it is not so much her fault that she regrets now, as having repented of it? Profitendieu raises himself.

'My poor Marguerite,' he says with dignity and severity, 'I am afraid you are a little stubborn tonight. It is late. We had better go to bed.'

He helps her up, leads her to her room, puts his lips to her forehead, then returns to his study and flings himself into an arm-chair. It is a curious thing that his liver attack has subsided – but he feels shattered. He sits with his head in his hands, too sad to cry. . . . He does not hear a knock at the door, but at the noise the door makes in opening, he raises his head – his son Charles!

'I came to say good night to you.'

He comes up. He wants to convey to his father that he has understood everything. He would like to manifest his pity, his tenderness, his devotion, but – who would think it of an advocate – he is extraordinarily awkward at expressing himself – or perhaps he becomes awkward precisely when his feelings are sincere. He kisses his father. The way in which he lays his head upon his shoulder, and leans and lingers there, convinces Profitendieu that his son has understood. He has understood so thoroughly that, raising his head a little, he asks in his usual clumsy fashion – but his heart is so anxious that he cannot refrain from asking:

'And Caloub?'

The question is absurd, for Caloub's looks are as strikingly like his family's as Bernard's are different.

Profitendieu pats Charles on the shoulder:

'No, no; it's all right. Only Bernard.'

Then Charles begins pompously:

'God has driven the intruder away...'

But Profitendieu stops him. He has no need of such words.

'Hush!'

Father and son have no more to say to each other. Let us leave them. It is nearly eleven o'clock. Let us leave Madame

Profitendieu in her room, seated on a small, straight, uncomfortable chair. She is not crying; she is not thinking. She too would like to run away. But she will not. When she was with her lover – Bernard's father (we need not concern ourselves with him) – she said to herself: 'No, no; try as I may, I shall never be anything but an honest woman.' She was afraid of liberty, of crime, of ease – so that after ten days, she returned repentant to her home. Her parents were right when they said to her: 'You never know your own mind.' Let us leave her. Cécile is already asleep. Caloub is gazing in despair at his candle; it will never last long enough for him to finish the story-book, with which he is distracting himself from thoughts of Bernard. I should be curious to know what Antoine can have told his friend the cook. But it is impossible to listen to everything. This is the hour appointed for Bernard to go to Olivier. I am not sure where he dined that evening – or even whether he dined at all. He has passed the porter's room without hindrance; he gropes his way stealthily up the stairs....

3

BERNARD AND OLIVIER

Plenty and peace breeds cowards; hardness ever
Of hardiness is mother.

Cymbeline, Act III, Sc. VI

OLIVIER had got into bed to receive his mother, who was in the habit of coming every evening to kiss her two younger sons good night before they went to sleep. He might have got up and dressed again to receive Bernard, but he was still uncertain whether he would come and was afraid of doing anything to rouse his younger brother's suspicions. George as a rule went to sleep early and woke up late; perhaps he would never notice that anything unusual was going on. When he heard a gentle scratching outside, Olivier sprang from his bed, thrust his feet hastily into his bedroom slippers, and ran to open the door. He did not light a candle; the moon gave light enough; there was no need for any other. Olivier hugged Bernard in his arms:

'How I was longing for you! I couldn't believe you would really come,' said Olivier, and in the dimness he saw Bernard shrug his shoulders. 'Do your parents know you are not sleeping at home tonight?'

Bernard looked straight in front of him into the dark.

'You think I ought to have asked their leave, eh?'

His tone of voice was so coldly ironical that Olivier at once felt the absurdity of his question. He had not yet grasped that Bernard had left 'for good'; he thought that he only meant to sleep out that one night and was a little perplexed as to the reason of this escapade. He began to question: When did Bernard think of going home? – Never!

Light began to dawn on Olivier. He was very anxious to be equal to the occasion and not to be surprised at anything; nevertheless an exclamation broke from him:

'What a tremendous decision!'

Bernard was by no means unwilling to astonish his friend a little; he was particularly flattered by the admiration which these words betrayed, but he shrugged his shoulders once more. Olivier took hold of his hand and asked very gravely and anxiously:

'But why are you leaving?'

'That, my dear fellow, is a family matter. I can't tell you.' And in order not to seem too serious he amused himself by trying to jerk off with the tip of his shoe the slipper that Olivier was swinging on his bare toes – for they were sitting down now on the side of the bed. There! Off it goes!

'Then where do you mean to live?'

'I don't know.'

'And how?'

'That remains to be seen.'

'Have you any money?'

'Enough for breakfast tomorrow.'

'And after that?'

'After that I shall look about me. Oh, I'm sure to find something. You'll see. I'll let you know.'

Olivier admires his friend with immense fervour. He knows him to be resolute; but he cannot help doubting; when he is at the end of his resources, and feeling, as soon he must, the pressure of want, won't he be obliged to go back? Bernard reassures him – he will do anything in the world rather than return to his people. And as he repeats several times over more and more savagely – 'anything in the world' – Olivier's heart is stabbed with a pang of terror. He wants to speak but dares not. At last with downcast head and unsteady voice, he begins:

'Bernard, all the same, you're not thinking of ...' but he stops. His friend raises his eyes and, though he cannot see him very distinctly, perceives his confusion.

'Of what?' he asks. 'What do you mean? Tell me. Of stealing?'

Olivier shakes his head. No, that's not it! Suddenly he bursts into tears and clasping Bernard convulsively in his arms:

'Promise me that you won't...'

Bernard kisses him, then pushes him away laughing. He has understood.

'Oh! yes! I promise . . . But all the same you must admit it would be the easiest way out.' But Olivier feels reassured; he knows that these last words are an affectation of cynicism.

'Your exam?'

'Yes; that's rather a bore. I don't want to be ploughed. I think I'm ready all right. It's more a question of feeling fit on the day. I must manage to get something fixed up very quickly. It's touch and go; but I *shall* manage. You'll see.'

They sit for a moment in silence. The second slipper has fallen.

Then Bernard: 'You'll catch cold. Get back into bed.'

'No; *you* must get into bed.'

'You're joking. Come along! quick!' and he forces Olivier to get into the bed which he has already lain down in and which is all tumbled.

'But you? Where are *you* going to sleep?'

'Anywhere. On the floor. In a corner. I must get accustomed to roughing it.'

'No. Look here! I want to tell you something, but I shan't be able to unless I feel you close to me. Get into my bed.' And when Bernard, after undressing himself in a twinkling, has got in beside him:

'You know . . . what I told you the other day . . . well, it's come off. I went.'

There was no need to say more for Bernard to understand. He pressed up against his friend.

'Well! it's disgusting . . . horrible . . . Afterwards I wanted to spit – to be sick – to tear my skin off – to kill myself.'

'You're exaggerating.'

'To kill *her*.'

'Who was it? You haven't been imprudent, have you?'

'No; it's some creature Dhurmer knows. He introduced me. It was her talk that was the most loathsome. She never once stopped jabbering. And oh! the deadly stupidity of it! Why can't people hold their tongues at such moments, I wonder? I should have liked to strangle her – to gag her.'

'Poor old Olivier! You didn't think that Dhurmer could get hold of anybody but an idiot, did you? Was she pretty, anyway?'

'D'you suppose I looked at her?'

'You're a donkey! You're a darling! ... Let's go to sleep. ... But ... did you bring it off all right?'

'God! That's the most disgusting thing about it. I was able to, in spite of everything ... just as if I'd desired her.'

'Well, it's magnificent, my dear boy.'

'Oh, shut up! If that's what they call love – I'm fed up with it.'

'What a baby you are!'

'What would *you* have been, pray?'

'Oh, you know, I'm not particularly keen; as I've told you before, I'm biding my time. In cold blood, like that, it doesn't appeal to me. All the same if I – '

'If you ... ?'

'If she ... Nothing! Let's go to sleep.'

And abruptly he turned his back, drawing a little away so as not to touch Olivier's body, which he feels uncomfortably warm. But Olivier, after a moment's silence, begins again:

'I say, do you think Barrès will get in?'

'Heavens! does that worry you?'

'I don't care a damn! I say, just listen to this a minute.' He presses on Bernard's shoulder, so as to make him turn round – 'My brother has got a mistress.'

'George?'

The youngster, who is pretending to be asleep, but who has been listening with all his might in the dark, holds his breath when he hears his name.

'You're crazy. I mean Vincent.' (Vincent is a few years older than Olivier and has just finished his medical training.)

'Did he tell you?'

'No. I found out without his suspecting. My parents know nothing about it.'

'What would they say if they knew?'

'I don't know. Mamma would be in despair. Papa would say he must break it off or else marry her.'

'Of course. A worthy bourgeois can't understand how one

can be worthy in any other fashion than his own. How did you find out?'

'Well, for some time past Vincent has been going out at night after my parents have gone to bed. He goes downstairs as quietly as he can, but I recognize his step in the street. Last week – Tuesday, I think, the night was so hot I couldn't stop in bed. I went to the window to get a breath of fresh air. I heard the door downstairs open and shut, so I leant out and, as he was passing under a lamp post, I recognized Vincent. It was past midnight. That was the first time – I mean the first time I noticed anything. But since then, I can't help listening – oh! without meaning to – and nearly every night I hear him go out. He's got a latchkey and our parents have arranged our old room – George's and mine – as a consulting-room for him when he has any patients. His room is by itself on the left of the entrance; the rest of our rooms are on the right. He can go out and come in without anyone knowing. As a rule I don't hear him come in, but the day before yesterday – Monday night – I don't know what was the matter with me – I was thinking of Dhurmer's scheme for a review . . . I couldn't go to sleep. I heard voices on the stairs. I thought it was Vincent.'

'What time was it?' asks Bernard, more to show that he is taking an interest than because he wants to know.

'Three in the morning, I think. I got up and put my ear to the door. Vincent was talking to a woman. Or rather, it was she who was talking.'

'Then how did you know it was he? All the people who live in the flat must pass by your door.'

'And a horrid nuisance it is, too. The later it is, the more row they make. They care no more about the people who are asleep than . . . It was certainly he. I heard the woman calling him by his name. She kept saying . . . Oh, I can't bear repeating it. It makes me sick. . . .'

'Go on.'

'She kept saying: "Vincent, my love – my lover . . . Oh, don't leave me!"'

'Did she say *you* to him and not *thou*?'

'Yes; isn't it odd?'

'Tell us some more.'

'"You have no right to desert me now. What is to become of me? Where am I to go? Say something to me! Oh, speak to me!" . . . And she called him again by his name, and went on repeating: "My lover! My lover!" And her voice became sadder and sadder and lower and lower. And then I heard a noise (they must have been standing on the stairs), a noise like something falling. I think she must have flung herself on her knees.'

'And didn't he answer anything? Nothing at all?'

'He must have gone up the last steps; I heard the door of the flat shut. And after that, she stayed a long time quite near – almost up against my door. I heard her sobbing.'

'You should have opened the door.'

'I didn't dare. Vincent would be furious if he thought I knew anything about his affairs. And then I was afraid it might embarrass her to be found crying. I don't know what I could have said to her.'

Bernard had turned towards Olivier:

'In your place I should have opened.'

'Oh, you! You're never afraid of anything. You do everything that comes into your head.'

'Is that a reproach?'

'Oh, no. It's envy.'

'Have you any idea who the woman is?'

'How on earth should I know? Good night.'

'I say, are you sure George hasn't heard us?' whispers Bernard in Olivier's ear. They listen a moment with bated breath.

'No,' Olivier goes on in his ordinary voice. 'He's asleep. And besides, he wouldn't understand. Do you know what he asked Papa the other day . . . ?'

At this, George can contain himself no longer. He sits up in his bed and breaks into his brother's sentence.

'You ass!' he cries. 'Didn't you see I was doing it on purpose? . . . Good Lord, yes! I've heard every word you've been saying. But you needn't excite yourselves. I've known all about Vincent for ever so long. And now, my young friends, talk a little lower please, because I'm sleepy – or else hold your tongues.'

Olivier turns toward the wall. Bernard, who cannot sleep, looks out into the room. It seems bigger in the moonlight. As a matter of fact, he hardly knows it. Olivier was never there during the daytime; the few times that Bernard had been to see him, it was in the flat upstairs. But it was after school hours, when they came out of the *lycée*, that the two friends usually met. The moonlight has reached the foot of the bed in which George has at last gone to sleep; he has heard almost everything that his brother has said. He has matter for his dreams. Above George's bed Bernard can just make out a little bookcase with two shelves full of school-books. On a table near Olivier's bed, he sees a larger sized book; he puts out his hand and takes it to look at the title – Tocqueville; but as he is putting it back on the table, he drops it and the noise wakes Olivier up.

'Are you reading Tocqueville now?'

'Dulac lent it me.'

'Do you like it?'

'It's rather boring, but some of it's very good.'

'I say, what are you doing tomorrow?'

Tomorrow is Thursday and there is no school. Bernard thinks he may meet his friend somewhere. He does not mean to go back to the *lycée*; he thinks he can do without the last lectures and finish preparing for his examination by himself.

'Tomorrow,' says Olivier, 'I'm going to St Lazare railway station at 11.30 to meet my Uncle Edouard, who is arriving from Le Havre, on his way from England. In the afternoon, I'm engaged to go to the Louvre with Dhurmer. The rest of the time I've got to work.'

'Your Uncle Edouard?'

'Yes. He's a half-brother of Mamma's. He's been away for six months and I hardly know him; but I like him very much. He doesn't know I'm going to meet him and I'm rather afraid I mayn't recognize him. He's not in the least like the rest of the family; he's somebody quite out of the common.'

'What does he do?'

'He writes. I've read nearly all his books; but he hasn't published anything for a long time.'

'Novels?'

'Yes; kind of novels.'

'Why have you never told me about them?'

'Because you'd have wanted to read them; and if you hadn't liked them . . .'

'Well, finish your sentence.'

'Well, I should have hated it. There!'

'What makes you say that he's out of the common?'

'I don't exactly know. I told you I hardly know him. It's more of a presentiment. I feel that he's interested in all sorts of things that don't interest my parents and that there's nothing that one couldn't talk to him about. One day – it was just before he went away – he had been to lunch with us; all the time he was talking to Papa I felt he kept looking at me and it began to make me uncomfortable; I was going to leave the room – it was the dining-room – where we had stayed on after coffee, but then he began to question Papa about me, which made me more uncomfortable than ever; and suddenly Papa got up and went to fetch some verses I had written and which I had been idiotic enough to show him.'

'Verses of yours?'

'Yes; you know – that poem you said you thought was like *Le Balcon*. I knew it wasn't any good – or hardly any – and I was furious with Papa for bringing it out. For a minute or two, while Papa was fetching the poem, we were alone together, Uncle Edouard and I, and I felt myself blushing horribly. I couldn't think of anything to say to him. I looked away – so did he, for that matter; he began by rolling a cigarette and lighting it and then to put me at my ease, no doubt, for he certainly saw I was blushing, he got up and went and looked out of the window. He was whistling. Then he suddenly said, 'I feel far more embarrassed than you do, you know.' But I think it was just kindness. At last Papa came back again; he handed my verses to Uncle Edouard, and he began to read them. I was in such a state that I think if he had paid me compliments, I should have insulted him. Evidently Papa expected him to – pay me compliments – and as my uncle said nothing, he asked him what he thought of them. But Uncle Edouard answered him, laughing, "I can't speak to him comfortably about them before you."

Then Papa laughed too and went out. And when we were alone again, he said he thought my verses were very bad, but I liked hearing him say so; and what I liked still more was that suddenly he put his finger down on two lines – the only two I cared for in the whole thing; he looked at me and said, "That's good!" Wasn't it nice? And if you only knew the tone in which he said it! I could have hugged him. Then he said my mistake was to start from an idea, and that I didn't allow myself to be guided sufficiently by the words. I didn't understand very well at first; but I think I see now what he meant – and that he was right. I'll explain it to you another time.'

'I understand now why you want to go and meet him.'

'Oh, all that's nothing and I don't know why I've told you about it. We said a great deal more to one another.'

'At 11.30 did you say? How do you know he's coming by that train?'

'Because he wrote and told Mamma on a postcard; and then I looked it up in the time-table.'

'Will you have lunch with him?'

'Oh, no. I must be back here by twelve. I shall just have time to shake hands with him. But that's enough for me. . . . Oh, one thing more before I go to sleep. When shall I see you again?'

'Not for some days. Not before I've got something fixed up.'

'All the same. . . Couldn't I help you somehow . . . ?'

'You? Help me? No. It wouldn't be fair play. I should feel as if I were cheating. Good night.'

4

VINCENT AND THE COMTE DE PASSAVANT

> Mon Père était une bête, mais ma mère avait de l'esprit; elle était quiétiste; c'était une petite femme douce qui me disait souvent: Mon fils, vous serez damné. Mais cela ne lui faisait pas de peine.
>
> FONTENELLE

No, it was not to see his mistress that Vincent Molinier went out every evening. Quickly as he walks, let us follow him. He goes along the rue Notre Dame des Champs, at the further end of which he lives, until he reaches the rue Placide, which is its prolongation; then he turns down the rue du Bac, where there are still a few belated passers-by. In the rue de Babylone, he stops in front of a *porte-cochère* which swings open to let him in. The Comte de Passavant lives here. If Vincent were not in the habit of coming often, he would enter this sumptuous mansion with a less confident air. The footman who comes to the door knows well enough how much timidity this feigned assurance hides. Vincent, with a touch of affectation, instead of handing him his hat, tosses it on to an arm-chair.

It is only recently that Vincent has taken to coming here. Robert de Passavant, who now calls himself his friend, is the friend of a great many people. I am not very sure how he and Vincent became acquainted. At the *lycée*, I expect – though Robert de Passavant is perceptibly older than Vincent; they had lost sight of each other for several years and then, quite lately, had met again one evening when, by some unusual chance, Olivier had gone with his brother to the theatre; during the *entr'acte* Passavant had invited them both to take an ice with him; he had learnt that Vincent had just finished his last medical examinations and was undecided as to whether he should take a place as house physician in a hospital; science attracted him more than medicine, but the necessity of earning his living . . . in short, Vincent accepted with pleasure the very remunerative offer Robert de Passavant had made him a little later of coming every evening, to attend his old father, who had lately undergone a very serious operation; it was a matter of bandages, of injections, of soundings – in fact, of whatever delicate services you please, which necessitate the ministrations of an expert hand.

But, added to this, the Vicomte had secret reasons for wishing a nearer acquaintance with Vincent; and Vincent had still others for consenting. Robert's secret reason we shall try to discover later on. As for Vincent's – it was this: he was urgently in need of money. When your heart is in the right place and a wholesome education has early instilled into you a sense of your responsibilities, you don't get a woman with child, without feeling yourself more or less bound to her – especially when the woman has left her husband to follow you.

Up till then, Vincent had lived on the whole virtuously. His adventure with Laura appeared to him alternately, according to the moment of the day in which he thought of it, as either monstrous or perfectly natural. It very often suffices to add together a quantity of little facts which, taken separately, are very simple and very natural, to arrive at a sum which is monstrous. He said all this to himself over and over again as he walked along, but it didn't get him out of his difficulties. No doubt, he had never thought of taking this woman permanently under his protection – of marrying her after a divorce, or of living with her without marrying; he was obliged to confess to himself that he had no very violent passion for her; but he knew she was in Paris without means of subsistence; he was the cause of her distress; at the very least he owed her that first precarious aid which he felt himself less and less able to give her – less today than yesterday. For last week he still possessed the five thousand francs which his mother had patiently and laboriously saved to give him a start in his profession; those five thousand francs would have sufficed, no doubt, to pay for his mistress's confinement, for her stay in a nursing home, for the child's first necessaries. To what demon's advice then had he listened? What demon had hinted to him one evening that this sum which he had as good as given to Laura, which he had laid by for her, pledged to her – that this sum would be insufficient? No, it was not Robert de Passavant; Robert had never said anything of the kind; but his proposal to take Vincent with him to a gambling club fell out precisely the same evening. And Vincent had accepted.

The hell in question was a particularly treacherous one, inasmuch as the habitués were all people in society and the whole thing took place on a friendly footing. Robert introduced his friend Vincent to one and another. Vincent, who was taken unawares, was not able to play high that first evening. He had hardly anything on him and refused the notes which the Vicomte offered to advance him. But as he began by winning, he regretted not being able to stake more and promised to go back the next night.

'Everybody knows you now; there's no need for me to come with you again,' said Robert.

These meetings took place at Pierre de Brouville's, commonly known as Pedro. After this first evening Robert de Passavant had put his car at his friend's disposal. Vincent used to look in about eleven o'clock, smoke a cigarette with Robert, and after chatting for ten minutes or so, go upstairs. His stay there was more or less lengthy according to the Count's patience, temper or requirements; after this he drove in the car to Pedro's in the rue St Florentin, whence about an hour later the car took him back – not actually to his own door, for he was afraid of attracting attention, but to the nearest corner.

The night before last, Laura Douviers, seated on the steps which led to the Moliniers' flat, had waited for Vincent till three o'clock in the morning; it was not till then that he had come in. As a matter of fact, Vincent had not been at Pedro's that night. Two days had gone by since he had lost every penny of the five thousand francs. He had informed Laura of this; he had written that he could do nothing more for her; that he advised her to go back to her husband or her father – to confess everything. But things had gone so far, that confession seemed impossible to Laura and she could not contemplate it with any sort of calm. Her lover's objurgations merely aroused indignation in her – an indignation which only subsided to leave her a prey to despair. This was the state in which Vincent had found her. She had tried to keep him; he had torn himself from her grasp. Doubtless, he had to steel himself to do it, for he had a tender heart; but he was more of a pleasure-seeker than a lover and he had easily persuaded himself that duty itself demanded harshness. He had answered nothing to all her entreaties and lamentations, and as Olivier, who had heard them, told Bernard afterwards, when Vincent shut the door against her, she had sunk down on the steps and remained for a long time sobbing in the dark.

More than forty hours had gone by since that night. The day before, Vincent had not gone to Robert de Passavant's, whose father seemed to be recovering; but that evening a telegram had summoned him. Robert wished to see him. When Vincent entered the room in which Robert usually sat – a room which he used as his study and smoking-room and which he had been at some pains to decorate and fit up in his own fashion – Robert carelessly held out his hand to him over his shoulder, without rising.

Robert is writing. He is sitting at a bureau littered with books. Facing him the french window which gives on to the garden, stands wide open in the moonlight. He speaks without turning round.

'Do you know what I am writing? But you won't mention it, will you? You promise, eh? – a manifesto for the opening number of Dhurmer's review. I shan't sign it, of course – especially as I puff myself in it. . . . And then as it'll certainly come out in the long run that I'm financing it, I don't want it known too soon that I write for it. So mum's the word! But it's just occurred to me – didn't you say that young brother of yours wrote? What's his name again?'

'Olivier,' says Vincent.

'Olivier! Yes; I had forgotten. Don't stay standing there like that! Sit down in that arm-chair. You're not cold? Shall I shut the window? . . . It's poetry he writes, isn't it? He ought to bring me something to see. Of course, I don't promise to take it. . . . But, all the same, I should be surprised if it were bad. He looks an intelligent boy. And then he's obviously *au courant*. I should like to talk to him. Tell him to come and see me, eh? Mind, I count on it. A cigarette?' And he holds out his silver cigarette-case.

'With pleasure.'

'Now then, Vincent, listen to me. I must speak to you very seriously. You behaved like a child the other evening . . . so did I, for that matter. I don't say it was wrong of me to take you to Pedro's, but I feel responsible, a little, for the money you've lost. I don't know if that's what's meant by remorse, but, upon my word, it's beginning to disturb my sleep and my digestion. And then, when I think of that unhappy woman you told me about. . . . But that's another story. We won't speak of that. It's sacred. What I want to say is this – that I wish – yes, I'm absolutely determined to put at your disposal a sum of money equivalent to what you've lost. It was five thousand francs, wasn't it? And you're to risk it again. Once more, I repeat, I consider myself the cause of your losing this money – I owe it to you – there's no need to thank me. You'll pay me back if you win. If not – worse luck! We shall be quits. Go back to Pedro's this evening, as if nothing had happened. The car will take you there; then it'll come back here to take me to Lady Griffith's, where I'll ask you to join me later on. I count upon it, eh? The car will fetch you from Pedro's.'

He opens a drawer and takes out five notes which he hands to Vincent.

'Be off with you, now.'

'But your father?'

'Oh, yes; I forgot to tell you: he died about . . . ' He pulls out his watch and exclaims: 'By Jove! how late it is! Nearly midnight. . . . You must make haste. Yes, about four hours ago.'

All this is said without any quickening of his voice, on the contrary with a kind of nonchalance.

'And aren't you going to stay to . . . '

'To watch by the body?' interrupts Robert. 'No, that's my young brother's business. He is up there with his old nurse, who was on better terms with the deceased than I was.'

Then as Vincent remains motionless, he goes on:

'Look here, my dear fellow, I don't want to appear cynical, but I have a horror of reach-me-down sentiments. In my early days I cut out my filial love according to the pattern I had in my heart; but I soon saw that my measurements had been too ample, and I was obliged to take it in. The old man never in his life occasioned me anything but trouble and vexation and constraint. If he had any tenderness left, it was certainly not to me that he showed it. My first impulses of affection towards him, in the days before I knew how to behave, brought me nothing but snubs – and I learnt my lesson. You must have seen for yourself when you were attending him.... Did he ever thank you? Did you ever get the slightest look, the smallest smile from him? He always thought everything his due. Oh, he was what people call a *character*! I think he must have made my mother very unhappy, and yet he loved her – that is, if he ever really loved anyone. I think he made everyone who came near him suffer – his servants, his dogs, his horses, his mistresses; not his friends, for he had none. A general sigh of relief will go up at his death. He was, I believe, a man of great distinction in "his line", as people say; but I have never been able to discover what it was. He was very intelligent, undoubtedly. At heart, I had – I still have – a certain admiration for him – but as for making play with a handkerchief – as for wringing tears out . . . no, thank you, I'm no longer child enough for that. Be off with you now! And join me in an hour's time at Lilian's. What! you're not dressed? Absurd! What does it matter? But if it'll make you more comfortable, I'll promise not to change either. Agreed! Light a cigar before you go and send the car back quickly – it'll fetch you again afterwards.'

He watched Vincent go out, shrugged his shoulders, then went into his dressing-room to change into his dress suit, which was ready laid out for him on a sofa.

In a room on the first floor, the old count is lying on his death-bed. Someone has placed a crucifix on his breast, but has omitted to fold his hands over it. A beard of some days' growth softens the stubborn angle of his chin. Beneath his grey hair, which is brushed up *en brosse*, the wrinkles that line his forehead seem less deeply graven, as though they were relaxed. His eye is sunk beneath the arch of the brow and the shaggy growth of the eyebrow. I know that we shall never see him again, and that is the reason that I take a long look at him. Beside the head of the bed is an arm-chair, in which is seated the old nurse Séraphine. But she has risen. She goes up to a table where an old-fashioned lamp is dimly lighting the room; it needs turning up. A lamp-shade casts the light on to the book young Gontran is reading....

'You're tired, Master Gontran. You had better go to bed.'

The glance that Gontran raises from his book to rest upon Séraphine is very gentle. His fair hair, a lock of which he pushes back from his forehead, waves loosely over his temples. He is fifteen years old, and his face, which is still almost girlish, expresses nothing as yet but tenderness and love.

'And you?' he says. 'It is you who ought to go to bed, you poor old Fine. Last night, you were on your feet nearly the whole time.'

'Oh, I'm accustomed to sitting up. And besides I slept during the daytime – but you...'

'No, I'm all right. I don't feel tired; and it does me good to stay here thinking and reading. I knew Papa so little; I think I should forget him altogether if I didn't take a good look at him now. I will sit beside him till daylight. How long is it, Fine, since you came to us?'

'I came the year before you were born, and you're nearly sixteen.'

'Do you remember Mamma quite well?'

'Do I remember your Mamma? What a question! You might as well ask me if I remember my own name. To be sure, I remember your Mamma.'

'I remember her too – a little.... But not very well.... I was only five when she died. Used Papa to talk to her much?'

'It depended on his mood. Your Papa was never a one to talk much, and he didn't care to be spoken to first. All the same, in those days he was a little more talkative than he has been of late.... But there now! What's past is past, and it's better not to stir it up again. There's One above who's a better judge of these things than we are.'

'Do you really think that He concerns Himself about such things, dear Fine?'

'Why, if He doesn't, who should then?'

Gontran puts his lips on Séraphine's red, roughened hand. 'You really ought to go to bed now. I promise to wake you as soon as it is light, and then I'll take my turn to rest. Please!'

As soon as Séraphine has left him, Gontran falls upon his knees at the foot of the bed; he buries his head in the sheets, but he cannot succeed in weeping. No emotion stirs his heart; his eyes remain despairingly dry. Then he gets up and looks at the impassive face on the bed. At this solemn moment, he would like to have some rare, sublime experience – hear a message from the world beyond – send his thought flying into ethereal regions, inaccessible to mortal senses. But no! his thought remains obstinately grovelling on the earth; he looks at the dead man's bloodless hands and wonders for how much longer the nails will go on growing. The sight of the unclasped hands grates on him. He would like to join them, to make them hold the crucifix. What a good idea! He thinks of Séraphine's astonishment when she sees the dead hands folded together; the thought of Séraphine's astonishment amuses him; and then he despises himself for being amused. Nevertheless he stoops over the bed. He seizes the arm which is farthest from him. The arm is stiff and will not bend. Gontran tries to force it, but the whole body moves with it. He seizes the other arm, which seems a little less rigid. Gontran almost succeeds in putting the hand in the proper place. He takes the crucifix and tries to slip it between the fingers and the thumb, but the contact of the cold flesh turns him sick. He thinks he is going to faint. He has a mind to call Séraphine back. He gives up everything – the crucifix, which drops aslant on the tumbled sheet, and the lifeless arm, which falls back again into its first position; then, through the depths of the funereal silence, he suddenly hears a rough and brutal 'God damn!' which fills him with terror, as if someone else . . . He turns round – but no! he is alone. It was from his own lips, from his own heart, that that resounding curse broke forth – his, who until today has never uttered an oath! Then he sits down and plunges again into his reading.

5

VINCENT MEETS PASSAVANT AT LADY GRIFFITH'S

C'était une âme et un corps où n'entrait jamais l'aiguillon.

SAINTE-BEUVE

LILIAN half sat up and put the tips of her fingers on Robert's chestnut hair. 'Take care, my dear. You are hardly thirty yet and you're beginning to get thin on the top. Baldness wouldn't be at all becoming to you. You take life too seriously.'

Robert raised his face and looked at her, smiling. 'Not when I am with you, I assure you.'

'Did you tell Molinier to come?'

'Yes, as you asked me to.'

'And . . . you lent him money?'

'Five thousand francs, as I told you . . . and he'll lose it, like the rest.'

'Why should he lose it?'

'He's bound to. I saw him the first evening. He plays anyhow.'

'He's had time to learn. . . . Will you make a bet that tonight he'll win?'

'If you like.'

'Oh, please don't take it as a penance. I like people to do what they do willingly.'

'Don't be cross. Agreed then. If he wins, he'll pay the money back to you. But if he loses, it's you who'll pay me. Is that all right?'

She pressed a bell.

'Bring a bottle of Tokay and three glasses, please. . . . And if he comes back with the five thousand and no more – he shall keep it, eh? If he neither loses nor wins . . .'

'That's unheard of. It's odd what an interest you take in him.'

'It's odd that you don't think him interesting.'

'You think him interesting because you're in love with him.'

'Yes, my dear boy, that's true. One doesn't mind admitting

that to *you*. But that's not the reason he interests me. On the contrary – as a rule, when my head's attracted, the rest of me turns cold.'

A servant came in with wine and glasses on a tray.

'First of all let's seal our bet, and afterwards we'll have another glass in honour of the winner.'

The servant poured out the wine and they drank to each other.

'Personally, I think your Vincent a bore.'

'Oh, "my Vincent"!... As if it hadn't been you who brought him here! And then, I advise you not to go repeating everywhere that you think him a bore. Your reason for frequenting him would be too obvious.'

Robert turned a little to put his lips on Lilian's bare foot; she drew it away quickly and covered it with her fan.

'Must I blush?' said he.

'It's not worth while trying as far as I am concerned. You couldn't succeed.'

She emptied her glass, and then:

'D'you know what, my dear friend? You have all the qualities of a man of letters – you are vain, hypocritical, fickle, selfish....'

'You are too flattering!'

'Yes; that's all very charming – but you'll never be a good novelist.'

'Because?'

'Because you don't know how to listen.'

'It seems to me I'm listening admirably.'

'Pooh! *He* isn't a writer and he listens a great deal better. But when we are together, *I* am the one to listen.'

'He hardly knows how to speak.'

'That's because you never stop talking yourself.'

'I know everything he's going to say beforehand.'

'You think so? Do you know the story of his affair with that woman?'

'Oh! Love affairs! The dullest things in the world!'

'And then I like it when he talks about natural history.'

'Natural history is even duller than love affairs. Does he give you lectures then?'

'If I could only repeat what he says.... It's thrilling, my dear friend. He tells me all sorts of things about the deep seas; I've always been particularly curious about creatures that live in the sea. You know that in America they make boats with glass let into the sides, so that you can go to the bottom of the sea and look all round you. They say that the sights are simply marvellous – live coral and... and... what do you call them?... madrepores, and sponges, and sea-weeds, and great shoals of fish. Vincent says that there are certain kinds of fish which die according as the water becomes more salt or less, and that there are others, on the contrary, which can live in any degree of salt water; and that they swim about on the edge of the currents, where the water becomes less salt, so as to prey on the others when their strength fails them. You ought to get him to talk to you about it.... I assure you it's most curious. When he talks about things like that, he becomes extraordinary. You wouldn't recognize him... But you don't know how to get him to talk. ... It's like when he tells me about his affair with Laura Douviers – yes, that's her name.... Do you know how he got to know her?'

'Did he tell you?'

'People tell me everything. You know they do, you shocking creature!' And she stroked his face with the feathers of her closed fan.

'Did you suspect that he had been to see me every single day since the evening you first brought him?'

'Every day? No, really! I didn't suspect that.'

'On the fourth, he couldn't resist any longer; he came out with the whole thing. But on every day following, he kept adding details.'

'And it didn't bore you? You're a wonder!'

'I told you, my dear, that I love him.' And she seized his arm emphatically.

'And *he*... loves the other woman?'

Lilian laughed.

'He did love her. Oh, I had to pretend at first to be deeply interested in her. I even had to weep with him. And all the time I was horribly jealous. I'm not any more now. Just listen how it began. They were at Pau together in the same home – a sanatorium, where they had been sent because they were supposed to be tuberculous. In reality, they weren't, either of them. But they thought they were very ill. They were strangers, and the first time they saw each other was on the terrace in the garden, where they were lying side by side on their deck-chairs; and all round them were other patients, who spend the whole day lying out of doors in the sun to get cured. As they thought they were doomed to die an early death, they persuaded themselves that nothing they did would be of any consequence. He kept repeating all the time that they neither of them had more than a month to live – and it was the springtime. She was there all alone. Her husband is a little French professor in England. She left him to go to Pau. She had been married six months. He had to pinch and starve to send her there. He used to write to her every day. She's a young woman of very good family – very well brought up – very reserved – very shy. But once there – I don't exactly know what he can have said to her, but on the third day she confessed that though she lay with her husband and belonged to him, she did not know the meaning of the word pleasure.'

'And what did he say then?'

'He took her hand, as it hung down beside her chair, and pressed a long kiss upon it.'

'And when he told you that, what did *you* say?'

'I? Oh, frightful! Only fancy! I went off into a *fou rire*. I couldn't prevent myself, and once I had begun, I couldn't stop. ... It's not so much what he said that made me laugh – it was the air of interest and consternation which I thought it necessary to take, in order to encourage him to go on. I was afraid of seeming too much amused. And then, in reality, it was all very beautiful and touching. You can't imagine how moved he was when he told me about it. He had never spoken of it to anyone before. Of course his parents know nothing about it.'

'*You* are the person who ought to write novels.'

'*Parbleu*, *mon cher*, if only I knew what language to write them in! ... But what with Russian, English and French, I should never be able to choose. Well, the following night he went to his new friend's room and there taught her what her husband had never been able to teach – and I expect he made a very good master. Only as they were convinced that they had only a short time to live, they naturally took no precautions, and, naturally, after a little while, with the help of love, they both began to get much better. When she realized she was *enceinte*, they were in a terrible state. It was last month. It was beginning to get hot. Pau in the summer is intolerable. They came back to Paris together. Her husband thinks she is with her parents, who have a boarding school near the Luxembourg; but she didn't dare to go to them. Her parents, on the other hand, think she is still in Pau; but it must all come out soon. Vincent swore at first not to abandon her; he proposed going away with her – anywhere – to America – to the Pacific. But they had no money. It was just at that moment that he met you and began to play.'

'He didn't tell me any of all this.'

'Whatever happens, don't let him know that I've told you.'

She stopped and listened a moment.

'I thought I heard him. . . . He told me that, during the railway journey from Pau to Paris, he thought she was going mad. She had only just begun to realize she was going to have a child. She was sitting opposite him in the railway carriage; they were alone. She hadn't spoken to him the whole morning; he had had to make all the arrangements for the journey by himself – she was absolutely inert – she seemed not to know what was going on. He took her hands, but she looked straight in front of her with haggard eyes, as if she didn't see him, and her lips kept moving. He bent towards her. She was saying: "A lover! A lover! I've got a lover!" She kept on repeating it in the same tone; and still the same word kept coming from her over and over again, as if it were the only one she remembered. I assure you, Robert, that when he told me that, I didn't feel in the least inclined to laugh any more. I've never in my life heard anything more pathetic. But all the same, I felt that as he was speaking he was detaching himself more and more from the whole thing. It was as though his feeling were passing away in the same breath as his words; it was as though he were grateful to my emotion for coming to relay his own.'

'I don't know how you would say it in Russian or English,

but I assure you that, in French, you do it exceedingly well.'

'Thanks. I'm aware of it. – It was after that, that he began to talk to me about natural history; and I tried to persuade him that it would be monstrous to sacrifice his career to his love.'

'In other words, you advised him to sacrifice his love. And is it your intention to take the place of that love?'

Lilian remained silent.

'This time, I think it really is he,' went on Robert, rising. 'Quick! one word before he comes in. My father died this evening.'

'Ah!' she said simply.

'You haven't a fancy to become Comtesse de Passavant, have you?'

At this Lilian flung herself back with a burst of laughter.

'Oh, oh, my dear friend! The fact is I have a vague recollection that I've mislaid a husband somewhere or other in England. What! I never told you?'

'Not that I remember.'

'You might have guessed it; as a rule a Lady's accompanied by a Lord.'

The Comte de Passavant, who had never had much faith in the authenticity of his friend's title, smiled. She went on: 'Is it to cloak your own life, that you've taken it into your head to propose such a thing to me? No, my dear friend, no. Let's stay as we are. Friends, eh?' And she held out her hand, which he kissed.

'Ah! Ah! I thought as much,' cried Vincent, as he came into the room. 'The traitor! He has dressed!'

'Yes, I had promised not to change, so as to keep him in countenance,' said Robert. 'I'm sorry, my dear fellow, but I suddenly remembered I was in mourning.'

Vincent held his head high. An air of triumph and of joy breathed from his whole person. At his arrival, Lilian had sprung to her feet. She looked him up and down for a moment, then rushed joyously at Robert and began belabouring his back with her fists, jumping, dancing and exclaiming as she did so. (Lilian irritates me rather when she puts on this affection of childishness.)

'He has lost his bet! He has lost his bet!'

'What bet?' asked Vincent.

'He had bet that you would lose your money again tonight. Tell us! Quickly! You've won. How much?'

'I have had the extraordinary courage – and virtue – to leave off at fifty thousand and come away.'

Lilian gave a roar of delight.

'Bravo! Bravo! Bravo!' she cried. Then she flung her arms round Vincent's neck. From head to foot, he felt her glowing, lissom body, with its strange perfume of sandal-wood, pressed against his own; and Lilian kissed him on the forehead, on the cheeks, on the lips; Vincent staggered and freed himself. He took a bundle of banknotes out of his pocket.

'Here! take back what you advanced me,' he said, holding out five of them to Robert.

'No,' answered Robert. 'It is to Lady Lilian that you owe them now.' And he handed her the notes, which she flung on to the divan. She was panting. She went out on the terrace to breathe. It was that ambiguous hour when night is drawing to an end, and the devil casts up his accounts. Outside not a sound was to be heard. Vincent had seated himself on the divan. Lilian turned towards him:

'And now, what do you mean to do?' she asked; and for the first time she called him 'thou'.

He put his head between his hands and said with a kind of sob:

'I don't know.'

Lilian went up to him and put her hand on his forehead; he raised it and his eyes were dry and burning.

'In the meantime, we'll drink each other's health,' said she, and she filled the three glasses with Tokay. After they had drunk:

'Now you must go. It's late and I'm tired out.' She accompanied them into the antechamber and then, as Robert went out first, she slipped a little metal object into Vincent's hand. 'Go out with him,' she whispered, 'and come back in a quarter of an hour.'

In the antechamber a footman was dozing. She shook him by the arm.

'Light these gentlemen downstairs,' she said.

The staircase was dark. It would have been a simple matter, no doubt, to make use of electric light, but she made it a point that her visitors should always be shown out by a servant.

The footman lighted the candles in a big candelabra, which he held high above him and preceded Robert and Vincent downstairs. Robert's car was waiting outside the door, which the footman shut behind them.

'I think I shall walk home. I need a little exercise to steady my nerves,' said Vincent, as the other opened the door of the motor and signed to him to get in.

'Don't you really want me to take you home?' And Robert suddenly seized Vincent's left hand, which he was holding shut. 'Open your hand! Come! Show us what you've got there!'

Vincent was simpleton enough to be afraid of Robert's jealousy. He blushed as he loosened his fingers and a little key fell on to the pavement. Robert picked it up at once, looked at it and gave it back to Vincent with a laugh.

'Ho! Ho!' he said and shrugged his shoulders. Then as he was getting into his car, he turned back to Vincent, who was standing there looking a little foolish:

'It's Thursday morning. Tell your brother that I expect him this afternoon at four o'clock.' And he shut the door of the carriage quickly without giving Vincent time to answer.

The car went off. Vincent walked a few paces along the quay, crossed the Seine, and went on till he reached the part of the Tuileries which lies outside the railings; going up to the little fountain, he soaked his handkerchief in the water and pressed it on to his forehead and his temples. Then, slowly, he walked back towards Lilian's house. There let us leave him, while the devil watches him with amusement as he noiselessly slips the little key into the keyhole....

It is at this same hour that Laura, his yesterday's mistress, is at last dropping off to sleep in her gloomy little hotel room, after having long wept, long bemoaned herself. On the deck of the ship which is bringing him back to France, Edouard, in the first light of the dawn, is re-reading her letter – the plaintive letter in which she appeals for help. The gentle shores of his native land are already in sight, though scarcely visible through the morning mist to any but a practised eye. Not a cloud is in the heavens, where the glance of God will soon be smiling. The horizon is already lifting a rosy eyelid. How hot it is going to be in Paris! It is time to return to Bernard. Here he is, just awaking in Olivier's bed.

6

BERNARD AWAKENS

> We are all bastards;
> And that most venerable man which I
> Did call my father, was I know not where
> When I was stamped.
>
> SHAKESPEARE: *Cymbeline*

BERNARD has had an absurd dream. He doesn't remember his dream. He doesn't try to remember his dream, but to get out of it. He returns to the world of reality to feel Olivier's body pressing heavily against him. Whilst they were asleep (or at any rate while Bernard was asleep) his friend had come close up to him – and, for that matter, the bed was too narrow to allow of much distance; he had turned over; he is sleeping on his side now and Bernard feels Olivier's warm breath tickling his neck. Bernard has nothing on but his short day-shirt; one of Olivier's arms is flung across him, weighing oppressively and indiscreetly on his flesh. For a moment Bernard is not sure that Olivier is really asleep. He frees himself gently. He gets up without waking Olivier, dresses and then lies down again on the bed. It is still too early to be going. Four o'clock. The night is only just beginning to dwindle. One more hour of rest, one more hour for gathering strength to start the coming day valiantly. But there is no more sleep for him. Bernard stares at the glimmering window-pane, at the grey walls of the little room, at the iron bedstead where George is tossing in his dreams.

'In a moment,' he says to himself, 'I shall be setting out to meet my fate. Adventure! What a splendid word! The *Advent* of destiny! All the surprising unknown that awaits me! I don't know if everyone is like me, but as soon as I am awake, I like despising the people who are asleep. Olivier, my friend, I shall go off without waiting for your good-bye. Up! valorous Bernard! The time has come!'

He rubs his face with the corner of a towel dipped in water, brushes his hair, puts on his shoes and leaves the room noiselessly. Out at last!

Ah! the morning air that has not yet been breathed, how life-giving it seems to body and soul! Bernard follows the railings of the Luxembourg Gardens, goes down the rue Bonaparte, reaches the quays, crosses the Seine. He thinks of the new rule of life which he has only lately formulated: 'If *I* don't do it, who will? If I don't do it at once, when shall I?' He thinks: 'Great things to do!' He feels that he is going towards them. 'Great things!' he repeats to himself, as he walks along. If only he knew what they were! . . . In the meantime he knows that he is hungry; here he is at the Halles. He has eight sous in his pocket – not a sou more! He goes into a public-house and takes a roll and coffee, standing at the bar. Price six sous. He has two sous left; he gallantly leaves one on the counter and holds out the other to a ragamuffin who is grubbing in a dustbin. Charity? Swagger? What does it matter? He feels as happy as a king. He has nothing left – and the whole world is his!

'I expect anything and everything from Providence,' thinks he. 'If only it sets a handsome helping of roast beef before me at lunch-time, I shall be willing to strike a bargain' – for last night he had gone without his dinner. The sun has risen long ago. Bernard is back again on the quays now. He feels all lightness. When he runs he feels as though he were flying. His thoughts leap through his brain with delicious ease. He thinks:

'The difficulty in life is to take the same things seriously for long at a time. For instance, my mother's love for the person I used to call my father – I believed in it for fifteen years. I still believed in it yesterday. *She* wasn't able to take her love seriously, either. I wonder whether I despise her or esteem her the more for having made her son a bastard. . . . But in reality, I don't wonder as much as all that. The feelings one has for one's progenitors are among the things that it's better not to go into too deeply. As for Mr Cuckold, it's perfectly simple – for as far back as I can remember, I've always hated him; I must admit now that I didn't deserve much credit for it – and that's the only thing I regret. To think that if I hadn't broken open that drawer I might have gone on all my life believing that I harboured unnatural feelings in my breast towards a father! What a relief to know!... All the same I didn't exactly break open the drawer; I never even thought of opening it.... And there were extenuating circumstances: first of all I was horribly bored that day. And that curiosity of mine – that "fatal curiosity" as Fénelon calls it, it's certainly the surest thing I've inherited from my real father, for the Profitendieus haven't an ounce of it in their composition. I have never met anyone less curious than the gentleman who is my mother's husband – unless perhaps it's the children he has produced. I must think about them later on – after I have dined.... To lift up a marble slab off the top of a table and to see a drawer underneath is really not the same thing as picking a lock. I'm not a burglar. It might happen to anyone to lift the marble slab off a table. Theseus must have been about my age when he lifted the stone. The difficulty in the case of a table is the clock as a rule.... I shouldn't have dreamt of lifting the marble slab off the table if I hadn't wanted to mend the clock.... What doesn't happen to everyone is to find arms underneath – or guilty love-letters. Pooh! The important thing was that I should learn the facts. It isn't everyone who can indulge in the luxury of a ghost to reveal them, like Hamlet. Hamlet! It's curious how one's point of view changes according as one is the offspring of crime or legitimacy. I'll think about that later on – after I have dined.... Was it wrong of me to read those letters!... No, I should be feeling remorseful! And if I hadn't read the letters, I should have had to go on living in ignorance and falsehood and submission. Oh, for a draught of air! Oh, for the open sea! "Bernard! Bernard, that green youth of yours ..." as Bossuet says. Seat your youth on that bench, Bernard. What a beautiful morning! There really are days when the sun seems to be kissing the earth. If I could get rid of myself for a little, there's not a doubt but I should write poetry.'

And as he lay stretched on the bench, he got rid of himself so effectually that he fell asleep.

7

LILIAN AND VINCENT

THE sun, already high in the heavens, caresses Vincent's bare foot on the wide bed, where he is lying beside Lilian. She sits up and looks at him, not knowing that he is awake, and is astonished to see a look of anxiety on his face.

It is possible that Lady Griffith loved Vincent; but what she loved in him was success. Vincent was tall, handsome, slim, but he did not know how to hold himself, how to sit down or get up. He had an expressive face, but he did his hair badly. Above all she admired the boldness and robustness of his intellect; he was certainly highly educated, but she thought him uncultivated. With the instinct of a mistress and a mother, she hung over this big boy of hers and made it her task to form him. He was her creation – her statue. She taught him to polish his nails, to part his hair on one side instead of brushing it back, so that his brow, when it was half hidden by a stray lock, looked all the whiter and loftier. And then instead of the modest little ready-made bows he used to wear, she gave him really becoming neckties. Decidedly Lady Griffith loved Vincent; but she could not put up with him when he was silent or 'moody', as she called it.

She gently passes a finger over Vincent's forehead, as though to efface a wrinkle – those two deep vertical furrows which start from his eyebrows, and give his face a look almost of suffering.

'If you are going to bring me regrets, anxieties, remorse,' she murmurs, as she leans over him, 'it would be better never to come back.'

Vincent shuts his eyes as though to shut out too bright a light. The jubilation in Lilian's face dazzles him.

'You must treat this as if it were a mosque – take your shoes off before you come in, so as not to bring in any mud from the outside. Do you suppose I don't know what you are thinking of?' Then, as Vincent tries to put his hand on her mouth, she defends herself with the grace of a naughty child.

'No! Let me speak to you seriously. I have reflected a great deal about what you said the other day. People always think that women aren't capable of reflection, but you know, it depends upon the woman.... That thing you said the other day about the products of cross breeding ... and that it isn't by crossing that one gets satisfactory results so much as by selection.... Have I remembered your lesson, eh? Well, this morning I think you have bred a monster – a perfectly ridiculous creature – you'll never rear it! A cross between a bacchante and the Holy Ghost! Haven't you now?... You're disgusted with yourself for having chucked Laura. I can tell it from the lines on your forehead. If you want to go back to her, say so at once and leave me; I shall have been mistaken in you and I shan't mind in the least. But if you mean to stay with me, then get rid of that funereal countenance. You remind me of certain English people – the more emancipated their opinions, the more they cling to their morality; so that there are no severer Puritans than their free-thinkers.... You think I'm heartless? You're wrong. I understand perfectly that you are sorry for Laura. But then, what are you doing here?'

Then, as Vincent turned his head away:

'Look here! You must go to the bathroom now and try and wash your regrets off in the shower-bath. I shall ring for breakfast, eh? And when you come back, I'll explain something that you don't seem to understand.'

He had got up. She sprang after him.

'Don't dress just yet. In the cupboard on the right hand side of the bath, you'll find a collection of burnouses and haiks and pyjamas. Take anything you like.'

Vincent appeared twenty minutes later dressed in a pistachio-coloured silk jellabah.

'Oh, wait a minute – wait! Let me arrange you!' cried Lilian in delight. She pulled out of an oriental chest two wide purple scarves; wound the darker of the two as a sash round Vincent's waist, and the other as a turban round his head.

'My thoughts are always the same colour as my clothes,' she said. (She had put on crimson and silver lamé pyjamas.) 'I remember once, when I was quite a little girl at San Francisco, I was put into black because a sister of my mother's had died – an old aunt whom I had never seen. I cried the whole day long. I was terribly, terribly sad; I thought that I was very unhappy and that I was grieving deeply for my aunt's death – all because I was in black. Nowadays, if men are more serious than women, it's because their clothes are darker. I'll wager that your thoughts are quite different from what they were a little while ago. Sit down there on the bed; and when you've drunk a glass of vodka and a cup of tea and eaten two or three sandwiches, I'll tell you a story. Say when I'm to begin....'

She settled down on the rug beside the bed, crouching between Vincent's legs like an Egyptian statue, with her chin resting on her knees. When she had eaten and drunk, she began:

'I was on the *Bourgogne*, you know, on the day of the wreck. I was seventeen, so now you know how old I am. I was a very good swimmer, and to show you that I'm not hard-hearted, I'll tell you that if my first thought was to save myself, my second was to save someone else. I'm not quite sure even whether it wasn't my first. Or rather, I don't think I thought of anything; but nothing disgusts me so much in such moments as the people who only think of themselves – oh, yes – the women who scream. There was a first boatload, chiefly of women and children, and some of them yelled to such an extent that it was enough to make anyone lose his head. The boat was so badly handled that instead of dropping down on to the sea straight, it dived nose foremost and everyone in it was flung out before it even had time to fill with water. The whole scene took place by the light of torches and lanterns and searchlights. You can't imagine how ghastly it was. The waves were very big and everything that was not in the light was lost in darkness on the other side of the hill of water.

'I have never lived more intensely; but I was as incapable of reflection as a Newfoundland dog, I suppose, when he jumps into the water. I can't even understand now what happened; I only know that I had noticed a little girl in the boat – a darling thing of about five or six; and when I saw the boat overturn, I immediately made up my mind that it was her I would save. She was with her mother, but the poor woman was a bad swimmer;

and as usual in such cases, her skirts hampered her. As for me, I expect I undressed mechanically; I was called to take my place in the second boatload. I must have got in; and then I no doubt jumped straight into the sea out of the boat; all I can remember is swimming about for a long time with the child clinging to my neck. It was terrified and clutched me so tight that I couldn't breathe. Luckily the people in the boat saw us and either waited for us or rowed towards us. But that's not why I'm telling you this story. The recollection which remains most vividly with me and which nothing will ever efface from my mind and my heart is this: There were about forty or so of us in the boat, all crowded together, for a number of swimmers had been picked up at the last gasp like me. The water was almost on a level with the edge of the boat. I was in the stern and I was holding the little girl I had just saved tightly pressed against me to warm her – and to prevent her from seeing what I couldn't help seeing myself – two sailors, one armed with a hatchet and the other with a kitchen chopper. And what do you think they were doing? . . . They were hacking off the fingers and hands of the swimmers who were trying to get into our boat. One of these two sailors (the other was a Negro) turned to me, as I sat there, my teeth chattering with cold and fright and horror, and said, "If another single one gets in we shall be bloody well done for. The boat's full." And he added that it was a thing that had to be done in all shipwrecks, but that naturally one didn't mention it.

'I think I fainted then; at any rate, I can't remember anything more, just as one remains deaf for a long time after a noise that has been too tremendous.

'And when I came to myself on board the *X*, which picked us up, I realized that I was no longer the same, that I never could again be the same sentimental young girl I had been before; I realized that a part of myself had gone down with the *Bourgogne*; that henceforth there would be a whole heap of delicate feelings whose fingers and hands I should hack away to prevent them from climbing into my heart and wrecking it.'

She looked at Vincent out of the corner of her eye and, with a backward twist of her body, went on: 'It's a habit one must get into.'

Then, as her hair, which she had pinned up loosely, was coming down and falling over her shoulders, she rose, went up to a mirror and began to rearrange it, talking as she did so:

'When I left America a little later, I felt as if I were the golden fleece starting off in search of a conqueror. I may sometimes have been foolish . . . I may sometimes have made mistakes – perhaps I am making one now in talking to you like this – but you, on your side, don't imagine that because I have given myself to you, you have won me. Make certain of this – I abominate mediocrity, and I can love no one who isn't a conqueror. If you want me, it must be to help you to victory; if it's only to be pitied and consoled and made much of . . . no, my dear boy – I'd better say so at once – *I'm* not the person you need – it's Laura.'

She said all this without turning round and while she was continuing to arrange her rebellious locks, but Vincent caught her eye in the glass.

'May I give you my answer this evening?' he said, getting up and taking off his Oriental garments to get into his day clothes. 'I must go home quickly now so as to catch my brother Olivier before he goes out. I've got something to say to him.'

He said it by way of apology, to give colour to his departure; but when he went up to Lilian, she turned round to him smiling, and so lovely that he hesitated.

'Unless I leave a line for him to get at lunch-time,' he added.

'Do you see a great deal of him?'

'Hardly anything. No, it's an invitation for this afternoon, which I've got to pass on to him.'

'From Robert? . . . *Oh! I see!* * . . .' she said, smiling oddly. 'That's a person, too, I must talk to you about. . . . All right! Go at once. But come back at six o'clock, because at seven his car is coming to take us out to dinner in the Bois.'

Vincent walks home, meditating as he goes; he realizes that from the satisfaction of desire there may arise, accompanying joy and as it were sheltering behind it, something not unlike despair.

* In English in the original.

8

EDOUARD AND LAURA

Il faut choisir d'aimer les femmes ou de les connaître; il n'y a pas de milieu.

CHAMFORT

EDOUARD, as he sits in the Paris express, is reading Passavant's new book, *The Horizontal Bar*, which he has just bought at the Dieppe railway station. No doubt he will find the book waiting for him when he gets to Paris, but Edouard is impatient. People are talking of it everywhere. Not one of his own books has ever had the honour of figuring on station bookstalls. He has been told, it is true, that it would be an easy matter to arrange, but he doesn't care to. He repeats to himself that he hasn't the slightest desire to see his books in railway stations – but it is the sight of Passavant's book that makes him feel the need of repeating it. Everything that Passavant does, and everything that other people do round about him, rubs Edouard up the wrong way: the newspaper articles, for instance, in which his book is praised up to the skies. It's as if it were a wager; in every one of the three papers that he buys on landing, there is a eulogy of *The Horizontal Bar*. In the fourth there is a letter from Passavant, complaining of an article which had recently appeared in the same paper and which had been a trifle less flattering than the others. Passavant writes defending and explaining his book. This letter irritates Edouard even more than the articles. Passavant pretends to enlighten public opinion – in reality he cleverly directs it. None of Edouard's books has ever given rise to such a crop of articles; but, for that matter, Edouard has never made the slightest attempt to attract the favour of the critics. If they turn him the cold shoulder, it is a matter of indifference to him. But as he reads the articles on his rival's book, he feels the need of assuring himself again that it is a matter of indifference.

Not that he detests Passavant. He has met him occasionally and has thought him charming. Passavant, moreover, has always been particularly amiable to him. But he dislikes Passavant's books. He thinks Passavant not so much an artist as a juggler. Enough of Passavant!

Edouard takes Laura's letter out of his coat pocket – the letter he was reading on the boat; he reads it again:

Dear friend, – The last time I saw you – (do you remember? – it was in St James's Park, on the 2nd of April, the day before I left for the South?) you made me promise to write to you if ever I was in any difficulty. I am keeping my promise. To whom can I appeal but you? I cannot ask for help from those to whom I should most like to turn; it is just from them that I must hide my trouble. Dear friend, I am in very great trouble. Some day perhaps, I will tell you the story of my life after I parted from Felix. He took me out to Pau and then he had to return to Cambridge for his lectures. What came over me, when I was left out there all by myself – the spring – my convalescence – my solitude? . . . Dare I confess to you what it is impossible to tell Felix? The time has come when I ought to go back to him – but oh! I am no longer worthy to. The letters which I have been writing to him for some time past have been lying letters, and the ones he writes to me speak of nothing but his joy at hearing that I am better. I wish to heaven I had remained ill! I wish to heaven I had died out there! . . . My friend, the fact must be faced: I am expecting a child and it is not his. I left Felix more than three months ago; there's no possibility of blinding *him* at any rate. I dare not go back to him. I cannot. I will not. He is too good. He would forgive me, no doubt, and I don't deserve – I don't want his forgiveness. I daren't go back to my parents either. They think I am still at Pau. My father – if he knew, if he understood – is capable of cursing me. He would turn me away. And how could I face his virtue, his horror of evil, of lying, of everything that is impure? I am afraid too of grieving my mother and my sister. As for . . . but I will not accuse him; when he was in a position to help me, he promised to do so. Unfortunately, however, in order to be better able to help me, he took to gambling. He has lost the money which should have served to keep me until after my confinement. He has lost it all. I had thought at first of going away with him somewhere – anywhere; of living with him at any rate for a short time, for I didn't mean to hamper him – to be a burden to him; I should have ended by finding some way of earning my living, but I can't just yet. I can see that he is unhappy at having to abandon me and that it is the only thing that he can do. I don't blame him – but all the same he *is* abandoning me. I am here in Paris without any money. I am living on credit in a little hotel, but it can't go on much longer. I don't know what is to become of me. To think that ways so sweet should lead only to such depths as these! I am writing to the address in London which you gave me. But when will this letter reach you? And I who longed so to have a child! I do nothing but cry all day long. Advise me. You are the only hope I have left. Help me if you can, and if you can't . . . Oh! in other days I should have had more courage, but now it is not I alone who will die. If you don't come – if you write that you can do nothing for me, I shall have no word or thought of reproach for you. In bidding you good-bye, I shall try and not regret life too much, but I think that you never quite understood that the friendship you gave me is still the best thing in my life – never quite understood that what I called my friendship for you went by another name in my heart.

LAURA DOUVIERS

P.S.—Before putting this letter in the post I shall make another attempt. This evening I shall go and see him one last time more. If you get this therefore it will mean that really . . . Good-bye, good-bye! I don't know what I am writing.

Edouard had received this letter on the morning of the day he had left England. That is to say he had decided to leave as soon as he received it. In any case, he had not intended to stay much longer. I don't mean to insinuate that he would have been incapable of returning to Paris specially to help Laura; I merely say that he is glad to return. He has been kept terribly short of pleasure lately in England; and the first thing he means to do when he gets to Paris is to go to a house of ill-fame; and as he doesn't wish to take his private papers with him, he reaches his portmanteau down from the rack and opens it, so as to slip in Laura's letter.

The place for this letter is not among coats and shirts; he pulls out from beneath the clothes a cloth-bound MS. book, half filled with his writing; turns to the very beginning of the book, looks up certain pages which were written last year and re-reads them; it is between these that Laura's letter will find its proper place.

EDOUARD'S JOURNAL

Oct 18th. – Laura does not seem to suspect her power; but I, who can unravel the secrets of my own heart, know well enough that up till now I have never written a line that has not been indirectly inspired by her. I feel her still a child beside me, and all the skill of my discourse is due only to my constant desire to instruct, to convince, to captivate her. I see nothing – I hear nothing without asking myself what she would think of it. I forsake my own emotion to feel only hers. And I think that if she were not there to give definition to my personality, it would vanish in the excessive vagueness of its contours. It is only round her that I concentrate and define myself. By what illusion have I hitherto believed that I was fashioning her to my likeness, when, on the contrary, I was bending myself to hers? And I never noticed it! Or rather – the influence of love, by a curious action of give and take, made us both reciprocally alter our natures. Involuntarily – unconsciously – each one of a pair of lovers fashions himself to meet the other's requirements – endeavours by a continual effort to resemble that idol of himself which he beholds in the other's heart. . . . Whoever really loves abandons all sincerity.

This was the way in which she deluded me. Her thought everywhere conpanioned mine. I admired her taste, her curiosity, her culture, and did not realize that it was her love for me which made her take so passionate an interest in everything that I cared for. For she never discovered anything herself. Each one of her admirations – I see it now – was merely a couch on which she could lay her thought alongside of mine; there was nothing in all this that responded to any profound need of her nature. 'It was only for you that I adorned and decked myself,' she will say. Yes! But I could have wished that it had been only for *her* and that she had yielded in doing so to an intimate and personal necessity. But of all these things that she has added to herself for my sake, nothing will remain – not even a regret – not even a sense of something missing. A day comes when the true self, which time has slowly stripped of all its borrowed raiment, reappears, and then, if it was of these ornaments that the other was enamoured, he finds that he is pressing to his heart nothing but an empty dress – nothing but a memory – nothing but grief and despair.

Ah! with what virtues, with what perfections I had adorned her!

How vexing this question of sincerity is! *Sincerity!* When I say the word I think only of her. If it is myself that I consider, I cease to understand its meaning. I am never anything but what I think myself – and this varies so incessantly, that often, if I were not there to make them acquainted, my morning's self would not recognize my evening's. Nothing could be more different from me than myself. It is only sometimes when I am alone that the substratum emerges and that I attain a certain fundamental continuity; but at such times I feel that my life is slowing down, stopping, and that I am on the very verge of ceasing to exist. My heart beats only out of sympathy; I live only through others – by procuration, so to speak, and by espousals; and I never feel myself living so intensely as when I escape from myself to become no matter who.

This anti-egoistical force of decentralization is so great in me that it disintegrates my sense of property – and, as a consequence, of responsibility. Such a being is not of the kind that one can marry. How can I make Laura understand this?

Oct. 26th. – The only existence that anything (including myself) has for me, is poetical – I restore this word its full signification. It seems to me sometimes that I do not really exist, but that I merely imagine I exist. The thing that I have the greatest difficulty in believing in, is my own reality. I am constantly getting outside myself, and as I watch myself act I cannot understand how a person who acts is the same as the person who is watching him act, and who wonders in astonishment and doubt how he can be actor and watcher at the same moment.

Psychological analysis lost all interest for me from the moment that I became aware that men feel what they imagine they feel. From that to thinking that they imagine they feel what they feel was a very short step . . . ! I see it clearly in the case of my love for Laura: between loving her and imagining I love her – between imagining I love her less and loving her less – what God could tell the difference? In the domain of feeling, what is real is indistinguishable from what is imaginary. And if it is sufficient to imagine one loves, in order to love, so it is sufficient to say to oneself that when one loves one imagines one loves, in order to love a little less and even in order to detach oneself a little from one's love, or at any rate to detach some of the crystals from one's love. But if one is able to say such a thing to oneself, must one not already love a little less?

It is by such reasoning as this, that *X* in my book tries to detach himself from *Z* – and, still more, tries to detach her from himself.

Oct. 28th. – People are always talking of the sudden crystallization of love. Its slow *decrystallization*, which I never hear talked of, is a psychological phenomenon which interests me far more. I consider that it can be observed, after a longer or shorter period, in all love marriages. There will be no reason to fear this, indeed, in Laura's case (and so much the better) if she marries Felix Douviers, as reason, and her family, and I myself advise her to do. Douviers is a thoroughly estimable professor, with many excellent points, and very capable in his own line (I hear that he is greatly appreciated by his pupils). In process of time and in the wear of daily life, Laura is sure to discover in him all the more virtues for having had fewer illusions to begin with; when she praises him, indeed, she seems to me really not to give him his due. Douviers is worth more than she thinks.

What an admirable subject for a novel – the progressive and and reciprocal decrystallization of a husband and wife after fifteen or twenty years of married life. So long as he loves and desires to be loved, the lover cannot show himself as he really is, and moreover he does not see the beloved – but instead, an idol whom he decks out, a divinity whom he creates.

So I have warned Laura to be on her guard against both herself and me. I have tried to persuade her that our love could not bring either of us any lasting happiness. I hope I have more or less convinced her.

*

Edouard shrugs his shoulders, slips the letter in between the leaves of his journal, shuts it up and replaces it in his suitcase. He then takes a hundred-franc note out of his pocket-book and puts that too in his suitcase. This sum will be more than sufficient to last him till he can fetch his suitcase from the cloakroom, where he means to deposit it on his arrival. The tiresome thing is that it has got no key – or at any rate he has not got its key. He always loses the keys of his suitcases. Pooh! The cloakroom attendants are too busy during the daytime and never alone. He will fetch it out at about four o'clock and then go to comfort and help Laura; he will try and persuade her to come out to dinner with him.

Edouard dozes; insensibly his thoughts take another direction. He wonders whether he would have guessed merely by reading Laura's letter, that her hair was black. He says to himself that novelists, by a too exact description of their characters, hinder the reader's imagination rather than help it, and that they ought to allow each individual to picture their personages to himself according to his own fancy. He thinks of the novel which he is planning and which is to be like nothing else he has ever written. He is not sure that *The Counterfeiters* is a good title. He was wrong to have announced it beforehand. An absurd custom this of publishing the titles of books in advance, in order to whet the reader's appetite! It whets nobody's appetite and it ties one. He is not sure either that the subject is a very good one. He is continually thinking of it and has been thinking of it for a long time past; but he has not yet written a line of it. On the other hand, he puts down his notes and reflections in a little notebook. He takes this notebook out of his suitcase and a fountain-pen out of his pocket. He writes:

I should like to strip the novel of every element that does not specifically belong to the novel. Just as photography in the past freed painting from its concern for a certain sort of accuracy, so the phonograph will eventually no doubt rid the novel of the kind of dialogue which is drawn from the life and which realists take so much pride in. Outward events, accidents, traumatisms, belong to the cinema. The novel should leave them to it. Even the description of the characters does not seem to me properly to belong to the *genre*. No; this does not seem to me the business of the *pure* novel (and in art, as in everything else, purity is the only thing I care about). No more than it is the business of the drama. And don't let it be argued that the dramatist does not describe his characters because the spectator is intended to see them transposed alive on the stage; for how often on the stage an actor irritates and baffles us because he is so unlike the person our own imagination had figured better without him. The novelist does not as a rule rely sufficiently on the reader's imagination.

What is the station that has just flashed past? Asnières. He puts the notebook back in his suitcase. But, decidedly, the thought of Passavant vexes him. He takes the notebook out again and adds:

The work of art, as far as Passavant is concerned, is not so much an end as a means. The artistic convictions which he displays are asserted with so much vehemence merely because they lack depth; no secret exigence of his temperament necessitates them; they are evoked by the passing hour; their *mot d'ordre* is opportunism.

The Horizontal Bar! The things that soonest appear out of date are those that at first strike us as most modern. Every concession, every affectation is the promise of a wrinkle. But it is by these means that Passavant pleases the young. He snaps his fingers at the future. It is the generation of today that he is speaking to – which is certainly better than speaking to that of yesterday. But as what he writes is addressed only to that younger generation, it is in danger of disappearing with it. He is perfectly aware of this and does not build his hopes on surviving. This is the reason that he defends himself so fiercely, and that, not only when he is attacked, but at the slightest restrictions of the critics. If he felt that his work was lasting he would leave it to defend itself and would not so continually seek to justify it. More than that, misunderstanding, injustice, would rejoice him. So much the more food for tomorrow's critics to use their teeth upon!

He looks at his watch: 11.35. He ought to have arrived by now. Curious to know if by any impossible chance Olivier will be at the station to meet him? He hasn't the slightest expectation of it. How can he even suppose that his postcard has come to Olivier's notice – that postcard on which he informed Olivier's parents of his return, and incidentally, carelessly, absent-mindedly to all appearance, mentioned the day and hour of his arrival . . . as one takes a pleasure in stalking – in setting a trap for fate itself.

The train is stopping. Quick! A porter! No! His suitcase is not very heavy, nor the cloakroom very far. . . . Even supposing he were there, would they recognize each other in all this crowd? They have seen so little of each other. If only he hasn't grown out of recognition! . . . Ah! Great Heavens! Can that be he?

9

EDOUARD AND OLIVIER

We should have nothing to deplore of all that happened later if only Edouard's and Olivier's joy at meeting had been more demonstrative; but they both had a singular incapacity for gauging their credit in other people's hearts and minds; this now paralysed them; so that each, believing his emotion to be unshared, absorbed in his own joy, and half ashamed at finding it so great, was completely preoccupied by trying to hide its intensity from the other.

It was for this reason that Olivier, far from helping Edouard's joy by telling him with what eagerness he had come to meet him, thought fit to speak of some job or other which he had had to do in the neighbourhood that very morning, as if to excuse himself for having come. His conscience, scrupulous to excess, cunningly set about persuading him that he was perhaps in Edouard's way. The lie was hardly out of his mouth when he blushed. Edouard surprised the blush, and as he had at first seized Olivier's arm and passionately pressed it, he thought (scrupulous he, too) that it was this that had made him blush.

He had begun by saying:

'I tried to force myself to believe that you wouldn't come, but in reality I was certain that you would.'

Then it came over him that Olivier thought these words presumptuous. When he heard him answer in an off-hand way: 'I had a job to do in this very neighbourhood,' he dropped Olivier's arm and his spirits fell from their heights. He would have liked to ask Olivier whether he had understood that the postcard, which he had addressed to his parents, had been really intended for him; as he was on the point of putting the question, his heart failed him. Olivier, who was afraid of boring Edouard or of being misunderstood if he spoke of himself, kept silent. He looked at Edouard and was astonished at the trembling of his lip; then he dropped his eyes at once. Edouard was both longing for the look and afraid that Olivier would think him too old. He kept rolling a bit of paper nervously between his fingers. It was the ticket he had just been given at the cloak-room, but he did not think of that.

'If it was his cloakroom ticket,' thought Olivier, as he watched him crumple it up and throw it absent-mindedly away, 'he wouldn't throw it away like that.' And he glanced round for a second to see the wind carry it off along the pavement far behind them. If he had looked longer he might have seen a young man pick it up. It was Bernard, who had been following them ever since they had left the station. . . . In the meanwhile Olivier was in despair at finding nothing to say to Edouard, and the silence between them became intolerable.

'When we get opposite Condorcet,' he kept repeating to him-self, 'I shall say, "I must go home now; good-bye."'

Then, when they got opposite the Lycée, he gave himself till as far as the corner of the rue de Provence. But Edouard, on whom the silence was weighing quite as heavily, could not endure that they should part in this way. He drew his companion into a café. Perhaps the port wine which he ordered would help them to get the better of their embarrass-ment.

They drank to each other.

'Good luck to you!' said Edouard, raising his glass. 'When is the examination?'

'In ten days.'

'Do you feel ready?'

Olivier shrugged his shoulders. 'One never knows. If one doesn't happen to be in good form on the day . . .'

He didn't dare answer 'yes', for fear of seeming conceited. He was embarrassed, too, because he wanted and yet was afraid to say 'thou' to Edouard. He contented himself by giving his sentences an impersonal turn, so as to avoid at any rate saying 'you'; and by so doing he deprived Edouard of the opportunity of begging him to say 'thou' – which Edouard longed for him to do and which he remembered well enough he *had* done a few days before his leaving for England.

'Have you been working?'

'Pretty well, but not as well as I might have.'

'People who work well always think they might work better,' said Edouard rather pompously.

He said it in spite of himself and then thought his sentence ridiculous.

'Do you still write poetry?'

'Sometimes. . . . I badly want a little advice.' He raised his eyes to Edouard. '*Your* advice,' he wanted to say – '*thy* advice.' And his look, in default of his voice, said it so plainly that Edouard thought he was saying it out of deference – out of amiability. But why should he have answered – and so brusquely too . . . ?

'Oh, one must go to oneself for advice, or to companions of one's own age. One's elders are no use.'

Olivier thought: 'I didn't ask him. Why is he protesting?'

Each of them was vexed with himself for not being able to utter a word that didn't sound curt and stiff; and each of them, feeling the other's embarrassment and irritation, thought himself the cause and object of them. Such interviews lead to no good unless something comes to the rescue. Nothing came.

Olivier had begun the morning badly. When, on waking up, he had found that Bernard was no longer beside him, that he had left him without saying good-bye, his heart had been filled with unhappiness; though he had forgotten it for an instant in the joy of seeing Edouard, it now surged up in him anew like a black wave and submerged every other thought in his mind. He would have liked to talk about Bernard, to tell Edouard everything and anything, to make him interested in his friend.

But Edouard's slightest smile would have wounded him; and as the passionate and tumultuous feelings which were shaking him could not have been expressed without the risk of seeming exaggerated, he kept silence. He felt his features harden; he would have liked to fling himself into Edouard's arms and cry. Edouard misunderstood this silence of Olivier's and the look of sternness on his face; he loved him far too much to be able to behave with any ease. He hardly dared look at Olivier, whom he longed to take in his arms and fondle like a child, and when he met his eyes and saw their dull and lifeless expression:

'Of course!' he said to himself. 'I bore him – I bore him to death. Poor child! He's just waiting for a word from me to escape.' And irresistibly Edouard said the word – out of sheer pity: 'You'd better be off now. Your people are expecting you for lunch, I'm sure.'

Olivier, who was thinking the same things, misunderstood in the same way. He got up in a desperate hurry and held out his hand. At least he wanted to say to Edouard: 'Shall I see you – thee – again soon? Shall we see each other again soon?' ... Edouard was waiting for these words. Nothing came but a commonplace 'Good-bye!'

10

THE CLOAKROOM TICKET

THE sun woke Bernard. He rose from his bench with a violent headache. His gallant courage of the morning had left him. He felt abominably lonely and his heart was swelling with something brackish and bitter which he would not call unhappiness, but which brought the tears to his eyes. What should he do? Where should he go? . . . If his steps turned towards St Lazare Station at the time that he knew Olivier was due there, it was without any definite purpose and merely with the wish to see his friend again. He reproached himself for having left so abruptly that morning; perhaps Olivier had been hurt? . . . Was he not the creature in the world he liked best? . . . When he saw him arm in arm with Edouard a peculiar feeling made him follow the pair and at the same time not show himself; painfully conscious of being *de trop*, he would yet have liked to slip in between them. He thought Edouard looked charming; only a little taller than Olivier and with a scarcely less youthful figure. It was he whom he made up his mind to address; he would wait until Olivier left him. But address him? Upon what pretext?

It was at this moment that he caught sight of the little bit of crumpled paper as it escaped from Edouard's hand. He picked it up, saw that it was a cloakroom ticket . . . and, by Jove, here was the wished-for pretext!

He saw the two friends go into a café, hesitated a moment in perplexity, and then continued his monologue:

'Now a normal fathead would have nothing better to do than to return this paper at once,' he said to himself.

> '"How weary, stale, flat and unprofitable
> Seem to me all the uses of this world!"

as I have heard Hamlet remark. Bernard, Bernard, what thought is this that is tickling you? It was only yesterday that you were rifling a drawer. On what path are you entering? Consider, my boy, consider. . . . Consider that the cloakroom attendant who took Edouard's luggage will be gone to his lunch at twelve o'clock, and that there will be another one on duty. And didn't you promise your friend to stick at nothing?'

He reflected, however, that too much haste might spoil everything. The attendant might be surprised into thinking this haste suspicious; he might consult the entry book and think it unnatural that a piece of luggage deposited in the cloakroom a few minutes before twelve should be taken out immediately after. And besides, suppose some passer-by, some busybody, had seen him pick up the bit of paper. . . . Bernard forced himself to walk to the place de la Concorde without hurrying – in the time it would have taken another person to lunch. It is quite usual, isn't it to put one's luggage in the cloakroom whilst one is lunching and to take it out immediately after. . . . His headache had gone. As he was passing by a restaurant terrace, he boldly took a toothpick from one of the little bundles that were set out on the tables, and stood nibbling it at the cloakroom counter, in order to give himself the air of having lunched. He was lucky to have in his favour his good looks, his well-cut clothes, his distinction, the frankness of his eyes and smile, and that indefinable something in the whole appearance which denotes those who have been brought up in comfort and want for nothing. (But all this gets rather draggled by sleeping on benches.) . . .

He had a horrible turn when the attendant told him there were ten centimes to pay. He had not a single sou left. What should he do? The suitcase was there, on the counter. The slightest sign of hesitation would give the alarm – so would his want of money. But the demon is watching over him; he slips between Bernard's anxious fingers, as they go searching from pocket to pocket with a pretence of feigned despair, a fifty-centime bit, which had lain forgotten since goodness knows when in his waistcoat pocket. Bernard hands it to the attendant. He has not shown a sign of his agitation. He takes up the suitcase, and in the simplest, honestest fashion pockets the forty centimes change. Heavens! How hot he is! Where shall he go now? His legs are beginning to fail him and the suitcase feels heavy. What shall he do with it? . . . He suddenly remembers that he has no key. No! No! Certainly not! He will not break open the lock; what the devil, he isn't a thief! . . . But if he only knew what was in it. His arm is aching and he is perspiring with the heat. He stops for a moment and puts his burden down on the pavement. Of course he has every intention of returning the wretched thing to its owner; but he would like to question it first. He presses the lock at a venture. . . . Oh miracle! The two shells open and disclose a pearl – a pocket-book, which in its turn discloses a bundle of banknotes. Bernard seizes the pearl and shuts up the oyster.

And now that he has the wherewithal – quick! a hotel. He knows of one close by in the rue d'Amsterdam. He is dying of hunger. But before sitting down to table, he must put his suitcase in safety. A waiter carries it upstairs before him; three flights; a passage; a door which he locks upon his treasure. He goes down again.

Sitting at table in front of a beefsteak, Bernard did not dare examine the pocket-book. (One never knows who may be watching you.) But his left hand amorously caressed it, lying snug in his inside pocket.

'How to make Edouard understand that I'm not a thief – that's the trouble. What kind of fellow is Edouard? Perhaps the suitcase may shed a little light upon that. Attractive – so much is certain. But there are heaps of attractive fellows who have no taste for practical joking. If he thinks his suitcase has been stolen, no doubt he'll be glad to see it again. If he's the least decent he'll be grateful to me for bringing it back to him. I shall easily rouse his interest. Let's eat the sweet quickly and then go upstairs and examine the situation. Now for the bill and a soul-stirring tip for the waiter.'

A minute or two later he was back again in his room.

'Now, suitcase, a word with you! . . . A morning-suit, not more than a trifle too big for me, I expect. The material becoming and in good taste. Linen; toilet things. I'm not very sure that I shall give any of all this back. But what proves that I'm not a thief is that these papers interest me a great deal more than anything else. We'll begin by reading this.'

This was the notebook into which Edouard had slipped Laura's melancholy letter. We have already seen the first pages; this is what followed.

II

EDOUARD'S JOURNAL: GEORGE MOLINIER

Nov. 1st. – A fortnight ago...

– it was a mistake not to have noted it down at once. It was not so much that I hadn't time as that my heart was still full of Laura – or, to be more accurate, I did not wish to distract my thoughts from her; moreover, I do not care to note anything here that is casual or fortuitous, and at that time I did not think that what I am going to relate could lead to anything, or be, as people say, of any consequence; at any rate, I would not admit it to myself and it was, in a way, to prove the unimportance of this incident that I refrained from mentioning it in my journal. But I feel more and more – it would be vain to deny it – that it is Olivier's figure that has now become the magnet of my thoughts, that their current sets towards him and that without taking him into account I shall be able neither to explain nor to understand myself properly.

I was coming back that morning from Perrin's, the publisher's, where I had been seeing about the Press copies of the fresh edition of my old book. As the weather was fine, I was dawdling back along the quays until it should be time for lunch.

A little before getting to Vanier's, I stopped in front of a second-hand bookseller's. It was not so much the books that interested me as a small schoolboy, about thirteen years old, who was rummaging the outside shelves under the placid eye of a shop assistant, who sat watching on a rush-bottomed chair in the doorway. I pretended to be examining the bookstall, but I too kept a watch on the youngster out of the corner of my eye. He was dressed in a threadbare overcoat, the sleeves of which were too short and showed his other sleeves below them. Its side pocket was gaping, though it was obviously empty; a corner of the stuff had given way. I reflected that this coat must have already seen service with several elder brothers and that his brothers and he must have been in the habit of stuffing a great many, too many, things into their pockets. I reflected too that his mother must be either very neglectful or very busy not to have mended it. But just then the youngster turned round a little and I saw that the pocket on the other side was coarsely darned with stout black thread. And I seemed to hear the maternal exhortations: 'Don't put two books at a time into your pocket; you'll ruin your overcoat. Your pocket's all torn again. Next time, I warn you, I shan't darn it. Just look what a sight you are! . . .' Things which my own poor mother used to say to me, too, and to which I paid no more attention than he. The overcoat was unbuttoned and my eye was attracted by a kind of decoration, a bit of ribbon, or rather a yellow rosette which he was wearing in the buttonhole of his inside coat. I put all this down for the sake of discipline and for the very reason that it bores me to put it down.

At a certain moment the man on the chair was called into the shop; he did not stay more than a second and came back to his chair at once, but that second was enough to allow the boy to slip the book he was holding into his pocket; then he immediately began scanning the shelves again as if nothing had happened. At the same time he was uneasy; he raised his head, caught me looking at him and understood that I had seen him. At any rate, he said to himself that I might have seen him; he was probably not quite certain; but in his uncertainty he lost all his assurance, blushed and started a little performance in which he tried to appear quite at his ease, but which, on the contrary, showed extreme embarrassment. I did not take my eyes off him. He took the purloined book out of his pocket, thrust it back again, walked away a few steps, pulled out of his inside pocket a wretched little pocket-book, in which he pretended to look for some imaginary money; made a face, a kind of theatrical grimace, aimed at me, and signifying, 'Drat! Not enough!' and with a little shade of surprise in it as well, 'Odd! I thought I had enough!' The whole thing slightly exaggerated, slightly overdone, as when an actor is afraid of not being understood. Finally, under the pressure of my look, I might almost say, he went back to the shelf, pulled the book, this time decidedly, out of his pocket and put it back in its place. It was done so naturally that the assistant noticed nothing. Then the boy raised his head again, hoping that at last he would be rid of me. But not at all; my look was still upon him, like the eye that watched Cain – only my eye was a smiling one. I determined to speak to him and waited until he should have left the bookstall before going up to him; but he didn't budge and still stood planted in front of the books, and I understood that he wouldn't budge as long as I kept gazing at him. So, as at Puss in the Corner, when one tries to entice the pretence quarry to change places, I moved a little away as if I had seen enough and he started off at once in his own direction; but he had no sooner got into the open than I caught him up.

'What was that book?' I asked him out of the blue, at the same time putting as much amenity as I could into my voice and expression.

He looked me full in the face and I felt all his suspicions drop from him. He was not exactly handsome, perhaps, but what charming eyes he had! I saw every kind of feeling wavering in their depths like water weeds at the bottom of a stream.

'It's a guide-book for Algeria. But it's too dear. I'm not rich enough.'

'How much?'

'Two francs fifty.'

'All the same, if you hadn't seen me, you'd have made off with the book in your pocket.'

The little fellow made a movement of indignation. He expostulated in a tone of extreme vulgarity:

'Well, I never! What d'you take me for? A thief?' But he said it with such conviction that I almost began to doubt my own eyes. I felt that I should lose my hold over him if I went on. I took three coins out of my pocket:

'All right! Go and buy it. I'll wait for you.'

Two minutes later he came back turning over the pages of the coveted book. I took it out of his hands. It was an old guide-book of the year 1871.

'What's the good of that?' I said as I handed it back to him. 'It's too old. It's of no use.'

He protested that it was – that, besides, recent guide-books were much too dear, and that for all he could do with it the maps of this one were good enough. I don't attempt to quote his words, which would lose their savour without the extraordinarily vulgar accent with which he said them and which was all the more amusing because his sentences were not turned without a certain elegance.

*

This episode must be very much shortened. Precision in the reader's imagination should be obtained not by accumulating details but by two or three touches put in exactly the right places. I expect for that matter that it would be a better plan to make the boy tell the story himself; his point of view is of more signification than mine. He is flattered and at the same time made uncomfortable by the attention I pay him. But the weight of my look makes him deviate a little from his own real direction. A personality which is over tender and still too young to be conscious of itself, takes shelter behind an attitude. Nothing is more difficult to observe than creatures in the period of formation. One ought to look at them only sideways – in profile.

The youngster suddenly declared that what he liked best was geography! I suspected that an instinct for vagabonding was concealed behind this liking.

'You'd like to go to those parts?' I asked.

'Wouldn't I?' he answered, shrugging his shoulders.

The idea crossed my mind that he was unhappy at home. I asked him if he lived with his parents. 'Yes.' Didn't he get on with them? He protested rather luke-warmly that he did. He seemed afraid that he had given himself away by what he had just said. He added:

'Why do you ask that?'

'Oh, for nothing,' I answered, and then, touching the yellow ribbon in his buttonhole, 'What's that?'

'It's a ribbon. Can't you see?'

My questions evidently annoyed him. He turned towards me abruptly and almost vindictively, and in a jeering, insolent voice of which I should never have thought him capable which absolutely turned me sick:

'I say . . . do you often go about picking up schoolboys?'

Then as I was stammering out some kind of a confused answer, he opened the satchel he was carrying under his arm to slip his purchase into it. It held his lesson books and one or two copy-books, all covered with blue paper. I took one out; it was a history notebook. It's small owner had written his name on it in large letters. My heart gave a jump as I recognized that it was my nephew's.

GEORGE MOLINIER

(Bernard's heart gave a jump too as he read these lines and the whole story began to interest him prodigiously.)

It will be difficult to get it accepted that the character who stands for me in *The Counterfeiters* can have kept on good terms with his sister and yet not have known her children. I have always had the greatest difficulty in tampering with real facts. Even to alter the colour of a person's hair seems to me a piece of cheating which must lessen the verisimilitude of the truth. Everything hangs together and I always feel such a subtle interdependence between all the facts life offers me, that it seems to me impossible to change a single one without modifying the whole. And yet I can hardly explain that this boy's mother is only my half-sister by a first marriage of my father's; that I never saw her during the whole time my parents were alive; that we were brought into contact by business relating to the property they left. . . . All this is indispensable, however, and I don't see what else I can invent in order to avoid being indiscreet. I knew that my half-sister had three sons; I had met the eldest – a medical student – but I had caught only a sight even of him, as he has been obliged to interrupt his studies on account of a threatening of tuberculosis and has gone to some place in the south for treatment. The two others were never there when I went to see Pauline; the one who was now before me was certainly the youngest. I showed no trace of astonishment, but, taking an abrupt leave of young George after learning that he was going home to lunch, I jumped into a taxi in order to get to rue Notre Dame des Champs before him. I expected that at this hour of the morning Pauline would keep me to lunch – which was exactly what happened; I had brought away a copy of my book from Perrin's, and made up my mind to present it to her as an excuse for my unexpected visit.

It was the first time I had taken a meal at Pauline's. I was wrong to fight shy of my brother-in-law. I can hardly believe that he is a very remarkable jurist, but when we are together he has the sense to keep off his shop as much as I off mine, so that we get on very well.

Naturally when I got there that morning I did not breathe a word of my recent meeting:

'It will give me an opportunity, I hope, of making my nephews' acquaintance,' I said, when Pauline asked me to stay to lunch. 'For, you know, there are two of them I have never met.'

'Olivier will be a little late,' she said; 'he has a lesson; we will begin lunch without him. But I've just heard George come in, I'll call him.' And going to the door of the adjoining room, 'George,' she said, 'come and say "how-do-you-do" to your uncle.'

The boy came up and held out his hand. I kissed him ... children's power of dissembling fills me with amazement – he showed no surprise; one would have supposed he did not recognize me. He simply blushed deeply; but his mother must have thought it was from shyness. I suspected he was embarrassed at this meeting with the morning's 'tec', for he left us almost immediately and went back to the next room – the dining-room, which I understood is used by the boys as a schoolroom between meals. He reappeared, however, shortly after, when his father came into the room, and took advantage of the moment when we were going into the dining-room to come up to me and seize hold of my hand without his parents' seeing. At first I thought it was a sign of good fellowship, which amused me, but no! He opened my hand as I was clasping his, slipped into it a little note which he had obviously just written, then closed my fingers over it and gave them a tight squeeze. Needless to say, I played up to him; I hid the little note in my pocket and it was not till after lunch that I was able to take it out. This is what I read:

'If you tell my parents the story of the book, I shall' (he had crossed out *'detest you'*) *'say that you solicited me.'*

And at the bottom of the page:

'I come out of school every morning at 10 o'clock.'

Interrupted yesterday by a visit from X. His conversation upset me considerably.

Have been reflecting a great deal on what X. said. He knows nothing about my life, but I gave him a long account of the plan of my *Counterfeiters*. His advice is always salutary, because his point of view is different from mine. He is afraid that my work may be too factitious, that I am in danger of letting go the real subject for the shadow of the subject in my brain. What makes me uneasy is to feel that life (my life) at this juncture is parting company from my work, and my work moving away from my life. But I couldn't say that to him. Up till now – as is right – my tastes, my feelings, my personal experiences have all gone to feed my writings; in my best contrived phrases I still felt the beating of my heart. But henceforth the link is broken between what I think and what I feel. And I wonder whether this impediment which prevents my heart from speaking is not the real cause that is driving my work into abstraction and artificiality. As I was reflecting on this, the meaning of the fable of Apollo and Daphne suddenly flashed upon me: happy, thought I, the man who can clasp in one and the same embrace the laurel and the object of his love.

I related my meeting with George at such length that I was obliged to stop at the moment when Olivier came on the scene. I began this tale only to speak of him and I have managed to speak only of George. But now that the moment has come to speak of Olivier I understand that it was desire to defer that moment which was the cause of all my slowness. As soon as I saw him that first day, as soon as he sat down to the family meal, at my first look – or rather at *his* first look – I felt that look of his take possession of me wholly, and that my life was no longer mine to dispose of.

Pauline presses me to go and see her oftener. She begs me urgently to interest myself in her boys. She gives me to understand that their father knows very little about them. The more I talk to her, the more charming I think her. I cannot understand how I can have been so long without seeing more of her. The children have been brought up as Catholics; but she remembers her early Protestant training, and though she left our father's home at the time my mother entered it, I discover many points of resemblance between her and me. She sends her boys to school with Laura's parents, with whom I myself boarded for so long. This school (half a school and half a boarding-house) was founded by old Monsieur Azaïs (a friend of my father's), who is still the head of it. Though he started life as a pastor, he prides himself on keeping his school free from any denominational tendency – in my time there were even Turks there.

Pauline says she has good news from the sanatorium where Vincent is staying; he has almost completely recovered. She tells me that she writes to him about me and that she wishes I knew him better; for I have barely seen him. She builds great hopes on her eldest son; the family is stinting itself in order to enable him to set up for himself shortly – that is, to have rooms of his own where he can receive his patients. In the meantime, she has managed to set aside a part of their small apartment for him, by putting Olivier and George on the floor below in a room that happened to be vacant. The great question is whether the state of Vincent's health will oblige him to give up being house-physician.

To tell the truth, I take very little interest in Vincent, and if I talk to his mother about him, it is really to please her and so that we can then go on to talk about Olivier at greater length. As for George, he fights shy of me, hardly answers when I speak to him, and gives me a look of indescribable suspicion when we happen to pass each other. He seems unable to forgive me for not having gone to meet him outside the *lycée* – or to forgive himself for his advances to me.

I don't see much of Olivier either. When I visit his mother, I don't dare go into the room where I know he is at work; if I meet him by chance, I am so awkward and shy that I find nothing to say to him, and that makes me so unhappy that I prefer to call on his mother at the times when I know he will be out.

12

EDOUARD'S JOURNAL: LAURA'S WEDDING

Nov. 2nd. – Long conversation with Douviers. We met at Laura's parents, and he left at the same time as I and walked across the Luxembourg Gardens with me. He is preparing a thesis on Wordsworth, but from the few words he let fall, I feel certain that he misses the most characteristic points of Wordsworth's poetry; he had better have chosen Tennyson. There is something or other inadequate about Douviers – something abstract and simple-minded and credulous. He always takes everything – people and things – for what they set out to be. Perhaps because he himself never sets out to be anything but what he is.

'I know,' he said to me, 'that you are Laura's best friend. No doubt I ought to be a little jealous of you. But I can't be. On the contrary, everything she has told me about you has made me understand her better herself and wish to become your friend. I asked her the other day if you didn't bear me too much of a grudge for marrying her. She answered on the contrary, that you had advised her to.' (I really think he said it just as flatly as that.) 'I should like to thank you for it, and I hope you won't think it ridiculous, for I really do so most sincerely,' he added, forcing a smile, but with a trembling voice and tears in his eyes.

I didn't know what to answer him, for I felt far less moved than I should have been, and incapable of reciprocating his effusion. He must have thought me a little stony; but he irritated me. Nevertheless, I pressed his hand as warmly as I could when he held it out to me. These scenes, when one of the parties offers more of his heart than the other wants, are always painful. No doubt he thought he should capture my sympathy. If he had been a little more perspicacious he would have felt he was being cheated; but I saw that he was both overcome by gratitude for his own nobility and persuaded that he had raised a response to it in me. As for me, I said nothing, and as my silence perhaps made him feel uncomfortable: 'I count,' he added, 'on her being transplanted to Cambridge, to prevent her from making comparisons which might be disadvantageous to me.'

What did he mean by that? I did my best not to understand. Perhaps he wanted me to protest. But that would only have sunk us deeper into the bog. He is one of those shy people who cannot endure silences and who think they must fill them by being exaggeratedly forthcoming – the people who say to you afterwards, 'I have always been open with you.' The deuce they have! But the important thing is not so much to be open oneself as to allow the other person to be so. He ought to have realized that his openness was the very thing that prevented mine.

But if I cannot be a friend of his, at any rate I think he will make Laura an excellent husband; for in reality what I am reproaching him with are his qualities. We went on to talk of Cambridge, where I have promised to pay them a visit.

What absurd need had Laura to talk to him about me?

What an admirable thing in women is their need for devotion! The man they love is as a rule a kind of clothes-peg on which to hang their love. How easily and sincerely Laura has effected the transposition! I understand that she should marry Douviers; I was one of the first to advise it. But I had the right to hope for a little grief.

Some reviews of my book to hand. The qualities which people are the most willing to grant me are just the very ones I most detest. Was I right to republish this old stuff? It responds to nothing that I care for at present. But it is only at present that I see it does not. I don't so much think that I have actually changed, as that I am only just beginning to be aware of myself. Up till now I did not know who I was. Is it possible that I am always in need of another being to act as a plate-developer? This book of mine had crystallized according to Laura; and that is why I will not allow it to be my present portrait.

An insight, composed of sympathy, which would enable us to be in advance of the seasons – is this denied us? What are the problems which will exercise the minds of tomorrow? It is for them that I desire to write. To provide food for curiosities still unformed, to satisfy requirements not yet defined, so that the child of to-day may be astonished tomorrow to find me in his path.

How glad I am to feel in Olivier so much curiosity, so much impatient want of satisfaction with the past....

I sometimes think that poetry is the only thing that interests him. And I feel as I re-read our poets through his eyes, how few there are who have let themselves be guided by a feeling for art rather than by their hearts or minds. The odd thing is that when Oscar Molinier showed me some of Olivier's verses, I advised the boy to let himself be guided by the words rather than force them into submission. And now it seems to me that it is I who am learning it from him.

How depressingly, tiresomely and ridiculously sensible everything that I have hitherto written seems to be today!

Nov. 5th. – The wedding ceremony is over. It took place in the little chapel in rue Madame, to which I have not been for a long time past. The whole of the Vedel-Azaïs families were present. Laura's grandfather, father and mother, her two sisters, her young brother, besides quantities of uncles, aunts and cousins. The Douviers family was represented by three aunts in deep mourning (they would have certainly been nuns if they had been Catholics). They all three live together, and Douviers, since his parents' death, has lived with them. Azaïs's pupils sat in the gallery. The rest of the chapel was filled with the friends of the family. From my place near the door I saw my sister with Olivier. George, I suppose, was in the gallery with his school-fellows. Old La Pérouse was at the harmonium. His face has aged, but finer, nobler than ever – though his eye had lost that admirable fire and spirit I found so infectious in the days when he used to give me piano lessons. Our eyes met and there was so much sadness in the smile he gave me that I determined not to let him leave without speaking to him. Some persons moved and left an empty place beside Pauline. Olivier at once beckoned to me, and pushed his mother aside so that I might sit next him; then he took my hand and held it for a long time in his. It is the first time he has been so friendly with me. He kept his eyes shut during the whole of the minister's interminable address, so that I was able to take a long look at him; he is like the sleeping shepherd in a bas-relief in the Naples Museum, of which I have a photograph on my writing desk. I should have thought he was asleep himself, if it hadn't been for the quivering of his fingers. His hand fluttered in mine like a captured bird.

The old pastor thought it his duty to retrace the whole of the Azaïs family history, beginning with the grandfather, with whom he had been at school in Strasburg before the war, and who had also been a fellow-student of his later on at the faculty of theology. I thought he would never get to the end of a complicated sentence in which he tried to explain that in becoming the head of a school and devoting himself to the education of young children, his friend had, so to speak, never left the ministry. Then the next generation had its turn. He went on to speak with equal edification of the Douviers family, though he didn't seem to know much about them. The excellence of his sentiments palliated the deficiency of his oratory and I heard several members of the congregation blowing their noses. I should have liked to know what Olivier was thinking; I reflected that, as he had been brought up a Catholic, the Protestant service must be new to him and that this was probably his first visit to the chapel. The singular faculty of *depersonalization* which I possess and which enables me to feel other people's emotions as if they were my own, compelled me, as it were, to enter into Olivier's feelings – those that I imagined him to be experiencing; and though he kept his eyes shut, or perhaps for that very reason, I felt as if, like him, I were seeing for the first time the bare walls, the abstract and chilly light which fell upon the congregation, the relentless outline of the pulpit on the background of the white wall, the straightness of the lines, the rigidity of the columns which support the gallery, the whole spirit of this angular and colourless architecture and its repellent want of grace, its uncompromising inflexibility, its parsimony. It can only be because I have been accustomed to it since childhood, that I have not felt all this sooner. . . . I suddenly found myself thinking of my religious awakening and my first fervours; of Laura and the Sunday school where we used to meet and of which we were both monitors, of our zeal and our inability, in the ardour which consumed all that was impure in us, to distinguish the part which belonged to the other and the part that was God's. And then I fell to regretting that Olivier had never known this early starvation of the senses which drives the soul so perilously far beyond appearances – that his memories were not like mine; but to feel him so distant from the whole thing, helped me to escape from it myself. I passionately pressed the hand which he had left in mine, but which just then he withdrew abruptly. He opened his eyes to look at me, and then, with a boyish smile of roguish playfulness, which mitigated the extraordinary gravity of his brow, he leant towards me and whispered – while just at that moment the minister was reminding all Christians of their duties, and lavishing advice, precepts and pious exhortations upon the newly married couple:

'I don't care a damn about any of it. I'm a Catholic.'

Everything about him is attractive to me – and mysterious.

At the sacristy door, I came across old La Pérouse. He said, a little sadly but without any trace of reproach: 'You've almost forgotten me, I think.'

I mentioned some kind of occupation or other as an excuse for having been so long without going to see him and promised to go the day after tomorrow. I tried to persuade him to come back with me to the reception, which the Azaïses were giving after the ceremony and to which I was invited; but he said he was in too sombre a mood and was afraid of meeting too many people to whom he ought to speak, and would not be able to.

Pauline went away with George and left me with Olivier.

'I trust him to your care,' she said, laughing; but Olivier seemed irritated and turned away his face.

He drew me out into the street. 'I didn't know you knew the Azaïses so well.'

He was very much surprised when I told him that I had boarded with them for two years.

'How could you do that rather than live independently – anywhere else?'

'It was convenient,' I answered vaguely, for I couldn't say that at that time Laura was filling my thoughts and that I would have put up with the worst disagreeables for the pleasure of bearing them in her company.

'And weren't you suffocated in such a hole?' Then, as I didn't answer: 'For that matter, I can't think how I bear it myself – nor why in the world I am there. . . . But I'm only a half-boarder. Even that's too much.'

I explained to him the friendship that had existed between his grandfather and the master of the 'hole', and that his mother's choice was no doubt guided by that.

'Oh, well,' he went on, 'I have no points of comparison; I dare say all these cramming places are the same, and, most likely, from what people say, the others are worse. I shouldn't have gone there at all if I hadn't had to make up the time I lost when I was ill. And now, for a long time past, I have only gone there for the sake of Armand.'

Then I learnt that this young brother of Laura's was his schoolfellow. I told Olivier that I hardly knew him.

'And yet he's the most intelligent and the most interesting of the family.'

'That's to say the one who interests you most.'

'No, no, I assure you, he's very unusual. If you like, we'll go and see him in his room. I hope he won't be afraid to speak before you.'

We had reached the pension.

The Vedel–Azaïses had substituted for the traditional wedding breakfast a less costly tea. Pastor Vedel's reception-room and study had been thrown open to the guests. Only a few intimate friends were allowed into the pastoress's minute private sitting-room; but in order to prevent it from being overrun, the door between it and the reception-room had been locked – which made Armand answer, when people asked him how they could get to his mother: 'Through the chimney!'

The place was crowded and the heat suffocating. Except for a few 'members of the teaching body', colleagues of Douviers', the society was exclusively Protestant. The odour of Puritanism is peculiar to itself. In a meeting of Catholics or Jews, when they let themselves go in each other's company, the emanation is as strong, and perhaps even more stifling; but among Catholics you find a self-appreciation, and among Jews a self-depreciation, of which Protestants seem to me very rarely capable. If Jews' noses are too long, Protestants' are bunged up; no doubt of it. And I myself, all the time I was plunged in their atmosphere, didn't perceive its peculiar quality – something ineffably alpine and paradisaical and foolish.

At one end of the room was a table set out as a buffet; Rachel, Laura's elder sister, and Sarah, her younger, were serving the tea with a few of their young lady friends to help them. . . .

As soon as Laura saw me, she drew me into her father's study, where a considerable number of people had already gathered. We took refuge in the embrasure of a window, and were able to talk without being overheard. In the days gone by, we had written our two names on the window-frame.

'Come and see. They are still there,' she said. 'I don't think anybody has ever noticed them. How old were you then?'

Underneath our names we had written the date. I calculated:

'Twenty-eight.'

'And I was sixteen. Ten years ago.'

The moment was not very suitable for awakening these memories; I tried to turn the conversation, while she with a kind of uneasy insistence continually brought me back to it; then suddenly, as though she were afraid of growing emotional, she asked me if I remembered Strouvilhou?

Strouvilhou in those days was an independent boarder who was a great nuisance to her parents. He was supposed to be attending lectures, but when he was asked which ones, or what examinations he was studying for, he used to answer negligently:

'I vary.'

At first people pretended to take his insolences for jokes, in an attempt to make them appear less cutting, and he would himself accompany them by a loud laugh; but his laugh soon became more sarcastic, and his witticisms more aggressive, and

I could never understand why or how the pastor could put up with such an individual as boarder, unless it were for financial reasons, or because he had a feeling that was half affection, half pity, for Strouvilhou, and perhaps a vague hope that he might end by persuading – I mean converting – him. I couldn't understand either why Strouvilhou stayed on at the pension, when he might so easily have gone elsewhere; for he didn't appear to have any sentimental reason, like me; perhaps it was because of the evident pleasure he took in his passages with the poor pastor, who defended himself badly and always got the worst of it.

'Do you remember one day when he asked Papa if he kept his coat on underneath his gown, when he preached?'

'Yes, indeed. He asked him so insinuatingly that your poor father was completely taken in. It was at table. I can remember it all as if...'

'And Papa ingenuously answered that his gown was rather thin and that he was afraid of catching cold without his coat.'

'And then Strouvilhou's air of deep distress! And how he had to be pressed before he ended by saying, that of course it was of "very little importance", but that when your father gesticulated in preaching, the sleeves of his coat showed underneath his gown and that it had rather an unfortunate effect on some of the congregation.'

'And after that, poor Papa preached a whole sermon with his arms glued to his sides, so that none of his oratorical effects came off.'

'And the Sunday after that he came home with a bad cold, because he had taken his coat off. Oh! and the discussion about the barren fig-tree in the Gospel and about trees that don't bear fruit...."*I'm* not a fruit-tree. What I bear is shade. *Monsieur le Pasteur*, I cast you into the shade."'

'He said that too at table.'

'Of course. He never appeared except at meals.'

'And he said it in such a spiteful way too. It was that that made grandfather turn him out. Do you remember how he suddenly rose to his feet, though he usually sat all the time with his nose in his plate, and pointed to the door with his outstretched arm, and shouted: "Leave the room!"'

'He looked enormous – terrifying; he was enraged. I really believe Strouvilhou was frightened.'

'He flung his napkin on to the table and disappeared. He went off without paying us; we never saw him again.'

'I wonder what has become of him.'

'Poor grandfather!' Laura went on rather sadly. 'How I admired him that day! He's very fond of you, you know. You ought to go up and pay him a little visit in his study. I am sure you would give him a great deal of pleasure.'

I write down the whole of this at once, as I know by experience how difficult it is to recall the tone of dialogue after any interval. But from that moment I began to listen to Laura less attentively. I had just noticed – some way off it is true – Olivier, whom I had lost sight of when Laura drew me into her father's study. His eyes were shining and his face extraordinarily animated. I heard afterwards that Sarah had been amusing herself by making him drink six glasses of champagne, in succession. Armand was with him, and they were both following Sarah and an English girl of the same age as Sarah, who has been boarding with the family for over a year – pursuing them from group to group. At last Sarah and her friend left the room, and through the open door I saw the two boys rush upstairs after them. In my turn, I was on the point of leaving the room in response to Laura's request, when she made a movement towards me:

'Wait, Edouard, there's one thing more . . .' and her voice suddenly became very grave. 'It'll probably be a long time before we see each other again. I should like you to say . . . I should like to know whether I may still count on you . . . as a friend.'

Never did I feel more inclined to embrace her than at that moment – but I contented myself with kissing her hand tenderly and impetuously, and with murmuring: 'Come what come may.' And then, to hide the tears which I felt rising to my eyes, I hurried off to find Olivier.

He was sitting on the stairs with Armand, watching for me to come out. He was certainly a little tipsy. He got up and pulled me by the arm:

'Come along,' he said. 'We're going to have a cigarette in Sarah's room. She's expecting you.'

'In a moment. I must first go up and see Monsieur Azaïs. But I shall never be able to find the room.'

'Oh, yes. You know it very well. It's Laura's old room,' cried Armand. 'As it was one of the best rooms in the house, it was given to the parlour-boarder, but as she doesn't pay much, she shares it with Sarah. They put in two beds for form's sake – not that there was much need....'

'Don't listen to him,' said Olivier, laughing and giving him a shove, 'he's drunk.'

'And what about you?' answered Armand. 'Well then, you'll come, won't you? We shall expect you.'

I promised to rejoin them.

Now that he has cut his hair *en brosse*, old Azaïs doesn't look like Walt Whitman any more. He has handed over the first and second floors of the house to his son-in-law. From the windows of his study (mahogany, rep and horse-hair furniture) he can look over the playground and keep an eye on the pupils' goings and comings.

'You see how spoilt I am,' he said, pointing to a huge bouquet of chrysanthemums which was standing on the table, and which a mother of one of the pupils – an old friend of the family's – had just left for him. The atmosphere of the room was so austere that it seemed as if any flower must wither in it at once. 'I have left the party for a moment. I'm getting old and all this noisy talk tires me. But these flowers will keep me company. They have their own way of talking and tell the glory of God better than men' (or some such stuff).

The worthy man has no conception how much he bores his pupils with remarks of this kind; he is so sincere in making them, that one hasn't the heart to be ironical. Simple souls like his are certainly the ones I find it most difficult to understand. If one is a little less simple oneself, one is forced into a kind of pretence; not very honest, but what is one to do? It is impossible either to argue or to say what one thinks; one can only acquiesce. If one's opinions are the least bit different from his,

Azaïs forces one to be hypocritical. When I first used to frequent the family, the way in which his grandchildren lied to him made me indignant. I soon found myself obliged to follow suit.

Pastor Prosper Vedel is too busy; Madame Vedel, who is rather foolish, lives plunged in a religio-poetico daydream, in which she loses all sense of reality; the young people's moral bringing-up, as well as their education, has been taken in hand by their grandfather. Once a month at the time when I lived with them, I used to assist at a stormy scene of explanations, which would end up by effusive and pathetic appeals of this kind:

'Henceforth we will be perfectly frank and open with one another.' (He likes using several words to say the same thing – an odd habit, left him from the time of his pastorship.) 'There shall be no more concealments, we won't keep anything back in the future, will we? Everything is to be above board. We shall be able to look each other straight in the face. That's a bargain, isn't it?'

After which they sank deeper than ever into their bog – he of blindness – and the children of deceit.

These remarks were chiefly addressed to a brother of Laura's, a year younger than she; the sap of youth was working in him and he was making his first essays of love. (He went out to the colonies and I have lost sight of him.) One evening when the old man had been talking in this way, I went to speak to him in his study; I tried to make him understand that the sincerity which he demanded from his grandson was made impossible by his own severity. Azaïs almost lost his temper:

'He has only to do nothing of which he need be ashamed,' he exlaimed in a tone of voice which allowed of no reply.

All the same he is an excellent man – a paragon of virtue, and what people call a heart of gold; but his judgements are childish. His great esteem for me comes from the fact that, as far as he knows, I have no mistress. He did not conceal from me that he had hoped to see me marry Laura; he is afraid Douviers may not be the right husband for her, and he repeated several times: 'I am surprised at her choice'; then he added, 'Still he seems to me an excellent fellow.... What do you think?...'

To which I answered, 'Certainly.'

The deeper the soul plunges into religious devotion, the more it loses all sense of reality, all need, all desire, all love for reality. I have observed the same thing in Vedel upon the few occasions that I have spoken to him. The dazzling light of their faith blinds them to the surrounding world and to their own selves. As for me, who cares for nothing so much as to see the world and myself clearly, I am amazed at the coils of falsehood in which devout persons take delight.

I tried to get Azaïs to speak of Olivier, but he takes more interest in George.

'Don't let him see that you know what I am going to tell you,' he began; 'for that matter, it's entirely to his credit. Just fancy! your nephew with a few of his schoolfellows has started a kind of little society – a little mutual emulation league; the ones who are allowed into it must show themselves worthy and furnish proofs of their virtue – a kind of children's Legion of Honour. Isn't it charming? They all wear a little ribbon in their buttonhole – not very noticeable, certainly, but all the same I noticed it. I sent for the boy to my study and when I asked him the meaning of this badge, he began by being very much embarrassed. The dear little chap thought I was going to reprove him. Then with a great deal of confusion and many blushes, he told me about the starting of this little club. It's the kind of thing, you see, one must be very careful not to smile at; one might hurt all sorts of delicate feelings. . . . I asked him why he and his friends didn't do it openly, in the light of day? I told him what a wonderful power of propaganda, or proselytism, they would have, what fine things they might do! . . . But at that age, one likes mysteries. . . . To encourage his confidence, I told him that in my time – that's to say, when I was his age – I had been a member of a society of the same kind, and that we went by the grand name of Knights of Duty; the President of the society gave us each a notebook, in which we set down with absolute frankness our failures and our shortcomings. He smiled and I could see that the story of the notebooks had given him an idea; I didn't insist, but I shouldn't be surprised if he introduced the system of notebooks among his companions.

You see, these children must be taken in the right way; and in the first place, they must see that one understands them. I promised him not to breathe a word of all this to his parents; though, at the same time, I advised him to tell his mother all about it, as it would make her so happy. But it seems that the boys had given their word of honour to say nothing about it. It would have been a mistake to insist. But before he left me we joined together in a prayer for God to bless their society.'

Poor, dear old Azaïs! I am convinced the little rascal was pulling his leg and that there wasn't a word of truth in the whole thing. But what else could he have said? . . . I must try and find out what it's all about.

I did not at first recognize Laura's room. It has been re-papered; its whole atmosphere is changed. And Sarah too seemed to me unrecognizable. Yet I thought I knew her. She has always been exceedingly confidential with me. All her life I have been a person to whom one could say anything. But I had let a great many months go by without seeing the Vedels. Her neck and arms were bare. She seemed taller, bolder. She was sitting on one of the two beds beside Olivier and right up against him; he was lying down at full length and seemed to be asleep. He was certainly drunk; and as certainly I suffered at seeing him so, but I thought him more beautiful than ever. In fact they were all four of them more or less drunk. The English girl was bursting with laughter at Armand's ridiculous remarks – a shrill laughter which hurt my ears. Armand was saying anything that came into his head; he was excited and flattered by the girl's laughter and trying to be as stupid and vulgar as she was; he pretended to light his cigarette at the fire of his sister's and Olivier's flaming cheeks, and to burn his fingers, when he had the effrontery to seize their heads and pull them together by force. Olivier and Sarah lent themselves to his tomfoolery, and it was extremely painful to me. But I am anticipating. . . .

Olivier was still pretending to be asleep when Armand abruptly asked me what I thought of Douviers. I had sat down in a low arm-chair, and was feeling amused, excited and, at the same time, embarrassed to see their tipsiness and their want of restraint; and for that matter, flattered too, that they had invited me to join them, when it seemed so evident that it was not my place to be there.

'The young ladies here present . . .' he continued, as I found nothing to answer and contented myself with smiling blandly, so as to appear up to the mark. Just then, the English girl tried to prevent him from going on and ran after him to put her hand over his mouth. He wriggled away from her and called out: 'The young ladies are indignant at the idea of Laura's going to bed with him.'

The English girl let go of him and exclaimed in pretended fury: 'Oh, you mustn't believe what he says. He's a liar!'

'I have tried to make them understand,' went on Armand, more calmly, 'that with only twenty thousand francs for a dot, one could hardly look for anything better, and that, as a true Christian, she ought first of all to take into account his spiritual qualities, as our father the pastor would say. Yes, my children. And then, what would happen to the population, if nobody was allowed to marry who wasn't an Adonis . . . or an Olivier, shall we say? to refer to a more recent period?'

'What an idiot!' murmured Sarah. 'Don't listen to him. He doesn't know what he is saying.'

'I'm saying the truth.'

I had never heard Armand speak in this way before. I thought him – I still think him – a delicate, sensitive nature; his vulgarity seemed to me entirely put on – due in part to his being drunk, and still more to his desire to amuse the English girl. She was pretty enough, but must have been exceedingly silly to take any pleasure in such fooling; what kind of interest could Olivier find in all this? . . . I determined not to hide my disgust, as soon as we should be alone.

'But you,' went on Armand, turning suddenly towards me, 'you, who don't care about money and who have enough to indulge in fine sentiments, will you consent to tell us why you didn't marry Laura? – when it appears you were in love with her, and when, to common knowledge, she was pining away for you?'

Olivier, who up to that moment had been pretending to be

asleep, opened his eyes; they met mine and if I did not blush, it must certainly have been that not one of the others was in a fit state to observe me.

'Armand, you're unbearable,' said Sarah, as though to put me at my ease, for I found nothing to answer. She had hitherto been sitting on the bed, but at that point she lay down at full length beside Olivier, so that their two heads were touching. Upon which, Armand leapt up, seized a large screen which was standing folded against the wall, and with the antics of a clown spread it out so as to hide the couple; then, still clowning, he leant towards me and said without lowering his voice:

'Perhaps you didn't know that my sister was a whore?'

It was too much. I got up and pushed the screen roughly aside. Olivier and Sarah immediately sat up. Her hair had come down. Olivier rose, went to the washhand stand and bathed his face.

'Come here,' said Sarah, taking me by the arm. 'I want to show you something.'

She opened the door of the room and drew me out on to the landing.

'I thought it might be interesting to a novelist. It's a notebook I found accidentally – Papa's private diary. I can't think how he came to leave it lying about. Anybody might have read it. I took it to prevent Armand from seeing it. Don't tell him about it. It's not very long. You can read it in ten minutes and give it back to me before you go.'

'But, Sarah,' said I, looking at her fixedly, 'it's most frightfully indiscreet.'

She shrugged her shoulders. 'Oh, if that's what you think, you'll be disappointed. There's only one place in which it gets interesting – and even that – Look here; I'll show it you.'

She had taken out of her bodice a very small memorandum book, about four years old. She turned over its pages for a moment, and then gave it to me, pointing to a passage as she did so.

'Read it quickly.'

Under the date and in quotation marks, I first of all saw the Scripture text: 'He who is faithful in small things will be faithful also in great.' Then followed: 'Why do I always put off till tomorrow my resolution to stop smoking? If only not to grieve Mélanie' (the pastor's wife). 'Oh, Lord! give me strength to shake off the yoke of this shameful slavery.' (I quote it, I think exactly.) Then came notes of struggles, beseeching, prayers, efforts – which were evidently all in vain, as they were repeated day after day. Then I turned another page and there was no more mention of the subject.

'Rather touching, isn't it?' asked Sarah with the faintest touch of irony, when I had done reading.

'It's much odder than you think,' I couldn't help saying, though I reproached myself for it. 'Just think, I asked your father only ten days ago if he had ever tried to give up smoking. I thought I was smoking a good deal too much myself and . . . Anyway, do you know what he answered? First of all he said that the evil effects of tobacco were very much exaggerated, and that as far as he was concerned he had never felt any; and as I insisted: "Yes," said he, at last. "I have made up my mind once or twice to give it up for a time." "And did you succeed?" "Naturally," he answered, as if it followed as a matter of course – "since I made up my mind to." It's extraordinary! Perhaps, after all, he didn't remember,' I added, not wishing to let Sarah see the depths of hypocrisy I suspected.

'Or perhaps,' rejoined Sarah, 'it proves that "smoking" stood for something else.'

Was it really Sarah who spoke in this way? I was struck dumb. I looked at her, hardly daring to understand. . . . At that moment Olivier came out of the room. He had combed his hair, arranged his collar and seemed calmer.

'Suppose we go,' he said, paying no attention to Sarah, 'it's late.'

'I am afraid you may mistake me,' he said, as soon as we were in the street. 'You might think that I'm in love with Sarah. But I'm not. . . . Oh! I don't detest her . . . only I don't love her.'

I had taken his arm and pressed it without speaking.

'You mustn't judge Armand either from what he said today,' he went on. 'It's a kind of part he acts . . . in spite of himself. In reality he's not in the least like that. . . . I can't explain. He has a kind of desire to spoil everything he most cares for. He hasn't been like that long. I think he's very unhappy and that he jokes in order to hide it. He's very proud. His parents don't understand him at all. They wanted to make a pastor of him.'

Memo. – Motto for a chapter of *The Counterfeiters:*

"*La famille . . . cette cellule sociale.*"

PAUL BOURGET (*passim*)

Title of the chapter: THE CELLULAR SYSTEM

True, there exists no prison (intellectual, that is) from which a vigorous mind cannot escape; and nothing that incites to rebellion is definitely dangerous – although rebellion may in certain cases distort a character – driving it in upon itself, turning it to contradiction and stubbornness, and impiously prompting it to deceit; moreover the child who resists the influence of his family, wears out the first freshness of his energy in the attempt to free himself. But also the education which thwarts a child strengthens him by the very fact of hampering. The most lamentable victims of all are the victims of adulation. What force of character is needed to detest the things that flatter us! How many parents I have seen (the mother in especial) who delight in encouraging their children's silliest repugnances, their most unjust prejudices, their failures to understand, their unreasonable antipathies. . . . At table: 'You'd better leave that; can't you see, it's a bit of fat? Don't eat that skin. That's not cooked enough. . . .' Out of doors, at night: 'Oh, a bat! . . . Cover your head quickly; it'll get into your hair.' Etc., etc. . . . According to them, beetles bite, grasshoppers sting, earthworms give spots . . . and such-like absurdities in every domain, intellectual, moral, etc.

In the suburban train the day before yesterday, as I was coming back from Auteuil, I heard a young mother whispering to a little girl of ten, whom she was petting:

'You and me, darling, me and you – the others may go hang!'

(Oh, yes! I knew they were working people, but the people too have a right to our indignation. The husband was sitting in the corner of the carriage reading the paper – quiet, resigned, not even a cuckold, I dare say.)

Is it possible to conceive a more insidious poison?

It is to bastards that the future belongs. How full of meaning is the expression 'a natural child'! The bastard alone has the right to be natural.

Family egoism . . . hardly less hideous than personal egoism.

Nov. 6th. – I have never been able to invent anything. But I set myself in front of reality like a painter, who should say to his model: 'Take up such and such an attitude; put on such and such an expression.' I can make the models which society furnishes me act as I please, if I am acquainted with their springs; or at any rate I can put such and such problems before them to solve in their own way, so that I learn my lesson from their reactions. It is my novelist's instinct that is constantly pricking me on to intervene – to influence the course of their destiny. If I had more imagination, I should be able to spin invention intrigues; as it is, I provoke them, observe the actors, and then work at their dictation.

Nov. 7th. – Nothing that I wrote yesterday is true. Only this remains – that reality interests me inasmuch as it is plastic, and that I care more – infinitely more – for what may be than for what has been. I lean with a fearful attraction over the depths of each creature's possibilities and weep for all that lies atrophied under the heavy lid of custom and morality.

*

Here Bernard was obliged to pause. His eyes were blurred. He was gasping as if the eagerness with which he read had made him forget to breathe. He opened the window and filled his lungs before taking another plunge. His friendship for Olivier was no doubt very great; he had no better friend and there was no one in the world he loved so much, now that he could no longer love his parents; and indeed he clung to this affection in a manner that was almost excessive; but Olivier and he did not understand friendship quite in the same way. Bernard, as he progressed in his reading, felt with more and more astonishment and admiration, though with a little pain too, what diversity this friend he thought he knew so well, was capable of showing. Olivier had never told him anything of what the journal recounted. He hardly knew of the existence of Armand and Sarah. How different Olivier was with them to what he was with him! . . . In that room of Sarah's, on that bed, would Bernard have recognized his friend? There mingled with the immense curiosity which drove him on to read so precipitately, a queer feeling of discomfort – disgust or pique. He had felt a little of this pique a moment before, when he had seen Olivier on Edouard's arm – pique at being out of it. This kind of pique may lead very far and may make one commit all sorts of follies – like every kind of pique for that matter.

Well, we must go on. All this that I have been saying is only to put a little air between the pages of this journal. Now that Bernard has got his breath back again, we will return to it. He dives once more into its pages.

13

EDOUARD'S JOURNAL: FIRST VISIT TO LA PÉROUSE

On tire peu de service des vieillards.
VAUVENARGUES

Nov. 8th. – Old Monsieur and Madame de La Pérouse have changed houses again. Their new apartment, which I had never seen so far, is an *entresol* in the part of the Faubourg St Honoré which makes a little recess before it cuts across the boulevard Haussmann. I rang the bell. La Pérouse opened the door. He was in his shirt sleeves and was wearing a sort of yellowish whitish night-cap on his head, which I finally made out to be an old stocking (Madame de La Pérouse's no doubt) tied in a knot, so that the foot dangled on his cheek like a tassel. He was holding a bent poker in his hand. I had evidently caught him at some domestic job, and as he seemed rather confused:

'Would you like me to come back later?' I asked.

'No, no. . . . Come in here.' And he pushed me into a long, narrow room with two windows looking on to the street, just on a level with the street lamp. 'I was expecting a pupil at this very moment' (it was six o'clock); 'but she has telegraphed to say she can't come. I am so glad to see you.'

He laid his poker down on a small table, and, as though apologizing for his appearance:

'Madame de La Pérouse's maidservant has let the stove go out. She only comes in the morning; I've been obliged to empty it.'

'Shall I help you light it?'

'No, no; it's dirty work. . . . Will you excuse me while I go and put my coat on?'

He trotted out of the room and came back almost immediately dressed in an alpaca coat, with its buttons torn off, its elbows in holes, and its general appearance so threadbare, that one wouldn't have dared give it to a beggar. We sat down.

'You think I'm changed, don't you?'

I wanted to protest, but could hardly find anything to say, I was so painfully affected by the harassed expression of his face, which had once been so beautiful. He went on:

'Yes, I've grown very old lately. I'm beginning to lose my memory. When I want to go over one of Bach's fugues, I am obliged to refer to the book....'

'There are many young people who would be glad to have a memory like yours.'

He replied with a shrug: 'Oh, it's not only my memory that's failing. For instance, I think I still walk pretty quickly; but all the same everybody in the street passes me.'

'Oh,' said I, 'people walk much quicker nowadays.'

'Yes, don't they? ... It's the same with my lessons – my pupils think that my teaching keeps them back; they want to go quicker than I do. I'm losing them.... Everyone's in a hurry nowadays.'

He added in a whisper so low that I could hardly hear him: 'I've scarcely any left.'

I felt that he was in such great distress that I didn't dare question him.

'Madame de La Pérouse won't understand. She says I don't set about it in the right way – that I don't do anything to keep them and still less to get new ones.'

'The pupil you were expecting just now ...?' I asked awkwardly.

'Oh, she! I'm preparing her for the Conservatoire. She comes here to practise every day.'

'Which means she doesn't pay you.'

'Madame de La Pérouse is always reproaching me with it. She can't understand that those are the only lessons that interest me; yes, the only lessons I really care about ... giving. I have taken to reflecting a great deal lately. Here! there's something I should like to ask you. Why is it there is so little about old people in books? ... I suppose it's because old people aren't able to write themselves and young ones don't take any interest in them. No one's interested in an old man.... And yet there are a great many curious things that might be said about them. For instance: there are certain acts in my past life which I'm only just beginning to understand. Yes, I'm just beginning to understand that they haven't at all the meaning I attached to them in the old days when I did them. . . . I've only just begun to understand that I have been a dupe during the whole of my life. Madame de La Pérouse has fooled me; my son fooled me; everybody has fooled me; God has fooled me. . . .'

The evening was closing in. I could hardly make out my old master's features; but suddenly the light of the street lamp flashed out and showed me his cheeks glittering with tears. I looked anxiously at first at an odd mark on his temple, like a dint, like a hole; but as he moved a little, the spot changed places and I saw that it was only a shadow cast by a knob of the balustrade. I put my hand on his scraggy arm; he shivered.

'You'll catch cold,' I said. 'Really, shan't we light the fire? . . . Come along.'

'No, no; one must harden oneself.'

'What? Stoicism?'

'Yes, a little. It's because my throat was delicate that I never would wear a scarf. I have always struggled with myself.'

'That's all very well as long as one is victorious; but if one's body gives way . . .'

'That would be the real victory.'

He let go my hand and went on: 'I was afraid you would go away without coming to see me.'

'Go where?' I asked.

'I don't know. You travel so much. There's something I wanted to say to you. . . . I expect to be going away myself soon.'

'What! are you thinking of travelling?' I asked clumsily, pretending not to understand him, notwithstanding the mysterious solemnity of his voice. He shook his head.

'You know very well what I mean. . . . Yes, yes. I know it will soon be time. I am beginning to earn less than my keep; and I can't endure it. There's a certain point beyond which I have promised myself not to go.'

He spoke in an emotional tone which alarmed me.

'Do you think it is wrong? I have never been able to understand why it was forbidden by religion. I have reflected a great deal latterly. When I was young, I led a very austere life; I used to congratulate myself on my force of character every time I refused a solicitation in the street. I didn't understand, that when I thought I was freeing myself, in reality I was becoming more and more the slave of my own pride. Every one of these triumphs over myself was another turn of the key in the door of my prison. That's what I meant just now by saying that God had fooled me. He made me take my pride for virtue. He was laughing at me. It amuses him. I think he plays with us as a cat does with a mouse. He sends us temptations which he knows we shan't be able to resist; but when we do resist he revenges himself still worse. Why does he hate us so? And why . . . But I'm boring you with these old man's questions.'

He took his head in his hands like a moping child and remained silent so long that I began to wonder whether he had not forgotten my presence. I sat motionless in front of him, afraid of disturbing his meditations. Notwithstanding the noise of the street which was so close, the calm of the little room seemed to me extraordinary, and notwithstanding the glimmer of the street lamp, which shed its fantastic light upon us from down below, like footlights at the theatre, the shadow on each side of the window seemed to broaden, and the darkness round us to thicken, as in icy weather the water of a quiet pool thickens into immobility – till my heart itself thickened into ice too. At last, shaking myself free from the clutch that held me, I breathed loudly and, preparatory to taking my leave, I asked out of politeness and in order to break the spell:

'How is Madame de La Pérouse?'

The old man seemed to wake up out of a dream. He repeated:

'Madame de La Pérouse . . . ?' interrogatively, as if the words were syllables which had lost all meaning for him; then he suddenly leant towards me:

'Madame de La Pérouse is in a terrible state . . . most painful to me.'

'What kind of state?' I asked.

'Oh, no kind,' he said, shrugging his shoulders, as if there were nothing to explain. 'She is completely out of her mind. She doesn't know what to be up to next.'

I had long suspected that the old couple were in profound disagreement, but without any hope of knowing anything more definite.

'My poor friend,' I said pityingly, 'and since when?'

He reflected a moment, as if he had not understood my question.

'Oh, for a long time ... ever since I've known her.' Then, correcting himself almost immediately: 'No; in reality it was over my son's bringing-up that things went wrong.'

I made a gesture of surprise, for I had always thought that the La Pérouses had no children. He raised his head, which he had been holding in his hands, and went on more calmly:

'I never mentioned my son to you, eh? ... Well, I'll tell you everything. You must know all about it now. There's no one else I can tell.... Yes, it was over my son's bringing-up. As you see, it's a long time ago. The first years of our married life had been delightful. I was very pure when I married Madame de La Pérouse. I loved her with innocence ... yes, that's the best word for it, and I refused to allow that she had any faults. But we hadn't the same ideas about bringing up children. Every time that I wanted to reprove my son, Madame de La Pérouse took his side against me; according to her, he was to be allowed to do anything he liked. They were in league together against me. She taught him to lie.... When he was barely twenty he took a mistress. She was a pupil of mine – a Russian girl, with a great talent for music, to whom I was very much attached. Madame de La Pérouse knew all about it; but of course, as usual, everything was kept from me. And of course I didn't notice she was going to have a baby. Not a thing – I tell you; I never suspected a thing. One fine day, I am informed that my pupil is unwell, that she won't be able to come for some time. When I speak about going to see her, I am told that she has changed her address – that she is travelling.... It was not till long after that I learnt that she had gone to Poland for her confinement. My son joined her there.... They lived together for several years, but he died before marrying her.'

'And ... she? did you ever see her again?'

He seemed to be butting with his head against some obstacle:

'I couldn't forgive her for deceiving me. Madame de La Pérouse still corresponds with her. When I learnt she was in great poverty, I sent her some money for the child's sake. But Madame de La Pérouse knows nothing about that. No more does she . . . she doesn't know the money came from me.'

'And your grandson?'

A strange smile flitted over his face; he got up.

'Wait a moment. I'll show you his photograph.' And again he trotted quickly out of the room, poking his head out in front of him. When he came back, his fingers trembled as he looked for the picture in a large letter-case. He held it towards me and, bending forward, whispered in a low voice:

'I took it from Madame de La Pérouse without her noticing. She thinks she has lost it.'

'How old is he?' I asked.

'Thirteen. He looks older, doesn't he? He is very delicate.'

His eyes filled with tears once more; he held out his hand for the photograph, as if he were anxious to get it back again as quickly as possible. I leant forward to look at it in the dim light of the street lamp; I thought the child was like him; I recognized old La Pérouse's high, prominent forehead and dreamy eyes. I thought I should please him by saying so; he protested:

'No, no; it's my brother he's like – a brother I lost. . . .'

The child was oddly dressed in a Russian embroidered blouse.

'Where does he live?'

'How can I tell?' cried La Pérouse, in a kind of despair. 'They keep everything from me, I tell you.'

He had taken the photograph, and after having looked at it a moment, he put it back in the letter-case, which he slipped into his pocket.

'When his mother comes to Paris, she only sees Madame de La Pérouse; if I question her, she always answers: 'You had better ask her yourself.' She says that, but at heart she would hate me to see her. She has always been jealous. She has always tried to take away everything I care for. . . . Little Boris is being educated in Poland – at Warsaw, I believe. But he often travels with his mother.' Then, in great excitement: 'Oh, would you have thought it possible to love someone one has never seen?

. . . Well, this child is what I care for most in the world. . . . And he doesn't know!'

His words were broken by great sobs. He rose from his chair and threw himself – fell almost – into my arms. I would have done anything to give him some comfort – but what could I do? I got up, for I felt his poor shrunken form slipping to the ground and I thought he was going to fall on his knees. I held him up, embraced him, rocked him like a child. He mastered himself. Madame de La Pérouse was calling in the next room.

'She's coming. . . . You don't want to see her, do you? . . . Besides, she's stone deaf. Go quickly.' And as he saw me out on to the landing:

'Don't be too long without coming again.' (There was entreaty in his voice.) 'Good-bye; good-bye.'

Nov. 9th. – There is a kind of tragedy, it seems to me, which has hitherto almost entirely eluded literature. The novel has dealt with the contrariness of fate, good or evil fortune, social relationships, the conflicts of passions and of characters – but not with the very essence of man's being.

And yet, the whole effect of Christianity was to transfer the drama on to the moral plane. But properly speaking there are no Christian novels. There are novels whose purpose is edification; but that has nothing to do with what I mean. Moral tragedy – the tragedy, for instance, which gives such terrific meaning to the Gospel text: 'If the salt have lost his flavour wherewith shall it be salted?' – that is the tragedy with which I am concerned.

Nov. 10th. – Olivier's examination is coming on shortly. Pauline wants him to try for the *École Normale* afterwards. His career is all mapped out. . . . If only he had no parents, no connexions! I would have made him my secretary. But the thought of me never occurs to him; he has not even noticed my interest in him, and I should embarrass him if I showed it. It is because I don't want to embarrass him that I affect a kind of indifference in his presence, a kind of detachment. It is only when he does not see me that I dare look my full at him.

Sometimes I follow him in the street without his knowing it. Yesterday I was walking behind him in this way, when he turned suddenly round before I had time to hide.

'Where are you off to in such a hurry?' I asked him.

'Oh, nowhere particular. I always seem most in a hurry when I have nothing to do.'

We took a few steps together, but without finding anything to say to each other. He was certainly put out at having been met.

Nov. 12th. – He has parents, an elder brother, school friends. . . . I keep repeating this to myself all day long – and that there is no room for me. I should no doubt be able to make up anything that might be lacking to him, but nothing is. He needs nothing; and if his sweetness delights me, there is nothing in it that allows me for a moment to deceive myself. . . . Oh, foolish words, which I write in spite of myself and which discover the duplicity of my heart. . . . I am leaving for London tomorrow. I have suddenly made up my mind to go away. It is time.

To go away because one is too anxious to stay! . . . A certain love of the arduous – a horror of indulgence (towards oneself, I mean) is perhaps the part of my Puritan upbringing which I find it hardest to free myself from.

Yesterday, at Smith's, bought a copy-book (English already) in which to continue my diary. I will write nothing more in this one. A new copy-book! . . .

Ah! if it were myself I could leave behind!

14

BERNARD AND LAURA

Il arrive quelquefois des accidents dans la vie, d'où il faut être un peu fou pour se bien tirer.

LA ROCHEFOUCAULD

IT was with Laura's letter, which Edouard had inserted into his journal, that Bernard's reading came to an end. The truth flashed upon him; it was impossible to doubt that the woman whose words rang so beseechingly in this letter was the same despairing creature of whom Olivier had told him the night before – Vincent Molinier's discarded mistress. And it became suddenly evident to Bernard that, thanks to this twofold confidence, Olivier's, and Edouard's in his journal, he was as yet the only one to know the two sides of the intrigue. It was an advantage he could not keep long; he must play his cards quickly and skilfully. He made up his mind at once. Without forgetting, for that matter, any of the other things he had read, Bernard now fixed his attention upon Laura.

'This morning I was still uncertain as to what I ought to do; now I have no longer any doubt,' he said to himself, as he darted out of the room. 'The imperative, as they say, is categorical. I must save Laura. It was not perhaps my duty to take the suitcase, but having taken it, I have certainly found in the suitcase a lively sense of my duty. The important thing is to come upon Laura before Edouard can get to her; to introduce myself and offer my services in such a way that she cannot take me for a swindler. The rest will be easy. At this moment I have enough in my pocket-book to come to the rescue of misfortune as magnificently as the most generous and the most compassionate of Edouards. The only thing which bothers me is how to do it. For Laura is a Vedel, and though she is about to become a mother in defiance of the code, she is no doubt a sensitive creature. I imagine her the kind of woman who stands on her dignity and flings her contempt in your face, as she tears up the banknotes you offer her – with benevolence, but in too flimsy an envelope. How shall I present the notes? How shall I present *myself*? That's the rub! As soon as one leaves the high road of legality, in what a tangle one finds oneself! I really am rather young to mix myself up in an intrigue as stiff as this. But, hang it all, youth's my strong point. Let's invent a candid confession – a touching and interesting story. The trouble is that it's got to do for Edouard as well; the same one – and without giving myself away. Oh! I shall think of something. Let's trust to the inspiration of the moment....'

He had reached the address given by Laura, in the rue de Beaune. The hotel was exceedingly modest, but clean and respectable looking. Following the porter's directions, he went up three floors. Outside the door of No. 16 he stopped, tried to prepare his entry, to find some words; he could think of nothing; then he made a dash for it and knocked. A gentle, sister-like voice, with, he thought, a touch of fear in it, answered:

'Come in!'

Laura was very simply dressed, all in black; she looked as if she were in mourning. During the few days she had been in Paris, she had been vaguely waiting for something or somebody to get her out of her straits. She had taken the wrong road, not a doubt of it; she felt completely lost. She had the unfortunate habit of counting on the event rather than on herself. She was not without virtue, but now that she had been abandoned she felt that all her strength had left her. At Bernard's entrance, she raised one hand to her face, like someone who keeps back a cry or shades his eyes from too bright a light. She was standing, and took a step backwards; then, finding herself close to the window, with her other hand she caught hold of the curtain.

Bernard stopped, waiting for her to question him; but she too waited for him to speak. He looked at her; with a beating heart, he tried in vain to smile.

'Excuse me, Madame,' he said at last, 'for disturbing you in this manner. Edouard X., whom I believe you know, arrived in Paris this morning. I have something urgent to say to him; I thought you might be able to give me his address and . . . forgive me for coming so unceremoniously to ask for it.'

Had Bernard not been so young, Laura would doubtless have been frightened. But he was still a child, with eyes so frank, so clear a brow, so timid a bearing, a voice so ill-assured, that fear yielded to curiosity, to interest, to that irresistible sympathy which a simple and beautiful being always arouses. Bernard's voice gathered a little courage as he spoke.

'But I don't know his address,' said Laura. 'If he is in Paris, he will come to see me without delay, I hope. Tell me who you are. I will tell him.'

'Now's the moment to risk everything,' thought Bernard. Something wild flashed across his eyes. He looked Laura steadily in the face.

'Who am I? . . . Olivier Molinier's friend. . . .' He hesitated, still uncertain; but seeing her turn pale at his name, he ventured further: 'Olivier, Vincent's brother – the brother of your lover, who has so vilely abandoned you. . . .'

He had to stop. Laura was tottering. Her two hands, flung backwards, were anxiously searching for some support. But what upset Bernard more than anything was the moan she gave – a kind of wail which was scarcely human, more like that of some hunted, wounded animal (and the sportsman, suddenly filled with shame, feels himself an executioner); so odd a cry it was, so different from anything that Bernard expected, that he shuddered. He understood all of a sudden that this was a matter of real life, of veritable pain, and everything he had felt up till that moment seemed to him mere show and pretence. An emotion surged up in him so unfamiliar that he was unable to master it. It rose to his throat. . . . What! is he sobbing? Is it possible? . . . He, Bernard! . . . He rushes forward to hold her up, and kneels before her, and murmurs through his sobs:

'Oh, forgive me . . . forgive; I have hurt you. . . . I knew that you were in difficulties, and . . . I wanted to help you.'

But Laura, gasping for breath, felt that she was fainting. She cast round with her eyes for somewhere to sit down. Bernard, whose gaze was fixed upon her, understood her look. He sprang towards a small arm-chair at the foot of the bed, with a rapid movement pushed it towards her, and she dropped heavily into it.

At this moment there occurred a grotesque incident which I hesitate to relate, but it was decisive of Laura's and Bernard's relationship, by unexpectedly relieving them of their embarrassment. I shall therefore not attempt to embellish the scene by any artifices.

For the price which Laura paid for her room (I mean, which the hotel-keeper asked her) one could not have expected the furniture to be elegant, but one might have hoped it would be solid. Now the small arm-chair, which Bernard pushed towards Laura, was somewhat unsteady on its feet; that is to say, it had a great propensity to fold back one of its legs, as a bird does under its wing – which is natural enough in a bird, but unusual and regrettable in an arm-chair; this one, moreover, hid its infirmity as best it could beneath a thick fringe. Laura was well acquainted with her arm-chair, and knew that it must be handled with extreme precaution; but in her agitation she forgot this and only remembered it when she felt the chair giving way beneath her. She suddenly gave a little cry – quite different from the long moan she had uttered just before, slipped to one side, and a moment later found herself sitting on the floor, between the arms of Bernard, who had hurried to the rescue. Bashful, but amused, he had been obliged to put one knee on the ground. Laura's face therefore happened to be quite close to his; he watched her blush. She made an effort to get up; he helped her.

'You've not hurt yourself?'

'No; thanks to you. This arm-chair is ridiculous; it has been mended once already. . . . I think if the leg is put quite straight, it will hold.'

'I'll arrange it,' said Bernard. 'There! . . . Will you try it?' Then, thinking better of it: 'No; allow me. It would be safer for me to try it first. Look! It's all right now. I can move my legs' (which he did, laughing). Then, as he rose: 'Sit down now, and if you'll allow me to stay a moment or two longer, I'll take this chair. I'll sit near you, so that I shall be able to prevent you from falling. Don't be frightened. . . . I wish I could do more for you.'

There was so much ardour in his voice, so much reserve in his manners, and in his movements so much grace, that Laura could not forbear a smile.

'You haven't told me your name yet.'

'Bernard.'

'Yes. But your family name?'

'I have no family.'

'Well, your parents' name.'

'I have no parents. That is, I am what the child you are expecting will be – a bastard.'

The smile vanished from Laura's face; she was outraged by this insistent determination to force an entrance into her intimacy and to violate the secret of her life.

'But how do you know? . . . Who told you? . . . You have no right to know. . . .'

Bernard was launched now; he spoke loudly and boldly:

'I know both what my friend Olivier knows and what your friend Edouard knows. Only each of them as yet knows only half your secret. I am probably the only person besides yourself to know the whole of it. . . . So you see,' he added more gently, 'it's essential that I should be your friend.'

'Oh, how can people be so indiscreet?' murmured Laura sadly. 'But . . . if you haven't seen Edouard, he can't have spoken to you. Has he written to you? . . . Is it he who has sent you?' . . .

Bernard had given himself away; he had spoken too quickly and had not been able to resist bragging a little. He shook his head. Laura's face grew still darker. At that moment a knock was heard at the door.

Whether they will or no, a link is created between two creatures who experience a common emotion. Bernard felt himself trapped; Laura was vexed at being surprised in company. They looked at each other like two accomplices. Another knock was heard. Both together said:

'Come in.'

For some minutes Edouard had been listening outside the door, astonished at hearing voices in Laura's room. Bernard's last sentences had explained everything. He could not doubt their meaning; he could not doubt that the speaker was the stealer of his suitcase. His mind was immediately made up. For Edouard is one of those beings whose faculties, which seem benumbed in the ordinary routine of daily life, spring into activity at the call of the unexpected. He opened the door therefore, but remained on the threshold, smiling and looking alternately at Laura and Bernard, who had both risen.

'Allow me, my dear Laura,' said he, with a gesture as though to put off any effusions till later. 'I must first say a word or two to this gentleman, if he will be so good as to step into the passage for a moment.'

His smile became more ironical when Bernard joined him.

'I thought I should find you here.'

Bernard understood that the game was up. There was nothing for him to do but to put a bold face on it, which he did with the feeling that he was playing his last card:

'I hoped I should meet you.'

'In the first place – if you haven't done so already (for I'll do you the credit of believing that that is what you came for), you will go downstairs to the bureau and settle Madame Douviers' bill with the money you found in my suitcase and which you must have on you. Don't come up again for ten minutes.'

All this was said gravely but with nothing comminatory in the tone. In the meantime Bernard had recovered his self-possession.

'I did in fact come for that. You are not wrong. And I am beginning to think that *I* was not wrong either.'

'What do you mean by that?'

'That you really are the person I hoped you would be.'

Edouard was trying in vain to look severe. He was immensely entertained. He made a kind of slight mocking bow:

'Much obliged. It remains to be seen whether I shall be able to return the compliment. I suppose, since you are here, that you have read my papers?'

Bernard, who had endured without flinching the brunt of Edouard's gaze, smiled in his turn with boldness, amusement, impertinence; and bowing low, 'Don't doubt it,' he said. 'I am here to serve you.'

Then, quick as an elf, he darted downstairs.

When Edouard went back into the room, Laura was sobbing. He went up to her. She put her forehead down on his shoulder. Any manifestation of emotion embarrassed him almost unbearably. He found himself gently patting her on the back as one does a choking child:

'My poor Laura,' said he; 'come, come, be sensible.'

'Oh, let me cry a little; it does me good.'

'All the same we've got to consider what you are to do.'

'What is there I *can* do? Where can I go? To whom can I speak?'

'Your parents. . . .'

'You know what they are. It would plunge them in despair. And they did everything they could to make me happy.'

'Douviers? . . .'

'I shall never dare face him again. He is so good. You mustn't think I don't love him. . . . If you only knew . . . if you only knew . . . Oh, say you don't despise me too much.'

'On the contrary, my dear; on the contrary. How can you imagine such a thing?' And he began patting her on the back again.

'Yes; I don't feel ashamed any more, when I am with you.'

'How long have you been here?'

'I can't remember. I have only been living in the hopes that you would come. There were times when I thought I couldn't bear it. I feel now as if I couldn't stay here another day.'

Her sobs redoubled and she almost screamed out, though in a choking voice:

'Take me away! Take me away!'

Edouard felt more and more uncomfortable.

'Now Laura . . . You must be calm. That . . . that . . . I don't even know his name. . . .'

'Bernard,' murmured Laura.

Bernard will be back in a moment. Come now; pull yourself together. He mustn't see you in this state. Courage! We'll think of something, I promise you. Come, come! Dry your eyes. Crying does no good. Look at yourself in the glass. Your face is all swollen. You must bathe it. When I see you crying I can't think of anything. . . . There! Here he is! I can hear him.'

He went to the door and opened it to let in Bernard, while Laura, with her back turned at the dressing-table, set about restoring a semblance of calm to her features.

'And now, sir, may I ask when I shall be allowed to get possession of my belongings again?'

He looked Bernard full in the face as he spoke, with the same ironical smile on his lips as before.

'As soon as you please, sir; but at the same time, I feel obliged to confess that I shall certainly feel the loss of your belongings a good deal more than you do. I am sure you would understand if you only knew my story. But I'll just say this, that since this morning I am without a roof, without a family and with nothing better to do than throw myself into the river, if I hadn't met you. I followed you this morning for a long time while you were talking to my friend Olivier. He has spoken to me about you such a lot! I should have liked to go up to you. I was casting about for some excuse to do so, by hook or by crook. . . . When you threw your luggage ticket away, I blessed my stars. Oh, don't take me for a thief. If I lifted your suitcase, it was more than anything so as to get into touch with you.'

Bernard brought all this out almost in a single breath. An extraordinary animation fired his words and features – as though they were aflame with kindness. Edouard, to judge by his smile, thought him charming.

'And now . . . ?' asked he.

Bernard understood that he was gaining ground.

'And now, weren't you in need of a secretary? I can't believe I should fill the post badly – it would be with such joy.'

This time Edouard laughed outright. Laura watched them both with amusement.

'Ho! Ho! . . . We must think about that. Come and see me tomorrow at the same time, and here – if Madame Douviers will allow it – for I have a great many things to settle with her too. You're staying at a hotel, I suppose? Oh, I don't want to know where. It doesn't matter in the least. Till tomorrow.'

He held out his hand.

'Sir, before I leave you,' said Bernard, 'will you allow me to remind you that there is a poor old music-master, called La Pérouse, I think, who is living in the Faubourg St Honoré, and who would be made very happy by a visit from you?'

'Upon my word, that's not a bad beginning. You have a very fair notion of your future duties.'

'Then. . . Really? You consent?'

'We'll see about it tomorrow. Good-bye.'

Edouard, after having stayed a few moments longer with Laura, went to the Moliniers'. He hoped to see Olivier again; he wanted to speak to him about Bernard. He saw only Pauline, though he stayed on and on in desperation.

Olivier, that very afternoon, yielding to the pressing invitation passed on to him by his brother, had gone to visit the author of *The Horizontal Bar*, the Comte de Passavant.

15

OLIVIER VISITS THE COMTE DE PASSAVANT

'I WAS afraid your brother hadn't delivered my message,' said Robert on seeing Olivier come into the room.

'Am I late?' he asked, coming forward timidly and almost on tiptoe. He had kept his hat in his hand and Robert took it from him.

'Put that down. Make yourself comfortable. Here, in this arm-chair, I think you'll be all right. Not late at all, to judge by the clock. But my wish to see you went faster than the time. Do you smoke?'

'No, thank you,' said Olivier, waving aside the cigarette case, which the Comte de Passavant held out to him. He refused out of shyness, though he was really longing to try one of the slender, amber-scented cigarettes (Russian, no doubt), which lay ranged in the proffered case.

'Yes, I'm glad you were able to come. I was afraid you might be too much taken up with your examination. When is it?'

'The written is in ten days. But I'm not working much. I think I'm ready and I'm more afraid of being fagged when I go up.'

'Still, I suppose you'd refuse to undertake any other occupation just now?'

'No . . . if it isn't too absorbing, that is.'

'I'll tell you why I asked you to come. First, for the pleasure of seeing you again. The other night in the foyer, during the *entr'acte*, we were just getting into a talk. I was exceedingly interested by what you said. I expect you don't remember?'

'Oh yes, I do,' said Olivier, who was under the impression he had said nothing but stupidities.

'But today I have something special to say to you. . . . I think you know an individual of the Hebrew persuasion, called Dhurmer? Isn't he one of your schoolfellows?'

'I have just this moment left him.'

'Ah! You see a good deal of each other?'

'Yes. We met at the Louvre today to talk about a review of which he is to be the editor.'

Robert burst into a loud, affected laugh.

'Ha! Ha! Ha! the editor! . . . He's in a deuce of a hurry. . . . Did he really say that to you?'

'He has been talking to me about it for ever so long.'

'Yes. I have been thinking of it for some time past. The other day I asked him casually whether he'd agree to read over the manuscripts with me; that's what he at once called becoming editor – not even sub-editor; I didn't contradict him and he immediately . . . Just like him, isn't it? What a fellow! He wants taking down a peg or two. . . . Don't you really smoke?'

'After all, I think I will,' said Olivier, this time accepting. 'Thank you.'

'Well, allow me to say, Olivier . . . you don't mind my calling you Olivier, do you? I really can't say Monsieur; you're too young, and I'm too intimate with your brother Vincent to call you Molinier. Well then, Olivier, allow me to say that I have infinitely more confidence in your taste than in Mr Solomon Dhurmer's. Now would you consent to taking the literary direction? Under me a little, of course – at first, at any rate. But I prefer not to have my name on the cover. I'll tell you why later. . . . Perhaps you'd take a glass of port wine, eh? I've got some that's quite good.'

He stretched out his hand to a kind of little sideboard that stood near and took up a bottle of wine and two glasses, which he filled.

'Well! What do you think?'

'Yes, indeed; first-rate.'

'I wasn't talking of the port,' protested Robert, laughing; 'but of what I was saying just now.'

Olivier had pretended not to understand. He was afraid of accepting too quickly and of showing his joy too obviously. He blushed a little and stammered with confusion:

'My examination wouldn't. . .'

'You have just told me that you weren't giving much time to it,' interrupted Robert. 'And besides, the review won't come out yet awhile. I am wondering whether it wouldn't be better to put off launching it till after the holidays. But in any case I had to sound you. We must get several numbers ready before October and we ought to see each other a great deal this summer so as to talk things over. What are you going to do these holidays?'

'I don't know exactly. My people will probably be going to Normandy. They always do in the summer.'

'And you will have to go with them? . . . Couldn't you let yourself be unhitched for a bit? . . .'

'My mother would never consent.'

'I'm dining tonight with your brother. May I speak to him about it?'

'Oh, Vincent won't be with us.' Then, realizing that this sentence was no answer to the question, he added: 'Besides, it wouldn't do any good.'

'Well, but if we find a good reason to give Mamma?'

Olivier did not answer. He loved his mother tenderly and the mocking tone in which Robert alluded to her displeased him. Robert understood that he had gone too far.

'So you appreciate my port,' he said by way of diversion. 'Have another glass?'

'No, no, thank you; but it's excellent.'

'Yes, I was struck by the ripeness and sureness of your judgement the other night. Do you mean to go in for criticism?'

'No.'

'Poetry? . . . I know you write poetry.'

Olivier blushed again.

'Yes, your brother has betrayed you. And no doubt you know other young men who would be ready to contribute. This review must become a rallying ground for the younger generation. That's its *raison d'être*. I should like you to help me draw up a kind of prospectus, a manifesto, which would just give a sketch of the new tendencies without defining them too precisely. We'll talk it over later on. We must make a choice of two or three telling epithets; they mustn't be neologisms; no old words that are thoroughly hackneyed; we'll fill them with a brand new meaning and make the public swallow them. After

Flaubert there was "cadenced and rhythmic"; after Leconte de Lisle, "hieratic and definitive". . . . Oh! what would you say to "vital", eh? . . . "Unconscious and vital" . . . No? . . . "Elementary, unconscious and vital"?'

'I think we might find something better still,' Olivier took courage to say, smiling, though without seeming to approve much.

'Come, another glass of port. . . .'

'Not quite full, please.'

'You see, the great weakness of the symbolist school is that it brought nothing but an aesthetic with it; all the other great schools brought with them, besides their new styles, a new ethic, new tables, a new way of looking at things, of understanding love, of behaving oneself in life. As for the symbolist, it's perfectly simple; he didn't behave himself at all in life; he didn't attempt to understand it; he denied its existence; he turned his back on it. Absurd, don't you think? They were a set of people without greed – without appetites even. Not like us . . . eh?'

Olivier had finished his second glass of port and his second cigarette. Reclining in his comfortable arm-chair, with his eyes half shut, he said nothing, but signified his assent by slightly nodding his head from time to time. At this moment a ring was heard, and almost immediately afterwards a servant entered with a card which he presented to Robert. Robert took the card, glanced at it and put it on his writing desk beside him.

'Very well. Ask him to wait a moment.' The servant went out. 'Look here, my dear boy, I like you very much and I think we shall get on very well together. But somebody has just come whom I absolutely must see and he wants to speak to me alone.'

Olivier had risen.

'I'll show you out by the garden, if you'll allow me. . . . Ah! whilst I think of it. Would you care to have my new book? I've got a copy here, on hand-made paper. . . .'

'I haven't waited for that to read it,' said Olivier, who didn't much care for Passavant's book, and tried his best to be amiable without being fulsome.

Did Passavant detect in his tone a certain tincture of disdain?

He went on quickly: 'Oh, you needn't say anything about it. If you were to tell me you liked it, I should be obliged to doubt either your taste or your sincerity. No; no one knows better than I do what's lacking in the book. I wrote it much too quickly. To tell the truth, the whole time I was writing it I was thinking of my next one. Ah! that one is a different matter. I care about that one. Yes, I care about it exceedingly. You'll see; you'll see. . . . I'm so very sorry, but you really must leave me now. . . . Unless . . . No, no; we don't know each other well enough yet, and your people are certainly expecting you back for dinner. Well, good-bye; *au revoir*. I'll write your name in the book; allow me.'

He had risen; he went up to his writing desk. While he was stooping to write, Olivier stepped forward and glanced out of the corner of his eye at the card which the servant had just brought in:

VICTOR STROUVILHOU

The name meant nothing to him.

Passavant handed Olivier the copy of *The Horizontal Bar*, and as Olivier was preparing to read the inscription:

'Look at it later,' said Passavant, slipping the book under his arm.

It was not till he was in the street that Olivier read the manuscript motto with which the Comte de Passavant had adorned the first page and which he had culled out of the book itself:

'*Prithee, Orlando, a few steps further. I am not perfectly sure that I dare altogether take your meaning.*'

Underneath which he had added:

To OLIVIER MOLINIER
from his presumptive friend
COMTE ROBERT DE PASSAVANT

An ambiguous motto, which made Olivier wonder, but which after all he was perfectly free to interpret as he pleased.

Olivier got home just after Edouard had left, weary of waiting.

16

VINCENT AND LILIAN

VINCENT'S education, which had been materialistic in tendency, prevented him from believing in the supernatural – which gave the demon an immense advantage. The demon never made a frontal attack upon Vincent; he approached him crookedly and furtively. One of his cleverest manoeuvres consists in presenting us our defeats as if they were victories. What inclined Vincent to consider his behaviour to Laura as a victory of his will over his affections, was that, being naturally kind-hearted, he had been obliged to force himself, to steel himself to be hard to her.

Upon a closer examination of the evolution of Vincent's character in this intrigue, I discover various stages, which I will point out for the reader's edification:

1st. – The period of good motives. Probity. Conscientious need of repairing a wrong action. In actual fact: the moral obligation of devoting to Laura the money which his parents had laboriously saved to meet the initial expenses of his career. Is this not self-sacrifice? Is this motive not respectable, generous, charitable?

2nd. – The period of uneasiness. Scruples. Is not the fear that this sum may be insufficient, the first step towards yielding, when the demon dangles before Vincent's eyes the possibility of increasing it?

3rd. – Constancy and fortitude. Need after the loss of this sum to feel himself 'above adversity'. It is this 'fortitude' which enables him to confess his loss at cards to Laura; and which enables him by the same occasion to break with her.

4th. – Renunciation of good motives, regarded as a cheat, in the light of the new ethic which Vincent finds himself obliged to invent in order to legitimize his conduct; for he continues to be a moral being, and the devil will only get the better of him by furnishing him with reasons for self-approval. Theory of immanence, of totality in the moment; of gratuitous, immediate and motiveless joy.

5th. – Intoxication of the winner. Contempt of the reserve in hand. Supremacy.

After which the demon has won the game.

After which the being who believes himself freest is nothing but a tool at his service. The demon will never rest now till Vincent has sold his brother to that creature of perdition – Passavant.

And yet Vincent is not bad. All this, do what he will, leaves him unsatisfied, uncomfortable. Let us add a few words more:

The name '*exoticism*' is, I believe, given to those of Maia's iridescent folds which make the soul feel itself a stranger, which deprive it of points of contact. There are some whose virtue would resist, but that the devil, before attacking it, transplants them. No doubt, if Vincent and Laura had not been under other skies, far from their parents, from their past memories, from all that maintained them in consistency with themselves, she would not have yielded to him, nor he attempted to seduce her. No doubt it seemed to them out there that their act did not enter into the reckoning.... A great deal more might be said; but the above is enough as it is to explain Vincent to us better.

With Lilian too he felt himself in a foreign land.

'Don't laugh at me, Lilian,' he said to her that same evening. 'I know that you won't understand, and yet I have to speak to you as if you would, for I'm unable now to get you out of my mind.'

Lilian was lying on the low divan, and he, half reclining at her feet, let his head rest, lover-like, on his mistress's knees, while she, lover-like, caressed it.

'The thing that was on my mind this morning was . . . yes, I think it was fear. Can you keep serious for a moment? Can you try to understand me so far as to forget for a moment – not what you believe, for you believe in nothing – but just that very fact that you believe in nothing? I didn't believe in anything either; I believed that I didn't believe in anything – not in anything but ourselves, in you, in me, in what I am when I am with you, in what, thanks to you, I am going to become. . . .'

'Robert will be here at seven,' interrupted Lilian. 'I don't want to hurry you; but if you don't get on a little quicker he'll interrupt you just at the very moment you are beginning to get interesting. I don't suppose you'll want to go on when he's here. It's odd that you should think it necessary to take so many precautions today. You remind me of a blind man, who has first to feel every spot with his stick before he puts his foot on it. And yet you can see I'm keeping quite serious. Why haven't you more confidence?'

'Ever since I've known you, my confidence has become extraordinary,' went on Vincent. 'I'm capable of great things, I feel it; and you see that everything I do turns out successful. But that's exactly what terrifies me. No; be quiet.... All day long I've kept thinking of what you told me this morning about the wreck of the *Bourgogne* and of the people who wanted to get into the boat having their hands cut off. It seems to me that something wants to get into my boat – I'm using your image, so that you may understand me – something that I want to prevent getting in....'

'And you want me to help you drown it.... You old coward!'

He went on without looking at her:

'Something I keep off, but whose voice I hear... a voice you have never heard, that I listened to in my childhood....'

'And what does your voice say? You don't dare tell me. I'm not surprised. I bet there's a dash of the catechism in it, isn't there?'

'Oh, Lilian, try to understand; the only way for me to get rid of these thoughts is to tell them to you. If you laugh at them, I shall keep them to myself and they'll poison me.'

'Tell away, then,' said she with an air of resignation. Then, as he kept silent and hid his face like a child in Lilian's skirts: 'Well, what are you waiting for?'

She seized him by the hair and forced him to raise his head:

'Upon my word, he's really taking it seriously! Just look at him! He's quite pale. Now, listen to me, my dear boy; if you mean to behave like a child, it's not my affair at all. One must have the strength of one's convictions. And, besides, you know I don't like people who cheat. When you try on the sly to pull things into your boat which oughtn't to be there, you're cheating. I'm willing to play the game with you, but it must be aboveboard; and I warn you my object is to make you succeed. I think you're capable of becoming somebody important – really important; I feel great intelligence in you, and great strength. I want to help you. There are quite enough women who spoil the careers of the men they fall in love with; I want to do the contrary. You've already told me you wanted to give up doctoring in order to work at science and that you were sorry you hadn't enough money. . . . Now you have just won fifty thousand francs, which isn't bad to begin with. But you must promise me not to play any more. I'll put as much money as is necessary at your disposal, on condition that if people say you are being kept, you'll be strong-minded enough to shrug your shoulders.'

Vincent had risen. He went up to the window. Lilian went on:

'To begin with, I think one might as well finish up with Laura and send her the five thousand francs you promised her. Now that you've got the money, why don't you keep your word? I don't like it at all. I detest caddishness. You don't know how to cut hands off decently. When that's done, we'll go and spend the summer where it'll be most profitable for your work. . . . You mentioned Roskoff; personally, I should prefer Monaco, because I know the Prince, and he might take us for a cruise and perhaps give you a job in his laboratory.'

Vincent kept silent. He felt disinclined to say to Lilian (he only told her later) that before coming to see her, he had gone to the hotel where Laura had waited for him in such despair. Anxious to be at last quit of his debt, he had slipped the notes, on which she no longer counted, into an envelope. He had entrusted the envelope to a waiter, and then waited in the hall until he should hear it had been delivered to her personally. A few moments later the waiter had come downstairs bringing with him the envelope, across which Laura had written:

'Too late.'

Lilian rang and asked for her cloak. When the maid had left the room:

'Oh, I wanted to say to you, before Robert arrives, that if he proposes an investment for your fifty thousand francs – be careful. He is very rich, but he is always in want of money. There! look and see. I think I hear his horn. He's half an hour before the time; but so much the better. . . . For all we were saying! . . .'

'I'm early,' said Robert as he came into the room, 'because I thought it would be amusing to go and dine at Versailles. Do you agree?'

'No,' said Lady Griffith; 'the fountains bore me. I had rather go to Rambouillet; there's time. We shan't have such a good dinner, but we shall be able to talk more easily. I want Vincent to tell you his fish stories. He knows some marvellous ones. I don't know if what he says is true, but it's more amusing than the best novel in the world.'

'That's not perhaps what a novelist will think,' said Vincent.

Robert de Passavant held an evening paper in his hand.

'D'you know that Brugnard has just been made assistant-secretary at the Ministry of Justice? Now's the moment to get your father decorated,' said he, turning to Vincent. Vincent shrugged his shoulders.

'My dear Vincent,' went on Passavant, 'allow me to say that you'll very much offend him by not asking this little favour – which he'll be so delighted to refuse.'

'Suppose you were to start by asking it for yourself,' Vincent replied.

Robert made an affected little grimace:

'No; for my part, my vanity consists in never blushing – not even in my buttonhole.' Then, turning to Lilian:

'Do you know it's rare nowadays to find a man who has reached forty without either the syph or the legion of honour?'

Lilian smiled and shrugged her shoulders:

'For the sake of a *bon-mot* he actually consents to make himself out older than he is! I say, is it a quotation from your next book? It'll be tasty. . . . Go on downstairs. I'll get my cloak and follow you.'

'I thought you had given up seeing him,' said Vincent to Robert on the staircase.

'Who? Brugnard?'

'You said he was so stupid....'

'My dear friend,' replied Passavant, pausing on a step and holding up Molinier, for he saw Lady Griffith coming and wanted her to hear: 'you must know there's not a single one of my friends whom I've known a certain time, that hasn't given me unmistakable proofs of imbecility. I assure you that Brugnard resisted the test longer than a great many others.'

'Than I, perhaps?' asked Vincent.

'Which doesn't prevent me from being your best friend... as you see.'

'And that's what's called wit in Paris,' said Lilian, who had joined them. 'Take care, Robert; there's nothing fades quicker.'

'Don't be alarmed, dear lady; words only fade when they're printed.'

They took their places in the car and drove off. As their conversation continued to be very witty, it is useless to record it here. They sat down to table on the terrace of a hotel overlooking a garden where the shades of night were gathering. Under cover of the evening, their talk grew slower and graver; urged on by Lilian and Robert, Vincent found himself at last the only speaker.

17

THE EVENING AT RAMBOUILLET

'I SHOULD take more interest in animals if I were less interested in men,' Robert had said. And Vincent had replied:

'Perhaps you think them too different. Every single one of the great discoveries in zoology has left its mark upon the study of man. The whole subject is interlinked and interdependent, and I believe that a novelist who also prides himself upon being a psychologist can never turn aside his eyes from the spectacle of nature and remain ignorant of her laws without paying for it. In the Goncourts' Journal, which you gave me to read, I fell upon an account of a visit they paid to the Zoological houses in the Jardin des Plantes, in which your charming authors deplore Nature's – or the Lord's – lack of imagination. This paltry blasphemy merely serves to show up the stupidity and incomprehension of their small minds. On the contrary, what astonishing diversity! It seems as if Nature had essayed one after the other every possible manner of living and moving, as if she had taken advantage of every permission granted by matter and its laws. What a lesson can be read in the progressive abandonment of certain palaeontological experiments which proved irrational and inelegant; the economy which has enabled some forms to survive explains why the others were abandoned. Botany is instructive, too. When I examine a plant, I observe that at the place where each leaf springs from the stem, a bud lies sheltered, which is capable in its turn of shooting into life the following year. When I remark that out of all these buds, two at most are destined to come to anything, and that by the very fact of their growth they condemn all the others to atrophy, I cannot help thinking that the case is the same with men. The buds which develop naturally are always the terminal buds – that is to say, those that are farthest away from the parent trunk. It is only by pruning or layering that the sap is driven back and so forced to give life to those germs which are nearest the trunk and which would otherwise have lain dormant. And in this manner, the most recalcitrant plants, which, if left to themselves, would no doubt have produced nothing but leaves, are induced to bear fruit. Oh! an orchard or a garden is an excellent school! and a horticulturist would often make the best of pedagogues! There is more to be learnt, if one can use one's eyes, in a poultry-yard, or a kennel, or an aquarium, or a rabbit warren, or a stable, than in all your books, or even, believe me, in the society of men, where everything is more or less sophisticated.'

Then Vincent spoke of selection. He explained how in order to obtain the finest seedlings, the ordinary plan is to choose the most robust specimens; and then he told them of the fantastic experiment of one audacious horticulturist, who, out of a horror of routine – it really seemed almost like a challenge – took it into his head, on the contrary, to select the most weakly – with the result that he obtained blooms of incomparable beauty.

Robert, who had at first listened with only half an ear, like a person who merely expects to be bored, now made no attempts to interrupt. His attention delighted Lilian, who took it as a compliment to her lover.

'You ought to tell us,' said she, 'of what you were saying the other day about fish and their power of accommodation to the different amounts of salt in the sea. . . . That was it, wasn't it?'

'Except for certain regions,' went on Vincent, 'the sea's degree of saltness is pretty constant; and marine fauna as a rule tolerates only very slight variations of density. But the regions I was telling you about are nevertheless not uninhabited; the regions I mean are those which are subject to intense evaporation and in which, therefore, the proportion of water to salt is greatly reduced – or, on the contrary, those where the constant inflow of fresh water dilutes the salt and, so to speak, unsalts the sea – those that are near the mouths of great rivers, or such enormous currents as the Gulf Stream. In such regions the animals called *stenohaline* grow enfeebled to the point of perishing; and as they become incapable of defending themselves, they inevitably fall a prey to the animals called *euryhaline*, so that the *euryhalines* live by choice on the confines of the great currents, where the density of the water varies and where the *stenohalines* meet their death. You understand, don't you, that the *stenos* are those which can exist only in water whose degree of saltness is unvarying; whilst the *eurys*...

'Are the pickles,' interrupted Robert,* who always referred everything back to himself, and only took an interest in that part of a theory which he could turn to account.

'Most of them are ferocious,' added Vincent gravely.

'I told you it was better than any novel!' cried Lilian ecstatically.

Vincent seemed transfigured – indifferent to the impression he was making. He was extraordinarily grave and went on in a lower tone as if he were talking to himself:

'The most astonishing discovery of recent times – at any rate the one that has taught me most – is the discovery of the photogenic apparatus of deep-sea creatures.'

'Oh, tell us about it!' cried Lilian, letting her cigarette go out and her ice melt on her plate.

'You know, no doubt, that the light of day does not reach very far down into the sea. Its depths are dark ... huge gulfs, which for a long time were thought to be uninhabited; then people began dragging them, and quantities of strange animals were brought up from these infernal regions – animals that were blind, it was thought. What use would the sense of sight be in the dark? Evidently they had no eyes; they wouldn't, they couldn't have eyes. Nevertheless, on examination it was found to people's amazement that some of them *had* eyes; that they almost all had eyes, and sometimes antennae of extraordinary sensibility into the bargain. Still people doubted and wondered: why eyes with no means of seeing? Eyes that are sensitive – but sensitive to what? ... And at last it was discovered that each of these animals which people at first insisted were creatures of darkness, gives forth and projects before and around it its *own* light. Each of them shines, illuminates, irradiates. When they were brought up from the depths at night and turned out on to the ship's deck, the darkness blazed. Moving, many-coloured

* Robert here makes a pun impossible to translate. *Dessalé* (literally *unsalted*) is a slang expression meaning something like *unscrupulous*. – *Translator's note.*

fires, glowing, vibrating, changing – revolving beacon-lamps – sparkling of stars and jewels – a spectacle, say those who saw it, of unparalleled splendour.'

Vincent stopped. No one spoke for a long time.

'Let's go home,' said Lilian suddenly; 'I'm cold.'

Lady Lilian took her seat beside the chauffeur, so as to be sheltered by the glass screen. The two men at the back of the open carriage carried on their own conversation. Robert had hardly spoken during the whole of the dinner; he had listened to Vincent talking; now it was his turn.

'Fish, like us, my dear boy, perish in calm waters,' said he to begin with, giving his friend a thump on the shoulder. He allowed himself a few familiarities with Vincent, but would not have suffered him to reciprocate them; for that matter, Vincent was not disposed to. 'Do you know, I think you're simply splendid! What a lecturer you'd make! Upon my word, you ought to quit doctoring. I really can't see you prescribing laxatives and having no company but the sick. A chair of comparative biology, or something of that sort is what you want.'

'Yes,' said Vincent, 'I have sometimes thought so.'

'Lilian ought to be able to manage it. She could get her friend the Prince of Monaco to interest himself in your researches. It's his line, I believe. I must speak to her about it.'

'She has suggested it already.'

'Oh, so I see there's no possibility of doing you a service,' said he, pretending to be vexed. 'Just as I wanted to ask you one for myself, too.'

'It's your turn to be in my debt. You think I've got a very short memory.'

'What? You're still thinking of that five thousand francs? But you've paid it back, my dear fellow. You owe me nothing at all now – except a little friendship, perhaps.' He added these words in a voice that was almost tender, and with one hand on Vincent's arm. 'I want to appeal to it now.'

'I am listening,' said Vincent.

But at that, Passavant immediately protested, as if the impatience were Vincent's, and not his own:

'Goodness me! What a hurry you're in! Between this and Paris there's time enough surely.'

Passavant was particularly skilful in the art of fathering his own words – and anything else he preferred to disown – on other people. He made a feint of dropping his subject, like an angler who, for fear of startling his trout, makes a long cast with his bait and then draws it in again by imperceptible degrees.

'Apropos, thank you for sending me your brother. I was afraid you had forgotten.'

Vincent made a gesture and Robert went on:

'Have you seen him since? . . . Not had time, eh? . . . Then it's odd you shouldn't have asked me yet how the interview went off. At bottom, you don't in the least care. You don't take the faintest interest in your brother. What Olivier thinks and feels, what he is, what he wants to be, never concerns you in the least. . . .'

'Reproaching me?' asked Vincent.

'Upon my soul, yes. I can't understand – I can't swallow your indifference. When you were ill at Pau, it might pass; you could only think of yourself; selfishness was part of the cure. But now . . . What! you have growing up beside you a young nature quivering with life, a budding intelligence, full of promise, only waiting for a word of advice, of encouragement. . . .'

He forgot as he spoke that he too had a brother.

Vincent, however, was no fool; the very exaggeration of this attack showed him that it was not sincere and that his companion's indignation was merely brought forward to pave the way for something else. He waited in silence. But Robert stopped short suddenly; he had just surprised in the glimmer of Vincent's cigarette a curious curl of his lip, which he took for irony; now there was nothing in the world he was more afraid of than being laughed at. And yet, was it really that which made him change his tone? I wonder whether the sudden intuition of a kind of connivance between Vincent and himself . . . He assumed an air of perfect naturalness and started again in the tone of 'there's no need of any pretence with you':

'Well, I had a most delightful conversation with young Olivier. I like the boy exceedingly.'

Passavant tried to catch Vincent's expression (the night was not very dark); but he was looking fixedly in front of him.

'And now, my dear Molinier, the service I wished to ask you...'

But, here again, he felt the need of marking time, something like an actor who drops his part for a moment with the assurance that he has his audience well in hand, and wishes to prove that he has, both to himself and to them. He bent forward therefore to Lilian, and speaking in a loud voice as if to accentuate the confidential character of what he had been saying, and of what he was going to say:

'Are you sure, dear lady, that you aren't catching cold? We have a rug here that's doing nothing....'

Then, without waiting for an answer, he sank back into the corner of the carriage beside Vincent, and lowering his voice once more:

'This is what it is. I want to take your brother away with me this summer. Yes; I tell you so frankly; what's the use of beating about the bush between us two?... I haven't the honour of being acquainted with your parents and of course they wouldn't allow Olivier to come away with me unless you were to intervene on my behalf. No doubt you'll find a way of disposing them in my favour. You know what they're like, I suppose, and you'll be able to get round them. You'll do this for me, won't you?'

He waited a moment, and then, as Vincent kept silent, went on:

'Look here, Vincent... I'm leaving Paris soon... I don't know for where as yet. I absolutely must have a secretary.... You know I'm founding a review. I have spoken about it to Olivier. He seems to me to have all the necessary qualities.... But I don't want to look at it merely from my own selfish point of view: I also think that this will be an opportunity for him to show all his qualities. I have offered him the place of editor.... Editor of a review at his age!... You must admit that it's unusual.'

'So very unusual, that I'm afraid my parents may be rather alarmed by it,' said Vincent at last, turning his eyes on him and looking at him fixedly.

'Yes; you're no doubt right. Perhaps it would be better not to mention that. You might just put forward the interest and advantage it would be for him to go travelling with me, eh? Your parents must understand that at his age one wants to see the world a bit. At any rate, you'll arrange it with them, won't you?'

He took a breath, lighted another cigarette, and went on without changing his tone:

'And since you're going to be so nice, I'll try and do something for you. I think I can put you on to a thing which promises to turn out quite exceptionally. . . . A friend of mine in the highest banking circles is keeping it open for a few privileged persons. But please don't mention it; not a word to Lilian. In any case I can only dispose of a very limited number of shares; I can't offer them both to her and you. . . . Your last night's fifty thousand francs? . . .'

'I have already disposed of them,' answered Vincent rather shortly, for he remembered Lilian's warning.

'All right, all right . . .' rejoined Robert quickly, as though he were a little piqued; 'I'm not insisting.' Then with the air of saying: 'I can't be offended with you,' he added: 'If you change your mind, send me word at once . . . because after five o'clock tomorrow evening, it'll be too late.'

Vincent's admiration for the Comte de Passavant had become much greater since he had ceased to take him seriously.

18

EDOUARD'S JOURNAL: SECOND VISIT TO LA PÉROUSE

TWO O'CLOCK. Lost my suitcase. Serves me right. There was nothing in it I cared about but my journal. But I cared about that too much. In reality, very much amused by the adventure. All the same, I should like to have my papers back again. Who will read them? . . . Perhaps now that I have lost them, I exaggerate their importance. The book I have lost came to an end with my journey to England. When I was over there, I used another one, which I shall give up writing in, now that I am back in France. I shall take good care not to lose this one, in which I am writing now. It is my pocket-mirror. I cannot feel that anything that happens to me has any real existence until I see it reflected here. But since my return I seem to be walking in a dream. What a miserable uphill affair my conversation with Olivier was! And I had been looking forward to it with such joy. . . . I hope it has left him as ill-satisfied as it has me – as ill-satisfied with himself as with me. I was no more able to talk than to get him to talk. Oh, how difficult the slightest word is, when it involves the whole assent of the whole being! When the heart comes into play, it numbs and paralyses the brain.

Seven o'clock. Found my suitcase; or at any rate the person who took it. The fact that he is Olivier's most intimate friend makes a link between us which it rests only with me to tighten. The danger is that anything unexpected amuses me so intensely that I lose sight of my goal.

Seen Laura. My desire to oblige people becomes more acute if there is a difficulty to be encountered, if a struggle has to be waged with convention, banality and custom.

Visit to old La Pérouse. It was Madame de La Pérouse who opened the door to me. I have not seen her for more than two years; she recognized me, however, at once. (I don't suppose they have many visitors.) She herself for that matter is very little changed; but (is it because I have a prejudice against her?) I thought her features harder, her expression sourer, her smile falser than ever.

'I am afraid Monsieur de La Pérouse is in no state to receive you,' said she at once, with the obvious desire of getting me to herself; then, taking advantage of her deafness in order to answer before I had questioned her:

'No, no; you're not disturbing me in the least. Do come in.'

She showed me into the room where La Pérouse gives his music lessons, the two windows of which look on to the courtyard. And as soon as she had got me safely inside:

'I am particularly glad to have a word with you alone. Monsieur de La Pérouse – I know what an old and faithful friend of his you are – is in a state which causes me great anxiety. Couldn't you persuade him to take more care of himself? He listens to you; as for me, I might as well talk to the winds.'

And thereupon she entered upon an endless series of recriminations: the old gentleman refuses to take care of himself, simply in order to annoy her; he does everything he oughtn't to do and nothing that he ought; he goes out in all weathers and will never consent to put on a muffler; he refuses to eat at meals – 'Monsieur isn't hungry' – and nothing she can contrive tempts his appetite; but at night, he gets up and turns the kitchen upside down, cooking himself some mess or other.

I have no doubt the old lady didn't invent anything; I could make out from her tale that it was her interpretation alone which gave an offensive meaning to the most innocent little facts and that reality had cast a monstrous shadow on the walls of her narrow brain. But does not her old husband on his side misinterpret all his wife's attentions? She thinks herself a martyr, while he takes her for a torturer. As for judging them, understanding them, I give it up; or rather, as always happens, the better I understand them, the more tempered my judgement of them becomes. But this remains – that here are two beings tied to each other for life and causing each other abominable suffering. I have often noticed with married couples how intolerably irritating the slightest protuberance of character in the one may be to the other, because in the course of life in common it continually rubs up against the same place. And if the rub is reciprocal, married life is nothing but a hell.

Beneath her smoothly parted black wig, which makes the features of her chalky face look harder still, with her long black mittens, from which protrude little claw-like fingers, Madame de La Pérouse has the appearance of a harpy.

'He accuses me of spying on him,' she continued. 'He has always needed a great deal of sleep; but at night he makes a show of going to bed, and then when he thinks I am fast asleep he gets up again; he muddles about among his old papers, and sometimes stays up till morning reading his late brother's letters and crying over them. And he wants me to bear it all without a word!'

Then she went on to complain that he wanted to make her go into a home; which would be all the more painful to her, she added, as he was quite incapable of living alone and doing without her care. This was said in a tearful tone, which was only too obviously hypocritical.

Whilst she was continuing her grievances, the drawing-room door opened gently behind her and La Pérouse came in, without her hearing him. At his wife's last words he smiled at me ironically, and touched his head with his hand to signify she was mad. Then, with an impatience – a brutality even – of which I should not have thought him capable, and which seemed to justify the old woman's accusations (but it was due too to his having to raise his voice to a shout in order to make himself heard):

'Come, Madam,' he cried, 'you ought to understand that you are tiring this gentleman with your talk. He didn't come to see you. Leave the room.'

The old lady protested that the arm-chair she was sitting in was her own and that she was not going to quit it.

'In that case,' went on La Pérouse with a grim chuckle, '*we* will leave *you*.' Then, turning to me, he repeated in gentler tones, 'Come, let us leave her.'

I made a sketchy and embarrassed bow, and followed him into the next room – the same one in which I had paid him my last visit.

'I am glad you heard her,' he said; 'that's what it's like the whole day long.'

He shut the window.

'There's such a noise in the street, one can't hear oneself speak. I spend my time shutting the windows and Madame de La Pérouse spends hers opening them again. She declares she's stifling. She always exaggerates. She refuses to realize that it's hotter out of doors than in. And yet I've got a little thermometer; but when I show it to her, she says that figures prove nothing. She wants to be right even when she knows she's wrong. Her main object in life is to annoy me.'

He himself, while he was speaking, seemed to me a little off his balance; he went on with growing excitement:

'Everything she does amiss in life she sets down as a grievance against me. All her judgements are warped. I'll just explain to you how it is: You know our impressions of outside images come to us reversed and that there's an apparatus in our brains which sets them right again. Well, Madame de La Pérouse has no such apparatus for setting them right. In her brain they *remain* upside-down. You can see for yourself how painful it is.'

It was certainly a great relief to him to explain himself and I took care not to interrupt him. He went on:

'Madame de La Pérouse has always eaten much too much. Well, now she makes out that it's I who eat too much. If she sees me presently with a bit of chocolate (it's my chief nourishment) she'll be certain to mutter, "Munching again!..." She spies on me. She accuses me of getting up in the night to eat on the sly, because she once surprised me making myself a cup of chocolate in the kitchen.... What am I to do? When I see her opposite me at table, falling ravenously upon her food, as she does, it takes away my appetite entirely. Then she declares I'm pretending to be fastidious just to torment her.'

He paused, and then in a sort of lyrical outburst:

'Her reproaches amaze me!... For instance, when she is suffering from her sciatica, I condole with her. Then she stops me, shrugs her shoulders and says: "Don't pretend you have a heart." Everything I do or say is in order to give her pain.'

We had seated ourselves, but all the time he was speaking, he kept getting up and sitting down again, in a state of morbid restlessness.

'Would you believe that in each of these rooms there are some pieces of furniture which belong to her and others to me? You saw her just now with her arm-chair. She says to the charwoman, when she's doing the room, "No, that's Monsieur's chair; don't touch that." And the other day, when by mistake I put a bound music-book on a little table which belongs to her, Madam knocked it on to the ground. Its corners were broken. ... Oh, it can't last much longer. ... But, listen ...'

He seized me by the arm, and lowering his voice:

'I have taken steps. She is continually threatening me if I "go on!" to take refuge in a home. I have set aside a certain sum of money which ought to be enough to pay for her at Sainte-Périne's; I hear it's an excellent place. The few lessons I still give, bring me in hardly anything. In a little time I shall be at the end of my resources; I should be forced to break into this sum – and I'm determined not to. So I have made a resolution. ... It will be in a little over three months. Yes; I have fixed the date. If you only knew what a relief it is to think that every hour it draws nearer.'

He had bent towards me; he bent closer still:

'And I have put aside a Government bond. Oh, it's not much. But I couldn't do more. Madame de La Pérouse doesn't know about it. It's in my bureau in an envelope directed to you, with the necessary instructions. I know nothing about business, but a solicitor whom I consulted, told me that the interest could be paid directly to my grandson, until he is of age, and that then he would have the security. I thought it wouldn't be too great a tax on your friendship to ask you to see that this is done. I have so little confidence in solicitors! ... And even, if you wished to make me quite easy, you would take charge of the envelope at once.... You will, won't you? ... I'll go and fetch it.'

He trotted out in his usual fashion and came back with a large envelope in his hand.

'You'll excuse me for having sealed it; for form's sake,' said he. 'Take it.'

I glanced at it and saw under my name the words 'To be opened after my death' written in printed letters.

'Put it in your pocket quick, so that I may know it's safe. Thank you. . . . Oh I was so longing for you to come! . . .'

I have often experienced that, in moments as solemn as this, all human emotion is transformed into an almost mystic ecstasy, into a kind of enthusiasm, in which my whole being is magnified, or rather liberated from all selfishness, as though dispossessed of itself and depersonalized. Those who have never experienced this will certainly not understand me. But I felt that La Pérouse understood. Any protestation on my part would have been superfluous, would have seemed unbecoming, I thought, and I contented myself with pressing the hand which he gave me. His eyes were shining with a strange brightness. In his free hand, in which he had at first been holding the envelope, was another piece of paper.

'I have written his address down here. For I know now where he is. At Saas-Fée. Do you know it? It's in Switzerland. I looked for it on the map, but I couldn't find it.'

'Yes,' I said. 'It's a little village near the Matterhorn.'

'Is it very far?'

'Not so far but that I might perhaps go there.'

'Really? Would you really? . . . Oh, how good you are!' said he. 'As for me, I'm too old. And besides, I can't because of his mother. . . . All the same, I think . . .' He hesitated for a word, then went on: 'that I should depart more easily, if only I had been able to see him.'

'My poor friend. . . . Everything that is humanly possible to do to bring him to you, I will do. You shall see little Boris, I promise you.'

'Thank you! . . . Thank you!'

He pressed me convulsively in his arms.

'But promise me that you won't think of . . .'

'Oh, that's another matter,' said he, interrupting me abruptly. Then immediately and as if he were trying to prevent me from going on by distracting my attention:

'What do you think, the other day, the mother of one of my pupils insisted on taking me to the theatre! About a month ago.

It was a matinée at the Théâtre Français. I hadn't been inside a theatre for more than twenty years. They were giving *Hernani*, by Victor Hugo. You know it? It seems that it was very well acted. Everybody was in raptures. As for me, I suffered indescribably. If politeness hadn't kept me there, I shouldn't have been able to stay it out. . . . We were in a box. My friends did their best to calm me. I wanted to apostrophize the audience. Oh! how can people? How can people?. . .'

Not understanding at first what it was he objected to, I asked:

'You thought the actors very bad?'

'Of course. But how can people represent such abominations on the stage? . . . And the audience applauded. And there were children in the theatre – children, brought there by their parents, who knew the play. . . . Monstrous! And that, in a theatre subsidized by the State!'

The worthy man's indignation amused me. By now I was almost laughing. I protested that there could be no dramatic art without a portrayal of the passions. In his turn, he declared that the portrayal of the passions must necessarily be an undesirable example. The discussion continued in this way for some time; and as I was comparing this portrayal of the passions to the effect of letting loose the brass instruments in an orchestra:

'For instance, the entry of the trombones in such and such a symphony of Beethoven's which you admire. . . .'

'But I don't. I don't admire the entry of the trombones,' cried he, with extraordinary violence. 'Why do you want to make me admire what disturbs me?'

His whole body was trembling. The indignant – the almost hostile tone of his voice surprised me and seemed to astonish even himself, for he went on more calmly:

'Have you observed that the whole effect of modern music is to make bearable, and even agreeable, certain harmonies which we used to consider discords?'

'Exactly,' I rejoined. 'Everything must finally resolve into – be reduced to harmony.'

'Harmony!' he repeated, shrugging his shoulders. 'All that I can see in it is familiarization with evil – with sin. Sensibility is blunted; purity is tarnished; reactions are less vivid; one tolerates; one accepts....'

'To listen to you, one would never dare wean a child.'

But he went on without hearing me: 'If one could recover the uncompromising spirit of one's youth, one's greatest indignation would be for what one has become.'

It was impossible to start on a teleological argument; I tried to bring him back to his own ground:

'But you don't pretend to restrict music to the mere expression of serenity, do you? In that case, a single chord would suffice – a continuous common chord.'

He took both my hands in his, and in a burst of ecstasy, his eyes rapt in adoration, he repeated several times over:

'A continuous common chord;* yes, yes; a continuous common chord.... But our whole universe is a prey to discord,' he added sadly.

I took my leave. He accompanied me to the door and as he embraced me, murmured again:

'Oh! How long shall we have to wait for the resolution of the chord?'

* The technical word in French for the expression 'common chord' is, as the author pointed out to me, '*accord parfait*', which in my first translation I mistakenly rendered as *perfect chord*. I have now corrected this, thereby losing the associations and connotations of La Pérouse's lovely sentences, which become *common* instead of *perfect*. Alas! – *Translator*.

SECOND PART

SAAS-FÉE

I

FROM BERNARD TO OLIVIER

Monday.

MY DEAR OLD OLIVIER, – First I must tell you that I've cut the *bachot*. I expect you understood as much when I didn't turn up. I shall go in for it next October. An unparalleled opportunity to go travelling was offered me. I jumped at it and I'm not sorry I did. I had to make up my mind at once – without taking time to reflect – without even saying good-bye to you. Apropos, my travelling companion tells me to say how sorry he is he had to leave without seeing you again. For do you know who carried me off? You've guessed it already. . . . It was Edouard – yes! that same uncle of yours, whom I met the very day he arrived in Paris, in rather extraordinary and sensational circumstances, which I'll tell you about some day. But everything in this adventure is extraordinary, and when I think of it my head whirls. Even now, I can hardly believe it is true and that I am really here in Switzerland with Edouard and . . . Well! I see I must tell you the whole story, but mind you tear my letter up and never breathe a word about it to a soul.

Just think, the poor woman your brother Vincent abandoned, the one you heard sobbing outside your door (I must say, it was idiotic of you not to open it) turns out to be a great friend of Edouard's and moreover is actually a daughter of Vedel's and a sister of your friend Armand's. I oughtn't to be writing you all this, because a woman's honour is at stake, but I should burst if I didn't tell someone. . . . So, once more, don't breathe a word! You know that she married recently; perhaps you know that shortly after her marriage she fell ill and went for a cure to the South of France. That's where she met Vincent – in the sanatorium at Pau. Perhaps you know that, too. But what you don't know is that there were consequences. Yes, old boy! She's going to have a child and it's your clumsy ass of a brother's fault. She came back to Paris and didn't dare show herself to her parents; still less go back to her husband. And then your brother, as you know, chucked her. I'll spare you my comments; but I can tell you that Laura Douviers has not uttered a word against him, either of reproach or resentment. On the contrary, she says all she can think of to excuse his conduct. In a word, she's a very fine woman with a very beautiful nature. And another very fine person is Edouard. As she didn't know what to do or where to go, he proposed taking her to Switzerland; and at the same time he proposed that I should go with them, because he didn't care about travelling *tête à tête*, as he is only on terms of friendship with her. So off we started. It was all settled in a jiffy – just time to pack one's suitcase and for me to get a kit (for you know I left home without a thing). You can't imagine how nice Edouard was about it; and what's more he kept repeating all the time that it was I who was doing him a service. Yes, really, old boy, you were quite right, your uncle's perfectly splendid.

The journey was rather troublesome, because Laura got very tired and her condition (she's in her third month) necessitated a great deal of care; and the place where we had settled to go (it would be too long to explain why) is rather difficult to get at. Besides, Laura very often made things more complicated by refusing to take precautions; she had to be forced; she kept repeating that an accident was the best thing that could happen to her. You can imagine how we fussed over her. Oh, Olivier, how wonderful she is! I don't feel the same as I did before I knew her, and there are thoughts which I no longer dare put into words and impulses which I check, because I should be ashamed not to be worthy of her. Yes, really, when one is with her, one feels forced, as it were, to think nobly. That doesn't prevent the conversation between the three of us from being very free – Laura isn't at all prudish – and we talk about anything; but I assure you that when I am with her, there are heaps of things I don't feel inclined to scoff at any more and which seem to me now very serious.

You'll be thinking I'm in love with her. Well, old boy, you aren't far wrong. Crazy, isn't it? Can you imagine me in love with a woman who is going to have a child, whom naturally I respect and wouldn't venture to touch with my finger-tip? Hardly on the road to becoming a rake, am I? . . .

When we reached Saas-Fée, after no end of difficulties (we had a carrying-chair for Laura, as it's impossible to get here by driving), we found there were only two rooms available in the hotel – a big one with two beds, and a little one, which it was settled with the hotel-keeper should be for me – for Laura passes as Edouard's wife, so as to conceal her identity; but every night she sleeps in the little room and I join Edouard in his. Every morning there's a regular business carrying things backwards and forwards, for the sake of the servants. Fortunately the two rooms communicate, so that makes it easier.

We've been here six days; I didn't write to you sooner because I was rather in a state of bewilderment to begin with, and I had to get straight with myself. I am only just beginning to find my bearings.

Edouard and I have already done one or two little excursions in the mountains. Very amusing; but to tell the truth, I don't much care for this country. Edouard doesn't either. He says the scenery is 'declamatory'. That's exactly it.

The best thing about the place is the air – virgin air, which purifies one's lungs. And then we don't want to leave Laura alone for too long at a time, for of course she can't come with us. The company in the hotel is rather amusing. There are people of all sorts of nationalities. The person we see most of is a Polish woman doctor, who is spending the holidays here with her daughter and a little boy she is in charge of. In fact, it's because of this little boy that we have come here. He's got a kind of nervous illness, which the doctor is treating according to a new method. But what does the little fellow most good (he's really a very attractive little thing) is that he's madly in love with the doctor's daughter, who is a year or two older than he and the prettiest creature I have ever seen in my life. They never leave each other from morning till night. And they are so charming together that no one ever thinks of chaffing them.

I haven't worked much and not opened a book since I left; but I've thought a lot. Edouard's conversation is extraordinarily interesting. He doesn't speak to me much personally, though he pretends to treat me as his secretary, but I listen to him talking to the others; especially to Laura, with whom he likes discussing his ideas. You can't imagine how much I learn by it. There are days when I say to myself that I ought to take notes; but I think I can remember it all. There are days when I long for you madly; I say to myself that it's you who ought to be here; but I can't be sorry for what's happened to me, nor wish for anything to be different. At any rate, you may be sure that I never forget it's thanks to you that I know Edouard and that it's to you I owe my happiness. When you see me again, I think you'll find me changed; I remain, nevertheless, and more faithfully and devotedly than ever

YOUR FRIEND

P.S. – *Wednesday*. We have this moment come back from a tremendous expedition. Climbed the Hallalin – guides, ropes, glaciers, precipices, avalanches, etc. Spent the night in a refuge in the middle of the snows, packed in with other tourists; needless to say, we didn't sleep a wink. The next morning we started before dawn. . . . Well, old boy, I'll never speak ill of Switzerland again. When one gets up there, out of sight of all culture, of all vegetation, of everything that reminds one of the avarice and stupidity of men, one feels inclined to shout, to sing, to laugh, to cry, to fly, to dive head foremost into the sky, or to fall on one's knees. Yours,

BERNARD

Bernard was much too spontaneous, too natural, too pure – he knew too little of Olivier, to suspect the flood of hideous feelings his letter would raise in his friend's heart – a kind of tidal wave, in which pique, despair and rage were mingled. He felt himself supplanted in Bernard's affection and in Edouard's. The friendship of his two friends left no room for his. One sentence in particular of Bernard's letter tortured him – a sentence which Bernard would never have written had he imagined all that Olivier read into it: 'In the same room,' he repeated to himself – and the serpent of jealousy unrolled its abominable coils and writhed in his heart. 'They sleep in the same room!' What did he not imagine? His mind filled with impure visions which he did not even try to banish. He was not jealous in particular either of Edouard or of Bernard; but of the two. He pictured each of them in turn or both simultaneously, and at the same time envied them. He received the letter one forenoon. 'Ah! so that's how it is . . .' he kept saying to himself all the rest of the day. That night the fiends of hell inhabited him. Early next morning he rushed off to Robert's. The Comte de Passavant was waiting for him.

2

EDOUARD'S JOURNAL: LITTLE BORIS

I HAVE had no difficulty in finding little Boris. The day after our arrival, he appeared on the hotel terrace and began looking at the mountains through a telescope which stands outside, mounted on a swivel for the use of the tourists. I recognized him at once. A little girl, rather older than Boris, joined him after a short time. I was sitting nearby in the drawing-room, of which the french window was standing open, and I did not lose a word of their conversation. Though I wanted very much to speak to him, I thought it more prudent to wait till I could make the acquaintance of the little girl's mother – a Polish woman doctor, who is in charge of Boris and keeps very careful watch over him. Little Bronja is an exquisite creature; she must be about fifteen. She wears her fair hair in two thick plaits, which reach to her waist; the expression of her eyes and the sound of her voice are more angelic than human. I write down the two children's conversation:

'Boris, Mamma had rather we didn't touch the telescope. Won't you come for a walk?'

'Yes, I will. No, I won't.'

The two contradictory sentences were uttered in the same breath. Bronja only answered the second:

'Why not?'

'Because it's too hot, it's too cold.' He had come away from the telescope.

'Oh, Boris, do be nice! You know Mamma would like us to go out. Where's your hat?'

'Vibroskomenopatof. Blaf blaf.'

'What does that mean?'

'Nothing.'

'Then why do you say it?'

'So that you shouldn't understand.'

'If it doesn't mean anything, it doesn't matter about not understanding it.'

'But if it did mean something, anyhow you wouldn't be able to understand.'

'When one talks it's in order to be understood.'

'Shall we play at making words in order to understand them only us?'

'First of all, try to speak good grammar.'

'My mamma can speak French, English, Rumanian, Turkish, Polish, Italoscope, Perroquese and Xixitou.'

All this was said very fast, in a kind of lyrical ecstasy. Bronja began to laugh.

'Oh, Boris, why are you always saying things that aren't true?'

'Why do you never believe what I say?'

'I believe it when it's true.'

'How do you know when it's true? I believed *you* the other day when you told me about the angels. I say, Bronja, do you think that, if I were to pray very hard, I should see them too?'

'Perhaps you'll see them if you get out of the habit of telling lies, and if God wants to show them to you; but God won't show them to you if you pray to him only for that. There are heaps of beautiful things we should see if we weren't too naughty.'

'Bronja, you aren't naughty; that's why you can see the angels. I shall always be naughty.'

'Why don't you try not to be? Shall we go to' – some place whose name I didn't know – 'and pray together to God and the Blessèd Virgin to help you not to be naughty?'

'Yes. No; listen – let's take a stick; you shall hold one end and I the other. I will shut my eyes, and I promise not to open them until we get to the place.'

They walked away, and as they were going down the terrace steps I heard Boris again:

'Yes, no, not that end. Wait till I've wiped it.'

'Why?'

'I've touched it.'

Mme Sophroniska came up to me as I was sitting alone, just finishing my early breakfast and wondering how I could enter into conversation with her. I was surprised to see that she was holding my last book in her hand; she asked me with the most affable smile whether it was the author whom she had the pleasure of speaking to; then she immediately launched upon a long appreciation of my book. Her judgement – both praise and criticism – seemed to me more intelligent than what I am accustomed to hearing, though her point of view is anything but literary. She told me she was almost exclusively interested in questions of psychology and in anything that may shed a new light on the human soul. 'But how rare it is,' she added, 'to find a poet, or dramatist or novelist, who is not satisfied with a ready-made psychology –' the only kind, I told her, that satisfies their readers.

Little Boris has been confided to her for the holidays by his mother. I took care not to let her know my reasons for being interested in him.

'He is very delicate,' said Mme Sophroniska. 'His mother's companionship is not at all good for him. She wanted to come to Saas-Fée with us, but I would only consent to look after the child on condition that she left him entirely to my care; otherwise it would be impossible to answer for his being cured. Just imagine,' she went on, 'she keeps the poor little thing in a state of continual excitement – the very thing to develop the worst kind of nervous troubles in him. She has been obliged to earn her living since his father's death. She used to be a pianist and, I must say, a marvellous performer; but her playing was too subtle to please the ordinary public. She decided to take to singing at concerts, at casinos – to go on the stage. She used to take Boris with her to her dressing-room; I believe the artificial atmosphere of the theatre greatly contributed to upset the child's balance. His mother is very fond of him, but to tell the truth it is most desirable that he shouldn't live with her.'

'What is the matter with him exactly?' I asked.

She began to laugh.

'Is it the name of his illness you want to know? Oh, you wouldn't be much the wiser if I were to give you a fine scientific name for it.'

'Just tell me what he suffers from.'

'He suffers from a number of little troubles, tics, manias, which are the sign of what people call a "nervous child", and which are usually treated by rest, open air and hygiene. It is certain that a robust organism would not allow these disturbances to show themselves. But if debility favours them, it does not exactly cause them. I think their origin can always be traced to some early shock, brought about by a circumstance it is important to discover. The sufferer, as soon as he becomes conscious of this cause, is half cured. But this cause, more often than not, escapes his memory, as if it were concealing itself in the shadow of his illness; it is in this refuge that I look for it, so as to bring it out into the daylight – into the field of vision, I mean. I believe that the look of a clear-sighted eye cleanses the mind, as a ray of light purifies infected water.'

I repeated to Sophroniska the conversation I had overheard the day before, from which it appeared to me that Boris was very far from being cured.

'It's because I am far from knowing all that I need to know of Boris's past. It's only a short while ago that I began my treatment.'

'Of what does it consist?'

'Oh, simply in letting him talk. Every day I spend one or two hours with him. I question him, but very little. The important thing is to gain his confidence. I know a good many things already. I divine a good many others. But the child is still on the defensive; he is ashamed; if I insisted too strongly, tried to force his confidence too quickly, I should be going against the very thing I want to arrive at – a complete surrender. It would set his back up. So long as I shall not have vanquished his reserve, his modesty . . .'

An inquisition of this kind seemed to me so much in the nature of an assault that it was with difficulty I refrained from protesting; but my curiosity carried the day.

'Do you mean that you expect the child to make you any shameful revelations?'

It was she who protested.

'Oh, shameful? There's no more shame in it than allowing oneself to be sounded. I need to know everything and particularly what is most carefully hidden. I must bring Boris to make a complete confession; until I can do that, I shall not be able to cure him.'

'You suspect then that he has a confession to make? Are you quite sure – forgive me – that you won't yourself suggest what you want him to confess?'

'That is a preoccupation which must never leave me, and it is for that reason I work so slowly. I have seen clumsy magistrates who have unintentionally prompted a child to give evidence that was pure invention from beginning to end, and the child, under the pressure of the magistrate's examination, tells lies in perfect good faith and makes people believe in entirely imaginary misdeeds. My part is to suggest nothing. Extraordinary patience is needed.'

'It seems to me that in such cases the value of the method depends upon the value of the operator.'

'I shouldn't have dared say so. I assure you that after a little practice one gets extraordinarily clever at it; it's a kind of divination – intuition, if you prefer. However, one sometimes goes off on a wrong track; the important thing is not to persist in it. Do you know how all our conversations begin? Boris starts by telling me what he has dreamt the night before.'

'How do you know he doesn't invent?'

'And even if he did invent! ... All the inventions of a diseased imagination reveal something.'

She was silent for a moment or two, and then: '"*Invention*", "*diseased imagination*" ... no, no, that's not it. Words betray one's meaning. Boris dreams aloud in my presence. Every morning he consents to remain during one hour in that state of semi-somnolence in which the images which present themselves to us escape from the control of our reason. They no longer group and associate themselves according to ordinary logic, but according to unforeseen affinities; above all, they answer to a mysterious inward compulsion – which is the very thing I want to discover; and the ramblings of this child are far more instructive than the most intelligent analysis of the most conscious of minds could be. Many things escape the reason, and a person who should attempt to understand life by merely using his reason would be like a man trying to take hold of a flame with the tongs. Nothing remains but a bit of charred wood, which immediately stops flaming.'

She was again silent and began to turn over the pages of my book.

'How very little you penetrate into the human soul!' she cried; then she laughed and added abruptly:

'Oh, I don't mean you in particular; when I say *you*, I mean novelists in general. Most of your characters seem to be built on piles; they have neither foundations nor subsoil. I really think there's more truth to be found in the poets; everything which is created by the intelligence alone is false. But now I am talking of what isn't my business. . . . Do you know what puzzles me in Boris? I believe him to be exceedingly pure.'

'Why should that puzzle you?'

'Because I don't know where to look for the source of the evil. Nine times out of ten a derangement like his has its origin in some sort of ugly secret.'

'Such a one exists in every one of us, perhaps,' said I, 'but it doesn't make us all ill, thank Heaven!'

At that Mme Sophroniska rose; she had just seen Bronja pass by the window.

'Look!' said she, pointing her out to me; 'there is Boris's real doctor. She is looking for me; I must leave you; but I shall see you again, shan't I?'

For that matter, I understand what Sophroniska reproaches the novel for not giving her; but in this case, certain reasons of art escape her – higher reasons, which make me think that a good novelist will never be made out of a good naturalist.

I have introduced Laura to Mme Sophroniska. They seem to take to each other, and I am glad of it. I have fewer scruples about keeping to myself when I know they are chatting together. I am sorry that Bernard has no companion of his own age; but at any rate the preparation for his examination keeps him occupied for several hours a day. I have been able to start work again on my novel.

3

EDOUARD EXPLAINS HIS THEORY OF THE NOVEL

NOTWITHSTANDING first appearances, and though each of them did his best, Uncle Edouard and Bernard were only getting on together fairly well. Laura was not feeling satisfied, either. How should she be? Circumstances had forced her to assume a part for which she was not fitted; her respectability made her feel uncomfortable in it. Like those loving and docile creatures who make the most devoted wives, she had need of the proprieties to lean on, and felt herself without strength now that she was without the frame of her proper surroundings. Her situation as regards Edouard seemed to her more and more false every day. What she suffered from most and what she found unendurable, if she let her mind dwell on it, was the thought that she was living at the expense of this protector – or rather that she was giving him nothing in exchange – or more exactly that Edouard asked nothing of her in exchange, while she herself felt ready to give him everything. 'Benefits,' says Tacitus, through the mouth of Montaigne, 'are only agreeable as long as one can repay them'; no doubt this is only true of noble souls, but without question Laura was one of these. She, who would have liked to give, was on the contrary continually receiving, and this irritated her against Edouard. Moreover, when she went over the past in her mind, it seemed to her that Edouard had deluded her by awakening a love in her which she still felt strong within her and then by evading this love and leaving it without an object. Was not that the secret motive of her errors – of her marriage with Douviers, to which she had resigned herself, to which Edouard had led her – and then of her yielding so soon after to the solicitations of the springtime? For she must needs admit it to herself, in Vincent's arms it was still Edouard that she sought. And as she could not understand her lover's coldness, she accused herself of being responsible for it, and imagined that she might have vanquished him, had she had more beauty or more boldness; and as she could not succeed in hating him, it was herself she upbraided and depreciated, denying herself all value, and refusing to allow herself any reason for existing or the possession of any virtue.

Let us add further that this camping-out style of life, necessitated by the arrangement of the rooms, though it might seem amusing to her companions, hurt her delicacy in many sensitive places. And she could see no issue to the situation, which yet was one it would be difficult to prolong.

The only scrap of comfort and joy Laura was able to find in her present life, was by inventing for herself the duties of godmother or elder sister towards Bernard. The worship of a youth so charming touched her; the adoration he paid her prevented her from slipping down that slope of self-contempt and loathing which may lead even the most irresolute creature to the extremest resolutions. Bernard, every morning that he was not called off before daybreak by an expedition into the mountains (for he loved early rising), used to spend two good hours with her reading English. The examination he was going up for in October was a convenient excuse.

It cannot be said that his secretarial duties took up much of his time. They were ill-defined. When Bernard undertook them he imagined himself already seated at a desk, writing from Edouard's dictation, or copying out his manuscripts. Now Edouard never dictated, and his manuscripts, such as they were, remained at the bottom of his trunk; Bernard was free every hour of the day; but it only lay with Edouard to make more calls upon Bernard, who was most anxious to have his zeal made use of, so that Bernard was not particularly distressed by his want of occupation, or by the feeling that he was not earning his living – which, thanks to Edouard's munificence, was a very comfortable one. He was quite determined not to let himself be embarrassed by scruples. He believed, I dare not say in Providence, but at any rate in his star, and that a certain amount of happiness was due to him, as the air is to the lungs which breathe it; Edouard was its dispenser in the same way as the sacred orator, according to Bossuet, is the dispenser of divine wisdom. Moreover, Bernard considered the present state of affairs as merely temporary, and was convinced that some day he would be able to acquit his debt, as soon as he could bring to the mint the uncoined riches whose abundance he felt in his heart. What vexed him more was that Edouard made no demand upon certain gifts which he felt within himself and which it seemed to him Edouard lacked. 'He doesn't know how to make use of me,' thought Bernard, who thereupon checked his self-conceit and wisely added: 'Worse luck!'

But then what was the reason of this uncomfortable feeling between Edouard and Bernard? Bernard seems to me to be one of those people who find their self-assurance in opposition. He could not endure that Edouard should have any ascendancy over him and, rather than yield to his influence, rebelled against it. Edouard, who never dreamed of coercing him, was alternately vexed and grieved to feel him so restive and so constantly on the alert to defend – or, at any rate, to protect – himself. He came to the pitch of doubting whether he had not committed an act of folly in taking away with him these two beings, whom he seemed only to have united in order that they should league together against him. Incapable of penetrating Laura's secret sentiments, he took her reserve and her reticence for coldness. It would have made him exceedingly uncomfortable if he had been able to see more clearly; and Laura understood this; so that her unrequited love spent all its strength in keeping hidden and silent.

Tea-time found them as a rule all assembled in the big sitting-room; it often happened that, at their invitation, Mme Sophroniska joined them, generally on the days when Boris and Bronja were out walking. She left them very free in spite of their youthfulness; she had perfect confidence in Bronja and knew that she was very prudent, especially with Boris, who was always particularly amenable with her. The country was quite safe; for of course there was no question of their adventuring on to the mountains, or even of their climbing the rocks near the hotel. One day when the two children had obtained leave to go to the foot of the glacier, on condition they did not leave the road, Mme Sophroniska, who had been invited to tea, was emboldened, with Bernard's and Laura's encouragement, to beg Edouard to tell them about his next novel – that is, if he had no objection.

'None at all; but I can't tell you its story.'

And yet he seemed almost to lose his temper when Laura asked him (evidently a tactless question) what the book would be like?

'Nothing!' he exclaimed; then, immediately and as if he had only been waiting for this provocation: 'What is the use of doing over again what other people have done already, or what I myself have done already, or what other people might do?'

Edouard had no sooner uttered these words than he felt how improper, how outrageous and how absurd they were; at any rate they seemed to him improper and absurd; or he was afraid that this was how they would strike Bernard.

Edouard was very sensitive. As soon as he began talking of his work, and especially when other people made him talk of it, he seemed to lose his head.

He had the most perfect contempt for the usual fatuity of authors; he snuffed out his own as well as he could; but he was not unwilling to seek a reinforcement of his modesty in other people's consideration; if this consideration failed him, modesty immediately went by the board. He attached extreme importance to Bernard's esteem. Was it with a view to conquering this that, when Bernard was with him, he set his Pegasus prancing? It was the worst way possible. Edouard knew it; he said so to himself over and over again; but in spite of all his resolutions, as soon as he was in Bernard's company, he behaved quite differently from what he wished, and spoke in a manner which immediately appeared absurd to him (and which indeed was so). This might almost make one suppose that he loved Bernard? . . . No; I think not. But a little vanity is quite as effectual in making us pose as a great deal of love.

'Is it because the novel, of all literary *genres*, is the freest, the most *lawless*,' held forth Edouard, '. . . is it for that very reason, for fear of that very liberty (the artists who are always sighing after liberty are often the most bewildered when they get it), that the novel has always clung to reality with such timidity?

And I am not speaking only of the French novel. It is the same with the English novel; and the Russian novel, for all its throwing off of constraints, is a slave to resemblance. The only progress it looks to is to get still nearer to nature. The novel has never known that "formidable erosion of contours", as Nietzsche calls it; that deliberate avoidance of life, which gave style to the works of the Greek dramatists, for instance, or to the tragedies of the French seventeenth century. Is there anything more perfectly and deeply human than these works? But that's just it – they are human only in their depths; they don't pride themselves on appearing so – or, at any rate, on appearing real. They remain works of art.'

Edouard had got up, and, for fear of seeming to give a lecture, began to pour out the tea as he spoke; then he moved up and down, then squeezed a lemon into his cup, but, nevertheless, continued speaking:

'Because Balzac was a genius, and because every genius seems to bring to his art a final and conclusive solution, it has been decreed that the proper function of the novel is to rival the *état-civil*.* Balzac constructed his work; he never claimed to codify the novel; his article on Stendhal proves it. Rival the *état-civil*! As if there weren't enough fools and boors in the world as it is! What have I to do with the *état-civil*? *L'état c'est moi!* I, the artist; civil or not, my work doesn't pretend to rival anything.'

Edouard, who was getting excited – a little factitiously, perhaps – sat down. He affected not to look at Bernard; but it was for him that he was speaking. If he had been alone with him, he would not have been able to say a word; he was grateful to the two women for setting him on.

'Sometimes it seems to me there is nothing in all literature I admire so much as, for instance, the discussion between Mithridate and his two sons in Racine; it's a scene in which the characters speak in a way we know perfectly well no father and no sons could ever have spoken in, and yet (I ought to say for that very reason) it's a scene in which all fathers and all sons can

* The State records of each individual citizen, in which are noted the legal facts of his existence.

see themselves. By localizing and specifying one restricts. It is true that there is no psychological truth unless it be particular; but on the other hand there is no art unless it be general. The whole problem lies just in that – how to express the general by the particular – how to make the particular express the general. May I light my pipe?'

'Do, do,' said Sophroniska.

'Well, I should like a novel which should be at the same time as true and as far from reality, as particular and at the same time as general, as human and as fictious as *Athalie*, or *Tartuffe* or *Cinna*.'

'And . . . the subject of this novel?'

'It hasn't got one,' answered Edouard brusquely, 'and perhaps that's the most astonishing thing about it. My novel hasn't got a subject. Yes, I know, it sounds stupid. Let's say, if you prefer it, it hasn't got *one* subject . . . "a slice of life", the naturalist school said. The great defect of that school is that it always cuts its slice in the same direction; in time, lengthwise. Why not in breadth? Or in depth? As for me I should like not to cut at all. Please understand; I should like to put everything into my novel. I don't want any cut of the scissors to limit its substance at one point rather than at another. For more than a year now that I have been working at it, nothing happens to me that I don't put into it – everything I see, everything I know, everything that other people's lives and my own teach me. . . .'

'And the whole thing stylized into art?' said Sophroniska, feigning the most lively attention, but no doubt a little ironically. Laura could not suppress a smile. Edouard shrugged his shoulders slightly and went on:

'And even that isn't what I want to do. What I want is to represent reality on the one hand, and on the other that effort to stylize it into art of which I have just been speaking.'

'My poor dear friend, you will make your readers die of boredom,' said Laura; as she could no longer hide her smile, she had made up her mind to laugh outright.

'Not at all. In order to arrive at this effect – do you follow me? – I invent the character of a novelist, whom I make my central figure; and the subject of the book, if you must have one, is just that very struggle between what reality offers him and what he himself desires to make of it.'

'Yes, yes; I'm beginning to see,' said Sophroniska politely, though Laura's laugh was very near conquering her. 'But you know it's always dangerous to represent intellectuals in novels. The public is bored by them; one only manages to make them say absurdities and they give an air of abstraction to everything they touch.'

'And then I see exactly what will happen,' cried Laura; 'in this novelist of yours you won't be able to help painting yourself.'

She had lately adopted in talking to Edouard a jeering tone which astonished herself and upset Edouard all the more that he saw a reflection of it in Bernard's mocking eyes. Edouard protested:

'No, no. I shall take care to make him very disagreeable.'

Laura was fairly started.

'That's just it; everybody will recognize you,' she said, bursting into such hearty laughter that the others were caught by its infection.

'And is the plan of the book made up?' inquired Sophroniska, trying to regain her seriousness.

'Of course not.'

'What do you mean? Of course not!'

'You ought to understand that it's essentially out of the question for a book of this kind to have a plan. Everything would be falsified if anything were settled beforehand. I wait for reality to dictate to me.'

'But I thought you wanted to abandon reality.'

'My novelist wants to abandon it; but I shall continually bring him back to it. In fact that will be the subject; the struggle between the facts presented by reality and the ideal reality.'

The illogical nature of his remarks was flagrant – painfully obvious to everyone. It was clear that Edouard housed in his brain two incompatible requirements and that he was wearing himself out in the desire to reconcile them.

'Have you got on far with it?' asked Sophroniska politely.

'It depends on what you mean by far. To tell the truth, of the actual book not a line has been written. But I have worked at it a great deal. I think of it every day and incessantly. I work at it in a very odd manner, as I'll tell you. Day by day in a notebook, I note the state of the novel in my mind; yes, it's a kind of diary that I keep as one might do of a child. . . . That is to say, that instead of contenting myself with resolving each difficulty as it presents itself (and every work of art is only the sum or the product of the solutions of a quantity of small difficulties), I set forth each of these difficulties and study it. My notebook contains, as it were, a running criticism of my novel – or rather of the novel in general. Just think how interesting such a notebook kept by Dickens or Balzac would be; if we had the diary of the *Education Sentimentale* or of *The Brothers Karamazof*! – the story of the work – of its gestation! How thrilling it would be . . . more interesting than the work itself. . . .'

Edouard vaguely hoped that someone would ask him to read these notes. But not one of the three showed the slightest curiosity. Instead:

'My poor friend,' said Laura, with a touch of sadness, 'it's quite clear that you'll never write this novel of yours.'

'Well, let me tell you,' cried Edouard impetuously, 'that I don't care. Yes, if I don't succeed in writing the book, it'll be because the history of the book will have interested me more than the book itself – taken the book's place; and it'll be a very good thing.'

'Aren't you afraid, when you abandon reality in this way, of losing yourself in regions of deadly abstraction and of making a novel about ideas instead of about human beings?' asked Sophroniska kindly.

'And even so!' cried Edouard with redoubled energy. 'Must we condemn the novel of ideas because of the groping and stumbling of the incapable people who have tried their hands at it? Up till now we have been given nothing but novels with a purpose parading as novels of ideas. But that's not it at all, as you may imagine. Ideas . . . ideas, I must confess, interest me more than men – interest me more than anything. They live; they fight; they perish like men. Of course it may be said that our only knowledge of them is through men, just as our only knowledge of the wind is through the reeds that it bends; but all the same the wind is of more importance than the reeds.'

'The wind exists independently of the reed,' ventured Bernard. His intervention made Edouard, who had long been waiting for it, start afresh with renewed spirit:

'Yes, I know; ideas exist only because of men; but that's what's so pathetic; they live at their expense.'

Bernard had listened to all this with great attention; he was full of scepticism and very near taking Edouard for a mere dreamer; but during the last few moments he had been touched by his eloquence and had felt his mind waver in its breath; 'But,' thought Bernard, 'the reed lifts its head again as soon as the wind has passed.' He remembered what he had been taught at school – that man is swayed by his passions and not by ideas. In the meantime Edouard was going on:

'What I should like to do is something like the art of fugue writing. And I can't see why what was possible in music should be impossible in literature....'

To which Sophroniska rejoined that music is a mathematical art, and moreover that Bach, by dealing only with figures and by banishing all pathos and all humanity, had achieved an abstract *chef d'œuvre* of boredom, a kind of astronomical temple, open only to the few rare initiated. Edouard at once protested that, for his part, he though the temple admirable, and considered it the apex and crowning point of all Bach's career.

'After which,' added Laura, 'people were cured of the fugue for a long time to come. Human emotion, when it could no longer inhabit it, sought a dwelling place elsewhere.'

The discussion tailed off in an unprofitable argument. Bernard, who until then had kept silent, but who was beginning to fidget on his chair, at last could bear it no longer; with extreme, even exaggerated deference, as was his habit whenever he spoke to Edouard, but with a kind of sprightliness, which seemed to make a jest of his deference:

'Forgive me, sir,' said he, 'for knowing the title of your book, since I learnt it through my own indiscretion – which however you have been kind enough to pass over. But the title seemed to me to announce a story.'

'Oh, tell us what the title is!' said Laura.

'Certainly, my dear Laura, if you wish it. . . . But I warn you that I may possibly change it. I am afraid it's rather deceptive. . . . Well, tell it them, Bernard.'

'May I? . . . *The Counterfeiters*,' said Bernard. 'But now *you* tell us – who are these Counterfeiters?'

'Oh dear! I don't know,' said Edouard.

Bernard and Laura looked at each other and then looked at Sophroniska. There was a long sigh; I think it was drawn by Laura.

In reality, Edouard had in the first place been thinking of certain of his fellow novelists when he began to think of *The Counterfeiters*, and in particular of the Comte de Passavant. But this attribution had been considerably widened; according as the wind blew from Rome or from elsewhere, his heroes became in turn either priests or freemasons. If he allowed his mind to follow its bent, it soon tumbled headlong into abstractions, where it was as comfortable as a fish in water. Ideas of exchange, of depreciation, of inflation, etc., gradually invaded his book (like the theory of clothes in Carlyle's *Sartor Resartus*) and usurped the place of the characters. As it was impossible for Edouard to speak of this, he kept silent in the most awkward manner, and his silence, which seemed like an admission of penury, began to make the other three very uncomfortable.

'Has it ever happened to you to hold a counterfeit coin in your hands?' he asked at last.

'Yes,' said Bernard; but the two women's 'No' drowned his voice.

'Well, imagine a false ten-franc gold piece. In reality it's not worth two sous. But it will be worth ten francs as long as no one recognizes it to be false. So if I start from the idea that . . .'

'But why start from an idea?' interrupted Bernard impatiently. 'If you were to start from a fact and make a good exposition of it, the idea would come of its own accord to inhabit it. If I were writing *The Counterfeiters* I should begin by showing the counterfeit coin – the little ten-franc piece you were speaking of just now.'

So saying, he pulled out of his pocket a small coin, which he flung on to the table.

'Just hear how true it rings. Almost the same sound as the real one. One would swear it was gold. I was taken in by it this morning, just as the grocer who passed it on to me had been taken in himself, he told me. It isn't quite the same weight, I think; but it has the brightness and the sound of a real piece; it is coated with gold, so that, all the same, it is worth a little more than two sous; but it's made of glass. It'll wear transparent. No; don't rub it; you'll spoil it. One can almost see through it, as it is.'

Edouard had seized it and was considering it with the utmost curiosity.

'But where did the grocer get it from?'

'He didn't know. He thinks he has had it in his drawer some days. He amused himself by passing it off on me to see whether I should be taken in. Upon my word, I was just going to accept it! But as he's an honest man, he undeceived me; then he let me have it for five francs. He wanted to keep it to show to what he calls "amateurs". I thought there couldn't be a better one than the author of *The Counterfeiters*; and it was to show you that I took it. But now that you have examined it, give it back to me! I'm sorry that the reality doesn't interest you.'

'Yes, it does,' said Edouard, 'but it disturbs me too.'

'That's a pity,' rejoined Bernard.

EDOUARD'S JOURNAL

Tuesday evening. – Sophroniska, Bernard and Laura have been questioning me about my novel. Why did I let myself be carried away into speaking of it? I said nothing but stupidities. Interrupted fortunately by the return of the two children. They were red and out of breath, as if they had been running. As soon as she came in, Bronja fell into her mother's arms; I thought she was going to burst into sobs.

'Mamma!' she cried, 'do scold Boris. He wanted to undress and lie down in the snow without any clothes on.'

Sophroniska looked at Boris, who was standing in the doorway, his head down, his eyes with a look in them of almost hatred; she seemed not to notice the little boy's strange expression, but with admirable calm:

'Listen, Boris,' she said. 'That's a thing you mustn't do in the evening. If you like we'll go there tomorrow morning; first of all you must begin with bare feet...'

She was gently stroking her daughter's forehead; but the little girl suddenly fell on the ground and began rolling about in convulsions. It was rather alarming. Sophroniska lifted her and laid her on the sofa. Boris stood motionless, watching the scene with a dazed, bewildered expression.

Sophroniska's methods of education seem to me excellent in theory, but perhaps she miscalculates the children's powers of resistance.

'You behave,' said I, when I was alone with her a little later (after the evening meal I had gone to inquire after Bronja, who was too unwell to come downstairs), 'as if good were always sure to triumph over evil.'

'It is true,' she said, 'I firmly believe that good must triumph. I have confidence.'

'And yet, through excess of confidence you might make a mistake....'

'Every time I have made a mistake, it has been because my confidence was not great enough. Today, when I allowed the children to go out, I couldn't help showing them I was a little uneasy. They felt it. All the rest followed from that.'

She had taken my hand.

'You don't seem to believe in the virtue of convictions.... I mean in their power as an active principle.'

'You are right,' I said laughing. 'I am not a mystic.'

'Well, as for me,' she cried in an admirable burst of enthusiasm, 'I believe with my whole soul that without mysticism nothing great, nothing fine can be accomplished in this world.'

Discovered the name of Victor Strouvilhou in the visitors' book. From what the hotel-keeper says, he must have left Saas-Fée two days before our arrival, after staying here nearly a month. I should have been curious to see him again. No doubt Sophroniska talked to him. I must ask her about him.

4
BERNARD AND LAURA

'I WANTED to ask you, Laura,' said Bernard, 'whether you think there exists anything in this world that mayn't become a subject of doubt.... So much so, that I wonder whether one couldn't take doubt itself as a starting point; for that, at any rate, will never fail us. I may doubt the reality of everything, but not the reality of my doubt. I should like... Forgive me if I express myself pedantically – I am not pedantic by nature, but I have just left the *lycée*, and you have no idea what a stamp is impressed on the mind by the philosophical training of our last year; I will get rid of it I promise you.'

'Why this parenthesis? You would like...?'

'I should like to write a story of a person who starts by listening to everyone, who consults everyone like Panurge, before deciding to do anything; after having discovered that the opinions of all these people are contradictory in every point, he makes up his mind to consult no one but himself, and thereupon becomes a person of great capacity.'

'It's the idea of an old man,' said Laura.

'I am more mature than you think. A few days ago I began to keep a notebook, like Edouard; I write down an opinion on the right-hand page, whenever I can write the opposite opinion, facing it, on the left-hand page. For instance, the other evening Sophroniska told us that she made Bronja and Boris sleep with their windows open. Everything she said in support of this régime seemed to us perfectly reasonable and convincing, didn't it? Well, yesterday in the smoking-room, I heard that German professor who has just arrived maintain the contrary theory, which seemed to me, I must admit, more reasonable still and better grounded. The important thing during sleep, said he, is to restrict as much as possible all expenditure and the traffic of exchanges in which life consists – carburation, he called it; it is only then that sleep becomes really restorative. He gave as example the birds who sleep with their heads under their wings, and the animals who snuggle down when they go to sleep, so as to be hardly able to breathe at all; in the same way, he said, the races that are nearest to Nature, the peasants who are least cultivated, stuff themselves up at night in little closets; and Arabs, who are forced to sleep in the open, at any rate cover their faces up with the hood of their burnouses. But to return to Sophroniska and the two children she is bringing up, I come round to thinking she is not wrong after all, and that what is good for others would be harmful for these two, because, if I understand rightly, they have the germs of tubercle in them. In short, I said to myself . . . But I'm boring you.'

'Never mind about that. You said to yourself . . . ?'

'I've forgotten.'

'Now, now, that's naughty. You mustn't be ashamed of your thoughts.'

'I said to myself that nothing is good for everyone, but only relatively to some people; that nothing is true for everyone, but only relatively to the person who believes it is; that there is no method and no theory which can be applied indifferently to all alike; that if, in order to act, we must make a choice, at any rate we are free to choose; and that if we aren't free to choose, the thing is simpler still; the belief that becomes truth for me (not absolutely, no doubt, but relatively to me) is that which allows me the best use of my strength, the best means of putting my virtues into action. For I can't prevent myself from doubting, and at the same time I loathe indecision. The soft and comfortable pillow Montaigne talks of, is not for my head, for I'm not sleepy yet and I don't want to rest. It's a long way that leads from what I thought I was to what perhaps I really am. I am afraid sometimes that I got up too early in the morning.'

'Afraid?'

'No; I'm afraid of nothing. But, d'you know, I have already changed a great deal; that is, my mind's landscape is not at all what it was the day I left home; since then I have met you. As soon as I did that I stopped putting my freedom first. Perhaps you haven't realized that I am at your service.'

'What do you mean by that?'

'Oh, you know quite well. Why do you want to make me say

it? Do you expect a declaration? . . . No, no; please don't cloud your smile, or I shall catch cold.'

'Come now, my dear boy, you are not going to pretend that you are beginning to love me.'

'Oh, I'm not beginning,' said Bernard. 'It's you who are beginning to feel it, perhaps; but you can't prevent me.'

'It was so delightful for me not to have to be on my guard with you. And now, if I've got to treat you like inflammable matter and not dare go near you without taking precautions . . . But think of the deformed, swollen creature I shall soon be. The mere look of me will be enough to cure you.'

'Yes, if it were only your looks that I loved. And then, in the first place, I'm not ill; or if it is being ill to love you, I prefer not to be cured.'

He said all this gravely, almost sadly; he looked at her more tenderly than ever Edouard had done, or Douviers, but so respectfully that she could not take umbrage. She was holding an English book they had been reading, on her lap, and was turning over its pages absently; she seemed not to be listening, so that Bernard went on without too much embarrassment:

'I used to imagine love as something volcanic – at all events the love I was destined to feel. Yes; I really thought I should only be able to love in a savage, devastating way, *à la* Byron. How ill I knew myself! It was you, Laura, who taught me to know myself; so different from what I thought I was! I was playing the part of a dreadful person and making desperate efforts to resemble him. When I think of the letter I wrote my supposed father before I left home, I feel very much ashamed, I assure you. I took myself for a rebel, an outlaw, who tramples underfoot everything that opposes his desire; and now here I find that when I am with you I have no desires. I longed for liberty as the supreme good, and no sooner was I free, than I bowed myself to your . . . Oh, if you only knew how maddening it is to have in one's head quantities of phrases from great authors, which come irresistibly to one's lips when one wants to express a sincere feeling. This feeling of mine is so new to me that I haven't yet been able to invent a language for it. Let's say it isn't love, since you dislike that word; let's call it devotion.

It's as though this liberty which seemed to me so infinite, had had limits set to it by your laws. It's as though all the turbulent and unformed things that were stirring within me, were dancing an harmonious round, with you for their centre. If one of my thoughts happens to stray from you, I leave it . . . Laura, I don't ask you to love me – I'm nothing but a schoolboy; I'm not worth your notice; but everything I want to do now is in order to deserve your . . . (oh! the word is frightful!) . . . your esteem. . . .'

He had gone down on his knees before her, and though she had at first drawn her chair away a little, Bernard's forehead was on her dress, and his arms thrown back behind him, in sign of adoration; but when he felt Laura's hand laid upon his forehead, he seized the hand and pressed his lips to it.

'What a child you are, Bernard! I am not free, either,' she said, taking away her hand. 'Here! Read this.'

She took from her bodice a crumpled piece of paper, which she held out to Bernard.

Bernard saw the signature first of all. As he feared, it was Felix Douviers'. One moment he kept the letter in his hand without reading it; he raised his eyes to look at Laura. She was crying. Then Bernard felt one more bond burst in his heart – one of the secret ties which bind each one of us to himself, to his selfish past. Then he read:

MY BELOVED LAURA, – In the name of the little child who is to be born, and whom I swear to love as if I were its father, I beseech you to come back. Don't think that any reproaches will meet you here. Don't blame yourself too much – that is what hurts me most. Don't delay. My whole soul awaits you, adores you, is laid humbly at your feet.

Bernard was sitting on the floor in front of Laura, but it was without looking at her that he asked:

'When did you get this?'

'This morning.'

'I thought he knew nothing about it. Did you write and tell him?'

'Yes; I told him everything.'

'Does Edouard know this?'

'He knows nothing about it.'

Bernard remained silent a little while with downcast head; then turning towards her once more:

'And . . . what do you mean to do now?'

'Do you really ask? . . . Return to him. It is with him that my place is – with him that I ought to live. You know it.'

'Yes,' said Bernard.

There was a very long silence. Bernard broke it:

'Do you believe one can love someone else's child as much as one's own, really?'

'I don't know if I believe it, but I hope it.'

'For my part, I believe one can. And, on the contrary, I don't believe in what people call so foolishly "the blood speaking". I believe this idea that the blood speaks is a mere myth. I have read somewhere that among certain tribes of South Sea Islanders, it is the custom to adopt other people's children, and that these adopted children are often preferred to the others. The book said – I remember it quite well – "made more of". Do you know what I think now? . . . I think that my supposed father, who stood in my father's place, never said or did anything that could let it be suspected that I was not his real son; that in writing to him as I did, that I had always felt the difference, I was lying; that, on the contrary, he showed a kind of predilection for me, which I felt perfectly, so that my ingratitude towards him was all the more abominable; and that I behaved very ill to him. Laura, my friend, I should like to ask you . . . Do you think I ought to beg his pardon and go back to him?'

'No,' said Laura.

'Why not? Since you are going back to Douviers?'

'You were telling me just now, that what was true for one is not true for another. I feel I am weak; you are strong. Monsieur Profitendieu may love you; but from what you have told me, you are not of the kind to understand each other. . . . Or, at any rate, wait a little. Don't go back to him worsted. Do you want to know what I really think? – that it is for me and not for him that you are proposing it – to get what you called "my esteem". You will only get it, Bernard, if I feel you are not seeking for it.

I can only care for you as you are naturally. Leave repentance to me. It is not for you, Bernard.'

'I almost get to like my name when I hear it on your lips. Do you know what my chief horror was at home? The luxury. So much comfort, so many facilities . . . I felt myself becoming an anarchist. Now, on the contrary, I think I'm veering towards conservatism. I realized that the other day because of the indignation that seized me when I heard the tourist at the frontier speak of his pleasure in cheating the customs. "Robbing the State is robbing no one," he said. My feeling of antagonism made me suddenly understand what the State was. And I began to have an affection for it, simply because it was being injured. I had never thought about it before. "The State is nothing but a convention," he said, too. What a fine thing a convention would be that rested on the bona fides of every individual! . . . if only there were nothing but honest folk. Why, if anyone were to ask me today what virtue I considered the finest, I should answer without hesitation – honesty. Oh, Laura! I should like all my life long, at the very smallest shock, to ring true, with a pure, authentic sound. Nearly all the people I have known ring false. To be worth exactly what one seems to be worth – not to try to seem to be worth more. . . . One wants to deceive people, and one is so much occupied with seeming, that one ends by not knowing what one really is. . . . Forgive me for talking like this. They are my last night's reflections.'

'You were thinking of the little coin you showed us yesterday. When I go away . . .'

She could not finish her sentence; the tears rose to her eyes and in the effort she made to keep them back, Bernard saw her lips tremble.

'Then you are going away, Laura . . .' he went on sadly. 'I am afraid that when I no longer feel you near me, I shall be worth nothing at all – or hardly anything. . . . But, tell me – I should like to ask you . . . would you be going away – would you have made this confession, if Edouard . . . I don't know how to say it . . .' (and as Laura blushed), 'if Edouard had been worth more? Oh, don't protest. I know so well what you think of him.'

'You say that, because yesterday you caught me smiling at what he said; you immediately jumped to the conclusion that we were judging him in the same way. But it's not so. Don't deceive yourself. In reality I don't know what I think of him. He is never the same for long together. He is attached to nothing, but nothing is more attractive than this elusiveness. He is perpetually forming, unforming, re-forming himself. One thinks one has grasped him. . . . Proteus! He takes the shape of what he loves, and oneself must love him to understand him.'

'You love him. Oh, Laura! it's not of Douviers I feel jealous, nor of Vincent; it's of Edouard.'

'Why jealous? I love Douviers; I love Edouard, but differently. If I am to love you, it must be with yet another love.'

'Laura, Laura, you don't love Douviers. You feel affection for him, pity, esteem; but that's not love. I think the secret of your sadness (for you are sad, Laura) is that life has divided you; love has only consented to take you, incomplete; you distribute among several what you would have liked to give to one only. As for me, I feel I am indivisible; I can only give the whole of myself.'

'You are too young to speak so. You cannot tell yet whether life will not "divide" you too, as you call it. I can only accept from you the . . . devotion which you offer me. The rest will have its exigencies and will have to be satisfied elsewhere.'

'Can it be true? Do you want to disgust me beforehand with myself and with life, too?'

'You know nothing of life. Everything is before you. Do you know what my mistake was? To think there was nothing more for me. It was when I thought, alas! that there was nothing more for me, that I let myself go. I lived that last spring at Pau as if I were never to see another – as if nothing mattered any more. I can tell you now, Bernard, now that I've been punished for it – Never despair of life!'

Of what use is it to speak so to a young creature full of fire? And indeed Laura was hardly speaking to Bernard. Touched by his sympathy, and almost in spite of herself, she was thinking aloud in his presence. She was unapt at feigning, unapt at self-control. As she had yielded a moment ago to the impulsive feeling which carried her away whenever she thought of Edouard, and which betrayed her love for him, so now she had given way to a certain tendency to sermonize, which she had no doubt inherited from her father. But Bernard had a horror of recommendations and advice, even if they should come from Laura; his smile told her as much and she went on more calmly:

'Are you thinking of keeping on as Edouard's secretary when you go back to Paris?'

'Yes, if he is willing to employ me; but he gives me nothing to do. Do you know what would amuse me? To write that book of his with him; for he'll never write it alone; you told him so yesterday. That method of working he described to us seemed to me absurd. A good novel gets itself written more naïvely than that. And first of all, one must believe in one's own story – don't you think so – and tell it quite simply? I thought at one time I might help him. If he had wanted a detective I might perhaps have done the job. He could have worked on the facts that my police work would have furnished him. . . . But with an idea-monger there's nothing doing. When I'm with him, I feel that I have the soul of a reporter. If he sticks to his mistaken ways, I shall work on my own account. I must earn my living. I shall offer my services to a newspaper. Between times I shall write verses.'

'For when you are with reporters, you'll certainly feel yourself the soul of a poet.'

'Oh! don't laugh at me. I know I'm ridiculous. Don't rub it in too much.'

'Stay with Edouard; you'll help him; and let him help you. He is very good.'

The luncheon bell rang. Bernard rose. Laura took his hand:

'Just one thing – that little coin you showed us yesterday . . . in remembrance of you, when I go away' – she pulled herself together and this time was able to finish her sentence – 'would you give it me?'

'Here it is,' said Bernard, 'take it.'

5

EDOUARD'S JOURNAL: CONVERSATION WITH SOPHRONISKA

C'est ce qui arrive de presque toutes les maladies de l'esprit humain qu'on se flatte d'avoir guéries. On les répercute seulement, comme on dit en médecine, et on leur en substitue d'autres.

SAINTE-BEUVE: *Lundis*, I, p. 19

I AM beginning to catch sight of what I might call the 'deep-lying subject' of my book. It is – it will be – no doubt, the rivalry between the real world and the representation of it which we make to ourselves. The manner in which the world of appearances imposes itself upon us, and the manner in which we try to impose on the outside world our own interpretation – this is the drama of our lives. The resistance of facts invites us to transport our ideal construction into the realm of dreams, of hope, of belief in a future life, which is fed by all the disappointments and disillusions of our present one. Realists start from facts – fit their ideas to suit the facts. Bernard is a realist. I am afraid we shall never understand each other.

How could I agree when Sophroniska told me I had nothing of the mystic in me? I am quite ready to recognize, as she does, that without mysticism man can achieve nothing great. But is it not precisely my mysticism which Laura incriminates when I speak of my book? ... Well, let them settle the argument as they please.

Sophroniska has been speaking to me again about Boris, from whom she thinks she has succeeded in obtaining a full confession. The poor child has not got the smallest covert, the smallest tuft left in him, where he can take shelter from the doctor's scrutiny. He has been driven into the open. Sophroniska takes to bits the innermost wheels of his mental organism and spreads them out in the broad daylight, like a watchmaker cleaning the works of a clock. If after that he does not keep good time, it's a hopeless job. This is what Sophroniska told me:

When Boris was about nine years old, he was sent to school at Warsaw. He there made friends with a schoolfellow one or two years older than himself – one Baptistin Kraft, who initiated him into certain clandestine practices, which the children in their ignorance and astonishment believed to be 'magic'. This is the name they bestowed upon their vice, from having heard or read that magic enables one in some mysterious way to gain possession of what one wishes for, that it gives unlimited powers and so forth. . . . They believed in all good faith that they had discovered a secret which made up for real absence by illusory presence, and they freely put themselves in a state of hallucination and ecstasy, gloating over an empty void, which their heated imagination, stimulated by their desire for pleasure, filled to overflowing with marvels. Needless to say, Sophroniska did not make use of these terms; I should have liked her to repeat exactly what Boris said, but she declares she only succeeded in making out the above – though she certified its accuracy – through a tangle of pretences, reticence and vagueness.

'I have at last found out the explanation of something I have been trying to discover for a long time past,' she added, '– of a bit of parchment which Boris used always to wear hanging round his neck in a little sachet, along with the religious medallions his mother forces him to wear. There were six words on it, written in capital letters in a childish, painstaking hand – six words whose meaning he never would tell me.

"GAS . . . TELEPHONE . . . ONE HUNDRED THOUSAND ROUBLES

'"But it means nothing – it's magic," he used always to answer whenever I pressed him. That was all I could get out of him. I know that these enigmatic words are in young Baptistin's handwriting – the grand master and professor of magic – and that these six words were the boys' formula of incantation – the "Open Sesame" of the shameful Paradise, into which their pleasure plunged them. Boris called this bit of parchment, his *talisman*. I had great difficulty in persuading him to let me see it and still greater in persuading him to give it up (it was at the beginning of our stay here); for I wanted him to give it up, as I know now that he had already given up his bad habits. I had hopes that the tics and manias from which he suffers would disappear with the *talisman*. But he clung to it and his illness clung to it as to a last refuge.'

'But you said he had already given up his bad habits....'

'His nervous illness only began after that. It arose no doubt from the constraint Boris was obliged to exercise in order to get free from them. I have just learnt from him that his mother caught him one day in the act of "doing magic", as he says. Why did she never tell me?...out of false shame?...'

'And no doubt because she knew he was cured.'

'Absurd!...And that is why I have been in the dark so long. I told you that I thought Boris was perfectly pure.'

'You even told me that you were embarrassed by it.'

'You see how right I was!... The mother ought to have warned me. Boris would be cured already if I had known this from the beginning.'

'You said these troubles only began later on....'

'I said they arose as a protestation. His mother, I imagine, scolded, begged, preached. Then his father died. Boris was convinced that this was the punishment of these secret practices he had been told were so wicked; he held himself responsible for his father's death; he thought himself criminal, damned. He took fright; and it was then that his weakly organism, like a tracked animal, invented all these little subterfuges, by means of which he works off his secret sense of guilt, and which are so many avowals.'

'If I understand you rightly, you think it would have been less prejudicial to Boris if he had gone quietly on with his "magic"?'

'I think he might have been cured without being frightened. The change of life which was made necessary by his father's death would have been enough, no doubt, to distract his attention, and when they left Warsaw he would have been removed from his friend's influence. No good result is to be arrived at by terror. Once I knew the facts, I talked the whole thing over with him, and made him ashamed of having preferred the possession of imaginary goods to the real goods which are, I told him, the reward of effort. Far from attempting to blacken his vice, I represented it to him simply as one of the forms of laziness; and I really believe it is – the most subtle – the most perfidious.'

These words brought back to my mind some lines of La Rochefoucauld, which I thought I should like to show her, and, though I might have quoted them by heart, I went to fetch the little book of *Maxims*, without which I never travel. I read her the following:

> Of all the passions, the one about which we ourselves know least is laziness, the fiercest and the most evil of them all, though its violence goes unperceived and the havoc it causes lies hidden. . . . The repose of laziness has a secret charm for the soul, suddenly suspending its most ardent pursuits and most obstinate resolutions. To give, in fine, some idea of this passion, it should be said that laziness is like a state of beatitude, in which the soul is consoled for all its losses, and which stands in lieu to it of all its possessions.*

'Do you mean to say,' said Sophroniska then, 'that La Rochefoucauld was hinting at what we have been speaking of, when he wrote that?'

'Possibly; but I don't think so. Our classical authors have a right to all the interpretations they allow of. That is why they are so rich. Their precision is all the more admirable in that it does not claim to be exclusive.'

I asked her to show me this wonderful *talisman* of Boris's. She told me it was no longer in her possession, as she had given it to a person who was interested in Boris and who had asked her for it as a souvenir. 'A certain M. Strouvilhou, whom I met here some time before your arrival.'

* *De toutes les passions, celle qui est la plus inconnue à nous-mêmes, c'est la paresse; elle est la plus ardente et la plus maligne de toutes, quoique sa violence soit insensible et que les dommages qu'elle cause soient très-cachés . . . Le repos de la paresse est un charme secret de l'âme qui suspend soudainement les plus ardentes poursuites et les plus opiniâtres résolutions. Pour donner enfin la véritable idée de cette passion, il faut dire que la paresse est comme une béatitude de l'âme, qui la console de toutes ses pertes et qui lui tient lieu de tous ses biens.* – LA ROCHEFOUCAULD.

I told Sophroniska then, that I had seen the name in the visitors' book, and that as I had formerly known a Strouvilhou, I was curious to learn whether it was the same. From the description she gave of him it was impossible to doubt it. But she could tell me nothing that satisfied my curiosity. I merely learnt that he was very polite, very attentive, that he seemed to her exceedingly intelligent, but a little lazy, 'if I dare still use the word,' she added, laughing. In my turn I told her all I knew of Strouvilhou, and that led me to speak of the boarding-school where we had first met, of Laura's parents (she too had been confiding in her), and finally of old La Pérouse, of his relationship with Boris, and of the promise I had made him to bring the child back to Paris. As Sophroniska had previously said that it was not desirable Boris should live with his mother, 'Why don't you send him to Azaïs's school?' I asked. In suggesting this, I was thinking especially of his grandfather's immense joy at having him so near, and staying with friends where he could see him whenever he liked. Sophroniska said she would think it over; extremely interested by everything I told her.

Sophroniska goes on repeating that little Boris is cured – a cure which is supposed to corroborate her method; but I am afraid she is anticipating a little. Of course I don't want to set my opinion against hers, and I admit that his tics, his way of contradicting himself, his hesitations of speech have almost entirely disappeared; but, to my mind, the malady has simply taken refuge in some deeper recess of his being, as though to escape the doctor's inquisitorial glance, and now it is his soul itself which is the seat of mischief. Just as onanism was succeeded by nervous movements, so these movements have given place to some strange undefinable, invisible state of terror. Sophroniska, it is true, is uneasy at seeing Boris, following upon Bronja's lead, fling himself into a sort of puerile mysticism; she is too intelligent not to understand that this new 'beatitude' which Boris is now seeking, is not very different after all from the one he at first provoked by artifice, and that though it may be less wasteful, less ruinous to the organism, it turns him aside quite as much from effort and realization. But when I say this she replies that creatures like Boris and Bronja cannot do without some idealistic food, and that if they were deprived of it, they would succumb – Bronja to despair, and Boris to a vulgar materialism; she thinks she has no right to destroy the children's confidence, and though she thinks their belief is untrue, she must needs see in it a sublimation of low instincts, a higher postulation, an incitement, a safeguard, what-not. . . . Without herself believing in the dogmas of the Church, she believes in the efficacy of faith. She speaks with emotion of the two children's piety, of how they read the Apocalypse together, of their fervour, their talk with angels, their white-robed souls. Like all women, she is full of contradictions. But she was right – I am decidedly not a mystic . . . any more than I am lazy. I rely on the atmosphere of Azaïs's school to turn Boris into a worker; to cure him in a word of seeking after *imaginary goods*. That is where his salvation lies. Sophroniska, I think, is coming round to the idea of confiding him to my care; but she will no doubt accompany him to Paris so as to be able to settle him into the school herself, and so reassure his mother, whose consent she makes sure of obtaining.

6

FROM OLIVIER TO BERNARD

Il y a de certains défauts qui, bien mis en oeuvres brillent plus que la vertu même.

LA ROCHEFOUCAULD

DEAR OLD FELLOW, – I must first tell you that I have passed my *bachot* all right. But that's of no importance. A unique opportunity came in my way of travelling for a bit. I was still hesitating; but after reading your letter, I jumped at it. My mother made some objections at first; but Vincent soon got over them. He has been nicer than I could have hoped. I cannot believe that in the circumstances you allude to, he can have behaved like a cad. At our age, we have an unfortunate tendency to judge people severely and condemn them without appeal. Many actions appear to us reprehensible – odious even – simply because we don't enter sufficiently into their motives. Vincent didn't . . . but this would take too long and I have too many things to say to you.

You must know that the writer of this letter is no less a person than the editor-in-chief of the new review, the *Vanguard*. After some reflection I agreed to take up this responsible position, as Comte Robert de Passavant considered I should fill it worthily. It is he who is financing the review, though he doesn't care about its being known just yet, and my name is to figure alone on the cover. We shall come out in October; try to send me something for the first number; I should be heart-broken if your name didn't adorn the first list of contents alongside of mine. Passavant would like the first number to contain something rather shocking and spicy, for he thinks the most appalling thing that can be said against a new review is that it is mealy-mouthed. I'm inclined to agree with him. We discuss it a great deal. He has asked me to write the thing in question and has provided me with a rather risky subject for a short story; it worries me a little because of my mother, who may be hurt by it. But it can't be helped. As Passavant says, the younger one is, the less compromising the scandal.

I am writing this from Vizzavone. Vizzavone is a little place half-way up one of the highest mountains in Corsica, buried in a thick forest. The hotel in which we are staying is some way off the village and is used by tourists as a starting place for their excursions. We have been here only a few days. We began by staying in an inn not far from the beautiful bay of Porto, where we bathed every morning; it is absolutely deserted and one can spend the whole day without a stitch on one. It was marvellous; but the weather turned too hot and we had to go up to the mountains.

Passavant is a delightful companion; he isn't at all stuck up about his title; he likes me to call him Robert; and the name he has invented for me is Olive – isn't it charming? He does all he can to make me forget his age and I assure you he does. My mother was rather alarmed at the idea of my going away with him, for she hardly knows him at all. I hesitated at first for fear of distressing her. Before your letter came I had almost given it up. Vincent persuaded her, however, and your letter suddenly gave me courage. We spent the last days before starting in doing a round of shops. Passavant is so generous that he is always wanting to give me things and I had to stop him all the time. But he thought my wretched rags frightful; shirts, ties, socks – nothing I had pleased him; he kept repeating that if we were to spend some time together, it would be too painful to him not to see me properly dressed – that is to say, as he likes. Naturally everything we bought was sent to his house, for fear of making my mother uncomfortable. He himself is exquisitely elegant; but above all his taste is very good, and a great many things which I used to think quite bearable now seem odious to me. You can't imagine how amusing he was in the shops. He is really very witty. I should like to give you an idea of it. One day, we were at Brentano's, where he was having a fountain pen mended. There was a huge Englishman just behind him who wanted to be served before his turn, and as Robert pushed him away rather roughly, he began to jabber something or other in his lingo; Robert turned round very calmly and said:

'It's not a bit of use. I don't understand English.'

The Englishman was in a rage and answered back in the purest French:

'Then you ought to.'

To which Robert answered with a polite smile:

'I told you it wasn't a bit of use.'

The Englishman was boiling over, but he hadn't another word to say. It was killing.

Another day we were at the Olympia. During the *entr' acte* we were in the promenade with a lot of prostitutes walking round. Two of them – rather decayed-looking creatures – accosted him:

'Stand us a glass of beer, dearie?'

We sat down at a table with them.

'Waiter! A glass of beer for these ladies.'

'And for you and the young gentleman, sir?'

'Oh, for us? We'll take champagne,' he said carelessly. He ordered a bottle of Moet, and we blew it all to ourselves. You should have seen the poor things' faces! . . . I think he has a loathing for prostitutes. He confided to me that he has never been inside a brothel, and gave me to understand that he would be very angry with me if I ever went. So you see he's perfectly all right in spite of his airs and his cynical talk – as, for instance, when he says he calls it a 'dull day' if he hasn't met at least five people before lunch with whom he wants to go to bed. (I must tell you by the way, that I haven't tried again . . . you know what.)

He has a particularly odd and amusing way of moralizing. The other day he said to me:

'You see, my dear boy, the important thing in life is not to step on to the downward path. One thing leads on to another and one never can tell how it will end. For instance, I once knew a very worthy young man who was engaged to marry my cook's daughter. One night he chanced to go into a small jeweller's shop; he killed the owner; then he robbed; after that he dissembled. You see where it leads. The last time I saw him he had taken to lying. So do be careful.'

He's like that the whole time. So there's no chance of being bored. We left with the idea of getting through a lot of work, but so far we've done nothing but bathe, dry in the sun and talk. He has extremely original ideas and opinions about everything. I am trying to persuade him all I can to write about some new theories he has on deep-sea fishes and what he calls their 'private lights', which enables them to do without the light of the sun – which he compares to grace and revelation. Told baldly like that it doesn't sound anything, but I assure you that when he talks about it, it's as interesting as a novel. People don't know that he's extremely well up in natural history; but he kind of prides himself on hiding his knowledge – what he calls his secret jewels. He says it's only snobs who like showing off all their possessions – especially if they're imitation.

He knows admirably well how to make use of ideas, images, people, things; that is, he gets something out of everything. He says the great art of life is not so much to enjoy things as to make the most of them.

I have written a few verses, but I don't care enough about them to send them to you.

Good-bye, old boy. Till October. You will find me changed, too. Every day I get a little more self-confidence. I am glad to hear you are in Switzerland, but you see that I have no cause to envy you.

OLIVIER

Bernard held this letter out to Edouard, who read it without showing any sign of the feelings that agitated him.

Everything that Olivier said of Robert with such complacency filled him with indignation and put the final touch to his detestation. What hurt him more than anything was that Olivier had not even mentioned him in his letter and seemed to have forgotten him. He tried in vain to decipher three lines of postscript, which had been heavily inked over and which had run as follows:

Tell Uncle E. that I think of him constantly; that I cannot forgive him for having chucked me and that my heart has been mortally wounded.

These lines were the only sincere ones in a letter which had been written for show and inspired by pique. Olivier had crossed them out.

Edouard gave the horrible letter back to Bernard without breathing a word; without breathing a word, Bernard took it. I have said before that they didn't speak to each other much – a kind of strange, inexplicable constraint weighed upon them when they were alone together. (I confess I don't like the word 'inexplicable' and use it only because I am momentarily at a loss.) But that evening, when they were alone in their room and getting ready to go to bed, Bernard, with a great effort and the words sticking in his throat a little, asked:

'I suppose Laura has shown you Douviers' letters?'

'I never doubted that Douviers would take it properly,' said Edouard, getting into bed. 'He's an excellent fellow – a little weak, perhaps, but still excellent. He'll adore the child, I'm sure. And it'll certainly be more robust than if it were his own. For he doesn't strike me as being much of a Hercules.'

Bernard was much too fond of Laura not to be shocked by Edouard's cool way of talking; but he did not let it be seen.

'So!' went on Edouard, putting out his candle. 'I am glad to see that after all there is to be a satisfactory ending to this affair, which at one time seemed as if it could only lead to despair. Anybody may make a false start; the important thing is not to persist in . . .'

'Evidently,' interrupted Bernard, who wanted to change the subject.

'I must confess, Bernard, that I am afraid I have made one with you.'

'A false start?'

'Yes; I'm afraid so. In spite of all the affection I have for you, I have been thinking for the last few days that we aren't the sort to understand each other and that . . .' (he hesitated a few seconds to find his words) '. . . staying with me longer would set you on the wrong track.'

Bernard had been thinking the same till Edouard spoke; but Edouard could certainly have said nothing more likely to bring Bernard back. The instinct of contradiction carried the day and he protested.

'You don't know me yet, and I don't know myself. You haven't put me to the test. If you have no complaint against me, mayn't I ask you to wait a little longer? I admit that we aren't at all like each other: but my idea was precisely that it was better for each of us that we shouldn't be too much alike. I think that if I can help you, it'll be above all by being different and by the new things I may be able to bring you. If I am wrong, it will be always time enough to tell me so. I am not the kind of person to complain or recriminate. See here – this is what I propose – it may be idiotic. . . . Little Boris, I understand, is to go to the Vedel–Azaïs school. Wasn't Sophroniska telling you that she was afraid he would feel a little lost there? Supposing I were to go there myself, with a recommendation from Laura; couldn't I get some kind of place – under-master – usher – something or other? I have got to earn my living. I shouldn't ask much – just my board and lodging. . . . Sophroniska seems to trust me and I get on very well with Boris. I would look after him, help him, tutor him, be his friend and protector. But at the same time I should remain at your disposition, work for you in the intervals and be at hand at your smallest sign. Tell me what you say to that?'

And as if to give 'that' greater weight, he added:

'I have been thinking of it for the last two days.'

Which wasn't true. If he hadn't invented it on the spur of the moment, he would have already spoken to Laura about it. But what was true, and what he didn't say, was that ever since his indiscreet reading of Edouard's journal, and since his meeting with Laura, his thoughts often turned to the Vedels' boarding-school; he wanted to know Armand, Olivier's friend, of whom he never spoke; he wanted still more to know Sarah, the younger sister; but his curiosity remained a secret one; out of consideration for Laura, he did not even own it to himself.

Edouard said nothing; and yet Bernard's plan in so far as it provided him with a domicile, pleased him. He didn't at all care for the idea of taking him in himself. Bernard blew out his candle, and then went on:

'Don't think that I didn't understand what you said about your book and about the conflict you imagine between brute reality and . . .'

'I don't imagine it,' said Edouard, 'it exists.'

'But for that very reason, wouldn't it be a good thing if I were to beat in a few facts for you, so as to give you something to fight with? I could do your observing for you.'

Edouard had a suspicion that he was laughing at him a little. The truth is he felt humiliated by Bernard. He expressed himself too well. . . .

'We'll think it over,' said Edouard.

A long time went by. Bernard tried in vain to sleep. Olivier's letter kept tormenting him. Finally, unable to hold out any longer, and hearing Edouard tossing in his bed, he murmured:

'If you aren't asleep, I should like to ask you one thing more. . . . What do you think of the Comte de Passavant?'

'I should think you could pretty well imagine,' said Edouard. Then, after a moment: 'And you?'

'I?' said Bernard savagely, '. . . I could kill him.'

7

THE AUTHOR REVIEWS HIS CHARACTERS

THE traveller, having reached the top of the hill, sits down and looks about him before continuing his journey, which henceforward lies all downhill. He seeks to distinguish in the darkness – for night is falling – where the winding path he has chosen is leading him. So the undiscerning author stops awhile to regain his breath, and wonders with some anxiety where his tale will take him.

I am afraid that Edouard, in confiding little Boris to Azaïs's care, is committing an imprudence. Every creature acts according to his own law and Edouard's leads him to constant experimentalizing. He has a kind heart, no doubt, but for the sake of others I should prefer to see him act out of self-interest; for the generosity which impels him is often merely the accompaniment of a curiosity which is liable to turn into cruelty. He knows Azaïs's school; he knows the poisonous air that reigns in it, under the stifling cover of morality and religion. He knows Boris – how tender he is – how fragile. He ought to foresee the rubs to which he is exposing him. But he refuses to consider anything but the protection, the help, the support, which old Azaïs's austerity will afford the little boy's precarious purity. To what sophisms does he not lend an ear? They must be the promptings of the devil, for if they came from anyone else, he would not listen to them.

Edouard has irritated me more than once (when he speaks of Douviers, for instance) – enraged me even; I hope I haven't shown it too much; but now I may be allowed to say so. His behaviour to Laura – at times so generous – has at times seemed to me revolting.

What I dislike about Edouard are the reasons he gives himself. Why does he try and persuade himself that he is conspiring for Boris's good? Does the torrent which drowns a child pretend that it is giving him drink? . . . I do not deny that there are actions in the world that are noble, generous and even disinterested; I only say that there often lies hidden behind the good motive a devil who is clever enough to find his profit in the very thing one thought one was wresting from him.

Let us make use of this summer season which disperses our characters to examine them at leisure. And besides, we have reached that middle point of our story, when its pace seems to slacken, in order to gather a new impetus and rush on again with swifter speed to its end. Bernard is assuredly much too young to take direction of an intrigue. He is convinced he will be able to guard Boris; but the very utmost he will be able to do is to observe him. We have already seen Bernard change; passions may come which will modify him still more. I find in a notebook a sentence or two in which I have written down what I thought of him some time ago:

'I ought to have been mistrustful of behaviour as excessive as Bernard's at the beginning of his story. It seems to me, to judge by his subsequent state, that this behaviour exhausted all his reserves of anarchy, which would no doubt have been kept replenished if he had continued to vegetate, as is fitting, in the midst of his family's oppression. And from that time onwards his life was, so to speak, a reaction and a protest against this original action. The habit he had formed of rebellion and opposition incited him to rebel against his very rebellion. Without a doubt not one of my heroes has disappointed me more than he, for perhaps there was not one who had given me greater hopes. Perhaps he gave way too early to his own bent.'

But this does not seem very true to me any longer. I think we ought to allow him a little more credit. There is a great deal of generosity in him; virility too and strength; he is capable of indignation. He enjoys hearing himself talk a little too much; but it's a fact that he talks well. I mistrust feelings that find their expression too quickly. He is very good at his studies, but new feelings do not easily fill forms that have been learnt by heart. A little invention would make him stammer. He has already read too much, remembered too much, and learnt a great deal more from books than from life.

I cannot console myself for the turn of chance which made

him take Olivier's place beside Edouard. Events fell out badly. It was Olivier that Edouard loved. With what care he would have ripened him! With what lover-like respect he would have guided, supported, raised him to his own level! Passavant will ruin him to a certainty. Nothing could be more pernicious for him than to be enveloped in so unscrupulous an atmosphere. I had hoped that Olivier would have defended himself a little better; but his is a tender nature and sensitive to flattery. Everything goes to his head. Moreover, I seem to gather from certain accents in his letter to Bernard that he is a little vain. Sensuality, pique, vanity – to what does not all this lay him open? When Edouard finds him again, I very much fear it will be too late. But he is still young and one has the right to hope.

Passavant ...? Best not speak of him, I think. Nothing spreads more ruin or receives more applause than men of his stamp – unless it be women like Lady Griffith. At the beginning, I must confess, she rather took me in. But I soon recognized my mistake. People like her are cut out of a cloth which has no thickness. America exports a great many of them, but is not the only country to breed them. Fortune, intelligence, beauty – they seem to possess everything, except a soul. Vincent, we may be sure, will soon find it out. No past weighs upon them – no constraint; they have neither laws, nor masters, nor scruples; by their freedom and spontaneity, they make the novelist's despair; he can get nothing from them but worthless reactions. I hope not to see Lady Griffith again for a long time to come. I am sorry she has carried off Vincent, who interested me more, but who becomes commonplace by frequenting her. Rolling in her wake, he loses his angles. It's a pity; he had rather fine ones.

If it ever happens to me to invent another story, I shall allow only well-tempered characters to inhabit it – characters that life, instead of blunting, sharpens. Laura, Douviers, La Pérouse, Azaïs . . . what is to be done with such people as these? It was not I who sought them out; while following Bernard and Olivier I found them in my path. So much the worse for me; henceforth it is my duty to attend them.

THIRD PART

PARIS

When we are in possession of a few more local monographs – then, and only then, by grouping their data, by minutely confronting and comparing them, we shall be able to reconsider the subject as a whole, and take a new and decisive step forward. To proceed otherwise, would be merely to start, armed with two or three rough and simple ideas, on a kind of rapid excursion. It would be, in most cases, to pass by everything that is particular, individual, irregular – that is to say, everything, on the whole, that is most interesting.

LUCIEN FÈBVRE: *La Terre et L'Evolution Humaine*

I

EDOUARD'S JOURNAL: OSCAR MOLINIER

Son retour à Paris ne lui causa point de plaisir.
FLAUBERT: *L'Education Sentimentale*

Sept. 22nd. – Hot; bored. Have come back to Paris a week too soon. My eagerness always makes me respond before I am summoned. Curiosity rather than zeal; desire to anticipate. I have never been able to come to terms with my thirst.

Took Boris to see his grandfather. Sophroniska, who had been the day before to prepare him, tells me that Madame de La Pérouse has gone into the home. Heavens! What a relief!

I left the little boy on the landing, after ringing the bell, thinking it would be more discreet not to be present at the first meeting; I was afraid of the old fellow's thanks. Questioned the boy later on, but could get nothing out of him. Sophroniska, when I saw her later, told me he had not said anything to her either. When she went to fetch him after an hour's interval, as had been arranged, a maidservant opened the door; she found the old gentleman sitting in front of a game of draughts and the child sulking by himself in a corner at the other end of the room.

'It's odd,' said La Pérouse, very much out of countenance, 'he seemed to be amused, but all of a sudden he got tired of it. I am afraid he is a little wanting in patience.'

It was a mistake to leave them alone together too long.

Sept. 27th. – This morning met Molinier under the arcades of the Odéon. Pauline and George are not coming back till the day after tomorrow. If Molinier, who has been by himself in Paris since yesterday, was as bored as I am, it's no wonder that he seemed enchanted to see me. We went and sat down in the Luxembourg, till it should be time for lunch, and agreed to take it together.

Molinier, when he is with me, affects a rather jocose – even, at times, a kind of rakish tone – which he no doubt thinks the correct thing to please an artist. A desire too to show that he is still full of beans.

'At heart,' he declared, 'I am a passionate man.' I understand that what he really meant was that he was a libidinous one. I smiled, as one would if one heard a woman declare she had very fine legs – a smile which signifies 'I never doubted it for a moment.' Until that day I had only seen the magistrate; the man at last threw aside his toga.

I waited till we were seated at table at Foyot's before speaking to him of Olivier; I told him that I had recently had news of him through one of his schoolfellows, and that I had heard he was travelling in Corsica with the Comte de Passavant.

'Yes, he's a friend of Vincent's: he offered to take him with him. As Olivier had just passed his *bachot* rather brilliantly, his mother thought it would be hard to refuse him such a pleasure. . . . The Comte de Passavant is a writer. I expect you know him.'

I did not conceal that I had no great liking for either his books or his person.

'Amongst *confrères* one is sometimes apt to be a little severe in one's judgements,' he retorted. 'I tried to read his last novel; certain critics think very highly of it. I didn't see much in it myself; but it's not my line, you know. . . .' Then as I expressed my fear as to the influence Passavant might have over Olivier:

'In reality,' he added in his rather woolly way, 'I personally didn't approve of this expedition. But it's no good not realizing that when they get to a certain age our children escape from our control. It's in the nature of things and there's nothing to be done. Pauline would like to go on hanging over them for ever. She's like all mothers. I sometimes say to her: "But you worry your sons to death. Leave them alone. It's you who put things into their heads with all your questions. . . ." For my part I consider it does no good to watch over them too long. The important thing is that a few good principles should be inculcated into them during their early education. The important thing above all is that they should come of a good stock. Heredity, my dear friend, heredity triumphs over everything.

There are certain bad lots whom nothing can improve – the predestined, we call them. Those must have a tight hand kept over them. But when one has to do with well-conditioned natures, one can let them go a bit easy.'

'But you were telling me,' I insisted, 'that you didn't approve of Olivier's being carried off in this way.'

'Oh! approve . . . approve!' he said with his nose in his plate, 'there's no need for my approval. There are many households, you know – and those the most united – where it isn't always the husband who settles things. But you aren't married; such things don't interest you. . . .'

'Oh!' said I, laughing, 'but I'm a novelist.'

'Then you have no doubt remarked that it isn't always from weakness of character that a man allows himself to be led by his wife.'

'Yes,' I conceded by way of flattery, 'there are strong and even dominating men whom one discovers to be of a lamb-like docility in their married life.'

'And do you know why?' he went on. 'Nine times out of ten, when the husband submits to his wife, it is because he has something to be forgiven him. A virtuous woman, my dear fellow, takes advantage of everything. If the man stoops for a second, there she is sitting on his shoulders. Oh! we poor husbands are sometimes greatly to be pitied. When we are young, our one wish is to have chaste wives, without a thought of how much their virtue is going to cost us.'

I gazed at Molinier, sitting there with his elbows on the table and his chin in his hands. The poor man little suspected how naturally his backbone fell into the stooping attitude of which he complained; he kept mopping his forehead, ate a great deal – not like a gourmet, but like a glutton – and seemed particularly to appreciate the old Burgundy which we had ordered. Happy to feel himself listened to, understood, and, no doubt he thought, approved, he overflowed in confessions.

'In my capacity as magistrate,' he continued, 'I have known women who only lent themselves to their husbands against the grain of their heart and senses . . . and who yet are indignant when the poor wretch who has been repulsed, seeks his provender elsewhere.'

The magistrate had begun his sentence in the past; the husband finished it in the present, with an unmistakable allusion to himself. He added sententiously between two mouthfuls:

'Other people's appetites easily appear excessive when one doesn't share them.' He drank a long draught of wine, then: 'And this explains, my dear friend, how a husband loses the direction of his household.'

I understood, indeed – it was clear under the apparent incoherence of his talk – his desire to make the responsibility of his own shortcomings fall upon his wife's virtue. Creatures as disjointed as this puppet, I said to myself, need every scrap of their egoism to bind together the disconnected elements of which they are formed. A moment's self-forgetfulness, and they would fall to pieces. He was silent. I felt I must pour a few reflections over him, as one pours oil on an engine that has accomplished a bout of work; and to set him going again I remarked:

'Fortunately Pauline is intelligent.'

He prolonged his 'ye-e-s' till it turned into a query; then:

'But still there are things she doesn't understand. However intelligent a woman may be, you know . . . Still, I must admit that in the circumstances I didn't manage very cleverly. I began telling her about a little affair of mine at a time when I thought – when I was absolutely convinced – that it wouldn't go any further. It did go further . . . and Pauline's suspicions too. It was a mistake to put her on the "*qui vive*", as people say. I have been obliged to hide things from her – to tell lies. . . . That's what comes of not holding one's tongue to begin with. It's not my fault. I'm naturally confiding. . . . But Pauline's jealousy is alarming. You can't imagine how careful I have had to be.'

'Was it long ago?' I asked.

'Oh, it's been going on for about five years now; and I flatter myself I had completely reassured her. But now the whole thing has to begin all over again. What do you think! When I got back home the day before yesterday . . . Suppose we order another bottle of Pommard, eh?'

'Not for me, please.'

'Perhaps I could have a half-bottle. I'll go home and take a little nap after lunch. I feel this heat so. . . . Well, I was telling you that the day before yesterday, when I got back, I went to my writing desk to put some papers away. I pulled open the drawer where I had hidden . . . the person in question's letters. Imagine my stupefaction, my dear fellow; the drawer was empty! Deuce take it! I see exactly what has happened; about a fortnight ago, Pauline came up to Paris with George, to go to the wedding of the daughter of one of my colleagues. I wasn't able to attend it myself; I was away in Holland. . . . And besides, functions of that kind are women's business. Well, there she was, with nothing to do, in an empty flat; under pretence of putting things straight . . . you know what women are like – always rather curious . . . she began nosing about . . . oh! intending no ill – I'm not blaming her. But Pauline has always had a perfect mania for tidying. . . . Well, what on earth am I to say to her, now that she's got all the proofs? If only the silly little thing didn't call me by my Christian name! Such a united couple! When I think what I'm in for! . . .'

The poor man stuck in the slough of his confidences. He dabbed his forehead – fanned himself. I had drunk much less than he. The heart does not furnish compassion at command; I merely felt disgust for him. I could put up with him as the father of a family (though it was painful to me to think that he was Olivier's father), as a respectable, honest, retired bourgeois; but as a man in love, I could only imagine him ridiculous. I was especially made uncomfortable by the clumsiness and triviality of his words, of his pantomime; neither his face nor his voice seemed suited to the feelings he expressed; it was like a double bass trying to produce the effects of an alto; his instrument brought out nothing but squeaks.

'You said that she had George with her. . . .'

'Yes; she didn't want to leave him at the seaside alone. But naturally in Paris he wasn't in her pocket the whole time. . . . Why, my dear fellow, in twenty-six years of married life I have never had the smallest scene, the slightest altercation. . . . When I think of what's in store for me! . . . for Pauline's coming back in two days. . . . Oh! I say, let's talk of something else. Well, what do you think of Vincent? The Prince of Monaco – a cruise. . . . By Jove! . . .What! didn't you know? . . . Yes; he has gone out in charge of soundings and deep-sea fishing near the Azores. Ah! there's no need to be anxious about him, I assure you. *He'll* make his way all right, without help from anyone.'

'His health?'

'Completely restored. With his intelligence, I think he is on the high road to becoming famous. The Comte de Passavant made no bones about saying that he considered him one of the most remarkable men he ever met. He even said "the *most* remarkable" . . . but one must make allowances for exaggeration.'

The meal was finished; he lit a cigar.

'May I ask you,' he went on, 'who the friend is who gave you news of Olivier? I must tell you that I attach particular importance to the company my children keep. I consider that it's a thing it's impossible to pay too much attention to. My sons fortunately have a natural tendency to make friends with only the best people. Vincent, you see, with his prince; Olivier with the Comte de Passavant. . . . As for George, he has been going about at Houlgate with one of his schoolfellows – a young Adamanti – he's to be at the Vedel–Azaïs school next term too; a boy in whom one can have complete confidence; his father is senator for Corsica. But just see how prudent one has to be! Olivier had a friend who seemed to belong to an excellent family – a certain Bernard Profitendieu. I must tell you that old Profitendieu is a colleague of mine; a most distinguished man. I have particular esteem for him. But . . . (between ourselves) . . . it has just come to my knowledge that he is not the father of the boy who bears his name! What do you say to that?'

'Young Bernard Profitendieu is the very person who spoke to me about Olivier,' I said.

Molinier drew a few deep puffs from his cigar and raised his eyebrows very high, so that his forehead was covered with wrinkles:

'I had rather Olivier saw as little as possible of that young fellow. I have heard the most deplorable things about him – not that I'm much astonished at that. We must admit that there's no grounds for expecting any good from a boy who has been born in such unfortunate conditions. I don't mean to say that a natural child mayn't have great qualities – and even virtues; but the fruit of lawlessness and insubordination must necessarily be tainted with the germs of anarchy. Yes, my dear friend, what was bound to happen has happened. Young Bernard has suddenly left the shelter of the family which he ought never to have entered. He has gone "to live his life", as Emile Augier says; live Heaven knows how or where. Poor Profitendieu, when he told me about this extravagant behaviour, seemed exceedingly upset about it. I made him understand that he ought not to take it so much to heart. In reality the boy's departure puts everything to rights again.'

I protested that I knew Bernard well enough to vouch for his being a charming, well-behaved boy. (Needless to say I took good care not to mention the affair of the suitcase.) But Molinier only went on all the more vigorously.

'So! So! I see I must tell you more.'

Then, leaning forward and speaking in a whisper:

'My colleague Profitendieu has recently had to investigate an exceedingly shady and disagreeable affair, both on its own account and because of the scandalous consequences it may entail. It's a preposterous story and one would be only too glad if one could disbelieve it. . . . Imagine, my dear fellow, a regular concern of organized prostitution, in fact of a . . . no, I don't want to use bad words; let's say a tea-shop, with this particularly scandalous feature, that its habitués are mostly, almost exclusively, very young schoolboys. I tell you it's incredible. The children certainly don't realize the gravity of their acts, for they hardly attempt to conceal themselves. It takes place when they come out of school. They take tea, they talk, they amuse themselves with the ladies; and the play is carried further in the rooms which adjoin the tea rooms. Of course not everyone is allowed in. One has to be introduced, initiated. Who stands the expense of these orgies? Who pays the rent? It wouldn't have been very difficult to find out; but the investigations had to be conducted with extreme prudence, for fear of learning too much, of being carried further than one meant, of being forced to prosecute and compromise the respectable families whose children are suspected of being the principal clients of the affair. I did what I could therefore to moderate Profitendieu's zeal. He charged into the business like a bull, without suspecting that with the first stroke of his horns... (oh! I'm sorry; I didn't say it on purpose; ha! ha! ha! how funny! It came out quite unintentionally) . . . he ran the risk of sticking his own son. Fortunately the holidays broke everything up. The schoolboys were scattered and I hope the whole business will peter out, be hushed up after a warning or so and a few discreet penalties.'

'Are you quite sure Bernard Profitendieu was mixed up in it?'

'Not absolutely, but...'

'What makes you think so?'

'First, the fact that he is a natural child. You don't suppose that a boy of his age runs away from home without having touched the lowest depths? . . . And then I have an idea that Profitendieu was seized with some suspicions, for his zeal suddenly cooled down; more than that, he seemed to be backing out, and the last time I asked him how the affair was going on he seemed embarrassed; "I think, after all that nothing will come of it," he said and hastily changed the subject. Poor Profitendieu! I must say he doesn't deserve it. He's an honest man, and what's rarer perhaps, a good fellow. By the way, his daughter has just married exceedingly well. I wasn't able to go to the wedding because I was in Holland, but Pauline and George came back on purpose. Did I tell you that before? It's time I went and had my nap.... What! really? You want to pay it all? No, no! You mustn't. Bachelors – old friends – go shares.... No use? Well! well! Good-bye! Don't forget that Pauline is coming back in two days. Come and see us. And don't call me Molinier. Won't you say Oscar? . . . I've been meaning to ask you for a long time.'

This evening a note from Rachel, Laura's sister:

I have something very serious to say to you. Could you, without inconvenience, look in at the school tomorrow afternoon? It would be doing me a great service.

If she had wanted to speak about Laura, she wouldn't have waited so long. This is the first time she has written to me.

2

EDOUARD'S JOURNAL: AT THE VEDELS'

Sept. 28th. – I found Rachel standing at the door of the big classroom on the ground floor. Two servants were washing the boards. She herself had a servant's apron on and was holding a duster in her hand.

'I knew I could count on you,' she said, holding out her hand with a look on her face of tender, resigned sadness, and yet a look that was smiling too, and more touching than beauty itself. 'If you aren't in too great a hurry, the best thing would be for you first to go up and pay grandfather a little visit, and then Mamma. If they heard you had been here without seeing them, they would be hurt. But keep a little time for me; I simply must speak to you. You will find me here; you see, I am superintending the maids' work.'

Out of a kind of modesty, she never says 'my work'. Rachel has effaced herself all her life and nothing could be more discreet, more retiring than her virtue. Abnegation is so natural to her, that not one of her family is grateful to her for her perpetual self-sacrifice. She has the most beautiful woman's nature that I know.

I went up to the second floor to see old Azaïs. He hardly ever leaves his arm-chair nowadays. He made me sit down beside him and began talking about La Pérouse almost at once.

'It makes me feel anxious to know that he is living all alone, and I should like to persuade him to come and stay here. We are old friends, you know. I went to see him the other day. I am afraid he has been very much affected by his dear wife's leaving him to go to Sainte Périne. His maid told me he hardly eats anything. I consider that as a rule we eat too much; but there should be moderation in all things and we should avoid excess in both directions. He thinks it useless to have things cooked only for him; but if he took his meals with us, seeing others eat would encourage him to do the same. Moreover, he would be with his charming little grandson, whom he would otherwise see very little of; for rue Vavin is quite a long journey away from the Faubourg St Honoré. And moreover, I shouldn't much care to let the child go out by himself in Paris. I have known Anatole de La Pérouse for a long time. He was always eccentric. I don't mean it as a reproach, but he is a little proud by nature, and perhaps he wouldn't accept my hospitality without wishing to make some return. So I thought I might propose that he should take school preparation; it wouldn't be tiring, and moreover it would have the advantage of distracting him, of taking him out of himself a little. He is a good mathematician, and if necessary he might give algebra and geometry lessons. Now that he has no pupils left, his furniture and his piano are of no use to him; he ought to give notice; and as coming here would save his rent I thought we might agree on a little sum for his board and lodging, to put him more at his ease, so that he shouldn't feel himself too much under an obligation to me. You ought to try and persuade him – and without much delay, for with his poor style of living, I am afraid he may soon become too enfeebled. Moreover, the boys are coming back in two days; so it would be a good thing to know how the matter stands and whether we may count on him – as he may count on us.'

I promised to speak to La Pérouse the following day. As if relieved, he went on at once:

'Oh! by the bye, what a good fellow your young protégé Bernard is! He has kindly offered to make himself useful to us; he spoke of taking preparation in the lower school; but I'm afraid he's rather young himself and perhaps he might not be able to keep order. I talked to him for a long time and found him most attractive. He is the metal out of which the best Christians are forged. It is assuredly to be regretted that an unfortunate early education has turned aside his soul from the true path. He confessed that he was without faith; but the tone in which he said so filled me with hope. I replied that I trusted I should find in him all the qualities that go to the making of a good little Christian soldier, and that he ought to devote himself to the increase of those talents which God had vouchsafed to grant him. We read the parable together and I think the seed has not fallen on bad ground. He seemed moved by my words and promised to reflect on them.'

Bernard had already given me an account of this interview; I knew what he thought of it, so that I felt the conversation becoming a little painful. I had already got up to go, but old Azaïs, keeping the hand I held out to him in both his, went on:

'Oh! by the bye. I have seen our Laura. I know the dear child passed a whole delightful month with you in the mountains; it seems to have done her a great deal of good. I am happy to think she is with her husband once more; he must have been beginning to suffer from her long absence. It is regrettable that his work would not allow of his joining you.'

I was pulling away my hand to leave, more and more embarrassed, for I didn't know what Laura might have said, but with a sudden commanding gesture he drew me towards him, and bending forward, whispered in my ear:

'Laura confided her hopes to me; but hush! . . . She prefers it not to be known yet. I mention it to you because I know that you are in the secret and because we are both discreet. The poor child was quite abashed when she told me and blushed deeply; she is so reserved. As she had gone down on her knees before me, we thanked God together for having, in His goodness, blessed their union.'

I think that Laura might have put off this confidence, which her condition doesn't as yet necessitate. Had she consulted me, I should have told her to wait until she had seen Douviers before saying anything. Azaïs can't see an inch in front of his nose, but the rest of the family will not be taken in so easily.

The old fellow went on to execute a few further variations on divers pastoral themes; then he told me his daughter would be happy to see me and I went downstairs to the Vedels' floor.

Just re-read the above. In speaking so of Azaïs, it is myself that I render odious. I am fully aware of it, and add these few lines for Bernard's sake, in case his charming indiscretion leads him to poke his nose again into this notebook. He has only to go on frequenting him a little longer in order to understand what I mean. I like the old fellow very much, and 'moreover', as he says, I respect him; but when I am with him I have the greatest difficulty in containing myself; this doesn't tend to make me enjoy his society.

I like his daughter, the pastoress, very much. Madame Vedel is like Lamartine's Elvire – an elderly Elvire. Her conversation is not without charm. She has a frequent habit of leaving her sentences unfinished, which gives her reflections a kind of poetic vagueness. She reaches the infinite by way of the indeterminate and the indefinite. She expects from a future life all that is lacking to her in this one; this enables her to enlarge her hopes boundlessly. The very narrowness of her taking-off ground adds strength to her impetus. Seeing Vedel so rarely enables her to imagine that she loves him. The worthy man is incessantly on the go, in request on all sides, taken up by a hundred and one different ploys – sermons, congresses, visits to the sick, visits to the poor. He can only shake your hand in passing, but it is with all the greater cordiality.

'Too busy to talk today.'

'Never mind; we shall meet again in Heaven,' say I; but he hasn't had time to hear me.

'Not a moment to himself,' sighs Madame Vedel. 'If you only knew the things he gets put on his shoulders now that . . . As people know that he never refuses anything, everyone . . . When he comes home at night, he is sometimes so tired that I hardly dare speak to him for fear of . . . He gives so much of himself to others that there's nothing left for his own family.'

And while she was speaking I remembered some of Vedel's home-comings at the time I was staying at the pension. I sometimes saw him take his head between his hands and pant aloud for a little respite. But even then I used to think he feared a respite even more than he longed for it, and that nothing more painful could have been accorded him than a little time in which to reflect.

'You'll take a cup of tea, won't you?' asked Madame Vedel, as a little maid brought in a loaded tray.

'There's not enough sugar, Ma'am.'

'Haven't I said that you must tell Miss Rachel about it? Quick! . . . Have you let the young gentlemen know tea's ready?'

'Mr Bernard and Mr Boris have gone out.'

'Oh! And Mr Armand?... Make haste.'

Then, without waiting for the maid to leave the room:

'The poor girl has just arrived from Strasburg. She has no ... She has to be told everything. ... Well! What are you waiting for now?'

The maidservant turned round like a serpent whose tail has been trodden on:

'The tutor's downstairs; he wanted to come up. He says he won't go till he's been paid.'

Madame Vedel's features assumed an air of tragic boredom:

'How many times must I repeat that I have nothing to do with settling accounts. Tell him to go to Miss Rachel. Go along ... Not a moment's peace! What can Rachel be thinking of?'

'Aren't we going to wait tea for her?'

'She never takes tea. ... Oh! the beginning of term is a troublesome time for us. The tutors who apply ask exorbitant fees, or when their fees are possible, they themselves aren't. Papa was not at all pleased with the last; he was a great deal too weak with him; and now he comes threatening. You heard what the maid said. All these people think of nothing but money.... As if there were nothing more important than that in the world. ... In the meantime we don't know how to replace him. Prosper always thinks one has nothing to do but to pray to God for everything to go right....'

The maid came back with the sugar.

'Have you told Mr Armand?'

'Yes, Ma'am; he's coming directly.'

'And Sarah?' I asked.

'She won't be back for another two days. She's staying with friends in England; with the parents of the girl you saw here before the holidays. They have been very kind, and I'm glad that Sarah was able to ... And Laura. I thought she was looking much better. The stay in Switzerland coming after the South has done her a great deal of good, and it was very kind of you to persuade her to it. It's only poor Armand who hasn't left Paris all the holidays.'

'And Rachel?'

'Yes, of course; Rachel too. She had a great many invitations, but she preferred to stop in Paris. And then Grandfather needed her. Besides one doesn't always do what one wants in this life – as I am obliged to repeat to the children now and then. One must think of other people. Do you suppose I shouldn't have enjoyed going away for a change to Switzerland too? And Prosper? When he travels, do you suppose it's for his pleasure? ... Armand, you know I don't like you to come in here without a collar on,' she added, as she saw her son enter the room.

'My dear Mother, you religiously taught me to attach no importance to my personal appearance,' said he, offering me his hand; 'and with eminent *à propos* too, as the wash doesn't come home till Tuesday and all the rest of my collars are in rags.'

I remembered what Olivier had told me about his school-fellow, and it seemed to me that he was right and that an expression of profound anxiety lay hidden beneath the spiteful irony he affected. Armand's face had fined down; his nose was pinched; it curved hawk-like over lips which had grown thin and colourless. He went on:

'Have you informed your noble visitor that we have made several additions to our usual company of performers and engaged a few sensational stars for the opening of the winter season? The son of a distinguished senator and the Vicomte de Passavant, brother to the illustrious writer – without counting two recruits whom you know already, but who are all the more honourable on that account – Prince Boris and the Marquis de Profitendieu – besides some others whose titles and virtues remain to be discovered.'

'You see he hasn't changed,' said the poor mother, smiling at these witticisms.

I was so terribly afraid that he would begin to talk about Laura that I cut short my visit and went downstairs as fast as I could to find Rachel.

She had turned up her sleeves to help in the arrangement of the classroom; but she hastily pulled them down again as she saw me come up.

'It is extremely painful to me to have recourse to you,' she began, drawing me into a small room adjoining, which is used for private lessons. 'I meant to apply to Felix Douviers – he asked me to; but now that I have seen Laura, I understand it's impossible. . . .'

She was very pale, and as she said these last words, her chin and lips quivered so convulsively that for some moments she was unable to speak. I looked away from her, in the fear of adding to her discomfort. She had shut the door and was leaning against it. I tried to take her hand, but she tore it away from between mine. At last she went on again in a voice that seemed strangled by the immensity of her effort:

'Can you lend me ten thousand francs? The term promises to be fairly good and I hope to be able to pay you back soon.'

'When do you want it?'

She made no answer.

'I happen to have a little over a thousand francs on me,' I went on. 'I can complete the sum tomorrow morning – this evening, if necessary.'

'No; tomorrow will do. But if you can let me have a thousand francs at once without inconvenience . . .'

I took out my pocket-book and handed them to her.

'Would you like fourteen hundred?'

She lowered her head and uttered a 'yes' so faint that I could hardly hear it, then she tottered to a school bench, dropped down on it, and with her elbows leaning on the desk in front of her, stayed for a few moments, her face hidden in her hands. I thought she was crying, but when I put my hand on her shoulder, she raised her head and I saw that her eyes were dry.

'Rachel,' I said, 'don't mind having had to ask me this; I am glad to be able to oblige you.'

She looked at me gravely:

'What is painful to me is to have to ask you not to mention it either to Grandfather or to Mamma. Since they gave the accounts of the school over to me, I have let them think that . . . well, they don't know. Don't say anything, I beg you. Grandfather is old and Mamma takes so much trouble.'

'Rachel, it's not your mother who takes trouble. . . . It's you.'

'She *has* taken trouble. She's tired now. It's my turn. I have nothing else to do.'

It was quite simply that she said these simple words. I felt no bitterness in her resignation – on the contrary, a kind of serenity.

'But don't imagine that things are worse than they are. It's just a difficult moment to tide over, because some of the creditors are getting impatient.'

'I heard the maid just now mention a tutor who was asking to be paid.'

'Yes; he came and had a very painful scene with Grandfather, which unfortunately I was unable to prevent. He's a brutal, vulgar man. I must go and pay him.'

'Would you like me to do it for you?'

She hesitated a moment, trying in vain to force a smile.

'Thank you. No; I had better do it myself.... But come with me, will you? I'm rather frightened of him. If he sees you, he won't dare say anything.'

The school courtyard is separated from the garden by two or three steps and a balustrade, against which the tutor was leaning with his elbows thrust behind him. He had on an enormous soft felt hat and was smoking a pipe. While Rachel was engaging him, Armand came up to me.

'Rachel has been bleeding you,' he said cynically. 'You have come in the nick of time to save her from a horrid anxiety. It's Alexandre – my beast of a brother, who has been getting into debt again in the colonies. She wants to hide it from my parents. She has already given up half her *dot* to make Laura's a little larger; but this time all the rest of it has gone. She didn't tell you anything about that, I bet. Her modesty exasperates me. It's one of the most sinister jokes in this world below that every time anyone sacrifices himself for others, one may be perfectly certain he is worth more than they.... Just look at all she has done for Laura! And how she has rewarded her! The slut!...'

'Armand!' I cried indignantly. 'You have no right to judge your sister.'

But he continued in a jerky, hissing voice:

'On the contrary, it's because I am no better than she that I am able to judge her. I know all about it. Rachel doesn't judge us. Rachel never judges anyone.... Yes, the slut! the slut!... I didn't beat about the bush to tell her what I thought of her, I promise you. And you! To have covered it all up, to have protected it! You who knew! . . . Grandfather is as blind as a bat. Mamma tries all she can to understand nothing. As for Papa, he trusts in the Lord; it's the most convenient thing to do. Whenever there's a difficulty, he falls to praying and leaves Rachel to get out of it. All he asks is to remain in the dark. He rushes about like a lunatic; he's hardly ever at home. I'm not surprised he finds it stifling here. As for me, it's smothering me to death. He tries to stupefy himself, by Jove. In the meantime Mamma writes verses. Oh! I'm not blaming her; I write them myself. But at any rate, I know I'm nothing but a blackguard; and I've never pretended to be anything else. But, I say, isn't it disgusting – Grandfather setting up to do the charitable by La Pérouse, because he's in need of a tutor? . . .' Then, suddenly: 'What's that beast there daring to say to my sister? If he doesn't take his hat off to her when he goes, I'll black his bloody eyes for him. . . .'

He darted towards the Bohemian, and I thought for a moment he was going to hit him. But at Armand's approach, the man made a theatrical and ironical flourish with his hat and disappeared under the archway. At that moment the door into the street opened to let in the pastor. He was dressed in a frock-coat, chimney-pot hat and black gloves, like a person on his way back from a christening or a wedding. The ex-tutor and he exchanged a ceremonious bow.

Rachel and Armand came towards me; when Vedel joined them:

'It's all arranged,' said Rachel to her father.

He kissed her on the forehead.

'Didn't I tell you so, my child? God never abandons those who put their trust in Him.'

Then, holding out his hand to me:

'Going already? . . . Well, we shall see you again one of these days, shan't we?'

3

EDOUARD'S JOURNAL: THIRD VISIT TO LA PÉROUSE

Sept. 29th. – Visit to La Pérouse. The maid hesitated before letting me in. 'Monsieur won't see anyone.' I insisted so much that at last she showed me into the drawing-room. The shutters were shut; in the semi-obscurity I could hardly make out my old master, as he sat huddled up in a straight-backed arm-chair. He did not rise. He held out a limp hand, without looking at me, and let it fall again as soon as I had pressed it. I sat down beside him, so that I could see him only in profile. His features were hard and unbending. By moments his lips moved, but he said nothing. I actually doubted whether he recognized me. The clock struck four; then, as though he too were moved by clock-work, he slowly turned his head.

'Why,' he asked, and his voice was solemn and loud, but as toneless as though it came from beyond the grave, 'why did they let you in? I told the maid to say if anyone came, that Monsieur de La Pérouse was dead.'

I was greatly distressed, not so much by these absurd words, as by their tone – a declamatory tone – unspeakably affected, to which I was unaccustomed in my old master – so natural with me, as a rule – so confiding.

'The girl didn't want to tell a falsehood,' I said at last. 'Don't scold her for having let me in. I am happy to see you.'

He repeated stolidly: 'Monsieur de La Pérouse is dead,' and then plunged back into silence. I had a moment's ill temper and got up, meaning to leave, and put off till another day the task of finding a clue to this melancholy piece of acting. But at that moment the maid came back; she was carrying a cup of smoking chocolate:

'Make a little effort, sir; you haven't tasted anything all day.'

La Pérouse made an impatient gesture, like an actor whose effect has been spoilt by a clumsy super.

'Later. When the gentleman has gone.'

But the maid had no sooner shut the door, when:

'Be kind, my dear friend. Get me a glass of water – plain water. I'm dying of thirst.'

I found a water bottle and a glass in the dining-room. He filled the glass, emptied it at a draught, and wiped his lips on the sleeve of his old alpaca coat.

'Are you feverish?' I asked.

The words brought him back to the remembrance of the part he was playing.

'Monsieur de La Pérouse is not feverish. He is not anything. On Wednesday evening Monsieur de La Pérouse ceased to live.' I wondered whether it would not be best to humour him.

'Wasn't Wednesday the very day little Boris came to see you?'

He turned his head towards me; a smile, the ghost of the one he used to have at Boris's name, lighted up his features, and at last consenting to abandon his role:

'My friend,' he said, 'I can at any rate talk to you about it. That Wednesday was the last day I had left.' Then he went on in a lower voice: 'The very last day, in fact, which I had allowed myself before... putting an end to everything.'

It was with extreme pain that I heard La Pérouse revert to this sinister topic. I realized that I had never taken seriously what he had said about it before, for I had allowed it to slip from my memory; and now I reproached myself. Now I remembered everything clearly, but I was astonished, for he had at first mentioned a more distant date, and as I reminded him of this, he confessed, in a voice that had become natural again, and even a little ironical, that he had deceived me as to the date, in the fear that I should try and prevent him, or hasten my return from abroad; but that he had gone on his knees several nights running to pray God to allow him to see Boris before dying.

'And I had even agreed with Him,' added he, 'that if needs were, I should delay my departure for a few days... because of the assurance you had given me that you would bring him back with you, do you remember?'

I had taken his hand; it was icy and I chafed it between mine. He continued in a monotonous voice:

'Then when I saw that you weren't going to wait till the end of the holidays before coming back, and that I should be able to see the boy without putting off my departure, I thought . . . it seemed to me that God had heard my prayer. I thought that He approved me. Yes, I thought that. I didn't understand at first that He was laughing at me, as usual.'

He took his hand from between mine and went on in a more animated voice:

'So it was on Wednesday evening that I had resolved to put an end to myself; and it was on Wednesday afternoon that you brought me Boris. I must admit that I did not feel the joy I had looked forward to on seeing him. I thought it over afterwards. Evidently I had no right to expect that the child would be glad to see me. His mother has never talked to him about me.'

He stopped; his lips trembled and I thought he was going to cry.

'Boris asks no better than to love you,' I ventured, 'but give him time to know you.'

'After the boy had left me,' went on La Pérouse, without having heard me, 'when I found myself alone again in the evening (for you know that Madame de La Pérouse is no longer here), I said to myself: "The moment has come! Now for it!" You must know that my brother – the one I lost – left me a pair of pistols, which I always keep beside me, in a case, by my bedside. I went then to fetch the case. I sat down in an arm-chair; there, just as I am now. I loaded one of the pistols. . . .'

He turned towards me and abruptly, brutally, repeated, as if I had doubted his word:

'Yes, I did load it. You can see for yourself. It still is loaded. What happened? I can't succeed in understanding. I put the pistol to my forehead. I held it for a long time against my temple. And I didn't fire. I couldn't. . . . At the last moment – it's shameful . . . I hadn't the courage to fire.'

He had grown animated while speaking. His eye was livelier and his cheeks faintly flushed. He looked at me, nodding his head.

'How do you explain that? A thing I had resolved on; a thing I hadn't ceased thinking of for months. . . . Perhaps that's the very reason. Perhaps I had exhausted all my courage in thought beforehand.'

'As before Boris's arrival, you had exhausted the joy of seeing him,' said I; but he continued:

'I stayed a long time with the pistol to my temple. My finger was on the trigger. I pressed it a little; but not hard enough. I said to myself: "In another moment I shall press harder and it will go off." I felt the cold of the metal and I said to myself: "In another moment I shall not feel anything. But before that I shall hear a terrible noise".... Just think! So near to one's ear!.... That's the chief thing that prevented me – the fear of the noise. ... It's absurd, for as soon as one's dead ... Yes, but I hope for death as a sleep; and a detonation doesn't send one to sleep – it wakes one up.... Yes, certainly that was what I was afraid of. I was afraid that instead of going to sleep I should suddenly wake up.'

He seemed to be collecting himself, and for some moments his lips again moved without making a sound.

'I only said all that to myself,' he went on, 'afterwards. In reality, the reason I didn't kill myself is that I wasn't free. I say now that I was afraid; but no; it wasn't that. Something completely foreign to my will held me back. As if God didn't want to let me go. Imagine a marionette who should want to leave the stage before the end of the play.... Halt! You're wanted for the *finale*. Ah! Ah! you thought you would be able to go off whenever you liked! ... I understood that what we call our will is merely the threads which work the marionette, and which God pulls. Don't you see? Well, I'll explain. For instance, I say to myself: "Now I'm going to raise my right arm"; and I raise it.' (And he did raise it.) 'But it's because the string had already been pulled which made me think and say: "I'm going to raise my right arm." ... And the proof that I'm not free is that if it had been my left arm that I had had to raise, I should have said to you: "Now I'm going to raise my left arm." ... No; I see you don't understand.... You are not free to understand.... Oh! I realize now that God is playing with us. It amuses him to let us think that what he makes us do is what we wanted to do. That's his horrible game.... Do you think I'm going mad?

Apropos – Madame de La Pérouse . . . you know she has gone into a home? . . . Well, what do you think? She is convinced that it's a lunatic asylum and that I have had her shut up to get rid of her – that I am passing her off for mad. . . . You must grant that it's rather a curious thing that the first passer-by in the street would understand one better than the woman one has given one's life to. . . . At first I went to see her every day. But as soon as she caught sight of me, she used to call out: "Ah! there you are again! come to spy on me! . . ." I had to give up my visits, as they only irritated her. How can you expect one to care about life, when one's of no good to anyone?'

His voice was stifled by sobs. He dropped his head and I thought he was going to relapse again into his dejection. But with a sudden start:

'Do you know what she did before she left? She broke open my drawer and burnt all my late brother's letters. She has always been jealous of my brother; especially since he died. She used to make scenes when she found me reading his letters at night. She used to cry out: "Ah you wanted me to go to bed! You do things on the sly!" Or else: "You had far better go to bed and sleep. You're tiring your eyes." One would have said she was full of attentions; but I know her; it was jealousy. She didn't want to leave me alone with him.'

'Because she loved you. There's no jealousy without love.'

'Well, you must allow it's a melancholy business when love, instead of making the happiness of life, becomes its calamity. . . . That's no doubt the way God loves us.'

He had become excited while he was speaking and all of a sudden he exclaimed:

'I'm hungry. When I want to eat, that servant always brings me chocolate. I suppose Madame de La Pérouse must have told her that I never took anything else. It would be very kind of you to go to the kitchen . . . the second door on the right in the passage . . . and see whether there aren't any eggs. I think she told me there were some . . .'

'Would you like her to get you a poached egg?'

'I think I could eat two. Will you be so kind? I can't make myself understood.'

'My dear friend,' said I when I came back, 'your eggs will be ready in a moment. If you'll allow me I'll stay and see you eat them; yes; it will be a pleasure. I was very much distressed just now to hear you say that you were of no good to anyone. You seem to forget your grandson. Your friend, Monsieur Azaïs, proposes that you should go and live with him, at the school. He commissioned me to tell you so. He thinks that now that Madame de La Pérouse is no longer here, there's nothing to keep you.'

I expected some resistance, but he hardly inquired the conditions of the new existence which was offered him.

'Though I didn't kill myself, I am none the less dead. Here or there, it doesn't matter to me. You can take me away.'

It was settled I should come and fetch him the next day but one; and that before then I should put at his disposal two trunks, for him to pack his clothes in and anything else he might want to take with him.

'And besides,' I added, 'as you will keep this apartment on till the expiration of your lease, you will always be able to come and fetch anything you need.'

The maid brought in the eggs, which he devoured hungrily. I ordered dinner for him, greatly relieved to see that nature at last was getting the upper hand.

'I give you a great deal of trouble,' he kept repeating. 'You are very kind.'

I should have liked him to hand over his pistols to me, and I told him he had no use for them now; but he would not consent to part with them.

'There's nothing to fear. What I didn't do that day, I know I shall never be able to do. But they are the only remembrances I have left of my brother – and I need them too to remind me that I am nothing but a plaything in God's hands.'

4

THE FIRST DAY OF THE TERM

THE day was very hot. Through the open windows of the Vedels' school could be seen the tree-tops of the Gardens, over which there still floated an immense, unexhausted store of summer.

The first day of the term was an opportunity old Azaïs never missed of making a speech. He stood at the foot of the master's desk, upright and facing the boys, as is proper. At the desk sat old La Pérouse. He had risen as the boys came in; but Azaïs, with a friendly gesture, signed to him to sit down again. His anxious eyes had gone straight to Boris, and this look of his embarrassed Boris all the more because Azaïs, in the speech in which he introduced the new master to his pupils, thought fit to allude to the relationship to one of them. La Pérouse, in the meantime, was distressed at receiving no answering look from Boris – indifference, he thought, coldness.

'Oh!' thought Boris, 'if only he would leave me alone! If only he wouldn't make me "an object"!' His schoolfellows terrified him. On coming out of the *lycée*, he had had to join them, and as he walked with them from the *lycée* to the Vedels', he had listened to their talk. He would have liked to fall in with it, for he had great need of sympathy, but he was of too fastidious and sensitive a nature, and he could not overcome his repugnance; the words froze on his lips; he reproached himself for his foolishness and tried hard not to let it show; tried hard even to laugh, so as not to be scoffed at; but it was no good; he looked like a girl among the others, and realized it sorrowfully.

They had broken up into groups almost immediately. A certain Léon Ghéridanisol was a central figure and was already beginning to take the lead. Rather older than the others, and more advanced in his studies, of a dark complexion, with black hair and black eyes, Ghéridanisol was neither very tall nor particularly strong – but he had what is called '*cheek*'. Really infernal lip! Even young George Molinier admitted that Ghéridanisol had 'made him sit up;' 'and you know, it takes a good deal to make me sit up!' Hadn't he seen him that very morning, with his own eyes, go up to a young woman who was carrying a child in her arms:

'Is that kid yours, madam?' (This with a low bow.) 'It's jolly ugly, I must say. But don't worry. It won't live.'

George was still rocking.

'No? Honour bright?' said Philippe Adamanti, his friend, when George told him the story.

This piece of insolence filled them with rapture; impossible to imagine anything funnier. A stale enough joke. Léon had learnt it from his cousin Strouvilhou, but that was no business of George's.

At school, Molinier and Adamanti got leave to sit on the same bench as Ghéridanisol – the fifth, so as not to be too near the usher. Molinier had Adamanti on his left hand and Ghéridanisol (Ghéri for short), on his right; at the end of the bench sat Boris. Behind him was Passavant.

Gontran de Passavant's life has been a sad one since his father's death – not that it had been very lively before it. He had long ago understood that he could expect no sympathy from his brother, no support. He had spent his holidays in Brittany, where his old nurse, the faithful Séraphine, had taken him to stay with her people. All his qualities are folded inwards; he devotes himself to his work. A secret desire spurs him on to prove to his brother that he is worth more than he. It is by his own choice that he is at school; out of a wish too not to go on living with his brother in the big house in the rue de Babylone, which has nothing but melancholy recollections for him. Séraphine has taken a lodging in Paris so as not to leave him alone; she is able to do this with the little pension specially left her by the late Count's will and served her by his two sons. Gontran has one of her rooms, and it is here that he spends his free time. He has furnished it to his own taste. He takes two meals a week with Séraphine; she looks after him and sees that he wants for nothing. When he is with her, Gontran chatters freely enough, though he can speak to her of hardly any of the things he has most at heart. At school he keeps his independence; he listens absent-mindedly to his schoolfellows' nonsense, and often refuses to join in their games. He prefers reading to any but out-of-door games. He likes sport – all kinds of sport – but preferably those that are solitary. For he is proud and will not associate with everyone. On Sundays, according to the season, he skates or swims, or boats, or takes immense walks in the country. He has repugnances and does not try to overcome them; nor does he try to widen his mind so much as to strengthen it. He is perhaps not so simple as he thinks – as he tries to make himself become; we have seen him at his father's death-bed; but he does not like mysteries and whenever he is unlike himself, he is disgusted. If he succeeds in remaining at the top of his class, it is through application, not through facility. Boris would find a protector in him, if he were only to look towards him, but it is his neighbour George who attracts him. As for George, he has eyes for no one but Ghéri, who has eyes for no one.

George had some important news to communicate to Philippe Adamanti, which he had judged it more prudent not to write.

That morning he had arrived at the *lycée* doors a quarter of an hour before the opening and had waited for him in vain. It was while he was waiting that he had heard Léon Ghéridanisol apostrophize the young woman so brilliantly, after which incident the two urchins had entered into conversation and had discovered to George's great joy that they were going to be schoolfellows.

On coming out of the *lycée*, George and Phiphi had at last succeeded in meeting. They walked to the Pension Azaïs in company with the other boys, but a little apart, so as to be able to talk freely.

'You had better hide that thing,' George had begun, pointing to the yellow rosette which Phiphi was still sporting in his buttonhole.

'Why?' asked Philippe, noticing that George was no longer wearing his.

'You run the risk of getting collared. I wanted to tell you

before school, my boy; why didn't you turn up earlier? I was waiting outside the doors to warn you.'

'But I didn't know,' Phiphi had answered.

'I didn't know. I didn't know,' George repeated, mimicking him. 'You might have guessed that there would be things to tell you when I didn't see you again at Houlgate.'

The perpetual aim and object of these two boys is to get the better of each other. His father's situation and fortune give Philippe certain advantages, but George is greatly superior in audacity and cynicism. Phiphi has to make an effort to keep up with him. He isn't a bad boy; but lacking in backbone.

'Well then, out with your things!' he had said.

Léon Ghéridanisol, who had come up, was listening to them. George was not ill pleased that he should overhear him; if Ghéri had filled him with admiration just now, George had a little surprise in store for Ghéri; he therefore answered Phiphi quite calmly:

'That girl Praline has got run in.'

'Praline!' cried Phiphi, thunderstruck by George's coolness. And Léon showed signs of being interested. Phiphi said to George:

'Can one tell him?'

'As you please,' said George, shrugging his shoulders. Then Phiphi, pointing to George:

'She's his tart.' Then to George:

'How do you know?'

'I met Germaine and she told me.'

And he went on to tell Phiphi how, when he had come up to Paris a fortnight before, he had wanted to visit the apartment which the procureur Molinier had once called 'the scene of the orgies', and had found the doors closed; that a little later as he was strolling about the neighbourhood, he had met Germaine (Phiphi's tart) and she had given him the news: the place had been raided by the police at the beginning of the holidays. What neither the women nor the boys knew, was that Profitendieu had taken good care to wait before taking this action until the younger delinquents should have left Paris, so that their parents might be spared the scandal of their being caught.

'Oh, Lord! . . .' repeated Phiphi without comments. 'Oh Lord! . . .' It had been a narrow squeak, thought he, for George and him.

'Makes your marrow freeze, eh?' said George, with a grin. He considered it perfectly useless to confess – especially before Ghéridanisol, that he had himself been terrified.

From the dialogue here recorded, these children might be thought more depraved than they actually are. I feel convinced that it is chiefly to show off that they talk in this way. There is a good deal of bravado in their case. No matter: Ghéridanisol is listening to them. He listens and leads them on. His cousin Strouvilhou will be greatly amused when he reports the conversation to him this evening.

That same evening Bernard went to see Edouard.

'Well? Did the first day go off all right?'

'Pretty well.' And then as he said no more:

'Master Bernard, if you are not in the humour to talk of your own accord, don't expect me to pump you. There's nothing I dislike so much. But allow me to remind you that you offered me your services and that I have a right to expect a few stories. . . .'

'What do you want to know?' rejoined Bernard, with no very good grace. 'That old Azaïs made a solemn speech and exhorted the boys to "press forward in a common endeavour and with the impetuous ardour of youth . . ."? I remember those words because they occurred three times. Armand declares the old boy regularly puts them into all his pi-jaws. He and I were sitting on the last bench at the back of the classroom watching the boys come into school – like Noah, watching the animals come into the Ark. There were every kind and sort – ruminants, pachyderms, molluscs and other invertebrates. When they began to talk to each other after the speech, Armand and I calculated that four sentences out of ten began with: "I bet you won't . . ."'

'And the other six?'

'"As for me, *I* . . ."'

'Not badly observed, I'm afraid. What else?'

'Some of them seem to me to have a *fabricated* personality.'

'What do you mean by that?' asked Edouard.

'I am thinking particularly of a boy who sat beside young Passavant. (Passavant himself just seems to me a good boy.) His neighbour, whom I watched for a long time, appears to have adopted the "*Ne quid nimis*" of the ancients as his rule of life. Doesn't that strike you as an absurd device at his age? His clothes are meagre; his necktie exiguous; even his bootlaces are only just long enough to tie. In the course of the few moments I spent talking to him, he found time to say that he saw everywhere about him a waste of energies, and to repeat, like a refrain: "Let's have no useless efforts!"'

'A plague upon the economical!' said Edouard. 'In art they turn into the prolix.'

'Why?'

'Because they can't bear to lose anything. What else? You have said nothing about Armand.'

'He's an odd chap. To tell you the truth, I don't much care for him. I don't like contortionists. He's by no means stupid; but he uses his intelligence for mere destruction; for that matter, it's against himself that he's the most ferocious; everything that's good in him, that's generous, or noble, or tender, he's ashamed of. He ought to go in for sport – take the air. Being shut up indoors all day is turning him sour. He seems to like my company. I don't avoid him; but I can't get accustomed to his cast of mind.'

'Don't you think that his sarcasm and his irony are the veil of excessive sensitiveness – and perhaps of great suffering? Olivier thinks so.'

'It may be. I have sometimes wondered. I don't know him well enough to say yet. The rest of my reflections are not ripe. I must think them over. I'll tell you about them – but later. This evening, forgive me if I leave you. I've got my examination in two days; and besides, I may as well own up to it . . . I'm feeling sad.'

5

OLIVIER MEETS BERNARD

Il ne faut prendre, si je ne me trompe, que la fleur de chaque objet. . . .

FÉNELON

OLIVIER, who had returned to Paris the day before, arose that morning fresh and rested. The air was warm, the sky pure. When he went out, after his shave and his shower-bath, elegantly dressed, conscious of his strength, his youth, his beauty, Passavant was still sleeping.

Olivier hastened to the Sorbonne. This was the morning that Bernard had to go up for his examination. How did Olivier know that? But perhaps he didn't know it. He was going to find out.

He quickened his step. He had not seen his friend since the night that Bernard came to take refuge in his room. What changes since then! Who knows whether he was not more anxious to show himself to his friend than to see him. A pity that Bernard cared so little about elegance. But it's a taste that sometimes comes with affluence. Olivier knew that by experience, thanks to the Comte de Passavant.

Bernard was doing his written examination this morning. He wouldn't be out before twelve. Olivier waited for him in the quadrangle. He recognized a few of his schoolfellows, shook a few hands. He felt slightly embarrassed by his clothes. He felt still more so when Bernard, free at last, came up to him in the quadrangle and exclaimed, with outstretched hand:

'Oh, dear! how lovely he is!'

Olivier, who *had* thought he would never blush again, blushed. He could not but feel the irony of these words, notwithstanding the cordiality of their tone. As for Bernard, he was still wearing the same suit he had on the evening of his flight. He had not been expecting to see Olivier. With his arm in his, he drew him along, questioning as they went. He felt a sudden shock of joy at seeing him. If at first he smiled a little at the refinement of his dress, it was with no malice; his heart was good; he was without bitterness.

'You'll lunch with me, won't you? Yes; I have got to go back at one-thirty for Latin. This morning it was French.'

'Pleased?'

'*I* am, yes; but I don't know whether the examiners will be. We had to discuss these lines from La Fontaine:

> ' "*Papillon du Parnasse, et semblable aux abeilles*
> *À qui le bon Platon compare nos merveilles,*
> *Je suis chose légére et vole à tout sujet,*
> *Je vais de fleur en fleur et d'objet en objet.*"

How would you have done it?'

Olivier could not resist a desire to shine:

'I should have said that La Fontaine, in painting himself, had painted the portrait of the artist – of the man who consents to take merely the outside of things, their surface, their bloom. Then I should have contrasted with that the portrait of the scholar, the seeker, the man who goes deep into things, and I should have shown that while the scholar seeks, the artist finds; that the man who goes deep, gets stuck, the man who gets stuck, gets sunk – up to his eyes and over them; that the truth is the appearance of things, that their secret is their form and that what is deepest in man is his skin.'

This last phrase Olivier had stolen from Passavant, who himself had gathered it from the lips of Paul-Ambroise, as he was discoursing one day in a lady's drawing-room. Everything that was not printed was fish for Passavant's net; what he called 'ideas in the air' – that is to say – other people's.

Something or other in Olivier's tone showed Bernard that this phrase was not his own. Olivier's voice did not seem at home in it. Bernard was on the point of asking: 'Whose?' But besides not wishing to hurt his friend, he was afraid of hearing Passavant's name, which up till now had not been pronounced. Bernard contented himself with giving his friend a searching look; and Olivier, for the second time, blushed.

Bernard's surprise at hearing the sentimental Olivier give

voice to ideas which were entirely different from those which he had once known him to have, immediately gave place to violent indignation; he was overwhelmed by something as sudden and surprising and irresistible as a cyclone. And it was not precisely against the ideas themselves that he was angry – though they struck him as absurd. And even perhaps, after all, they were not as absurd as all that. In his collection of contradictory opinions, he might have written them down on the page facing his own. Had they been genuinely Olivier's ideas, he would not have been angry either with him or with them; but he felt there was someone hidden behind them; it was with Passavant that he was angry.

'It's with ideas like those that France is being poisoned!' he cried in a muffled, vehement voice. He took a high stand. He wished to outsoar Passavant. And he was himself surprised at what he said – as if his words had preceded his thoughts; and yet it was these very thoughts he had developed that morning in his essay; but he felt shamefaced at expressing what he called 'fine sentiments', particularly when he was talking to Olivier. As soon as they were put into words, they seemed to him less sincere. So that Olivier had never heard his friend speak of the interests of 'France'; it was his turn to be surprised. He opened his eyes wide, without even thinking of smiling. Was it really Bernard? He repeated stupidly:

'France? . . .' Then, so as to disengage his responsibility – for Bernard was decidedly not joking:

'But, old boy, it isn't *I* who think so, it's La Fontaine.'

Bernard became almost aggressive:

'By Jove, I know well enough it isn't you who think so. But my dear fellow, it isn't La Fontaine either. If he had only had that lightness, which, for that matter, he regretted and apologized for at the end of his life, he would never have been the artist we admire. That's just what I said in my essay this morning, and I brought a great many quotations in support of my theory – for you know I've a fairly good memory. But I soon left La Fontaine, and taking as my text the justification these lines might afford to a certain class of superficial minds, I just let myself go in a tirade against the spirit of carelessness, of flippancy, of irony, of what is called "French wit", which some people think is the spirit of France, and which sometimes gives us such a deplorable reputation among foreigners. I said that we ought not to consider all this as even the smile of France, but as her grimace; that the real spirit of France was a spirit of investigation, of logic, of devotedness, of patient thoroughness; and if La Fontaine had not been animated by that spirit, he might have written his tales, but never his fables nor the admirable epistle (I showed that I knew it) from which the lines we had to comment upon were taken. Yes, old boy, a violent attack – perhaps I shall get ploughed for it. But I don't care two straws; I had to say it.'

Olivier had not particularly meant what he had said just before. He had yielded to his desire to be brilliant and to bring out, as it were carelessly, a sentence which he thought would tremendously impress his friend. But now that Bernard took it in this way, there was nothing for him to do but to beat a retreat. But his great weakness lay in the fact that he was in much more need of Bernard's affection than Bernard of his. Bernard's speech had humiliated, mortified him. He was vexed with himself for having spoken too soon. It was too late now to go back on it – to agree with Bernard, as he certainly would have done if he had let him speak first. But how could he have foreseen that Bernard, whom he remembered so scathingly subversive, would set up as a defender of feelings and ideas which Passavant had taught him could not be considered without a smile? But he really had no desire to smile now; he was ashamed. And as he could neither retract nor contradict Bernard, whose genuine emotion he couldn't help respecting, his one idea was to protect himself – to slip out of it.

'Oh! well, if you put that in your essay, it wasn't against me that you were saying it. . . . I'm glad of that.'

He spoke as though he were vexed – not at all in the tone he would have liked.

'But it *is* against you that I am saying it now,' retorted Bernard.

These words cut straight at Olivier's heart. Bernard had certainly not said them with a hostile intention, but how else could they be taken? Olivier was silent. Between Bernard and him a gulf was yawning. He tried to think of some question to fling from one side of the gulf to the other which might re-establish the contact. He tried, without much hope of succeeding. 'Doesn't he understand how miserable I am?' he said to himself, and he grew more miserable still. He did not have to force back his tears, perhaps, but he said to himself that it was enough to make anyone cry. It was his own fault, too; his meeting with Bernard would have seemed less sad if he had looked forward to it with less joy. When two months before he had hurried off to meet Edouard, it had been the same thing. It would always be the same thing, he said to himself. He wanted to go away – anywhere – by himself – to chuck Bernard – to forget Passavant. Edouard. . . . An unexpected meeting suddenly interrupted these melancholy thoughts.

A few steps in front of them, going up the boulevard Saint-Michel, along which he and Bernard were walking, Olivier caught sight of his young brother George. He seized Bernard's arm, and turning sharply on his heel, drew him hurriedly along with him.

'Do you think he saw us?... My people don't know I'm back.'

Young George was not alone. Léon Ghéridanisol and Philippe Adamanti were with him. The conversation of the three boys was exceedingly animated; but George's interest in it did not prevent him from keeping 'his eyes skinned', as he said. In order to listen to the children's talk, we will leave Olivier and Bernard for a moment; especially since our two friends have gone into a restaurant, and are for the moment more occupied in eating than in talking – to Olivier's great relief.

'Well then, *you* do it,' says Phiphi to George.

'Oh, he's got the dithers! He's got the dithers!' retorts George, putting what cold contempt he can into his voice, so as to goad Philippe to action. Then says Ghéridanisol with calm superiority:

'Look here, my lambs, if you aren't game, you had better say so at once. I shan't have any difficulty in finding fellows with a little more pluck than you. Here! Give it back!'

He turns to George, who is holding a small coin in his tight-shut hand.

'I'll do it!' cries George, in a sudden burst of courage. 'Won't I just! Come on!' (They are opposite a tobacco shop.)

'No,' says Léon; 'we'll wait for you at the corner. Come along, Phiphi.'

A moment later George comes out of the shop; he has a packet of so-called 'de luxe' cigarettes in his hand and offers them to his friends.

'Well?' asks Phiphi anxiously.

'Well, what?' replies George with an air of affected indifference, as if what he has just done has suddenly become so natural that it wasn't worth mentioning.

But Philippe insists:

'Did you pass it?'

'Good Lord! Didn't I?'

'And nobody said anything?'

George shrugged his shoulders:

'What on earth should they say?'

'And they gave you back the change?'

This time George doesn't even deign to answer. But as Philippe, still a little sceptical and fearful, insists again: 'Show us,' George pulls the money out of his pocket. Philippe counts – the seven francs are there right enough. He feels inclined to ask: 'Are you sure *they* aren't false too?' But he refrains.

George had given one franc for the false coin. It had been agreed that the money should be divided between them. He holds out three francs to Ghéridanisol. As for Phiphi, he shan't have a farthing; at the outside a cigarette; it'll be a lesson to him.

Encouraged by this first success, Phiphi is now anxious to try for himself. He asks Léon to sell him another coin. But Léon considers Phiphi a muff, and in order to screw him up to the right pitch, he affects contempt for his former cowardice and pretends to hold back. He had only to make up his mind sooner; they could very well do without him. Besides which, Léon thinks it imprudent to risk another attempt so close upon the first. And then it's too late now. His cousin Strouvilhou is expecting him to lunch.

Ghéridanisol is not such a duffer that he can't pass his false coins by himself; but his big cousin's instructions are that he is to get himself accomplices. He goes off now to give him an account of his successfully performed mission.

'The kids we want, you see, are those who come of good families, because then if rumours get about, their parents do all they can to stifle them.' (It is Cousin Strouvilhou who is talking in this way, while the two are having lunch together.) 'Only with this system of selling the coins one by one, they get put into circulation too slowly. I've got fifty-two boxes containing twenty coins each, to dispose of. They must be sold for twenty francs a box; but not to anyone, you understand. The best thing would be to form an association to which no one should be admitted who didn't furnish pledges. The kids must be made to compromise themselves, and hand over something or other which will give us a hold over their parents. Before letting them have the coins, they must be made to understand that – oh! without frightening them. One must never frighten children. You told me Molinier's father was a magistrate? Good. And Adamanti's father?'

'A senator.'

'Better still. You're old enough now to grasp that there's no family without some skeleton or other in the cupboard, which the people concerned are terrified of having discovered. The kids must be set hunting; it'll give them something to do. Family life as a rule is so boring! And then it'll teach them to observe, to look about them. It's quite simple. Those who contribute nothing will get nothing. When certain parents understand that they are in our hands, they'll pay a high price for our silence. What the deuce! we have no intention of blackmailing them; we are honest folk. We merely want to have a hold on them. Their silence for ours. Let them keep silent and make other people keep silent, and then we'll keep silent too. Here's a health to them!'

Strouvilhou filled two glasses. They drank to each other.

'It's a good – it's even an indispensable thing,' he went on, 'to create ties of reciprocity between citizens; by so doing societies are solidly established. We all hold together, good Lord! *We* have a hold on the children, who have a hold on their parents, who have a hold on us. A perfect arrangement. Twig?'

Léon twigged admirably. He chuckled.

'That little George...' he began.

'Well, what about him? That little George...?'

'Molinier. I think he's pretty well screwed up. He has laid his hands on some letters to his father from an Olympia chorus girl.'

'Have you seen them?'

'He showed them to me. I overheard him talking to Adamanti. I think they were pleased at my listening to them; at any rate, they didn't hide from me; I had already taken steps and treated them to a little entertainment in your style, to inspire them with confidence. George said to Phiphi (to give him a stunner): "My father's got a mistress." Upon which, Phiphi, not to be outdone, answered: "*My* father's got two." It was idiotic and really nothing to make a fuss about; but I went up to George and said: "How do you know?" I've seen some letters," he answered. I pretended I didn't believe him and said: "Rubbish!"... Well, I went on at him, until at last he said he had got them with him; he pulled them out of a big letter-case and showed them to me.'

'Did you read them?'

'I didn't have time to. I only saw they were all in the same handwriting; one of them began: "My darling old ducky."'

'And signed?'

'"Your little white mousie." I asked George how he had got hold of them. He grinned and pulled out of his trouser pocket an enormous bunch of keys.... "To fit every drawer in the universe," said he.'

'And what did Master Phiphi say?'

'Nothing. I think he was jealous.'

'Would George give you the letters?'

'If necessary I'll get him to. I don't want to take them from him. He'll give them if Phiphi joins in, too. They each of them egg the other on.'

'That's what goes by the name of emulation. And you don't see anyone else at the school?'

'I'll look about.'

'One thing more I wanted to say. . . . I think there must be a little boy called Boris amongst the boarders. You're to leave him alone'; he paused a moment and then added in a whisper: 'for the moment.'

Olivier and Bernard are seated at a table in one of the Boulevard restaurants. Olivier's unhappiness melts like hoar-frost in the warmth of his friend's smile. Bernard avoids pronouncing Passavant's name; Olivier feels it; a secret instinct warns him; but the name is on the tip of his tongue; he must speak, come what may.

'Yes; I didn't let my people know we were coming back so soon. This evening the *Argonauts* are giving a dinner. Passavant particularly wants me to be present. He wishes our new review to be on good terms with its elder and not to set up as a rival. . . . You ought to come; and I tell you what . . . you ought to bring Edouard. . . . Perhaps not to dinner, because one's got to be invited, but immediately after. It's to be in the upstairs room of the Taverne du Panthéon. The principal members of the *Argonaut* staff will be there and a good many of our own *Vanguard* contributors. Our first number is nearly ready; but, I say, why didn't you send me anything?'

'Because I hadn't anything ready,' he answers rather curtly.

Olivier's voice becomes almost imploring:

'I put your name down next to mine in the list of contents. . . . We could wait a little, if necessary . . . no matter what; anything. . . . You had almost promised.'

It grieves Bernard to hurt his friend; but he hardens himself:

'Look here, old boy, I had better tell you at once – I'm afraid I shouldn't hit it off with Passavant very well.'

'But it's I who am the editor. He leaves me perfectly free.'

'And then I dislike the idea of sending you *no matter what*; I don't want to write *no matter what*.'

'I said *no matter what*, because I knew that no matter what you wrote would be good . . . that it would never really be *no matter what*.'

He doesn't know what to say. He is just floundering. If he

cannot feel his friend beside him, all his interest in the review vanishes. It had been such a delightful dream, this of making their début together.

'And then, old fellow, if I'm beginning to know what I don't want to do, I don't know yet what I *do* want to do. I don't even know whether I shall write.'

This declaration fills Olivier with consternation. But Bernard goes on:

'Nothing that I could write easily tempts me. It's because I can turn my sentences easily that I have a detestation of well-turned sentences. Not that I like difficulty for its own sake; but I really do think that writers of the present time take things a bit too easy. I don't know enough about other people's lives to write a novel; and I haven't yet had a life of my own. Poetry bores me. The alexandrine is worn threadbare; the *vers libre* is formless. The only poet who satisfies me nowadays is Rimbaud.'

'That's exactly what I say in our manifesto.'

'Then it's not worth while my repeating it. No, old boy; no; I don't know whether I shall write. It sometimes seems to me that writing prevents one from living, and that one can express oneself better by acts than by words.'

'Works of art are acts that endure,' ventured Olivier timidly; but Bernard was not listening.

'That's what I admire most of all in Rimbaud – to have preferred life.'

'He made a mess of his own.'

'What do you know about it?'

'Oh! really, old boy! . . .'

'One can't judge other people's lives from the outside. But anyhow, let's grant he was a failure; with ill-luck, poverty, illness to bear. . . . Even so, I envy him his life; yes, I envy it more – even with its sordid ending – more than the life of . . .'

Bernard did not finish his sentence; on the point of naming an illustrious contemporary, he hesitated between too many of them. He shrugged his shoulders and went on:

'I have a confused feeling in myself of extraordinary aspirations, surgings, stirrings, incomprehensible agitations, which I don't want to understand – which I don't even want to observe, for fear of preventing them. Not so long ago, I was constantly talking to myself. Now, even if I wanted to, I shouldn't be able to. It was a mania that came to an end suddenly, without my even being aware of it. I think that this habit of soliloquizing – of inward dialogue, as our professor used to call it – necessitated a kind of division of the personality, which I ceased to be capable of, the day that I began to love someone else better than myself.'

'You mean Laura,' said Olivier. 'Do you still love her as much as ever?'

'No,' said Bernard; 'more than ever. I think it's the special quality of love not to be able to remain stationary, to be obliged to increase under pain of diminishing; and that's what distinguishes it from friendship.'

'Friendship, too, can grow less,' said Olivier sadly.

'I think that the margins of friendship aren't so wide.'

'I say . . . you won't be angry if I ask you something?'

'Try.'

'I don't want to make you angry.'

'If you keep your questions to yourself, you'll make me more angry still.'

'I want to know whether you feel . . . desire for Laura.'

Bernard suddenly became very grave.

'If it weren't you . . .' he began. 'Well, old boy, it's a curious thing that's happened to me: ever since I have come to know her, all my desires have gone; I have none left at all. You remember in the old days how I used to be all fire and flame for twenty women at once whom I happened to pass by in the street (and that's the very thing that prevented me from choosing any one of them); well, now it seems to me that I shall never be touched again by any other form of beauty than hers; that I shall never be able to love any other forehead than hers; her lips, her eyes. But what I feel for her is veneration; when I am with her every carnal thought seems an impiety. I think I was mistaken about myself, and that in reality I am very chaste by nature. Thanks to Laura, my instincts have been sublimated. I feel I have within me great unemployed forces. I should like to make them take up service. I envy the Carthusian who bends his pride to the rule of his order; the person to whom one says: "I count upon you." I envy the soldier. . . . Or, rather, no; I envy no one; but the turbulence I feel within me oppresses me and my aspiration is to discipline it. It's like steam inside me; it may whistle as it escapes (that's poetry), put in motion wheels and pistons; or even burst the engine. Do you know the act which I sometimes think would express me best? It's . . . Oh! I know well enough I shan't kill myself; but I understand Dmitri Karamazof perfectly when he asks his brother if he understands a person killing himself out of enthusiasm, out of sheer excess of life . . . just *bursting*.'

An extraordinary radiance shone from his whole being. How well he expressed himself! Olivier gazed at him in a kind of ecstasy.

'So do I,' he murmured timidly. 'I understand killing oneself too; but it would be after having tasted a joy so great, that all one's life to come would seem pale beside it; a joy so great, that it would make one feel: "I have had enough. I am content; never again shall I . . ."'

But Bernard was not listening. He stopped. What was the use of talking to empty air? All his sky clouded over again. Bernard took out his watch:

'I must be off. Well then, this evening, you say? . . . What time?'

'Oh, I should think ten would be early enough. Will you come?'

'Yes. I'll try to bring Edouard, too. But you know he doesn't much care for Passavant; and literary gatherings bore him. It would only be to see you. I say, can't we meet somewhere after my Latin paper?' Olivier did not immediately answer. He reflected with despair that he had promised to meet Passavant that afternoon at the printer's to talk over the printing of the *Vanguard*. What would he not have given to be free?

'I should like to, but I'm engaged.'

No trace of his unhappiness was apparent; and Bernard answered:

'Oh well, it doesn't matter.'

And at that the two friends parted.

Olivier had said nothing to Bernard of all he had meant and hoped to say. He was afraid Bernard had taken a dislike to him. He took a dislike to himself. He, so gay, so smart that morning, walked now with lowered head. Passavant's friendship, of which at first he had been so proud, began to be irksome to him; for he felt Bernard's reprobation weighing upon it. Even if he were to meet his friend at the dinner that evening, he would be unable to speak to him in front of all those people. He would be unable to enjoy the dinner if they had not come to an understanding beforehand. And what an unfortunate idea his vanity had suggested to him of trying to get Uncle Edouard to come too! There, in the presence of Passavant, surrounded by elder men, by other writers, by the future contributors to the *Vanguard*, he would be obliged to show off. Edouard would misjudge him still more – misjudge him no doubt irrevocably.... If only he could see him before this evening! ... see him at once; he would fling his arms round his neck; he would cry perhaps; he would tell all his troubles.... From now till four o'clock, he has the time. Quick! a taxi.

He gives the address to the chauffeur. He reaches the door with a beating heart; he rings.... Edouard is out.

Poor Olivier! Instead of hiding from his parents, why did he not simply return home? He would have found his Uncle Edouard sitting with his mother.

6

EDOUARD'S JOURNAL: MADAME MOLINIER

THOSE novelists deceive us who show the individual's development without taking into account the pressure of surroundings. The forest fashions the tree. To each one how small a place is given! How many buds are atrophied! One shoots one's branches where one can. The mystic bough is due more often than not to stifling. The only escape is upwards. I cannot understand how Pauline manages not to grow a mystic bough, nor what further pressure she needs. She has talked to me more intimately than ever before. I did not suspect, I confess, the amount of disillusionment and resignation she hides beneath the appearance of happiness. But I recognize that she would have had to have a very vulgar nature not to have been disappointed in Molinier. In my conversation with her the day before yesterday, I was able to gauge his limits. How in the world could Pauline have married him? . . . Alas! the most lamentable lack of all – lack of character – is a hidden one, to be revealed only by time and usage.

Pauline puts all her efforts into palliating Oscar's insufficiencies and weaknesses, into hiding them from everyone; and especially from his children. Her utmost ingenuity is employed in enabling them to respect their father; and she is really hard put to it; but she does it in such a way that I myself was deceived. She speaks of her husband without contempt, but with a kind of indulgence which is expressive enough. She deplored his want of authority over the boys; and, as I expressed my regrets at Olivier's being with Passavant, I understood that if it had depended on her, the trip to Corsica would not have taken place.

'I didn't approve of it,' she said, 'and to tell you the truth, I don't much care about that Monsieur Passavant. But what could I do? When I see that I can't prevent a thing, I prefer granting it with a good grace. As for Oscar, he always gives in; he gives in to me, too. But when I think it's my duty to oppose any plan of the children's – stand out against them in any way, he never supports me in the least. On this occasion Vincent stepped in as well. After that, how could I oppose Olivier without risking the loss of his confidence? And it's that I care about most.'

She was darning old socks – the socks, I said to myself, which were no longer good enough for Olivier. She stopped to thread her needle, and then went on again in a lower voice, more confidingly and more sadly:

'His confidence.... If I were only sure I still had it. But no; I've lost it....'

The protest I attempted – without conviction – made her smile. She dropped her work and went on:

'For instance, I know he is in Paris. George met him this morning; he mentioned it casually, and I pretended not to hear, for I don't like him to tell tales about his brother. But still I know it. Olivier hides things from me. When I see him again, he will think himself obliged to lie to me, and I shall pretend to believe him, as I pretend to believe his father every time *he* hides things from me.'

'It's for fear of paining you.'

'He pains me a great deal more as it is. I am not intolerant. There are a number of little short-comings that I tolerate, that I shut my eyes to.'

'Of whom are you talking now?'

'Oh! of the father as well as the sons.'

'When you pretend not to see them, *you* are lying too.'

'But what am I to do? It's enough not to complain. I really can't approve! No, I say to myself that, sooner or later, one loses hold, that the tenderest affection is helpless. More than that. It's in the way; it's a nuisance. I have come to the pitch of hiding my love itself.'

'Now you are talking of your sons.'

'Why do you say that? Do you mean that I can't love Oscar any more? Sometimes I think so, but I think too that it's for fear of suffering too much that I don't love him more. And... Yes, I suppose you are right – in Olivier's case, I prefer to suffer.'

'And Vincent?'

'A few years ago everything I now say of Olivier would have been true of Vincent.'

'My poor friend. . . . Soon you will be saying the same of George.'

'But one becomes resigned, slowly. And yet one didn't ask so much of life. One learns to ask less . . . less and less.' Then she added softly: 'And of oneself, more and more.'

'With ideas of that kind, one is almost a Christian,' said I, smiling in my turn.

'I sometimes think so too. But having them isn't enough to make one a Christian.'

'Any more than being a Christian is enough to make one have them.'

'I have often thought – will you let me say so? – that in their father's default, *you* might speak to the boys.'

'Vincent is not here.'

'It is too late for him. I am thinking of Olivier. It's with you that I should have liked him to go away.'

At these words, which gave me the sudden imagination of what might have been if I had not so thoughtlessly listened to the appeal of passing adventure, a dreadful emotion wrung my heart, and at first I could find nothing to say; then, as the tears started to my eyes, and wishing to give some appearance of a motive to my disturbance:

'Too late, I fear, for him, too,' I sighed.

Pauline seized my hand:

'How good you are!' she cried.

Embarrassed at seeing her thus mistake me, and unable to undeceive her, I could only turn aside the conversation from a subject which put me too ill at my ease.

'And George?' I asked.

'He makes me more anxious than the other two put together,' she answered. 'I can't say that with him I am losing my hold, for he has never been either confiding or obedient.'

She hesitated a few moments. It obviously cost her a great deal to say what follows.

'This summer something very serious happened,' she went on at last, 'something it's a little painful for me to speak to you about, especially as I am still not very sure. . . . A hundred-franc note disappeared from a cupboard in which I was in the habit of keeping my money. The fear of being wrong in my suspicions prevented me from bringing any accusation; the maid who waited on us at the hotel was a very young girl and seemed to me honest. I said I had lost the note before George; I might as well admit that my suspicions fell upon him. He didn't appear disturbed; he didn't blush. . . . I felt ashamed of having suspected him; I tried to persuade myself I had made a mistake. I did my accounts over again; unfortunately there was no possibility of a doubt – a hundred francs were missing. I shrank from questioning him, and finally I didn't. The fear of seeing him add a lie to a theft kept me back. Was I wrong? . . . Yes, I reproach myself now for not having insisted; perhaps it was out of a fear that I should have to be too severe – or that I shouldn't be severe enough. Once again, I played the part of a person who knows nothing, but with a very anxious heart, I assure you. I had let the time go by, and I said to myself it was too late and that the punishment would come too long after the fault. And how punish him? I did nothing; I reproach myself for it . . . but what could I have done?

'I had thought of sending him to England; I even wanted to ask your advice about it, but I didn't know where you were. . . . At any rate, I didn't hide my trouble from him – my anxiety; I think he must have felt it, for, you know, he has a good heart. I count more on his own conscience to reproach him than on anything I could have said. He won't do it again, I feel certain. He used to go about with a very rich boy at the seaside, and he was no doubt led on to spend money. No doubt I must have left the cupboard open; and I repeat, I'm not really sure it was he. There were a great many people coming and going in the hotel. . . . .'

I admired the ingenious way in which she put forward every possible consideration that might exonerate her child.

'I should have liked him to put the money back,' I said.

'I hoped he would. And when he didn't, I thought it must be a proof of his innocence. And then I said to myself that he was afraid to.'

'Did you tell his father?'

She hesitated a few moments:

'No,' she said at last, 'I prefer him to know nothing about it.'

No doubt she thought she heard a noise in the next room; she went to make sure there was no one there; then she sat down again beside me.

'Oscar told me you lunched together the other day. He was so loud in your praise, that I suppose what you chiefly did was to listen to him.' (She smiled sadly, as she said these words.) 'If he confided in you, I have no desire not to respect his confidences . . . though in reality I know a great deal more about his private life than he imagines. But since I got back, I can't understand what has come over him. He is so gentle – I was almost going to say – so humble. . . . It's almost embarrassing. He goes on as if he were afraid of me. He needn't be. For a long time past I've been aware that he has been carrying on. . . . I even know with whom. He thinks I know nothing about it and takes enormous pains to hide it; but his precautions are so obvious, that the more he hides, the more he gives himself away. Every time he goes out with an affectation of being busy, worried, anxious, I know that he is off to his pleasure. I feel inclined to say to him: "But, my dear friend, I'm not keeping you; are you afraid I'm jealous?" I should laugh if I had the heart to. My only fear is that the children may notice something; he's so careless – so clumsy! Sometimes, without his suspecting it, I find myself forced to help him, as if I were playing his game. I assure you I end by being almost amused by it; I invent excuses for him; I put the letters he leaves lying about back in his coat pocket.'

'That's just it,' I said; 'he's afraid you have discovered some letters.'

'Did he tell you so?'

'And that's what's making him so nervous.'

'Do you think I want to read them?'

A kind of wounded pride made her draw herself up; I was obliged to add:

'It's not a question of the letters he may have mislaid inadvertently; but of some letters he had put in a drawer and which he says he can't find. He thinks you have taken them.'

At these words, I saw Pauline turn pale, and the horrible suspicion which darted upon her, forced itself suddenly into my mind too. I regretted having spoken, but it was too late. She looked away from me and murmured:

'Would to Heaven it *were* I!'

She seemed overcome.

'What am I to do?' she repeated. 'What am I to do?' Then raising her eyes to mine again: 'You? Couldn't *you* speak to him?'

Although she avoided, as I did, pronouncing George's name it was clear that she was thinking of him.

'I will try. I will think it over,' I said, rising. And as she accompanied me to the front door:

'Say nothing about it to Oscar, please. Let him go on suspecting me – thinking what he thinks. . . . It is better so. Come and see me again.'

7

OLIVIER AND ARMAND

IN the meantime, Olivier, deeply disappointed at not having found his Uncle Edouard, and unable to bear his solitude, turned his thoughts towards Armand with a heart aching for friendship. He made his way to the Pension Vedel.

Armand received him in his bedroom. It was a small, narrow room, reached by the backstairs. Its window looked on to an inner courtyard, on to which the water-closets and kitchens of the next-door house opened also. The light came from a corrugated zinc reflector, which caught it from above and cast it down, pallid, leaden and dreary. The room was badly ventilated; an unpleasant odour pervaded it.

'But one gets accustomed to it,' said Armand. 'My parents, you understand, keep the best rooms for the boarders who pay best. It's only natural. I have given up the room I had last year to a Vicomte – the brother of your illustrious friend Passavant. A princely room – but under the observation of Rachel's. There are heaps of rooms here, but not all of them are independent. For instance, poor Sarah, who came back from England this morning, is obliged to pass, either through our parents' room (which doesn't suit her at all) to get to her new abode, or else through mine, which, truth to tell, is really nothing but a dressing-room or box-room. At any rate, I have the advantage here of being able to go out and in as I please, without being spied upon by anyone. I prefer that to the attics, where the servants live. To tell the truth, I rather like being uncomfortably lodged; my father would call it the "love of maceration", and would explain that what is hurtful to the body leads to the salvation of the soul. For that matter, he has never been inside the place. He has other things to do, you understand, than worrying over his son's habitat. My papa's a wonderful fellow. He has by heart a number of consoling phrases for the principal events of life. It's magnificent to hear him. A pity he never has any time for a little chat. . . . You're looking at my picture gallery; one can enjoy it better in the morning. That is a colour print by a pupil of Paolo Ucello's – for the use of veterinaries. In an admirable attempt at synthesis, the artist has concentrated on a single horse all the ills by means of which Providence chastens the equine soul; you observe the spirituality of the look. . . . That is a symbolical picture of the ages of life from the cradle to the grave. As a drawing, not much can be said for it; its chief value lies in its intention. Further on you will note with admiration the photograph of one of Titian's courtesans, which I have put over my bed in order to give myself libidinous thoughts. That is the door into Sarah's room.'

The almost sordid aspect of the place made a melancholy impression on Olivier; the bed was not made and the basin on the wash-stand was not emptied.

'Yes, I fix up my room myself,' said Armand, in response to his anxious look. 'Here, you see, is my writing table. You have no idea how the atmosphere of the room inspires me. . . . "*L'atmosphère d'un cher réduit*. . . ." I even owe it the idea of my last poem – *The Nocturnal Vase*.'

Olivier had come to see Armand with the intention of speaking about his review and asking him to contribute to it; he no longer dared to. But Armand's own conversation was coming round to the subject.

'*The Nocturnal Vase* – eh? What a magnificent title! . . . With this motto from Baudelaire:

'" Funereal vase, what tears awaitest thou?" * BAUDELAIRE

'I take up once more the ancient (and ever young) comparison of the potter creator, who fashions every human being as a vase destined to hold – ah! what? And I compare myself in a lyrical outburst to the above-mentioned vase – an idea which, as I was telling you, came to me as the natural result of breathing the odour of this chamber. I am particularly pleased with the opening line:

'"Whoe'er at forty boasts no haemorrhoids . . ."

* *Es-tu vase funèbre attendant quelques pleurs?*

I had first of all written, in order to reassure the reader, "Whoe'er at fifty ..." but I should have missed the assonance. As for "haemorrhoids" it is undoubtedly the finest word in the French language – independently of its meaning,' he added with a saturnine laugh.

Olivier, a pain at his heart, kept silent. Armand went on:

'Needless to say, the night vase is particularly flattered when it receives a visit from a pot filled with aromatics like yourself.'

'And haven't you written anything but that?' asked Olivier at last, desperately.

'I was going to offer my *Nocturnal Vase* to your great and glorious review, but from the tone in which you have just said "*that*," I see there isn't much likelihood of its pleasing you. In such cases the poet always has the resource of arguing: "I don't write to please," and of persuading himself that he has brought forth a masterpiece. But I cannot conceal from you that I consider my poem execrably bad. For that matter, I have so far only written the first line. And when I say *written*, it's a figure of speech, for I have this very moment composed it in your honour. ... No, really? were you thinking of publishing something of mine? You actually desired my collaboration? You judged me, then, not incapable of writing something decent? Can you have discerned on my pale brow the revealing stigmata of genius? I know the light here is not very favourable for looking at oneself in the glass, but when – like another Narcissus – I gaze at my reflection, I can see nothing but the features of a failure. After all, perhaps it's an effect of chiaroscuro. ... No, my dear Olivier, no; I have done nothing this summer, and if you are counting on me for your review, you may go to blazes. But that's enough about me. ... Did all go well in Corsica? Did you enjoy your trip? Did it do you good? Did you rest after your labours? Did you ...'

Olivier could bear it no longer:

'Oh! do shut up, old boy. Stop playing the ass. If you imagine I think it's funny ...'

'And what about me?' cried Armand. 'No, my dear fellow, no; all the same I'm not so stupid as all that. I've still intelligence enough to understand that everything I've been saying is idiotic.'

'Can't you ever talk seriously?'

'Very well; we'll talk seriously, since seriousness is the style you favour. Rachel, my eldest sister, is going blind. Her sight has been getting very bad lately. For the last two years, she hasn't been able to read without glasses. I thought at first it would be all right if she were to change them. But it wasn't. At my request, she went to see an oculist. It seems the sensitiveness of the retina is failing. You understand there are two very different things – on the one hand, a defective power of accomodation of the crystalline, which can be remedied by glasses. But even after they have brought the visual image to the proper focus, that image may make an insufficient impression on the retina and be only dimly transmitted to the brain. Do I make myself clear? You hardly know Rachel, so don't imagine that I am trying to arouse your pity for her. Then why am I telling you all this? . . . Because, reflecting on my own case, I became aware that not only images but ideas may strike the brain with more or less clearness. A person with a dull mind receives only confused perceptions; but for that very reason he cannot realize clearly that he is dull. He would only begin to suffer from his stupidity if he were conscious of it; and in order to be conscious of it, he would have to become intelligent. Now imagine for a moment such a monster – an imbecile who is intelligent enough to understand that he is stupid.'

'Why, he would cease to be an imbecile.'

'No, my dear fellow; you may believe me, because as a matter of fact, *I* am that very imbecile.'

Olivier shrugged his shoulders. Armand went on:

'A real imbecile has no consciousness of any idea beyond his own. *I* am conscious of the *beyond*. But all the same I'm an imbecile, because I know that I shall never be able to attain that "*beyond*"! . . .'

'But, old fellow,' said Olivier, in a burst of sympathy, 'we are all made so that we might be better, and I think the greatest intelligence is precisely the one that suffers most from its own limitations.'

Armand shook off the hand that Olivier had placed affectionately on his arm.

'Others,' said he, 'have the feeling of what they possess; I have only the feeling of what I lack. Lack of money, lack of strength, lack of intelligence, lack of love – an everlasting deficit. I shall never be anything but below the mark.'

He went up to the toilette table, dipped a hairbrush in the dirty water in the basin and plastered his hair down in hideous fashion over his forehead.

'I told you I hadn't written anything; but a few days ago, I did have an idea for an essay, which I should have called: *On Incapacity*. But of course I was incapable of writing it. I should have said . . . But I'm boring you.'

'No; go on; you bore me when you make jokes; you're interesting me very much now.'

'I should have tried to find throughout nature the dividing line, below which nothing exists. An example will show you what I mean. The newspapers the other day had an account of a workman who was electrocuted. He was handling some live wires carelessly; the voltage was not very high; but it seems his body was in a state of perspiration. His death is attributed to the layer of humidity which enabled the current to envelop his body. If his body had been drier, the accident wouldn't have taken place. But now let's imagine the perspiration added drop by drop. . . . One more drop – there you are!'

'I don't understand,' said Olivier.

'Because my example is badly chosen. I always choose my examples badly. Here's another: Six shipwrecked persons are picked up in a boat. They have been adrift for ten days in the storm. Three are dead; two are saved. The sixth is expiring. It was hoped he might be restored to life; but his organism had reached the extreme limit.'

'Yes, I understand,' said Olivier. 'An hour sooner and he might have been saved.'

'An hour! How you go it! I am calculating the extremest point. It is possible. It is still possible. . . . It is no longer possible! My mind walks along that narrow ridge. That dividing line between existence and non-existence is the one I keep trying to trace everywhere. The limit of resistance to – well, for instance, to what my father would call temptation. One holds out; the cord on which the devil pulls is stretched to breaking. ... A tiny bit more, the cord snaps – one is damned. Do you understand now? A tiny bit less – non-existence. God would not have created the world. Nothing would have been. "The face of the world would have been changed," says Pascal. But it's not enough for me to think – "if Cleopatra's nose had been shorter." I insist. I ask: shorter, by how much? For it might have been a tiny bit shorter, mightn't it? ... Gradation; gradation; and then a sudden leap. ... *Natura non fecit saltus.* What absurd rubbish! As for me, I am like the Arab in the desert who is dying of thirst. I am at that precise point, you see, when a drop of water might still save him ... or a tear. ...'

His voice trailed away; there had come into it a note of pathos which surprised Olivier and disturbed him. He went on more gently – almost tenderly:

'You remember: "I shed that very tear for thee ..."'

Olivier remembered Pascal's words; he was even a little put out that his friend had not quoted them exactly. He could not refrain from correcting: '"I shed that very drop of blood for thee ..."'

Armand's emotion dropped at once. He shrugged his shoulders:

'What can we do? There are some who get through with more than enough and to spare. ... Do you understand now what it is to feel that one is always "on the border line"? As for me, I shall always have one mark too little.'

He had begun to laugh again. Olivier thought that it was for fear of crying. He would have liked to speak in his turn, to tell Armand how much his words had moved him, and how he felt all the sickness of heart that lay beneath his exasperating irony. But the time for his rendezvous with Passavant was pressing him; he pulled out his watch.

'I must go now. Are you free this evening?'

'What for?'

'To come and meet me at the Taverne du Panthéon. The *Argonauts* are giving a dinner. You might look in afterwards.

There'll be a lot of fellows there – some of them more or less well known – and most of them rather drunk. Bernard Profitendieu has promised to come. It might be funny.'

'I'm not shaved,' said Armand a little crossly. 'And then what should I do among a lot of celebrities? But, I say – why don't you ask Sarah? She got back from England this very morning. I'm sure it would amuse her. Shall I invite her from you? Bernard could take her.'

'All right, old chap,' said Olivier.

8

THE *ARGONAUTS'* DINNER

IT had been agreed then that Bernard and Edouard, after having dined together, should pick up Sarah a little before ten o'clock. She had delightedly accepted the proposal passed on to her by Armand. At about half past nine, she had gone up to her bedroom, accompanied by her mother. She had to pass through her parents' room in order to reach hers; but another door, which was supposed to be kept shut, led from Sarah's room to Armand's, which in its turn opened, as we have seen, on to the backstairs.

Sarah, in her mother's presence, made as though she were going to bed, and asked to be left to go to sleep; but as soon as she was alone, she went up to her dressing-table to put an added touch of brilliancy to her lips and cheeks. The toilette table had been placed in front of the closed door, but it was not too heavy for Sarah to lift noiselessly. She opened the door.

Sarah was afraid of meeting her brother, whose sarcasms she dreaded. Armand, it is true, encouraged her most audacious exploits; it was as though he took pleasure in them – but only with a kind of temporary indulgence, for it was to judge them later on with all the greater severity; so that Sarah wondered whether his complaisance itself was not calculated to play the censor's game.

Armand's room was empty. Sarah sat down on a little low chair and, as she was waiting, meditated. She cultivated a facile contempt for all the domestic virtues as a kind of preventive protest. The constraint of family life had intensified her energies and exasperated her instinct for revolt. During her stay in England, she had worked herself up into a white heat of courage. Like Miss Aberdeen, the English girl boarder, she was resolved to conquer her liberty, to grant herself every licence, to dare all. She felt ready to affront scorn and blame on every side, capable of every defiance. In the advances she had made to Olivier, she had already triumphed over natural modesty and many an instinctive reluctance. The example of her two sisters had taught her her lesson; she looked upon Rachel's pious resignation as the delusion of a dupe, and saw in Laura's marriage nothing but a lugubrious barter with slavery as its upshot. The education she had received, that which she had given herself, that which she had taken, inclined her very little to what she called 'conjugal piety'. She did not see in what particular the man she might marry could be her superior. Hadn't she passed her examinations like a man? Hadn't she her opinions and ideas on any and every subject? On the equality of the sexes in particular; and it even seemed to her that in the conduct of life, and consequently of business, and even, if need were, of politics, women often gave proof of more sense than many men....

Steps on the staircase. She listened and then opened the door gently.

Bernard and Sarah had never met. There was no light in the passage. They could hardly distinguish each other in the dark.

'Mademoiselle Sarah Vedel?' whispered Bernard. She took his arm without more ado.

'Edouard is waiting for us at the corner of the street in a taxi. He didn't want to get down for fear of meeting your parents. It didn't matter for me; you know I am staying in the house.'

Bernard had been careful to leave the door into the street ajar, so as not to attract the porter's attention. A few minutes later, the taxi deposited them all three in front of the Taverne du Panthéon. As Edouard was paying the taxi, they heard a clock strike ten.

Dinner was finished. The table had been cleared, but it was still covered with coffee-cups, bottles and glasses. Everyone was smoking and the atmosphere was stifling. Madame des Brousses, the wife of the editor of the *Argonauts*, called for fresh air in a strident voice, which rang out shrilly above the hum of general talk. Someone opened a window. But Justinien, who wanted to put in a speech, had it shut almost immediately 'for acoustics' sake'. He rose to his feet and struck on his glass with a spoon, but failed to attract anyone's attention. The editor of the *Argonauts*, whom people called the Président des Brousses, interposed, and having at last succeeded in obtaining a modicum of silence, Justinien's voice gushed forth in a copious stream of dullness. A flood of metaphors covered the triteness of his ideas. He spoke with an emphasis which took the place of wit, and managed to ladle out to everyone in turn a handsome helping of grandiloquent flummery. At the first pause, and just as Edouard, Bernard and Sarah were making their entry, there was a loud burst of polite applause. Some of the company prolonged it, no doubt a little ironically, and as if hoping to put an end to the speech; but in vain – Justinien started off afresh; nothing could daunt his eloquence. At that moment it was the Comte de Passavant whom he was bestrewing with the flowers of his rhetoric. He spoke of *The Horizontal Bar* as of another *Iliad*. Passavant's health was drunk. Edouard had no glass, neither had Bernard nor Sarah, so that they were dispensed from joining in the toast.

Justinien's speech ended with a few heartfelt wishes for the prosperity of the new review and a few elegant compliments to its future editor – 'the young and gifted Molinier – the darling of the Muses, whose pure and lofty brow would not long have to wait for its crown of laurels.'

Olivier was standing near the door, so as to welcome his friends as soon as they should arrive. Justinien's blatant compliments obviously embarrassed him, but he was obliged to respond to the little ovation which followed them.

The three new arrivals had dined too soberly to feel in tune with the rest of the assembly. In this sort of gathering, late-comers understand ill – or only too well – the others' excitement. They judge, when they have no business to judge, and exercise, even though involuntarily, a criticism which is without indulgence; this was the case at any rate with Edouard and Bernard. As for Sarah, in this milieu, everything was new to her; her one idea was to learn what she could, her one anxiety to be up to the mark.

Bernard knew no one. Olivier, who had taken him by the arm, wanted to introduce him to Passavant and des Brousses. He refused. Passavant, however, forced the situation by coming up to him and holding out a hand, which he could not in decency refuse:

'I have heard you spoken of so often that I feel as if I knew you already.'

'The same with me,' said Bernard in such a tone that Passavant's amenity froze. He at once turned to Edouard.

Though often abroad travelling, and keeping, even when he was in Paris, a great deal to himself, Edouard was nevertheless acquainted with several of the guests and feeling perfectly at his ease. Little liked, but at the same time esteemed, by his *confrères*, he did not object to being thought proud, when, in reality, he was only distant. He was more willing to listen than to speak.

'From what your nephew said, I was hoping you would come tonight,' began Passavant in a gentle voice that was almost a whisper. 'I was delighted because...'

Edouard's ironical look cut short the rest of his sentence. Skilful in the arts of pleasing and accustomed to please, Passavant, in order to shine, had need to feel himself confronted by a flattering mirror. He collected himself, however, for he was not the man to lose his self-possession for long or to let himself be easily snubbed. He raised his head, and his eyes were charged with insolence. If Edouard would not follow his lead with a good grace, he would find means to worst him.

'I was wanting to ask you...' he went on, as if he were continuing his first remark, 'whether you had any news of your other nephew, Vincent? It was he who was my special friend.'

'No,' said Edouard dryly.

This 'no' upset Passavant once more; he did not know whether to take it as a provocative contradiction, or as a simple answer to his question. His disturbance lasted only a second; it was Edouard who unintentionally restored him to his balance by adding almost at once:

'I have merely heard from his father that he was travelling with the Prince of Monaco.'

'Yes, I asked a lady, who is a friend of mine, to introduce him to the Prince. I was glad to hit upon this diversion to distract him a little from his unlucky affair with that Madame Douviers.

. . . You know her, so Olivier told me. He was in danger of wrecking his whole life over it.'

Passavant handled disdain, contempt, condescension with marvellous skill; but he was satisfied with having won this bout and with keeping Edouard at sword's length. Edouard indeed was racking his brains for some cutting answer. He was singularly lacking in presence of mind. That was no doubt the reason he cared so little for society – he had none of the qualities which are necessary to shine in it. His eyebrows however began to look frowningly. Passavant was quick to notice; when anything disagreeable was coming to him, he sniffed it in the air, and veered about. Without even stopping to take breath, and with a sudden change of tone:

'But who is that delightful girl who is with you?' he asked smiling.

'It is Mademoiselle Sarah Vedel, the sister of the very lady you were mentioning – my friend Madame Douviers.'

In default of any better repartee, he sharpened the words 'my friend' like an arrow – but an arrow which fell short, and Passavant, letting it lie, went on:

'It would be very kind of you to introduce me.'

He had said these last words and the sentence which preceded them loud enough for Sarah to hear, and as she turned towards them, Edouard was unable to escape:

'Sarah, the Comte de Passavant desires the honour of your acquaintance,' said he with a forced smile.

Passavant had sent for three fresh glasses, which he filled with kümmel. They all four drank Olivier's health. The bottle was almost empty, and as Sarah was astonished to see the crystals remaining at the bottom, Passavant tried to dislodge them with a straw. A strange kind of clown, with a befloured face, a black beady eye, and hair plastered down on his head like a skull-cap, came up.

'You won't do it,' he said, munching out each one of his syllables with an effort which was obviously assumed. 'Pass me the bottle. I'll smash it.'

He seized it, broke it with a blow against the window ledge, and presenting the bottom of the bottle to Sarah:

'With a few of these little sharp-edged polyhedra, the charming young lady will easily induce a perforation of her gizzard.'

'Who is that pierrot?' she asked Passavant, who had made her sit down and was sitting beside her.

'It's Alfred Jarry, the author of *Ubu Roi*. The *Argonauts* have dubbed him a genius because the public have just damned his play. All the same, it's the most interesting thing that's been put on the stage for a long time.'

'I like *Ubu Roi* very much,' said Sarah, 'and I'm delighted to see Jarry. I had heard he was always drunk.'

'I should think he must be tonight. I saw him drink two glasses of neat absinthe at dinner. He doesn't seem any the worse for it. Won't you have a cigarette? One has to smoke oneself so as not to be smothered by the other people's smoke.'

He bent towards her to give her a light. She crunched a few of the crystals.

'Why! it's nothing but sugar-candy,' said she, a little disappointed. 'I hoped it was going to be something strong.'

All the time she was talking to Passavant, she kept smiling at Bernard, who had stayed beside her. Her dancing eyes shone with an extraordinary brightness. Bernard, who had not been able to see her before because of the dark, was struck by her likeness to Laura. The same forehead, the same lips.... In her features, it is true, there breathed a less angelic grace, and her looks stirred he knew not what troubled depths in his heart. Feeling a little uncomfortable, he turned to Olivier:

'Introduce me to your friend Bercail.'

He had already met Bercail in the Luxembourg, but he had never spoken to him. Bercail was feeling rather out of it in this milieu into which Olivier had introduced him, and which he was too timid not to find distasteful, and every time Olivier presented him as one of the chief contributors to the *Vanguard* he blushed. The fact is, that the allegorical poem of which he had spoken to Olivier at the beginning of our story, was to appear on the first page of the new review, immediately after the manifesto.

'In the place I had kept for you,' said Olivier to Bernard. 'I'm sure you'll like it. It's by far the best thing in the number. And so original!'

Olivier took more pleasure in praising his friends than in hearing himself praised. At Bernard's approach, Bercail rose; he was holding his cup of coffee in his hand so awkwardly that in his agitation he spilled half of it down his waistcoat. At that moment, Jarry's mechanical voice was heard close at hand:

'Little Bercail will be poisoned. I've put poison in his cup.'

Bercail's timidity amused Jarry, and he liked putting him out of countenance. But Bercail was not afraid of Jarry. He shrugged his shoulders and finished his coffee calmly.

'Who is that?' asked Bernard.

'What! Don't you know the author of *Ubu Roi*?'

'Not possible! *That* Jarry? I took him for a servant.'

'Oh, all the same,' said Olivier, a little vexed, for he took a pride in his great men. 'Look at him more carefully. Don't you think he's extraordinary?'

'He does all he can to appear so,' said Bernard, who only esteemed what was natural, and who nevertheless was full of consideration for *Ubu*.

Everything about Jarry, who was got up to look like the traditional circus clown, smacked of affectation – his way of talking in particular; several of the *Argonauts* did their utmost to imitate it, snapping out their syllables, inventing odd words, and oddly mangling others; but it was only Jarry who could succeed in producing that toneless voice of his – a voice without warmth or intonation, or accent or emphasis.

'When one knows him, he is charming, really,' went on Olivier.

'I prefer not to know him. He looks ferocious.'

'Oh, that's just the way he has. Passavant thinks that in reality he is the kindest of creatures. But he has drunk a terrible lot tonight; and not a drop of water, you may be sure – nor even of wine; nothing but absinthe and spirits. Passavant's afraid he may do something eccentric.'

In spite of himself, Passavant's name kept recurring to his lips, and all the more obstinately that he wanted to avoid it.

Exasperated at feeling so little able to control himself, and as if he were trying to escape from his own pursuit, he changed his ground:

'You should talk to Dhurmer a little. I'm afraid he bears me a deadly grudge for having stepped into his shoes at the *Vanguard*; but it really wasn't my fault; I simply had to accept. You might try and make him see it and calm him down a bit. Pass . . . I'm told he's fearfully worked up against me.'

He had tripped, but this time he had not fallen.

'I hope he has taken his copy with him. I don't like what he writes,' said Bercail; then turning to Bernard: 'But, you, Monsieur Profitendieu, I thought that you . . .'

'Oh, please don't call me Monsieur . . . I know I've got a ridiculous mouthful of a name . . . I mean to take a pseudonym, if I write.'

'Why haven't you contributed anything?'

'Because I hadn't anything ready.'

Olivier, leaving his two friends to talk together, went up to Edouard.

'How nice of you to come! I was longing to see you again. But I would rather have met you anywhere but here. . . . This afternoon, I went and rang at your door. Did they tell you? I was so sorry not to find you; if I had known where you were . . .'

He was quite pleased to be able to express himself so easily, remembering a time when his emotion in Edouard's presence kept him dumb. This ease of his was due, alas! to his potations and to the banality of his words.

Edouard realized it sadly.

'I was at your mother's.' (And for the first time he said 'you' to Olivier instead of 'thou'.)

'Were you?' said Olivier, who was in a state of consternation at Edouard's style of address. He hesitated whether he should not tell him so.

'Is it in this milieu that you mean to live for the future?' asked Edouard, looking at him fixedly.

'Oh, I don't let it encroach on me.'

'Are you quite sure of that?'

These words were said in so grave, so tender, so fraternal a tone . . . Olivier felt his self-assurance tottering within him.

'You think I am wrong to frequent these people?'

'Not all of them, perhaps; but certainly some.'

Olivier took this as a direct allusion to Passavant, and in his inward sky, a flash of blinding, painful light shot through the bank of clouds which ever since the morning had been thickening and darkening in his heart. He loved Bernard, he loved Edouard far too well to bear the loss of their esteem. Edouard's presence exalted all that was best in him; Passavant's all that was worst; he acknowledged it now; and indeed, had he not always known it? Had not his blindness as regards Passavant been deliberate? His gratitude for all that the count had done for him turned to loathing. With his whole soul, he cast him off. What he now saw put the finishing touch to his hatred.

Passavant, leaning towards Sarah, had passed his arm round her waist and was becoming more and more pressing. Aware of the unpleasant rumours which were rife concerning his relations with Olivier, he thought he would give them the lie, and to make his behaviour more public, he had determined to get Sarah to sit on his knees. Sarah had so far put up very little defence, but her eyes sought Bernard's, and when they met them, her smile seemed to say:

'See how far a person may go with me!'

But Passavant was afraid of overdoing it; he was lacking in experience.

'If I can only get her to drink a little more, I'll risk it,' he said to himself, putting out his free hand towards a bottle of curaçao.

Olivier, who was watching him, was beforehand with him; he snatched up the bottle, simply to prevent Passavant from getting it; but as soon as he took hold of it, it seemed to him that the liqueur would restore him a little of his courage – the courage he felt failing within him – the courage he needed to utter, loud enough for Edouard to hear, the complaint that was trembling on his lips:

'If only you had chosen...'

Olivier filled his glass and emptied it at a draught. Just at that moment, he heard Jarry, who was moving about from group to group, say in a half-whisper, as he passed behind Bercail:

'And now we're going to ki-kill little Bercail.'

Bercail turned round sharply:

'Just say that again out loud.'

Jarry had already moved away. He waited until he had got round the table and then repeated in a falsetto voice:

'And now we're going to ki-kill little Bercail'; then, taking out of his pocket a large pistol, with which the *Argonauts* had often seen him playing about, he raised it to his shoulder.

Jarry had acquired the reputation of being a good shot. Protests were heard. In the drunken state in which he now was, people were not very sure that he would confine himself to play-acting. But little Bercail was determined to show he was not afraid; he got on to a chair, and with his arms folded behind his back, took up a Napoleonic attitude. He was just a little ridiculous and some tittering was heard, but it was at once drowned by applause.

Passavant said to Sarah very quickly:

'It may end unpleasantly. He's completely drunk. Get under the table.'

Des Brousses tried to catch hold of Jarry, but he shook him off and got on to a chair in his turn (Bernard noticed he was wearing patent leather pumps). Standing there straight opposite Bercail, he stretched out his arm and took aim.

'Put the light out! Put the light out!' cried des Brousses.

Edouard, who was still standing by the door, turned the switch.

Sarah had risen in obedience to Passavant's injunction; and as soon as it was dark, she pressed up against Bernard, to pull him under the table with her.

The shot went off. The pistol was only loaded with a blank cartridge. But a cry of pain was heard. It came from Justinien, who had been hit in the eye by the wad.

And, when the light was turned on again, there, to everyone's admiration, stood Bercail, still on his chair in the same attitude, motionless and barely a shade paler.

In the meantime the President's lady was indulging in a fit of hysterics. Her friends crowded round her.

'Idiotic to give people such a turn.'

As there was no water on the table, Jarry, who had climbed

down from his pedestal, dipped a handkerchief in brandy to rub her temples with, by way of apology.

Bernard had stayed only a second under the table, just long enough to feel Sarah's two burning lips crushed voluptuously against his. Olivier had followed them; out of friendship, out of jealousy. . . . That horrible feeling which he knew so well, of being out of it, was exacerbated by his being drunk. When, in his turn, he came out from underneath the table, his head was swimming. He heard Dhurmer exclaim:

'Look at Molinier! He's as funky as a girl!'

It was too much. Olivier, hardly knowing what he was doing, darted towards Dhurmer with his hand raised. He seemed to be moving in a dream. Dhurmer dodged the blow. As in a dream, Olivier's hand met nothing but empty air.

The confusion became general, and while some of the guests were fussing over the President's lady, who was still gesticulating wildly and uttering shrill little yelps as she did so, others crowded round Dhurmer, who called out: 'He didn't touch me! He didn't touch me!' . . . and others round Olivier, who, with a scarlet face, wanted to rush at him again, and was with great difficulty restrained.

Touched or not, Dhurmer must consider that he had had his ears boxed; so Justinien, as he dabbed his eye, endeavoured to make him understand. It was a question of dignity. But Dhurmer was not in the least inclined to receive lessons in dignity from Justinien. He kept on repeating obstinately:

'Didn't touch me! . . . Didn't touch me!'

'Can't you leave him alone?' said des Brousses. 'One can't force a fellow to fight if he doesn't want to.'

Olivier, however, declared in a loud voice, that if Dhurmer wasn't satisfied, he was ready to box his ears again; and, determined to force a duel, asked Bernard and Bercail to be his seconds. Neither of them knew anything about so-called 'affairs of honour'; but Olivier didn't dare apply to Edouard. His neck-tie had come undone; his hair had fallen over his forehead, which was dank with sweat; his hands trembled convulsively.

Edouard took him by the arm:

'Come and bathe your face a little. You look like a lunatic.'

He led him away to a lavatory.

As soon as he was out of the room, Olivier understood how drunk he was. When he had felt Edouard's hand laid upon his arm, he thought he was going to faint, and let himself be led away unresisting. Of all that Edouard had said to him, he only understood that he had called him 'thou'. As a storm-cloud bursts into rain, he felt his heart suddenly dissolve in tears. A damp towel which Edouard put to his forehead brought him finally to his sober senses again. What had happened? He was vaguely conscious of having behaved like a child, like a brute. He felt himself ridiculous, abject. . . . Then, quivering with distress and tenderness, he flung himself towards Edouard, pressed up against him and sobbed out:

'Take me away!'

Edouard was extremely moved himself:

'Your parents?' he asked.

'They don't know I'm back.'

As they were going through the café downstairs on the way out, Olivier said to his companion that he had a line to write.

'If I post it tonight it'll get there tomorrow morning.'

Seated at a table in the café, he wrote as follows:

MY DEAR GEORGE, – Yes, this letter is from me, and it's to ask you to do something for me. I don't suppose it's news to you to hear I am back in Paris, for I think you saw me this morning near the Sorbonne. I was staying with the Comte de Passavant (rue de Babylone); my things are still there. For reasons it would be too long to explain and which wouldn't interest you, I prefer not to go back to him. You are the only person I can ask to go and fetch them away – my things, I mean. You'll do this for me, won't you? I'll remember it when it's your turn. There's a locked trunk. As for the things in the room, put them yourself into my suitcase, and bring the lot to Uncle Edouard's. I'll pay for the taxi. Tomorrow's Sunday fortunately; you'll be able to do it as soon as you get this line. I can count upon you, can't I?

Your affectionate brother
OLIVIER

P.S. – I know you're sharp enough and you'll be able to manage all right. But mind, that if you have any direct dealings with Passavant, you are to be very distant with him.

Those who had not heard Dhurmer's insulting words could not understand the reason of Olivier's sudden assault. He seemed to have lost his head. If he had kept cool, Bernard would have approved him; he didn't like Dhurmer; but he had to admit that Olivier had behaved like a madman and put himself entirely in the wrong. It pained Bernard to hear him judged severely. He went up to Bercail and made an appointment with him. However absurd the affair was, they were both anxious to conduct it correctly. They agreed to go and call on their client at nine o'clock the next morning.

When his two friends had gone, Bernard had neither reason nor inclination to stay. He looked round the room in search of Sarah and his heart swelled with a kind of rage to see her sitting on Passavant's knee. They both seemed drunk; Sarah, however, rose when she saw Bernard coming up.

'Let's go,' she said, taking his arm.

She wanted to walk home. It was not far. They spoke not a word on the way. At the pension all the lights were out. Fearful of attracting attention, they groped their way to the backstairs, and there struck matches. Armand was waiting for them. When he heard them coming upstairs, he went out on to the landing with a lamp in his hand.

'Take the lamp,' said he to Bernard. 'Light Sarah; there's no candle in her room . . . and give me your matches so that I can light mine.' Bernard accompanied Sarah into the inner room. They were no sooner inside than Armand, leaning over from behind them, blew the lamp out at a single breath, then, with a chuckle:

'Good night!' said he. 'But don't make a row. The parents are sleeping next door.'

Then, suddenly stepping back, he shut the door on them; and bolted it.

9

OLIVIER AND EDOUARD

ARMAND has lain down in his clothes. He knows he will not be able to sleep. He waits for the night to come to an end. He meditates. He listens. The house is resting, the town, the whole of nature; not a sound.

As soon as a faint light, cast down by the reflector from the narrow strip of sky above, enables him to distinguish once more the hideous squalor of his room, he rises. He goes towards the door which he bolted the night before; opens it gently....

The curtains of Sarah's room are not drawn. The rising dawn whitens the window-pane. Armand goes up to the bed where his sister and Bernard are resting. A sheet half hides them as they lie with limbs entwined. How beautiful they are! Armand gazes at them and gazes. He would like to be their sleep, their kisses. At first he smiles, then, at the foot of the bed, among the coverings they have flung aside, he suddenly kneels down. To what god can he be praying thus with folded hands? An unspeakable emotion shakes him. His lips are trembling... he rises....

But on the threshold of the door, he turns. He wants to wake Bernard so that he may gain his own room before anyone in the house is awake. At the slight noise Armand makes, Bernard opens his eyes. Armand hurries away, leaving the door open. He leaves his room, goes downstairs; he will hide no matter where; his presence would embarrass Bernard; he does not want to meet him.

From a window in the class-room a few minutes later, he sees him go by, skirting the walls like a thief....

Bernard has not slept much. But that night he has tasted a forgetfulness more restful than sleep – the exaltation at once and the annihilation of self. Strange to himself, ethereal, buoyant, calm and tense as a god, he glides into another day. He has left Sarah still asleep – disengaged himself furtively from her arms. What! without one more kiss? Without a last lover's look? Without a supreme embrace? Is it through insensibility that he leaves her in this way? I cannot tell. He cannot tell himself. He tries not to think; it is a difficult task to incorporate this unprecedented night with all the preceding nights of his history. No; it is an appendix, an annexe, which can find no place in the body of the book – a book where the story of his life will continue, surely, will take up the thread again, as if nothing had happened.

He goes upstairs to the room he shares with little Boris. What a child! He is fast asleep. Bernard undoes his bed, rumples the bed-clothes, so as to give it the look of having been slept in. He sluices himself with water. But the sight of Boris takes him back to Saas-Fée. He recalls what Laura once said to him there: 'I can only accept from you the devotion which you offer me. The rest will have its exigences and will have to be satisfied elsewhere.' This sentence had revolted him. He seems to hear it again. He had ceased to think of it, but this morning his memory is extraordinarily active. His mind works in spite of himself with marvellous alacrity. Bernard thrusts aside Laura's image, tries to smother these recollections; and, to prevent himself from thinking, he seizes a lesson book and forces himself to read for his examination. But the room is stifling. He goes down to work in the garden. He would like to go out into the street, walk, run, get into the open, breathe the fresh air. He watches the street door; as soon as the porter opens it, he makes off.

He reaches the Luxembourg with his book, and sits down on a bench. He spins his thoughts like silk; but how fragile! If he pulls it, the thread breaks. As soon as he tries to work, indiscreet memories wander obtrusively between his book and him; and not the memories of the keenest moments of his joy, but ridiculous, trifling little details – so many thorns, which catch and scratch and mortify his vanity. Another time he will show himself less of a novice.

About nine o'clock, he gets up to go and fetch Lucien Bercail. Together they make their way to Edouard's.

Edouard lived at Passy on the top floor of an apartment house. His room opened on to a vast studio. When, in the early dawn, Olivier had risen, Edouard at first had felt no anxiety.

'I'm going to lie down a little on the sofa,' Olivier had said. And as Edouard was afraid he might catch cold, he had told Olivier to take some blankets with him. A little later, Edouard in his turn had risen. He had certainly been asleep without being aware of it, for he was astonished to find that it was now broad daylight. He wanted to see whether Olivier was comfortable; he wanted to see him again; and perhaps an obscure presentiment guided him....

The studio was empty. The blankets were lying at the foot of the couch unfolded. A horrible smell of gas gave him the alarm. Opening out of the studio, there was a little room which served as a bathroom. The smell no doubt came from there. He ran to the door; but at first was unable to push it open; there was some obstacle – it was Olivier's body, sunk in a heap beside the bath, undressed, icy, livid and horribly soiled with vomiting.

Edouard turned off the gas which was coming from the jet. What had happened? An accident? A stroke?... He could not believe it. The bath was empty. He took the dying boy in his arms, carried him into the studio, laid him on the carpet, in front of the wide open window. On his knees, stooping tenderly, he put his ear to his chest. Olivier was still breathing, but faintly. Then Edouard, desperately, set all his ingenuity to work to rekindle the little spark of life so near extinction; he moved the limp arms rhythmically up and down, pressed the flanks, rubbed the thorax, tried everything he had heard should be done in a case of suffocation, in despair that he could not do everything at once. Olivier's eyes remained shut. Edouard raised his eyelids with his fingers, but they dropped at once over lifeless eyes. But yet his heart was beating. He searched in vain for brandy, for smelling salts. He heated some water, washed the upper part of the body and the face. Then he laid this inanimate body on the couch and covered it with blankets. He wanted to send for a doctor, but was afraid to absent himself. A charwoman was in the habit of coming every morning to do the housework; but not before nine o'clock. As soon as he heard her, he sent her off at once to fetch the nearest doctor; then he called her back, fearing he might be exposed to an enquiry.

Olivier, in the meantime, was slowly coming back to life.

Edouard sat beside his couch. He gazed at the shut book of his face, baffled by its riddle. Why? Why? One may act thoughtlessly at night in the heat of intoxication, but the resolutions of early morning carry with them their full weight of virtue. He gave up trying to understand, until at last the moment should come when Olivier would be able to speak. Until that moment came he would not leave him. He had taken one of his hands in his and concentrated his interrogation, his thoughts, his whole life into that contact. At last it seemed to him that he felt Olivier's hand responding feebly to his clasp. . . . Then he bent down, and set his lips on the forehead, where an immense and mysterious suffering had drawn its lines.

A ring was heard at the door. Edouard rose to open it. It was Bernard and Lucien Bercail. Edouard kept them in the hall and told them what had happened; then, taking Bernard aside, he asked if he knew whether Olivier was subject to attacks of giddiness, to fits of any kind? . . . Bernard suddenly remembered their conversation of the day before, and, in particular, some words of Olivier's which he had hardly listened to at the time, but which came back to him now, as distinctly as if he heard them over again.

'It was I who began to speak of suicide,' said he to Edouard. 'I asked him if he understood a person's killing himself out of mere excess of life, "out of enthusiasm", as Dmitri Karamazof says. I was absorbed in my thought and at the time I paid no attention to anything but my own words; but I remember now what he answered.'

'What did he answer?' insisted Edouard, for Bernard stopped as though he were reluctant to say anything more.

'That he understood killing oneself, but only after having reached such heights of joy, that anything afterwards must be a descent.'

They both looked at each other and added nothing further. Light was beginning to dawn on them. Edouard at last turned away his eyes; and Bernard was angry with himself for having spoken. They went up to Bercail.

'The tiresome thing is,' said he, 'that people may think he has tried to kill himself in order to avoid fighting.'

Edouard had forgotten all about the duel.

'Behave as if nothing had happened,' said he. 'Go and find Dhurmer, and ask him to tell you who his seconds are. It is to them that you must explain matters, if the idiotic business doesn't settle itself. Dhurmer didn't seem particularly keen.'

'We will tell him nothing,' said Lucien, 'and leave him all the shame of retreating. For he will shuffle out of it, I'm certain.'

Bernard asked if he might see Olivier. But Edouard thought he had better be kept quiet.

Bernard and Lucien were just leaving, when young George arrived. He came from Passavant's, but had not been able to get hold of his brother's things.

'Monsieur le Comte is not at home,' he had been told. 'He has left no orders.'

And the servant had shut the door in his face.

A certain gravity in Edouard's tone, in the bearing of the two others, alarmed George. He scented something out of the way – made inquiries. Edouard was obliged to tell him.

'But say nothing about it to your parents.'

George was delighted to be let into a secret.

'A fellow can hold his tongue,' said he. And as he had nothing to do that morning, he proposed to accompany Bernard and Lucien on their way to Dhurmer's.

After his three visitors had left him, Edouard called the charwoman. Next to his own room was a spare room, which he told her to get ready, so that Olivier might be put into it. Then he went noiselessly back to the studio. Olivier was resting. Edouard sat down again beside him. He had taken a book, but he soon threw it aside without having opened it, and watched his friend sleeping.

10

OLIVIER'S CONVALESCENCE

Rien n'est simple de ce qui s'offre à l'âme; et l'âme ne s'offre jamais simple à aucun sujet.

PASCAL

'I THINK he will be glad to see you,' said Edouard to Bernard next morning. 'He asked me this morning if you hadn't come yesterday. He must have heard your voice, at the time when I thought he was unconscious. . . . He keeps his eyes shut, but he doesn't speak. He often puts his hand to his forehead, as if it were aching. Whenever I speak to him he frowns; but if I go away, he calls me back and makes me sit beside him. . . . No, he isn't in the studio. I have put him in the spare room next to mine, so that I can receive visitors without disturbing him.'

They went into it.

'I've come to inquire after you,' said Bernard very softly.

Olivier's features brightened at the sound of his friend's voice. It was almost a smile already.

'I was expecting you.'

'I'll go away if I tire you.'

'Stay.'

But as he said the word, Olivier put his finger on his lips. He didn't want to be spoken to. Bernard, who was going up for his *viva voce* in three days' time, never moved without carrying in his pocket one of those manuals which contain a concentrated elixir of the bitter stuff which is the subject matter of examinations. He sat down beside his bed and plunged into his reading. Edouard had gone to his own room, which communicated with Olivier's; the door between them had been left open, and from time to time he appeared at it. Every two hours he made Olivier drink a glass of milk, but only since that morning. During the whole of the preceding day, the patient had been unable to take any food.

A long time went by. Bernard rose to go. Olivier turned round, held out his hand, and with an attempt at a smile:

'You'll come back tomorrow?'

At the last moment he called him back, signed to him to stoop down, as if he were afraid of not making himself heard, and whispered:

'Did you ever know such an idiot?'

Then, as though to forestall Bernard's protest, put his finger again to his lips.

'No, no; I'll explain later.'

The next morning Edouard received a letter from Laura, when Bernard came, he gave it to him to read:

MY DEAR FRIEND, – I am writing to you in a great hurry to try and prevent an absurd disaster. You will help me, I am sure, if only this letter reaches you in time.

Felix has just left for Paris, with the intention of going to see you. His idea is to get from you the explanation which I refuse to give him; he wants you to tell him the name of the person, whom he wishes to challenge. I have done all I can to stop him, but nothing has any effect and all I say merely serves to make him more determined. You are the only person who will perhaps be able to dissuade him. He has confidence in you and will, I hope, listen to you. Remember that he has never in his life held a pistol or a foil in his hands. The idea that he may risk his life for my sake is intolerable to me; but – I hardly dare own it – I am really more afraid of his covering himself with ridicule.

Since I got back, Felix has been all that is attentive and tender and kind; but I cannot bring myself to show more love for him than I feel. He suffers from this; and I believe it is his desire to force my esteem, my admiration, that is making him take this step, which will no doubt appear to you unconsidered, but of which he thinks day and night, and which, since my return, has become an *idée fixe* with him. He has certainly forgiven me; but he bears . . . a mortal grudge.

Please, I beg of you, welcome him as affectionately as you would welcome myself; no proof of your friendship could touch me more. Forgive me for not having written to you sooner to tell you once more how grateful I am for all the care and kindness you lavished on me during our stay in Switzerland. The recollection of that time keeps me warm and helps me to bear my life.

Your ever anxious and ever confident friend

LAURA

'What do you mean to do?' asked Bernard, as he gave the letter back.

'What *can* I do?' replied Edouard, slightly irritated, not so much by Bernard's question, as by the fact that he had already put it to himself. 'If he comes, I will receive him to the best of my abilities. If he asks my advice, I will give him the best I can; and try to persuade him that the most sensible thing he can do is to keep quiet. People like poor Douviers are always wrong to put themselves forward. You'd think the same if you knew him, believe me. Laura, on the other hand, was cut out for a leading role. Each of us assumes the drama that suits his measure, and is allotted his share of tragedy. What can we do about it? Laura's drama is to have married a super. There's no help for that.'

'And Douviers' drama is to have married someone who will always be his superior, do what he may,' rejoined Bernard.

'Do what he may ...' echoed, Edouard '– and do what Laura may. The admirable thing is that Laura, out of regret for her fault, out of repentance, wanted to humble herself before him; but he immediately prostrated himself lower still; so that all that each of them did merely served to make *him* smaller and *her* greater.'

'I pity him very much,' said Bernard. 'But why won't you allow that he too may become greater by prostrating himself?'

'Because he lacks the lyrical spirit,' said Edouard irrefutably.

'What *do* you mean?'

'He never forgets himself in what he feels, so that he never feels anything great. Don't push me too hard. I have my own ideas; but they don't lend themselves to the yard measure, and I don't care to measure them. Paul-Ambroise is in the habit of saying that he refuses to take count of anything that can't be put down in figures; I think he is playing on the words "take count"; for if that were the case, we should be obliged to leave God out of "the account". That of course is where he is tending and what he desires.... Well, for instance, I think I call *lyrical* the state of the man who consents to be vanquished by God.'

'Isn't that exactly what the word *enthusiasm* means?'

'And perhaps the word *inspiration*. Yes, that is just what I mean: Douviers is a being who is incapable of inspiration. I admit that Paul-Ambroise is right when he considers inspiration as one of the most harmful things in art; and I am willing to believe that one can only be an artist on condition of mastering the lyrical state; but in order to master it, one must first of all experience it.'

'Don't you think that this state of divine visitation can be physiologically explained by . . .'

'Much good that will do!' interrupted Edouard. 'Such considerations as that, even if they are true, only embarrass fools. No doubt there is no mystical movement that has not its corresponding material manifestation. What then? Mind, in order to bear its witness, cannot do without matter. Hence the mystery of the incarnation.'

'On the other hand, matter does admirably without mind.'

'Oh, ho! we don't know about that!' said Edouard, laughing.

Bernard was very much amused to hear him talk in this way. As a rule Edouard was more reserved. The mood he was in today came from Olivier's presence. Bernard understood it.

'He is talking to me as he would like already to be talking to him,' thought he. 'It is Olivier who ought to be his secretary. As soon as Olivier is well again, I shall retire. My place is not here.'

He thought this without bitterness, entirely taken up as he now was by Sarah, with whom he had spent the preceding night and whom he was to see that night too.

'We've left Douviers a long way behind,' he said, laughing in his turn. 'Will you tell him about Vincent?'

'Goodness no! What for?'

'Don't you think it's poisoning Douviers' life not to know whom to suspect?'

'Perhaps you are right. But you must say that to Laura. I couldn't tell him without betraying her. . . . Besides I don't even know where he is.'

'Vincent? . . . Passavant must know.'

A ring at the door interrupted them. Madame Molinier had come to inquire for her son. Edouard joined her in the studio.

11

EDOUARD'S JOURNAL: PAULINE

VISIT from Pauline. I was a little puzzled how to let her know, and yet I could not keep her in ignorance of her son's illness. I thought it useless to say anything about the incomprehensible attempt at suicide and spoke simply of a violent liver attack, which, as a matter of fact, remains the clearest result of the proceedings.

'I am reassured already by knowing Olivier is with you,' said Pauline. 'I shouldn't nurse him better myself, for I feel that you love him as much as I do.'

As she said these last words, she looked at me with an odd insistence. Did I imagine the meaning she seemed to put in her look? I was feeling what one is accustomed to call 'a bad conscience' as regards Pauline, and was only able to stammer out something incoherent. I must also say that, sur-saturated as I have been with emotion for the last two days, I had entirely lost command of myself; my confusion must have been very apparent, for she added:

'Your blush is eloquent! ... My poor dear friend, don't expect reproaches from me. I should reproach you if you didn't love him.... Can I see him?'

I took her in to Olivier. Bernard had left the room as he heard us coming.

'How beautiful he is!' she murmured, bending over the bed. Then, turning towards me: 'You will kiss him from me. I am afraid of waking him.'

Pauline is decidedly an extraordinary woman. And today is not the first time that I have begun to think so. But I could not have hoped that she would push comprehension so far. And yet it seemed to me that behind the cordiality of her words and the pleasantness she put into her voice, I could distinguish a touch of constraint (perhaps because of the effort I myself made to hide my embarrassment); and I remembered a sentence of our last conversation – a sentence which seemed to me full of wisdom even then, when I was not interested in finding it so: 'I prefer granting with a good grace what I know I shan't be able to prevent.' Evidently Pauline was striving after good grace; and, as if in response to my secret thoughts, she went on again, as soon as we were back in the studio:

'By not being shocked just now, I am afraid it is I who have shocked you. There are certain liberties of thought of which men would like to keep the monopoly. And yet I can't pretend to have more reprobation for you than I feel. Life has not left me ignorant. I know what a precarious thing boys' purity is, even when it has the appearance of being most intact. And besides, I don't think that the youths who are chastest turn into the best husbands – nor even, unfortunately, the most faithful!' she added, smiling sadly. 'And then their father's example made me wish other virtues for my sons. But I am afraid of their taking to debauchery or to degrading liaisons. Olivier is easily led astray. You will have it at heart to keep him straight. I think you will be able to do him good. It only rests with you....'

These words filled me with confusion.

'You make me out better than I am.'

That is all I could find to say, in the stupidest, stiffest way. She went on with exquisite delicacy:

'It is Olivier who will make you better. With love's help what can one not obtain from oneself?'

'Does Oscar know he is with me?' I asked, to put a little air between us.

'He does not even know he is in Paris. I told you that he pays very little attention to his sons. That is why I counted on you to speak to George. Have you done so?'

'No – not yet.'

Pauline's brow grew suddenly sombre.

'I am becoming more and more anxious. He has an air of assurance, which seems to me a combination of recklessness, cynicism, presumption. He works well. His masters are pleased with him; my anxiety has nothing to lay hold of....'

Then all of a sudden, throwing aside her calm and speaking with an excitement such that I barely recognized her:

'Do you realize what my life is?' she exclaimed. 'I have

restricted my happiness; year by year, I have been obliged to narrow it down; one by one, I have curtailed my hopes. I have given in; I have tolerated; I have pretended not to understand, not to see. . . . But all the same, one clings to something, however small; and when even that fails one! . . . In the evening he comes and works beside me under the lamp; when sometimes he raises his head from his book, it isn't affection that I see in his look – it's defiance. I haven't deserved it. . . . Sometimes it seems to me suddenly that all my love for him is turned to hatred; and I wish that I had never had any children.'

Her voice trembled. I took her hand.

'Olivier will repay you, I vouch for it.'

She made an effort to recover herself.

'Yes, I am mad to speak so; as if I hadn't three sons. When I think of one, I forget the others. . . . You'll think me very unreasonable, but there are really moments when reason isn't enough.'

'And yet what I admire most about you is your reasonableness,' said I baldly, in the hopes of calming her. 'The other day, you talked about Oscar so wisely. . . .'

Pauline drew herself up abruptly. She looked at me and shrugged her shoulders.

'It's always when a woman appears most resigned that she seems the most reasonable,' she cried, almost vindictively.

This reflection irritated me, by reason of its very justice. In order not to show it, I asked:

'Anything new about the letters?'

'New? New? . . . What on earth that's new can happen between Oscar and me?'

'He was expecting an explanation.'

'So was I. I was expecting an explanation. All one's life long one expects explanations.'

'Well, but,' I continued, rather annoyed. 'Oscar felt that he was in a false situation.'

'But, my dear friend, you know well enough that nothing lasts more eternally than a false situation. It's the business of you novelists to try to solve them. In real life nothing is solved; everything continues. We remain in our uncertainty; and we *shall* remain to the very end without knowing what to make of things. In the meantime life goes on and on, the same as ever. And one gets resigned to that too; as one does to everything else... as one does to everything. Well, well, good-bye.'

I was painfully affected by a new note in the sound of her voice, which I had never heard before; a kind of aggressiveness, which forced me to think (not at the actual moment, perhaps, but when I recalled our conversation) that Pauline accepted my relations with Olivier much less easily than she said; less easily than all the rest. I am willing to believe that she does not exactly reprobate them, that from some points of view she is glad of them, as she lets me understand; but, perhaps without owning it to herself, she is none the less jealous of them.

This is the only explanation I can discover for her sudden outburst of revolt, so soon after, and on a subject which, on the whole, she had much less at heart. It was as though by granting me at first what cost her more, she had exhausted her whole stock of benignity and suddenly found herself with none left. Hence her intemperate, her almost extravagant language, which must have astonished her herself, when she came to recall it, and in which her jealousy unconsciously betrayed itself.

In reality, I ask myself, what can be the state of mind of a woman who is not resigned? An 'honest woman', I mean. ... As if what is called 'honesty' in woman did not always imply resignation!

This evening Olivier is perceptibly better. But returning life brings anxiety along with it. I reassure him by every device in my power.

'His duel?' – Dhurmer has run away into the country. One really can't run after him.

'The review?' – Bercail is in charge of it.

'The things he had left at Passavant's?' – This is the thorniest point. I had to admit that George had been unable to get possession of them; but I have promised to go and fetch them myself tomorrow. He is afraid, from what I can gather, that Passavant may keep them as a hostage; inadmissible for a single moment!

Yesterday, I was sitting up late in the studio, after having written this, when I heard Olivier call me. In a moment I was by his side.

'I should have come myself, only I was too weak,' he said. 'I tried to get up, but when I stand, my heard turns round and I was afraid of falling. No, no, I'm not feeling worse; on the contrary. But I had to speak to you.

'You must promise me something. . . . Never to try and find out why I wanted to kill myself the other night. I don't think I know myself. I can't remember. Even if I tried to tell you, upon my honour, I shouldn't be able to. . . . But you mustn't think that it's because of anything mysterious in my life, anything you don't know about.' Then, in a whisper: 'And don't imagine either that it was because I was ashamed. . . .'

Although we were in the dark, he hid his face in my shoulder.

'Or if I am ashamed, it is of the dinner the other evening; of being drunk, of losing my temper, of crying; and of this summer . . . and of having waited for you so badly.'

Then he protested that none of all that was part of him any more; that it was all that that he had wanted to kill – that he had killed – that he had wiped out of his life.

I felt, in his very agitation, how weak he still was, and rocked him in my arms, like a child, without saying anything. He was in need of rest; his silence made me hope he was asleep; but at last I heard him murmur:

'When I am with you, I am too happy to sleep.'

He did not let me leave him till morning.

12

EDOUARD AND THEN STROUVILHOU VISIT PASSAVANT

BERNARD arrived that morning. Olivier was still asleep. As on the preceding days, Bernard settled himself down at his friend's bedside with a book, which allowed Edouard to go off guard, in order to call on the Comte de Passavant, as he had promised. At such an early hour he was sure to be in.

The sun was shining; a keen air was scouring the trees of their last leaves; everything seemed limpid, bathed in azure. Edouard had not been out for three days. His heart was dilated by an immense joy; and even his whole being, like an opened, empty wrapping, seemed floating on a shoreless sea, a divine ocean of loving-kindness. Love and fine weather have this power of boundlessly enlarging our contours.

Edouard knew that he would want a taxi to bring back Olivier's things; but he was in no hurry to take one; he enjoyed walking. The state of benevolence in which he felt himself towards the whole world, was no good preparation for facing Passavant. He told himself that he ought to execrate him; he went over in his mind all his grievances – but they had ceased to sting. This rival, whom only yesterday he had so detested, he could detest no longer – he had ousted him too completely. At any rate he could not detest him that morning. And as, on the other hand, he thought it prudent that no trace of this reversal of feeling should appear, for fear of its betraying his happiness, he would have gladly evaded the interview. And indeed, why the dickens was he going to it? He! Edouard! Going to the rue de Babylone, to ask for Olivier's things – on what pretext? He had undertaken the commission very thoughtlessly, he told himself, as he walked along; it would imply that Olivier had chosen to take up his abode with him – exactly what he wanted to conceal. . . . Too late, however, to draw back; Olivier had his promise. At any rate, he must be very cold with Passavant, very firm. A taxi went by and he hailed it.

Edouard knew Passavant ill. He was ignorant of one of the chief traits of his character. No one had ever succeeded in catching Passavant out; it was unbearable to him to be worsted. In order not to acknowledge his defeats to himself, he always affected to have desired his fate, and whatever happened to him, he pretended that that was what he wished. As soon as he understood that Olivier was escaping him, his one care was to dissemble his rage. Far from attempting to run after him, and risk being ridiculous, he forced himself to keep a stiff lip and shrug his shoulders. His emotions were never too violent to keep under control. Some people congratulate themselves on this, and refuse to acknowledge that they owe their mastery over themselves less to their force of character than to a certain poverty of temperament. I don't allow myself to generalize; let us suppose that what I have said applies only to Passavant. He did not therefore find much difficulty in persuading himself that he had had enough of Olivier; that during these two summer months he had exhausted the charm of an adventure which ran the risk of encumbering his life; that, for the rest, he had exaggerated the boy's beauty, his grace and his intellectual resources; that, indeed, it was high time he should open his eyes to the inconveniences of confiding the management of a review to anyone so young and inexperienced. Taking everything into consideration, Strouvilhou would serve his purpose far better (as regards the review, that is). He had written to him and appointed him to come and see him that very morning.

Let us add too that Passavant was mistaken as to the cause of Olivier's desertion. He thought he had made him jealous by his attentions to Sarah; he was pleased with this idea which flattered his self-conceit; his vexation was soothed by it.

He was expecting Strouvilhou; and as he had given orders that he was to be let in at once, Edouard benefited by the instructions and was shown in to Passavant without being announced.

Passavant gave no signs of his surprise. Fortunately for him, the part he had to play was suited to his temperament and he was easily able to switch his mind on to it. As soon as Edouard had explained the motive of his visit:

'I'm delighted to hear what you say. Then really? You're willing to look after him? It doesn't put you out too much?... Olivier is a charming boy, but he was beginning to be terribly in my way here. I didn't like to let him feel it – he's so nice.... And I knew he didn't want to go back to his parents.... Once one has left one's parents, you know ... Oh! but now I come to think of it, his mother is a half-sister of yours, isn't she?... Or something of that kind? Olivier must have told me so, I expect. Then, nothing could be more natural than that he should stay with you. No one can possibly smile at it' (though he himself didn't fail to do so as he said the words). 'With me, you understand, it was rather more shady. In fact, that was one of the reasons that made me anxious for him to go.... Though I am by no means in the habit of minding public opinion. No; it was in his own interest rather....'

The conversation had not begun badly; but Passavant could not resist the pleasure of pouring a few drops of his poisonous perfidy on Edouard's happiness. He always kept a supply on hand; one never knows what may happen.

Edouard felt his patience giving way. But he suddenly thought of Vincent; Passavant would probably have news of him. He had indeed determined not to answer Douviers, should he question him; but he thought it would be a good thing to be himself acquainted with the facts, in order the better to avoid his inquiries. It would strengthen his resistance. He seized this pretext as a diversion.

'Vincent has not written to me,' said Passavant; 'but I have had a letter from Lady Griffith – you know – the successor – in which she speaks of him at length. See, here it is.... After all, I don't know why you shouldn't read it.'

He handed him the letter, and Edouard read:

25th August.

MY DEAR,*– The prince's yacht is leaving Dakar without us. Who knows where we shall be when you get this letter which it is taking with it? Perhaps on the banks of the Casamance, where Vincent wants to botanize, and I to shoot. I don't exactly know whether it is I who am carrying him off, or he me; or whether it isn't

* In English in the original.

rather that we have both of us fallen into the clutches of the demon of adventure. He was introduced to us by the demon of boredom, whose acquaintance we made on board ship. . . . *Ah, cher!* one must live on a yacht to know what boredom is. In rough weather life is just bearable; one has one's share of the vessel's agitation. But after Teneriffe not a breath; not a wrinkle on the sea.

. . . grand miroir
De mon désespoir.

And do you know what I have been engaged in doing ever since? In hating Vincent. Yes, my dear, love seemed too tasteless, so we have gone in for hating each other. In reality it began long before; really, as soon as we got on board; at first it was only irritation, a smouldering animosity, which didn't prevent closer encounters. With the fine weather, it became ferocious. Oh! I know now what it is to feel passion for someone. . . .

The letter went on for some time longer.

'I don't need to read any further,' said Edouard, giving it back to Passavant. 'When is he coming back?'

'Lady Griffith doesn't speak of returning.'

Passavant was mortified that Edouard showed so little appetite for this letter. Since he had allowed him to read it, such a lack of curiosity must be considered as an affront. He enjoyed rejecting other people's offers, but could not endure to have his own disdained. Lilian's letter had filled him with delight. He had a certain affection for her and Vincent; and had even proved to his own satisfaction that he was capable of being kind to them and helpful; but as soon as one got on without it, his affection dwindled. That his two friends should not have set sail for perfect bliss when they left him, tempted him to think: 'Serves them right!'

As for Edouard, his early morning felicity was too genuine for him not to be made uncomfortable by the picture of such outrageous feelings. It was quite unaffectedly that he gave the letter back.

Passavant felt it essential to recover the lead at once:

'Oh! I wanted to say too – you know that I had thought of making Olivier editor of a review. Of course, there's no further question of that.'

'Of course not,' rejoined Edouard, whom Passavant had unwittingly relieved of a considerable anxiety. He understood by Edouard's tone that he had played into his hand, and without even giving himself the time to bite his lips:

'Olivier's things are in the room he was occupying. You have a taxi, I suppose? I'll have them brought down to you. By the bye, how is he?'

'Very well.'

Passavant had risen. Edouard did the same. They parted with the coldest of bows.

The Comte de Passavant had been terribly put out by Edouard's visit. He heaved a sigh of relief when Strouvilhou came into the room.

Although Strouvilhou, on his side, was perfectly able to hold his own, Passavant felt at ease with him – or, to be more accurate, treated him in a free and easy manner. No doubt his opponent was by no means despicable, but he considered himself his match, and piqued himself on proving it.

'My dear Strouvilhou, take a seat,' said he, pushing an armchair towards him. 'I am really glad to see you again.'

'Monsieur le Comte sent for me. Here I am entirely at his service.'

Strouvilhou liked affecting a kind of flunkey's insolence with Passavant, but Passavant knew him of old.

'Let's get to the point; it's time to come out into the open. You've already tried your hand at a good many trades. . . . I thought today of proposing you an actual dictatorship – only in the realms of literature, let us hasten to add.'

'A pity!' Then, as Passavant held out his cigarette case: 'If you'll allow me, I prefer . . .'

'I'll allow nothing of the kind. Your horrid contraband cigars make the room stink. I can't understand how anyone can smoke such stuff.'

'Oh! I don't pretend that I rave about them. But they're a nuisance to one's neighbours.'

'Playful as ever?'

'Not altogether an idiot, you know.'

And without replying directly to Passavant's proposal,

Strouvilhou thought proper to establish his positions; afterwards he would see. He went on:

'Philanthropy was never one of my strong points.'

'I know, I know,' said Passavant.

'Nor egoism either. That's what you don't know.... People want to make us believe that man's single escape from egoism is a still more disgusting altruism! As for me, I maintain that if there's anything more contemptible and more abject than a man, it's a lot of men. No reasoning will ever persuade me that the addition of a number of sordid units can result in an enchanting total. I never happen to get into a tram or a train without hoping that a good old accident will reduce the whole pack of living garbage to a pulp; yes, good Lord! and myself into the bargain. I never enter a theatre without praying that the chandelier may come crashing down, or that a bomb may go off; and even if I had to be blown up too, I'd be only too glad to bring it along in my coat pocket – if I weren't reserving myself for something better. You were saying?...'

'No, nothing; go on. I'm listening. You're not one of those orators who need the stimulus of contradiction to keep them going.'

'The fact is, I thought I heard you offer me some of your incomparable port.'

Passavant smiled.

'Keep the bottle beside you,' he said, as he passed it to him. 'Empty it if you like, but talk.'

Strouvilhou filled his glass, sat comfortably back in his big arm-chair and began:

'I don't know if I've got what people call a hard heart; in my opinion, I've got too much indignation, too much disgust in my composition – not that I care. It is true that for a long time past I have repressed in that particular organ of mine everything which ran the risk of softening it. But I am not incapable of admiration, and of a sort of absurd devotion; for, in so far as I am a man, I despise and hate myself as much as I do my neighbours. I hear it repeated everywhere and constantly that literature, art and science work together in the long run for the good of mankind; and that's enough to make me loathe them. But there's nothing to prevent me from turning the proposition round, and then I breathe again. Yes, what for my part I like to imagine is, on the contrary, a servile humanity working towards the production of some cruel masterpiece; a Bernard Palissy (how they have deaved us with that fellow!) burning his wife and children to get a varnish for a fine plate. I like turning problems round; I can't help it, my mind is so constructed that they keep steadier when they are standing on their heads. And if I can't endure the thought of a Christ sacrificing himself for the thankless salvation of all the frightful people I knock up against daily, I imagine with some satisfaction, and indeed a kind of serenity, the rotting of that vile mob in order to produce a Christ . . . though, in reality, I should prefer something else; for all His teaching has only served to plunge us deeper into the mire. The trouble comes from the selfishness of the ferocious. Imagine what magnificent things an unselfish ferocity would produce! When we take care of the poor, the feeble, the rickety, the injured, we are making a great mistake; and that is why I hate religion – because it teaches us to. That deep peace, which philanthropists themselves pretend they derive from the contemplation of nature, and its fauna and flora, comes from this – that in the savage state, it is only robust creatures that flourish; all the rest is refuse and serves as manure. But people won't see it; won't admit it.'

'Yes, yes; I admit it willingly. Go on.'

'And tell me whether it isn't shameful, wretched . . . that men have done so much to get superb breeds of horses, cattle, poultry, cereals, flowers, and that they themselves are still seeking a relief for their sufferings in medicine, a palliative in charity, a consolation in religion, and oblivion in drink. What we ought to work at is the amelioration of the breed. But all selection implies the suppression of failures, and this is what our fool of a Christianized society cannot consent to. It will not even take upon itself to castrate degenerates – and those are the most prolific. What we want is not hospitals, but stud farms.'

'Upon my soul, Strouvilhou, I like you when you talk so.'

'I am afraid, Monsieur le Comte, that you have misunderstood me. You thought me a sceptic, and in reality I am an idealist, a mystic. Scepticism has never been any good. One knows for that matter where it leads – to tolerance! I consider sceptics people without imagination, without ideals – fools. . . . And I am not ignorant of all the delicacies, the sentimental subtleties which would be suppressed by the production of this robust humanity; but no one would be there to regret the delicacies, since the people capable of appreciating them would be suppressed too. Don't make any mistake – I am not without what is called culture, and I know that certain among the Greeks had caught a glimpse of my ideal; at any rate, I like imagining it, and remembering that Coré, daughter of Ceres, went down to Hades full of pity for the shades; but that after she had become queen, and Pluto's wife, Homer never calls her anything but "implacable Proserpine". See Odyssey, Bk. VI. "*Implacable*" – that's what every man who pretends to be virtuous owes it to himself to be.'

'Glad to see you come back to literature – that is, if we may be said ever to have left it. Well then, virtuous Strouvilhou, I want to know whether you'll consent to become the implacable editor of a review?'

'To tell the truth, my dear Count, I must own that of all nauseating human emanations, literature is one of those which disgust me most. I can see nothing in it but compromise and flattery. And I go so far as to doubt whether it can be anything else – at any rate until it has made a clean sweep of the past. We live upon nothing but feelings which have been taken for granted once for all and which the reader imagines he experiences, because he believes everything he sees in print; the author builds on this as he does on the conventions which he believes to be the foundations of his art. These feelings ring as false as counters, but they pass current. And as everyone knows that "bad money drives out good", a man who should offer the public real coins would seem to be defrauding us. In a world in which everyone cheats, it's the honest man who passes for a charlatan. I give you fair warning – if I edit a review, it will be in order to prick bladders – in order to demonetize fine feelings, and those promissory notes which go by the name of *words*.'

'Upon my soul, I should very much like to know how you'll set about it.'

'Let me alone and you'll soon see . . . I have often thought it over.'

'No one will understand what you're after; no one will follow you.'

'Oh, come now! The cleverest young men of the present day are already on their guard against poetical inflation. They perfectly recognize a gasbag when they see one – even in the disguise of scientifically elaborate metre, and trimmed up with all the hackneyed effusions of high-sounding lyrical verse. One can always find hands for a work of destruction. Shall we found a school with no other object but to pull things down? . . . Would you be afraid?'

'No. . . . So long as my garden isn't trampled on.'

'There's enough to be done elsewhere . . . *en attendant*. The moment is propitious. I know many a young man who is only waiting for the rallying cry; quite young ones. . . . Oh, yes, I know! That's what you like; but I warn you they aren't taking any. . . . I have often wondered by what miracle painting has gone so far ahead, and how it happens that literature has let itself be outdistanced. In painting today, just see how the "*motif*", as it used to be called, has fallen into discredit. *A fine subject!* It makes one laugh. Painters don't even dare venture on a portrait unless they can be sure of avoiding every trace of resemblance. If we manage our affairs well, and leave me alone for that, I don't ask for more than two years before a future poet will think himself dishonoured if anyone can understand a word of what he says. Yes, Monsieur le Comte, will you wager? All sense, all meaning will be considered anti-poetical. Illogicality shall be our guiding star. What a fine title for a review – *The Scavengers*!'

Passavant had listened without turning a hair.

'Do you count your young nephew among your acolytes?' he asked after a pause.

'Young Léon is one of the elect; he doesn't let the flies settle on him, either. Really, it's a pleasure teaching him. Last term he thought it would be a joke to cut out the swotters in his form and carry off all the prizes. Since he came back from the holidays he has let his work go to the deuce; I haven't the least idea what he's hatching; but I have every confidence in him, and I wouldn't for the world interfere.'

'Will you bring him to see me?'

'Monsieur le Comte is joking, no doubt.... Well, then, this review?'

'We'll see about it later. I must have time to let your plans mature in my mind. In the meantime, you might really find me a secretary. I'm not satisfied with the one I had.'

'I'll send you little Cob-Lafleur tomorrow. I shall be seeing him this afternoon, and I make no doubt he'll suit you.'

'Scavenger style?'

'A little.'

'*Ex uno*...'

'Oh, no; don't judge them all from him. He is one of the moderate ones. Just right for you.'

Strouvilhou rose.

'Apropos,' said Passavant, 'I haven't given you my book, I think. I'm sorry not to have a first edition left....'

'As I don't mean to sell it, it isn't of the slightest importance.'

'It's only because the print's better.'

'Oh! as I don't mean to read it either... *Au revoir*. And if the spirit moves you, I'm at your service. I wish you good morning.'

13

EDOUARD'S JOURNAL: DOUVIERS AND PROFITENDIEU

BROUGHT back Olivier's things from Passavant's. As soon as I got home, set to work on *The Counterfeiters*. My exaltation is calm and lucid. My joy is such as I have never known before. Wrote thirty pages without hesitation, without a single erasure. The whole drama, like a nocturnal landscape suddenly illuminated by a flash of lightning, emerges out of the darkness, very different from what I had been trying to invent. The books which I have hitherto written seem to me like the ornamental pools in public gardens – their contours are defined – perfect perhaps, but the water they contain is captive and lifeless. I wish it now to run freely, according to its bent, sometimes swift, sometimes slow; I choose not to foresee its windings.

X. maintains that a good novelist, before he begins to write his book, ought to know how it is going to finish. As for me, who let mine flow where it will, I consider that life never presents us with anything which may not be looked upon as a fresh starting point, no less than as a termination. 'Might be continued' – these are the words with which I should like to finish my *Counterfeiters*.

Visit from Douviers. He is certainly an excellent fellow.

As I exaggerated my sympathy for him, I was obliged to submit to his effusions, which were rather embarrassing. All the time I was talking to him, I kept repeating to myself La Rochefoucauld's words: 'I am very little susceptible to pity; and should like not to be so at all . . . I consider that one ought to content oneself with showing it and carefully refrain from feeling it.' And yet my sympathy was real, undeniable, and I was moved to tears. Truth to tell, my tears seemed to console him better than my words. I almost believe that he gave up being unhappy as soon as he saw me cry.

I was firmly resolved not to tell him the name of the seducer;

but to my surprise he did not ask it. I think his jealousy dies down as soon as he no longer feels Laura's eyes upon him. In any case, its energy had been somewhat diminished by the act of coming to see me.

There is something illogical in his case; he is indignant that the other man should have deserted Laura. I pointed out that if it had not been for his desertion, Laura would not have come back to him. He is resolved to love the child as if it were his own. Who knows whether he would ever have tasted the joys of paternity without the seducer? I took good care not to point this out to him, for at the recollection of his insufficiencies, his jealousy becomes more acute. But then it belongs to the domain of vanity and ceases to interest me.

That an Othello should be jealous is comprehensible; the image of his wife's pleasure obsesses him. But when a Douviers becomes jealous it can only be because he imagines he ought to be.

And no doubt he nurses this passion from a secret need to give body to his somewhat unsubstantial personage. Happiness would be natural to him; but he has to admire himself and he esteems only what is acquired, not what is natural. I did all I could therefore to persuade him that simple happiness was more meritorious than torments and very difficult to attain. I did not let him go till he was calm again.

Inconsistency. Characters in a novel or a play who act all the way through exactly as one expects them to. . . . This consistency of theirs, which is held up to our admiration, is on the contrary the very thing which makes us recognize that they are artificially composed.

Not that I pretend that inconsistency is a sure indication of naturalness, for one often meets, especially among women, affected inconsistencies; and on the other hand, in some few instances, there is reason to admire what is known as *esprit de suite*; but, as a rule, such consecutiveness is obtained only by vain and obstinate perseverance, and at the expense of all naturalness. The more fundamentally generous an individual is, and the more fertile in possibilities, the more liable he is to change, and the less willing to allow his future to be decided by his past. The '*justum et tenacem propositi virum*', who is held up to us as a model, more often than not offers a stony soil and is refractory to culture.

I have known some of yet another sort: these assiduously fabricate for themselves a self-conscious originality, and after having made a choice of certain practices, their principal preoccupation is never to depart from them, to remain for ever on their guard and allow themselves not a moment's relaxation. (I remember X., who refused to let me fill his glass with Montrachet 1904, saying: 'I don't like anything but Bordeaux.' As soon as I pretended it was a Bordeaux, he thought the Montrachet delectable.)

When I was younger, I used to make resolutions, which I imagined were virtuous. I was less anxious to be what I was, than to become what I wished to be. Now, I am not far from thinking that in irresolution lies the secret of not growing old.

Olivier has asked me what I am working at. I let myself be carried away into talking of my book, and even – he seemed so much interested – into reading him the pages I had just written. I was afraid of what he would say, knowing how sweeping young people's judgements are and how difficult they find it to admit another point of view from their own. But the few remarks which he diffidently offered, seemed to me most judicious, and I immediately turned them to account.

My breath, my life comes to me from him – through him.

He is still anxious about the review he was going to edit, and particularly about the story which he wrote at Passavant's request and which he now repudiates. I told him that Passavant's new arrangements will necessitate the re-casting of the first number; he will be able to get his M S. back.

Just received a very unexpected visit from *M. le juge d'instruction* Profitendieu. He was mopping his forehead and breathing heavily, not so much, it seemed to me, from having come up my six flights of stairs, as from embarrassment. He kept his hat in his hand and did not sit down till I pressed him to. He is a handsome man, with a fine figure and considerable presence.

'I think you are President Molinier's brother-in-law,' he said. 'It is about his son George that I have taken the liberty of coming to see you. I feel sure you will excuse a step which at first sight may seem indiscreet, but which the affection and esteem I have for my colleague will, I hope, sufficiently explain.'

He paused. I got up and went to let down a *portière*, for fear the charwoman, who is very inquisitive, and who was, I knew, in the next room, should overhear. Profitendieu approved me with a smile.

'In my capacity as *juge d'instruction*, I have an affair on my hands which is causing me extreme embarrassment. Your young nephew has already been mixed up in a most compromising manner in a . . . this is quite between ourselves, I beg . . . in a somewhat scandalous adventure. I am willing to believe, considering his extreme youth, that he was taken by surprise, owing to his simplicity – his innocence; but I may say that it has required some skill on my part to . . . ahem . . . circumscribe this affair, without injuring the interests of justice. In the face of a second breach – of quite another kind, I hasten to add – I cannot answer for it that young George will get off so easily. I even doubt whether it is in the boy's own interest to *try* to get him off, notwithstanding all my desire as a friend to spare your brother-in-law such a scandal. Nevertheless, I *will* try; but I have officers, you understand, who are zealous, and whom I am not always able to restrain. Or, if you prefer it, I am still able to keep them in hand today, but tomorrow I shall be unable to. And I thought you might speak to your young nephew and warn him of the risk he is running.'

Profitendieu's visit (I might as well admit it) had at first alarmed me horribly; but as soon as I understood that he had come neither as an enemy nor as a judge, I began to be amused. I was a great deal more so when he went on:

'For some time past a certain number of counterfeit coins have been put into circulation. So far I am informed. But I have not yet succeeded in discovering their origin. I know, however, that young George – quite innocently, I am willing to believe – is one of those who circulate them. A few young boys of your nephew's age are lending themselves to this shameful traffic. I don't doubt that their simplicity is being abused and that these foolish children are tools in the hands of one or two unscrupulous elders. We should have had no difficulty in taking up the younger delinquents and making them confess the origin of the coins; but I am only too well aware that after a certain point a case escapes our control, so to speak; that is to say, we cannot go back on the police court proceedings, and we sometimes find ourselves forced to become acquainted with things we should prefer to ignore. Upon this occasion, I have no doubt I shall discover the real culprits without having recourse to the minors' evidence. I have given orders therefore not to alarm them. But my orders are only provisional. I don't want your nephew to force me to countermand them. He had better be told that the authorities' eyes are open. It wouldn't be a bad thing indeed to frighten him a little; he is on a downward course....'

I declared I would do my best to warn him, but Profitendieu seemed not to hear me. His eyes became vague. He repeated twice: 'on what is called a downward course,' and then was silent.

I do not know how long his silence lasted. Without his having to formulate his thoughts, I seemed to see them forming in his mind, and before he spoke, I already heard his words:

'I am a father myself, sir....'

Everything he had been saying disappeared; there was nothing left between us but Bernard. The rest was only a pretext; it was to talk of him that he had come.

If effusions make me feel uncomfortable, if exaggerated feelings irritate me, nothing, on the contrary, could have been more calculated to touch me than this restrained emotion. He kept it back as best he could, but with so great an effort that his lips and hands trembled. He was unable to continue. He suddenly hid his face in his hands, and the upper part of his body was shaken with sobs:

'You see,' he stammered, 'you see how miserable a child can make us.'

What was the good of pretending? Extremely moved myself, 'If Bernard were to see you,' I cried, 'his heart would melt; I can vouch for it.'

At the same time I felt in rather an awkward situation.

Bernard had hardly ever mentioned his father to me. I had morally accepted his having left his family, ready as I am to consider such desertions natural, and disposed to see in them nothing but what will be to the child's greatest advantage. In Bernard's case, there was the additional factor of his bastardy. ... But here was his false father discovering feelings which were all the stronger, no doubt, that they were beyond control, and all the more sincere that they were in no way obligatory. In the face of this love, this grief, I was forced to ask myself whether Bernard had done right to leave. I had no longer the heart to approve him.

'Make use of me, if you think I can be of any use,' I said, 'if you think that I ought to speak to him. He has a good heart.'

'I know. I know.... Yes, you can do a great deal. I know he was with you this summer. My police work is well done.... I know too that he is going up for his *viva voce* this very day. I chose the moment I knew he would be at the Sorbonne to come and see you. I was afraid of meeting him.'

For some minutes, my emotion had been dwindling, for I had just noticed that the verb 'to know' figured in nearly all his sentences. I immediately became less interested in what he was saying than in this trick of speech, which was perhaps professional.

He told me also that he 'knew' that Bernard had passed his written examination brilliantly. An obliging examiner, who happened to be a friend of his, had enabled him to see his son's French essay, which it appears was most remarkable. He spoke of Bernard with a kind of restrained admiration, which made me wonder whether after all he did not believe he was really his father.

'Heavens!' added he, 'whatever you do, don't tell him what I have just been saying. He is so proud by nature, so easily offended!... If he suspected that ever since he left I have never ceased thinking of him, following him... But all the same, you can tell him that you have seen me.' (He breathed painfully after each sentence.) 'You can tell him, what no one else can, that I am not angry with him'; then with a voice that grew fainter: 'that I have never ceased to love him ... like a son. Yes, I know that you know.... You can tell him too ...' and without looking at me, with difficulty, in a state of extreme confusion 'that his mother left me... yes, for good, this summer; and that if he... would come back, I...'

He was unable to finish.

When a big, strong, matter-of-fact man, who has made his way in life and is firmly established in his career, suddenly throws aside all decorum and pours out his heart before a stranger, he affords him (in this case it was I) a most singular spectacle. I was able once more to verify, as I have often done before, that I am more easily moved by the effusions of an outsider than by those of a familiar acquaintance. (Will examine into the reason of this another time.)

Profitendieu did not conceal that he had at first been prejudiced against me, not having understood, and still not understanding, why Bernard had left his home to join me. This was what had prevented him from coming to see me in the first place. I did not dare tell him the story of the suitcase, and merely spoke of his son's friendship for Olivier, which had quickly led to our becoming intimate in our turn.

'These young men,' went on Profitendieu, 'start off in life without knowing to what they are exposed. No doubt their ignorance of danger makes their strength. But we who know, we, their fathers, tremble for them. Our solicitude irritates them, and the best thing is to let them see it as little as possible. I know that it is sometimes very troublesome and clumsy. Rather than incessantly repeat to a child that fire burns, let us consent to his burning his fingers. Experience is a better instructor than advice. I always allowed Bernard the greatest possible liberty – so much so, that he fancied, I grieve to say, that I was indifferent to him. I am afraid that was his mistake and the reason of his running away. Even then, I thought it was better to let him be; though I kept a watch on him all the time without his suspecting it. Thank God, I had the means!' (Evidently the organization of his police was Profitendieu's special pride – this was the third time he had alluded to it.) 'I thought I must take care not to belittle the risks of his initiative in the boy's eyes. Shall I own to you that his rebellious conduct, notwithstanding the pain it gave me, has only made me fonder of him than ever? It seemed to me a proof of courage, of valour....'

Now that he felt himself on confidential terms, the worthy man would have gone on for ever. I tried to bring the conversation back to what interested me more and, cutting him short, asked him if he had ever seen one of the counterfeit coins of which he had spoken. I was curious to know whether they were like the little glass piece which Bernard had shown us. I had no sooner mentioned this, than Profitendieu's whole countenance changed; his eyelids half closed and a curious light burned in his eyes; crow's-feet appeared upon his temples, his lips tightened, his features were all drawn upwards in his effort at attention. There was no further question of anything that had passed before. The judge ousted the father and nothing existed for him but his profession. He pressed me with questions, took notes and spoke of sending a police officer to Saas-Fée to take the names of the visitors in the hotel books.

'Though in all likelihood,' he added, 'the coin you saw was given to the grocer by an adventurer who was merely passing through the place.'

To which I replied that Saas-Fée was at the further end of an *impasse* and that it was not easy to go there and back from it in the same day. He appeared particularly pleased with this piece of information, and after having thanked me warmly, left me, with an absorbed, delighted look on his face, and without having once recurred either to George or to Bernard.

14
BERNARD AND THE ANGEL

BERNARD was to experience that morning that for a nature as generous as his, there is no greater joy than to rejoice another being. This joy was denied him. He had just heard that he had passed his examination with honours, but finding no one near to whom he could communicate it, the news lost all its savour. Bernard knew well enough that the person who would have been most pleased to hear it, was his father. He even hesitated a moment whether he would not go there and then and tell him; but pride held him back. Edouard? Olivier? It was really giving too much importance to a certificate. He had passed his *baccalauréat*. Nothing to make a fuss about! It was now that the difficulties would begin.

In the Sorbonne quadrangle, he saw one of his schoolfellows, who had also been successful; but he had drawn apart from the others and was crying. The poor boy was in mourning. Bernard knew that he had just lost his mother. A great wave of sympathy drove him towards the orphan; then a feeling of absurd shyness made him pass on. The other boy, who had seen him come up and then go by, was ashamed of his tears; he esteemed Bernard and was hurt by what he took for contempt.

Bernard went into the Luxembourg gardens. He sat down on a bench in the same part of the gardens where he had gone to meet Olivier the evening he had sought shelter with him. The air was almost warm and the blue sky laughed down at him through the branches of the great trees, already stripped of their leaves. One could not believe that winter was really on the way; the cooing birds themselves were deceived. But Bernard did not look at the gardens; he saw the ocean of life spread out before him. People say there are paths on the sea, but they are not traced and Bernard did not know which one was his.

He had been meditating for some moments, when he saw coming towards him – gliding on so light a foot that one felt it might have rested on the waves – an angel. Bernard had never seen any angels, but he had not a moment's doubt, and when the angel said: 'Come!' he rose obediently and followed him. He was not more astonished than he would have been in a dream. He tried to remember afterwards if the angel had taken him by the hand; but in reality they did not touch each other and even kept a little apart. They returned together to the quadrangle where Bernard had left the orphan, firmly resolved to speak to him; but the quadrangle was empty.

Bernard walked, with the angel by his side, towards the church of the Sorbonne, into which the angel passed first – into which Bernard had never been before. Other angels were going to and fro in this place; but Bernard had not the eyes that were needed to see them. An unfamiliar peace enfolded him. The angel went up to the high altar, and Bernard, when he saw him kneel down, knelt down beside him. He did not believe in any god, so that he could not pray, but his heart was filled with a lover's longing for dedication, for sacrifice; he offered himself. His emotion was so confused that no word could have expressed it; but suddenly the organ's song arose.

'You offered yourself in the same way to Laura,' said the angel; and Bernard felt the tears streaming down his cheeks. 'Come, follow me.'

As the angel drew him along, Bernard almost knocked up against one of his old schoolfellows, who had also just passed his *viva voce*. Bernard considered him a dunce and was astonished that he had got through. The dunce did not notice Bernard, who saw him slip some money for a candle into the beadle's hand. Bernard shrugged his shoulders and went out.

When he found himself in the street again, he saw that the angel had left him. He went into a tobacco shop – the very same in which George, a week before, had risked his first false coin. He had passed a great many more since then. Bernard bought a packet of cigarettes and smoked. Why had the angel gone? Had Bernard and he then nothing to say to each other? . . . Noon struck. Bernard was hungry. Should he go back to the pension? Should he join Olivier and share with him Edouard's lunch? . . . He made sure that he had enough money in his pocket and went into a restaurant. As he was finishing his lunch, a soft voice murmured in his ear:

'The time has come to do your accounts.'

Bernard turned his head. The angel was again beside him.

'You will have to make up your mind,' he said. 'You have been living at haphazard. Do you mean to let chance dispose of your life? You want to be of service – but what do you wish to serve? That is the question.'

'Teach me; guide me,' said Bernard.

The angel led Bernard into a hall full of people. At the bottom of the hall was a platform and on the platform a table covered with a dark red cloth. A man, who was still young, was seated behind the table and was speaking.

'It is a very great folly,' he was saying, 'to imagine that there is anything we can discover. What have we that we have not received? It is the duty of each one of us to understand while we are still young, that we derive from the past, that we are bound to this past by every kind of obligation, and that the whole of our future is marked out by it.'

When he had finished developing this theme, another orator took his place; he began by approving the former and then raised his voice against the presumption of the man who thinks he can live without a doctrine, or guide himself by his own lights.

'A doctrine has been bequeathed us,' he said. 'It has already traversed many centuries. It is assuredly the best – the only one. The duty of each one of us is to prove this truth. It has been handed down to us by our masters. It is our country's and every time she repudiates it, she has to pay for her error dearly. No one can be a good Frenchman without holding it, nor succeed in anything good without conforming to it.'

To this second orator succeeded a third, who thanked the other two for having so ably traced what he called the theory of their programme; then he set forth that this programme consisted in nothing less than the regeneration of France, which was to be brought about by the united efforts of each single member of their party. He himself, he declared, was a man of action; he affirmed that the end and proof of every theory is in its practice, and that the duty of every good Frenchman is to be a combatant.

'But, alas!' he added, 'how many isolated efforts are wasted! Our country would be far greater, our activity would be far more widespread, all that is best in us would be brought forward, if every effort were coordinated, if every act contributed to the glory of law and order, if everyone were willing to serve in the ranks.'

And while he was speaking, a number of young men went round the audience, distributing printed forms of membership, which had only to be signed.

'You wanted to offer yourself,' said the angel then, 'What are you waiting for?'

Bernard took one of the papers which were handed him; it began with these words: 'I solemnly pledge myself to ...' He read it, then looked at the angel and saw that he was smiling; then he looked at the meeting and recognized among the young men present, the schoolfellow whom he had seen just before in the church, burning a candle in gratitude for having passed his examination; and suddenly, further on, he caught sight of his eldest brother, whom he had not seen since he had left home. Bernard did not like him and was a little jealous of the consideration with which their father seemed to treat him. He crumpled the paper nervously in his hand.

'Do you think I ought to sign?'

'Yes,' said the angel, 'certainly – if you have doubts of yourself.'

'I doubt no longer,' said Bernard, flinging the paper from him.

In the meantime the orator was still speaking. When Bernard began to listen to him again, he was teaching an infallible method for never making a mistake, which was to give up ever forming a judgement for oneself and always to defer to the judgements of one's superiors.

'And who are these superiors?' asked Bernard; and suddenly a great indignation seized him.

'If you went on to the platform,' he said to the angel, 'and grappled with him, you would be sure to throw him....'

'It is with *you* I will wrestle. This evening. Do you agree...?'

'Yes,' said Bernard.

They went out. They reached the boulevards. The crowds that were thronging them seemed entirely composed of rich people; each of them seemed sure of himself, indifferent to the others, but anxious.

'Is that the image of happiness?' asked Bernard, who felt the tears rising in his heart.

Then the angel took Bernard into the poor quarters of the town, whose wretchedness Bernard had never suspected. Evening was falling. They wandered for a long time among tall, sordid houses, inhabited by disease, prostitution, shame, crime and hunger. It was only then that Bernard took the angel's hand, and the angel turned aside to weep.

Bernard did not dine that evening; and when he went back to the pension he did not attempt to join Sarah, as he had done the other evenings, but went straight upstairs to the room he shared with Boris.

Boris was already in bed, but not asleep. He was re-reading, by the light of his candle, the letter he had received that very morning from Bronja.

'I am afraid,' wrote his friend, 'that I shall never see you again. I caught cold when we got back to Poland. I have a cough; and though the doctor hides it from me, I feel I cannot live much longer.'

When he heard Bernard coming up, Boris hid the letter under his pillow, and blew the candle out hurriedly.

Bernard came in in the dark. The angel was with him, but, although the night was not very dark, Boris saw only Bernard.

'Are you asleep?' asked Bernard in a whisper. And as Boris did not answer, he concluded he was sleeping.

'Then, now,' said Bernard to the angel, 'we'll have it out.'

And all that night, until the breaking of the day, they wrestled.

Boris dimly perceived that Bernard was struggling. He thought it was his way of praying and took care not to disturb him. And yet he would have liked to speak to him, for his unhappiness was very great. He got up and knelt down at the foot of his bed. He would have liked to pray, but he could only sob:

'Oh, Bronja! You who can see angels, you who were to have opened my eyes, you are leaving me! Without you, Bronja, what will become of me? What will become of me?'

Bernard and the angel were too busy to hear him. They wrestled together till daybreak. The angel departed without either of them having vanquished the other.

When, a little later, Bernard himself left the room, he met Rachel in the passage.

'I want to speak to you,' she said. Her voice was so sad that Bernard understood at once what it was she had to say to him. He answered nothing, bowed his head, and in his great pity for Rachel suddenly began to hate Sarah and to loathe the pleasure he took with her.

15
BERNARD VISITS EDOUARD

ABOUT ten o'clock, Bernard turned up at Edouard's with a hand-bag which was sufficient to contain the few clothes and books that he possessed. He had taken leave of Azaïs and of Madame Vedel, but had not attempted to see Sarah.

Bernard was grave. His struggle with the angel had matured him. He no longer resembled the careless youth who had stolen the suitcase and who thought that all that is needed in this world is to be daring. He was beginning to understand that boldness is often achieved at the expense of other people's happiness.

'I have come to ask for shelter,' said he to Edouard. 'Here I am again without a roof.'

'Why are you leaving the Vedels'?'

'For private reasons . . . forgive me for not telling you.'

Edouard had observed Bernard and Sarah on the evening of the dinner enough to guess at the meaning of this silence.

'All right,' he said smiling. 'The couch in my studio is at your service. But I must first tell you that your father came to see me yesterday.' And he repeated the part of their conversation which he thought likely to touch him. 'It is not in my house that you ought to spend the night, but in his. He is expecting you.'

Bernard, however, kept silent.

'I will think about it,' he said at last. 'Allow me in the meantime to leave my things here. May I see Olivier?'

'The weather is so fine, that I advised him to go out. I wanted to go with him, for he is still very weak, but he wouldn't let me. But it's more than an hour since he left and he will be back soon. You had better wait for him. . . . But I've just thought. . . . Your examination?'

'I've passed; but it's of no importance; the important thing is to know what I'm to do now. Do you know the chief reason that prevents me from going back to my father's? It's because I don't want to take his money. You'll think me absurd to fling away such an opportunity; but I made a vow that I would make my way without it. I feel I must prove to myself that I am a man of my word –someone I can count on.'

'It strikes me as pride more than anything else.'

'Call it by any name you please – pride, presumption, conceit . . . it's a feeling you won't succeed in cheapening in my eyes. But at the present moment, what I should like to know is this – is it necessary to fix one's eyes on a goal in order to guide oneself in life?'

'Explain.'

'I wrestled over it all last night. What am I to do with the strength I feel I possess? To what use am I to put it? How am I to get out of myself the best that's in me? Is it by aiming at a goal? But how choose such a goal? How know what it is before reaching it?'

'To live without a goal, is to give oneself up to chance.'

'I am afraid you don't understand. When Columbus discovered America did he know towards what he was sailing? His goal was to go ahead,straight in front of him. Himself was his goal, impelling him to go ahead. . . .'

'I have often thought,' interrupted Edouard, 'that in art, and particularly in literature, the only people who count are those who launch out on to unknown seas. One doesn't discover new lands without consenting to lose sight of the shore for a very long time. But our writers are afraid of the open; they are mere coasters.'

'Yesterday, when I came out from my examination,' Bernard said, without hearing him, 'some demon or other urged me into a hall where there was a public meeting going on. The talk was all about national honour, devotion to one's country, and a whole lot of things that made my heart beat. I came within an ace of signing a paper by which I pledged myself on my honour to devote my energies to the service of a cause, which certainly seemed to me a fine and noble one.'

'I am glad you didn't sign, but what prevented you?'

'No doubt some secret instinct. . . .' Bernard reflected a few moments, and then added, laughing: 'I think it was chiefly the looks of the audience – starting with my brother, whom I recognized among them. It seemed to me all the young men I saw there, were animated by the best of sentiments, and that they were doing quite right to abdicate their initiative (for it wouldn't have led them far) and their judgement (for it was inadequate) and their independence of mind (for it was still-born). I said to myself too, that it was a good thing for the country to count among its citizens a large number of these well-intentioned individuals with subservient wills, but that my will would never be of that kind. It was then that I began to ask myself how to establish a rule, since I did not accept life without a rule and yet would not accept a rule from anyone else.'

'The answer seems to me simple: to find the rule in oneself; to have for goal the development of oneself.'

'Yes . . . that, as a matter of fact, is what I said to myself. But I wasn't much further on. If I were certain of preferring what is best in myself, I might develop that rather than the rest. But I can't even find out what *is* best in myself. . . . I wrestled over it all night, I tell you. Towards morning I was so tired that I thought of enlisting – before I was called up.'

'Running away from the question doesn't solve it.'

'That's what I said to myself, and that even if I put the question off now, it would come up again more seriously than ever after my service. So I came to ask you your advice.'

'I have none to give you. You can only find counsel in yourself; you can only learn how you ought to live by living.'

'And if I live badly, whilst I'm waiting to decide how to live?'

'That in itself will teach you. It's a good thing to follow one's inclination, provided it leads uphill.'

'Are you joking? . . . No; I think I understand you, and I accept your formula. But while I am developing myself, as you say, I shall have to earn my living. What do you say to an alluring advertisement in the papers: "Young man of great promise requires a job. Could be employed in any capacity"?'

Edouard laughed.

'No job is so difficult to find as any job. Better be a little more explicit.'

'Perhaps one of the innumerable little wheels in the organization of a big newspaper would do? Oh! I'd accept any post however subordinate – proof-reader – printer's devil – anything. I need so little.'

He spoke with hesitation. In reality, it was a secretaryship he wanted; but he did not dare say so to Edouard, because of their mutual dissatisfaction with each other on this score. After all, it wasn't his, Bernard's, fault, that this trial of theirs had failed so lamentably.

'I might perhaps,' said Edouard, 'get you into the *Grand Journal*; I know the editor....'

While Bernard and Edouard were conversing in this manner, Sarah was having an extremely painful explanation with Rachel. Sarah had suddenly understood that Rachel's remonstrances were the cause of Bernard's abrupt departure; and she was indignant with her sister, who, she said, was a kill-joy. She had no right to impose upon others a virtue which her example was enough to render odious.

Rachel, who was terribly upset by these accusations, for she had always sacrificed herself, turned very white, and protested with trembling lips:

'I can't let you go to perdition.'

But Sarah sobbed and cried out:

'I don't believe in your heaven. I don't want to be saved.'

She decided on the spot to return to England, where she would go and stay with her friend. For, after all, she was free and claimed the right to live in any way she pleased. This melancholy quarrel left Rachel shattered.

16

EDOUARD WARNS GEORGE

EDOUARD took care to arrive at the pension before the boys came in. He had not seen La Pérouse since the beginning of the term and it was to him that he wanted to speak first. The old music master carried out his new duties as well as he could – that is to say, very badly. He had at first tried to make himself liked, but he had no authority; the boys took advantage of him; his indulgence passed for weakness, and they began to take strange liberties. La Pérouse tried to be severe, but too late; his exhortations, his threats, his reprimands finally set the boys against him. If he raised his voice, they laughed; if he thumped his fist resoundingly on his desk, they shrieked in pretended terror; they mimicked him; they called him by absurd nicknames; caricatures of him circulated from bench to bench; he – so kind and courteous – was portrayed armed with a pistol (the pistol which Ghéridanisol, George and Phiphi had found one day in the course of an indiscreet investigation of his room), ferociously massacring the boys; or else on his knees before them, with hands clasped, imploring, as he had done at first, for 'a little quiet, for pity's sake'. He was like a poor old stag at bay among a savage pack of hounds. Edouard knew nothing of all this.

EDOUARD'S JOURNAL

La Pérouse received me in a small classroom on the ground floor, which I recognized as the most uncomfortable one in the school. Its only furniture consisted of four benches attached to four desks, a blackboard and a straw chair, on which La Pérouse forced me to sit down, while he screwed himself up slantwise on to one of the benches, after vain endeavours to get his long legs under the desk.

'No, no. I'm perfectly comfortable, I assure you,' he declared, while the tone of his voice and the expression of his face said:

'I am horribly uncomfortable, and I hope it's obvious; but I prefer to be so; and the more uncomfortable I am, the less you will hear me complain.'

I tried to make a joke, but could not succeed in getting him to smile. His manner was ceremonious and stiff, as if he wished to keep me at a distance and imply: 'I owe it to you that I am here.'

At the same time he declared himself perfectly satisfied with everything, though all the while eluding my questions and seeming vexed at my insisting. I asked him, however, where his room was.

'Rather too far from the kitchen,' he suddenly exclaimed; and as I expressed my astonishment: 'Sometimes during the night, I want something to eat . . . when I can't sleep.'

I was near him; I came nearer still and put my hand gently on his arm. He went on in a more natural tone:

'I must tell you that I sleep very badly. When I do go to sleep, I never lose the feeling that I am asleep. That's not proper sleep, is it? A person who is properly asleep, doesn't feel that he is asleep. When he wakes up, he just knows that he has been asleep.'

Then, leaning towards me, he went on with a kind of finicky insistence:

'Sometimes I'm inclined to think that it's an illusion and that, all the same, I *am* properly asleep, when I think I'm not asleep. But the proof that I'm not properly asleep is that if I want to open my eyes, I open them. As a rule, I don't want to. You understand, don't you, that there's no object in it? What's the use of proving to myself that I'm not asleep? I always go on hoping that I shall go to sleep by persuading myself that I'm asleep already. . . .'

He bent still nearer and went on in a whisper:

'And then there's something that disturbs me. Don't tell anyone. . . . I haven't complained, because there's nothing to do about it; and if a thing can't be altered, there's no good complaining, is there? . . . Well, just imagine, in the wall, right against my bed and exactly on a level with my head, there's something that makes a noise.'

He had grown excited as he spoke. I suggested that he should take me to his room.

'Yes! Yes!' he said getting up suddenly. 'You might be able to tell me what it is . . . I can't succeed in making out. Come along.'

We went up two storeys and then down a longish passage. I had never been into that part of the house before.

La Pérouse's room looked on to the street. It was small but decent. On the bedside table, I noticed, next a prayer book, the case of pistols, which he had insisted on taking with him. He seized me by the arm, and pushing aside the bed a little:

'There! Now! . . . Put your ear to the wall. . . . Can you hear it?'

I listened for a long time with the greatest attention. But notwithstanding the best will in the world, I could not succeed in hearing anything. La Pérouse grew vexed. Just then a van drove by, shaking the house and making the windows rattle.

'At this time of day,' I said, in the hopes of pacifying him, 'the little noise that irritates you is drowned by the noise of the street. . . .'

'Drowned for you, because you can't distinguish it from the other noises,' he exclaimed with vehemence. 'As for me, I hear it all the same. In spite of everything, I go on hearing it. Sometimes I am so exasperated by it that I make up my mind to speak to Azaïs or to the landlord. . . . Oh, I don't suppose I shall get it to stop. . . .But, at any rate, I should like to know what it is.'

He seemed to reflect for a few moments, then went on: 'It sounds something like a nibbling. I've done everything I can think of not to hear it. I pull my bed away from the wall. I put cotton wool in my ears. I hang my watch (you see, I've put a little nail there) just at the place where the pipe (I suppose) passes, so that its ticking may prevent my hearing the other noise. . . . But then it's even more fatiguing, because I have to make an effort to distinguish it. Absurd, isn't it? But I really prefer to hear it without any disguise, since I know it's there all the same. . . . Oh! I oughtn't to talk to you in this way. You see, I'm nothing but an old man now.'

He sat down on the edge of the bed, and stayed for some time, as though sunk in a kind of dull misery. The sinister degradation of age is not so much attacking La Pérouse's intelligence as the innermost depths of his nature. The worm lodges itself in the fruit's core, I thought, as I saw him give way to his childish despair, and remembered him as he used to be, so firm – so proud. I tried to rouse him by speaking of Boris.

'Yes, his room is near mine,' said he, raising his head. 'I'll show it to you. Come along.'

He preceded me along the passage and opened a neighbouring door.

'The other bed you see there is young Bernard Profitendieu's.' (I judged it useless to tell him that Bernard had left that very day, and would not be coming back to sleep in it.) He went on: 'Boris likes having him as a companion and I think he gets on with him. But, you know, he doesn't talk to me much. He's very reserved. . . . I am afraid the child is rather unfeeling.'

He said this so sadly that I took upon myself to protest and to say that I could answer for his grandson's warm-heartedness.

'In that case, he might show it a little more,' went on La Pérouse.

'For instance, in the mornings, when he goes off to the *lycée* with the others, I lean out of my window to see him go by. He knows I do. . . . Well, he never turns round.'

I wanted to explain to him that no doubt Boris was afraid of making a spectacle of himself before his schoolfellows and dreaded being laughed at; but at that moment a clamour arose from the courtyard below.

La Pérouse seized me by the arm and, in an altered, agitated voice:

'Listen! Listen!' he cried, 'they are coming in.'

I looked at him. He had begun to tremble all over.

'Do the little wretches frighten you?' I asked.

'No, no,' he said in some confusion; 'how could you think such a thing? . . .' Then, very quickly: 'I must go down. Recreation only lasts a few minutes and you know I take preparation. Good-bye. Good-bye.'

He darted into the passage, without even shaking my hand. A moment later I heard him stumbling downstairs. I stayed for a few moments to listen, as I had no wish to go past the boys. I could hear them shouting, laughing and singing. Then a bell rang and silence was abruptly restored.

I went to see Azaïs and obtained permission for George to leave school in order to come and speak to me. He soon joined me in the same small room in which La Pérouse had received me a little while before.

As soon as he was in my presence, George thought fit to assume a jocular air. It was his way of concealing his embarrassment. But I wouldn't swear that he was the more embarrassed of the two. He was on the defensive; for no doubt he expected to be sermonized. He seemed trying as hastily as possible to lay hold of anything he could use as a weapon against me, for, before I had opened my mouth, he inquired after Olivier, in such a bantering tone of voice, that I should have had the greatest pleasure in boxing his ears. He was in a position to score off me. His ironical eyes, the mocking curl of his lips all seemed to say: 'I'm not afraid of you, you know.' I at once lost all my self-assurance and my one anxiety was to conceal the fact. The speech I had prepared suddenly struck me as inappropriate. I had not the prestige necessary to play the censor. At bottom, George amused me too much.

'I have not come to scold you,' I said at last; 'I only want to warn you.' (And, in spite of myself, my whole face was smiling).

'Tell me first whether it's Mamma who has sent you?'

'Yes and no. I have spoken about you to your mother; but that was some days ago. Yesterday I had a very important conversation about you with a very important person, whom you don't know. He came to see me on purpose to talk about you. A *juge d'instruction*. It's from him I've come. Do you know what a *juge d'instruction* is?'

George had turned suddenly pale, and no doubt his heart had stopped beating for a moment. He shrugged his shoulders, it is true, but his voice trembled a little:

'Oh! all right! Out with it! What did old Profitendieu say?'

The youngster's coolness took me aback. No doubt it would have been simpler to go straight to the point; but going straight to the point is a thing particularly foreign to my nature, whose irresistible bent is towards moving obliquely. In order to explain my conduct, which, though it afterwards appeared absurd to me, was quite spontaneous at the time, I must say that my last conversation with Pauline had greatly exercised me. I had immediately inserted the reflections it had suggested to me into my novel, putting them into the form of a dialogue, which exactly fitted in with certain of my characters. It very rarely happens that I make direct use of what occurs to me in real life, but for once I was able to take advantage of this affair of George's; it was as though my book had been waiting for it, it came in so pat; I hardly had to alter one or two details.

But I did not give a direct account of this affair (I mean his stealing). I merely showed it – with its consequences – by glimpses, in the course of conversations. I had put down some of these in a notebook, which I had at that very moment in my pocket. On the contrary, the story of the false coins, as related by Profitendieu, did not seem to me capable of being turned to account. And no doubt that is why, instead of making immediately for this particular point, which was the main object of my visit, I tacked about.

'I first want you to read these few lines,' I said. 'You will see why.' And I held him out my notebook, which I had opened at the page I thought might interest him.

I repeat it – this behaviour of mine now seems to me absurd. But in my novel, it is precisely by a similar reading that I thought of giving the youngest of my heroes a warning. I wanted to know what George's reaction would be; I hoped it might instruct me . . . and even as to the value of what I had written.

I transcribe the passage in question:

There was a whole obscure region in the boy's character which attracted Audibert's affectionate curiosity. It was not enough for him to know that young Eudolfe had committed thefts; he would have liked Eudolfe to tell him what had made him begin, and what he had felt on the occasion of his first theft. But the boy, even if he had been willing to confide in him, would no doubt have been incapable of explaining. And Audibert did not dare question him, for fear of inducing him to tell lies in self-defence.

One evening when Audibert was dining with Hildebrant, he spoke to him about Eudolfe – without naming him and altering the circumstances so that Hildebrant should not recognize him.

'Have you ever observed,' said Hildebrant, 'that the most decisive actions of our life – I mean those that are most likely to decide the whole course of our future – are, more often than not, unconsidered?'

'I easily believe it,' replied Audibert. 'Like a train into which one jumps without thinking, and without asking oneself where it is going. And more often than not, one does not even realize that the train is carrying one off, till it is too late to get down.'

'But perhaps the boy you are talking of has no wish to get down?'

'Not so far, doubtless. For the moment he is being carried along unresisting. The scenery amuses him, and he cares very little where he is going.'

'Do you mean to talk morals to him?'

'No indeed! It would be useless. He has been overdosed with morals till he is sick.'

'Why did he steal?'

'I don't exactly know. Certainly not from real need. But to get certain advantages – not to be outdone by his wealthier companions – Heaven knows what all! Innate propensity – sheer pleasure of stealing.'

'That's the worst.'

'Of course! Because he'll begin again.'

'Is he intelligent?'

'I thought for a long time that he was less so than his brothers. But I wonder now whether I wasn't mistaken, and whether my unfavourable impression was not caused by the fact that he does not as yet understand what his capabilities are. His curiosity has gone off the tracks – or, rather, it is still in the embryonic state – still at the stage of indiscretion.'

'Will you speak to him?'

'I propose making him put in the scales, on the one hand the little profit his thefts bring him, and on the other what his dishonesty loses him: the confidence of his friends and relations, their esteem, mine amongst others . . . things which can't be measured and the value of which can be calculated only by the enormousness of the effort needed later to regain them. There are men who have spent their whole lives over it. I shall tell him, what he is still too young to realize – that henceforth if anything doubtful or unpleasant happens in his neighbourhood, it will always be laid to his door. He may find himself accused wrongfully of serious misdeeds and be unable to defend himself. His past actions point to him. He is marked. And lastly what I should like to say . . . But I am afraid of his protestations.'

'You would like to say ?. . .'

'That what he has done has created a precedent, and that if some resolution is required for a first theft, for the ensuing ones nothing is needed but to drift with the current. All that follows is mere *laisser aller*. . . . What I should like to say is, that a first movement, which one makes almost without thinking, often begins to trace a line which irrevocably draws our figure, and which our after effort will never be able to efface. I should like . . . but no, I shan't know how to speak to him.'

'Why don't you write down our conversation of this evening ? You could give it him to read.'

'That's an idea,' said Audibert. 'Why not ?'

I did not take my eyes off George while he was reading; but his face showed no signs of what he was thinking.

'Am I to go on ?' he asked, preparing to turn the page.

'There's no need. The conversation ends there.'

'A great pity.'

He gave me back the notebook, and in a tone of voice that was almost playful:

'I should have liked to know what Eudolfe says when he has read the notebook.'

'Exactly. I want to know myself.'

'Eudolfe is a ridiculous name. Couldn't you have christened him something else ?'

'It's of no importance.'

'Nor what he answers either. And what becomes of him afterwards?'

'I don't know yet. It depends upon you. We shall see.'

'Then if I understand right, *I* am to help you go on with your book. No, really, you must admit that...'

He stopped as if he had some difficulty in expressing his ideas.

'That what?' I said to encourage him.

'You must admit that you'd be pretty well sold,' he went on, 'if Eudolfe...'

He stopped again. I thought I understood what he meant and finished his sentence for him.

'If he became an honest boy? ... No, my dear.' And suddenly the tears rose to my eyes. I put my hand on his shoulder. But he shook it off:

'For after all, if he hadn't been a thief, you wouldn't have written all that.'

It was only then that I understood my mistake. In reality, George was flattered at having occupied my thoughts for so long. He felt interesting. I had forgotten Profitendieu; it was George who reminded me of him.

'And what did your *juge d'instruction* say to you?'

'He commissioned me to warn you that he knew you were circulating false coins....'

George changed colour again. He understood denials would be useless, but he muttered indistinctly:

'I'm not the only one.'

'... and that if you and your pals don't stop your traffickings at once, he'll be obliged to arrest you.'

George had begun by turning very pale. Now his cheeks were burning. He stared fixedly in front of him and his knitted brows drew two deep wrinkles on his forehead.

'Good-bye,' I said, holding out my hand. 'I advise you to warn your companions as well. As for you, you won't be offered a second chance.'

He shook my hand silently and left the room without looking round.

On re-reading the pages of *The Counterfeiters* which I showed

George, I thought them on the whole rather bad. I transcribe them as George read them, but all this chapter must be rewritten. It would be better decidedly to speak to the child. I must discover how to touch him. Certainly, at the point he has reached, it would be difficult to bring Eudolfe (George is right; I must change his name) back into the path of honesty. But I mean to bring him back; and whatever George may think, this is what is most interesting, because it is most difficult. (Here am I reasoning like Douviers!) Let us leave realistic novelists to deal with the stories of those who drift.

*

As soon as he got back to the classroom, George told his two friends of Edouard's warnings. Everything his uncle had said about his pilferings slipped off the child's mind, without causing him the slightest emotion; but, when it came to the false coins, which ran the risk of getting them into trouble, he saw the importance of getting rid of them as quickly as possible. Each of the three boys had on him a certain number which he intended disposing of the next free afternoon. Ghéridanisol collected them and hurried off to throw them down the drains. That same evening he warned Strouvilhou, who immediately took his precautions.

17

ARMAND AND OLIVIER

THAT same evening, while Edouard was talking to his nephew George, Olivier, after Bernard had left him, received a visit from Armand.

Armand Vedel was unrecognizable; shaved, smiling, carrying his head high; he was dressed in a new suit, which was rather too smart and looked perhaps a trifle ridiculous; he felt it and showed that he felt it.

'I should have come to see you before, but I've had so much to do lately! ... Do you know that I've actually become Passavant's secretary? or, if you prefer it, the editor of his new review. I won't ask you to contribute, because Passavant seems rather worked up against you. Besides the review is decidedly going more and more to the left. That's the reason it has begun by dropping Bercail and his pastorals....'

'I'm sorry for the review,' said Olivier.

'And that's why, on the other hand, it has accepted my *Nocturnal Vase*, which, by the bye, is, without your permission, to be dedicated to you.'

'I'm sorry for me.'

'Passavant even wished my work of genius to open the first number; but my natural modesty, which was severely tried by his encomiums, was opposed to this. If I were not afraid of fatiguing a convalescent's ears, I would give you an account of my first interview with the illustrious author of *The Horizontal Bar*, whom I had only known up till then through you.'

'I have nothing better to do than to listen.'

'You don't mind smoke?'

'I'll smoke myself to show you.'

'I must tell you,' began Armand, lighting a cigarette, 'that your desertion left our beloved Count somewhat in a fix. Let it be said, without flattery, that it isn't easy to replace such a bundle of gifts, virtues, qualities as are united in your...'

'Get on,' interrupted Olivier, exasperated by this heavy-footed irony.

'Well, to get on, Passavant wanted a secretary. He happened to know a certain Strouvilhou, whom I happen to know myself, because he is the uncle of a certain individual in the school, who happened to know Jean Cob-Lafleur, whom you know.'

'Whom I don't know,' said Olivier.

'Well, my boy, you ought to know him. He's an extraordinary fellow; a kind of faded, wrinkled, painted baby, who lives on cocktails and writes charming verses when he's drunk. You'll see some in our first number. So Strouvilhou had the brilliant idea of sending him to Passavant, to take your place. You can imagine his entry into the rue de Babylone mansion. I must tell you that Cob-Lafleur's clothes are covered with stains; that he has flowing flaxen locks, which fall upon his shoulders; and that he looks as if he hadn't washed for a week. Passavant, who always wants to be master of the situation, declares that he took a great fancy to Cob-Lafleur. Cob-Lafleur has a gentle, smiling, timid way with him. When he chooses he can look like Banville's Gringoire. In a word, Passavant was taken by him and was on the point of engaging him. I must tell you that Lafleur hasn't got a penny piece. . . . So he gets up to take leave: – "Before leaving, Monsieur le Comte, I think it's only right to inform you that I have a few faults."–"Which of us has not?" – "And a few vices. I smoke opium."– "Is that all?" says Passavant, who isn't to be put off by a little thing of that kind; "I've got some excellent stuff to offer you." – "Yes, but when I smoke it, I completely lose every notion of spelling." Passavant took this for a joke, forced a laugh and held out his hand. Lafleur goes on: – "And then I take hasheesh." – "I have sometimes taken it myself," says Passavant. – "Yes, but when I am under the influence of hasheesh, I can't keep from stealing." Passavant began to see then that he was being made a fool of; and Lafleur, who was set going by now, rattled on, impulsively: – "And besides, I drink ether; and then I tear everything to bits – I smash everything I can lay my hands on," and he seizes a glass vase and makes as if he were going to throw it into the fire.

Passavant just had time to snatch it out of his hands. – "Much obliged to you for warning me."'

'And he chucked him out?'

'Yes; and watched out of the window to see Lafleur didn't drop a bomb into the cellar as he left.'

'But why did Lafleur behave so? From what you say, he was really in need of the place.'

'All the same, my dear fellow, you must admit that there are people who feel impelled to act against their interest. And then, if you want to know, Lafleur ... well, Passavant's luxury disgusted him – his elegance, his amiable manners, his condescension, his affectation of superiority. Yes; it turned his stomach. And I add that I perfectly understand him. ... At bottom, your Passavant makes one's gorge rise.'

'Why do you say "your Passavant"? You know quite well that I've given him up. And then why have you accepted his place, if you think him so disgusting?'

'For the very reason that I like things that disgust me ... to start with my own delightful – or disgusting – self. And then, in reality, Cob-Lafleur suffers from shyness; he wouldn't have said any of all that if he hadn't felt ill at ease.'

'Oh! come now!'

'Certainly. He was ill at ease, and he was furious at being made to feel ill at ease by someone he really despises. It was to conceal his shyness that he bluffed.'

'I call it stupid.'

'My dear fellow, everyone can't be as intelligent as you are.'

'You said that last time, too.'

'What a memory!'

Olivier was determined to hold his ground.

'I try,' said he, 'to forget your jokes. But last time you did at last talk to me seriously. You said things I can't forget.'

Armand's eyes grew troubled. He went off into a forced laugh.

'Oh, old fellow, last time I talked to you as you wanted to be talked to. You called for something in a minor key, so, in order to please you, I played my lament, with a soul like a corkscrew and anguish à la Pascal. ... It can't be helped, you know. I'm only sincere when I'm cracking jokes.'

'You'll never make me believe that you weren't sincere when you talked to me as you did that day. It's now that you are playing a part.'

'Oh, simplicity! What a pure angelic soul you possess! As if we weren't all playing parts more or less sincerely and consciously. Life, my dear fellow, is nothing but a comedy. But the difference between you and me is that I know I am playing a part, whilst...'

'Whilst...' repeated Olivier aggressively.

'Whilst my father, for instance, not to speak of you, is completely taken in when he plays at being a pastor. Whatever I say or do, there's always one part of myself which stays behind, and watches the other part compromise itself, which laughs at and hisses it, or applauds it. When one is divided in that way, how is it possible to be sincere? I have got to the point of ceasing to understand what the word means. It can't be helped; when I'm sad, I seem so grotesque to myself that it makes me laugh; when I'm cheerful, I make such idiotic jokes that I feel inclined to cry.'

'You make me feel inclined to cry too, my dear boy. I didn't think you were in such a bad way.'

Armand shrugged his shoulders and went on in a totally different tone of voice:

'To console you, should you like to know the contents of our first number? Well, there's my *Nocturnal Vase*; four songs by Cob-Lafleur; a dialogue by Jarry; some prose poems by young Ghérindanisol, one of our boarders; and then *The Flat Iron*, a vast essay in general criticism, in which the tendencies of the review will be more or less definitely laid down. Several of us have combined together to produce this *chef-d'œuvre*.'

Olivier, not knowing what to say, objected clumsily:

'No *chef-d'œuvre* was ever produced by several people together.'

Armand burst out laughing:

'But, my dear fellow, I said it was a *chef-d'œuvre* as a joke. It isn't a *chef-d'œuvre*; it isn't anything at all. And, for that matter, what does one mean by *chef-d'œuvre*? That's just what *The Flat Iron* tries to get to the bottom of. There are heaps of works one admires on faith, just because everyone else does, and because no one so far has thought of saying – or dared to say – that they were stupid. For instance, on the first page of this number, we are going to give a reproduction of the *Mona Lisa*, with a pair of moustaches stuck on to her face. You'll see! The effect is simply staggering.'

'Does that mean you consider the *Mona Lisa* a stupidity?'

'Not at all, my dear fellow. (Though I don't think it as marvellous as all that.) You don't understand me. The thing that's stupid is people's admiration for it. It's the habit they have got of speaking of what are called *chefs-d'œuvre* with bated breath. The object of *The Flat Iron* (it's to be the name of the review too) is to make this reverence appear grotesque – to hold up to the reader's admiration something absolutely idiotic (my *Nocturnal Vase* for instance) by an author who is absolutely senseless.'

'Does Passavant approve of all this?'

'He's very much amused by it.'

'I see I did well to retire.'

'Retire! . . . Sooner or later, old man, willy-nilly, one always has to end by retiring. This wise reflection naturally leads me to take my leave.'

'Stop a moment, you old clown. . . . What made you say just now that your father played the part of pastor? Don't you think he is in earnest?'

'My revered father has so arranged his life that he hasn't the right now – or even the power – not to be in earnest. Yes, it's his profession to be in earnest. He's a professor of earnestness. He inculcates faith; it's his *raison d'être*; it's the role he has chosen and he must go through with it to the very end. But as for knowing what goes on in what he calls his "inner consciousness" . . . it would be indiscreet to inquire. And I don't think he ever inquires himself. He manages in such a way that he never has time to. He has crammed his life full of a lot of obligations which would lose all meaning if his conviction failed; so that in a manner they necessitate his conviction and at the same time keep it going. He imagines he believes, because he continues to act as if he did. If his faith failed, my dear fellow, why, it would be a catastrophic collapse! And reflect, that at the same time my family would cease to have anything to live on. That's a fact that must be taken into consideration, old boy. Papa's faith is our means of subsistence. So that to come and ask me if Papa's faith is genuine, is not, you must admit, a very tactful proceeding on your part.'

'I thought you lived chiefly on what the school brings in.'

'Yes; there's some truth in that. But that's not very tactful either – to cut me short in my lyrical flights.'

'And you then? Don't you believe in anything?' asked Olivier sadly, for he was fond of Armand, and his ugliness pained him.

'*Jubes renovare dolorem*.... You seem to forget, my dear friend, that my parents wanted to make a pastor of me. They nourished me on pious precepts – fed me up with them, if I may say so.... But finally they were obliged to recognize that I hadn't the vocation. It's a pity. I might have made a first-class preacher. But my vocation was to write *The Nocturnal Vase*.'

'You poor old thing! If you knew how sorry I am for you!'

'You have always had what my father calls "a heart of gold". ... I won't trespass on it any longer.'

He took up his hat. He had almost left the room, when he suddenly turned round:

'You haven't asked after Sarah?'

'Because you could tell me nothing that I haven't heard from Bernard.'

'Did he tell you that he had left the pension?'

'He told me that your sister Rachel had requested him to leave.'

Armand had one hand on the door handle; with his walking-stick in the other, he pushed up the *portière*. The stick went into a hole in the *portière* and made it bigger.

'Account for it how you will,' said he, and his face became very grave. 'Rachel is, I believe, the only person in the world I love and respect. I respect her because she is virtuous. And I always behave in such a way as to offend her virtue. As for Bernard and Sarah, she had no suspicions. It was I who told her the whole thing.... And the oculist said she wasn't to cry! It's comic!'

'Am I to think you sincere now?'

'Yes, I think the most sincere thing about me is a horror – a hatred of everything people call Virtue. Don't try to understand. You have no idea what a Puritan bringing-up can do to one. It leaves one with an incurable resentment in one's heart . . . to judge by myself,' he added, with a jarring laugh.

He put down his hat and went up to the window. 'Just look here; on the inside of my lip?'

He stooped towards Olivier and lifted up his lip with his finger.

'I can't see anything.'

'Yes, you can; there; in the corner.'

Olivier saw a whitish spot near the corner. A little uneasily: 'It's a gumboil,' he said to reassure Armand.

But Armand shrugged his shoulders.

'Don't talk nonsense – such a serious fellow as you! A gumboil's soft and it goes away. This is hard and gets larger every week. And it gives me a kind of bad taste in my mouth.'

'Have you had it long?'

'It's more than a month since I first noticed it. But as the *chef-d'œuvre* says: "*Mon mal vient de plus loin. . . .*"'

'Well, old boy, if you're anxious about it, you had better consult a doctor.'

'You don't suppose I needed your advice for that.'

'What did he say?'

'I didn't need your advice to say to myself that I ought to consult a doctor. But all the same, I didn't consult one, because if it's what I think, I prefer not to know it.'

'It's idiotic.'

'Isn't it stupid? But so human, my friend, so human. . . .'

'The idiotic thing is not to be treated for it.'

'So that when one *is* treated, one can always say: "Too late!" That's what Cob-Lafleur expresses so well in one of his poems which you'll see in the review:

> '"*Il faut se rendre à l'évidence;*
> *Car, dans ce bas monde, la danse*
> *Précède souvent la chanson.*"'

'One can make literature out of anything.'

'Just so; out of anything. But, dear friend, it's not so easy as all that. Well, good-bye. ... Oh! there's one thing more I wanted to tell you. I've heard from Alexandre. ... Yes, you know – my eldest brother, who ran away to Africa. He began by coming to grief over his business and running through all the money Rachel sent him. He's settled now on the banks of the Casamance; and he has written to say that things are doing well and that he'll soon be able to pay everything back.'

'What kind of a business?'

'Heaven knows! Rubber, ivory, Negroes perhaps ... a lot of odds and ends. ... He has asked me to go out to him.'

'Will you go?'

'I would tomorrow, if it weren't for my military service. Alexandre is a kind of donkey, something in my style. I think I should get on with him very well. ... Here! would you like to see? I've got his letter with me.'

He took an envelope out of his pocket, and several sheets of notepaper out of the envelope; he chose one, and held it out to Olivier.

'There's no need to read it all. Begin here.'

Olivier read:

'For the last fortnight, I have been living in company wth a singular individual whom I have taken into my hut. The sun of these parts seems to have touched him in the upper story. I thought at first it was delirium, but there's no doubt it's just plain madness. This curious young man is about thirty years old, tall, strong, good-looking, and certainly "a gentleman", to judge from his manners, his language, and his hands, which are too delicate ever to have done any rough work. The strange thing about him is that he thinks himself possessed by the devil – or rather, as far as I can make out, he thinks he *is* the devil. He must have had some odd adventure or other, for when he is dreaming or half dozing, a state into which he often falls (and then he talks to himself as if I weren't there) he continually speaks of hands being cut off, and as at those times he gets extremely excited and rolls his eyes in an alarming manner, I take care that there shall be no weapons within reach. The rest of the time, he is a good fellow and an agreeable companion – which I appreciate, as you can imagine, after months of solitude. Besides which, he is of great assistance to me in my work. He never speaks of his past life, so that I can't succeed in discovering who he can be. He is particularly interested in plants and insects, and sometimes in his talk shows signs of being remarkably well educated. He seems to like staying with me and doesn't speak of leaving; I have decided to let him stay as long as he likes. I was wanting a help; all things considered, he has come just in the nick of time.

'A hideous Negro who came up the Casamance with him, and to whom I have talked a little, speaks of a woman who was with him, and who, I gather, must have been drowned in the river one day when their boat upset. I shouldn't be surprised to learn that my companion had had a finger in the accident. In this country, if one wants to get rid of anyone, there is a great choice of means, and no one ever asks a question. If one day I learn anything more, I'll write it to you – or rather I'll tell you about it when you come out. Yes, I know, there's your service.... Well, I'll wait. For you may be sure that if ever you want to see me again, you will have to make up your mind to come out. As for me, I want to come back less and less. I lead a life here which I like and which suits me down to the ground. My business is flourishing, and that badge of civilization – the starched collar – appears to me a straight waistcoat which I shall never be able to endure again.

'I enclose a money order which you can do what you like with. The last was for Rachel. Keep this for yourself....'

'The rest isn't interesting,' said Armand.

Olivier gave the letter back without saying anything. It never occurred to him that the murderer it spoke of was his brother. Vincent had given no news of himself for a long time; his parents thought he was in America. To tell the truth, Olivier did not trouble much about him.

18

'THE STRONG MEN'

It was only a month later that Boris heard of Bronja's death from Madame Sophroniska, who came to see him at the pension. Since his friend's last sad letter, Boris had been without news. Madame Sophroniska came into Madame Vedel's drawing-room one day when he was sitting there, as was his habit during recreation hour, and as she was in deep mourning, he understood everything before she said a word. They were alone in the room. Sophroniska took Boris in her arms and they cried together. She could only repeat: 'My poor little thing. . . . My poor little thing . . .' as if Boris was the person to be pitied, and as though she had forgotten her own maternal grief in the presence of the immense grief of the little boy.

Madame Vedel, who had been told of Madame Sophroniska's arrival, came in, and Boris, still convulsed with sobs, drew aside to let the two ladies talk to each other. He would have liked them not to speak of Bronja. Madame Vedel, who had not known her, spoke of her as she would of any ordinary child. Even the questions which she asked seemed to Boris tactless and common-place. He would have liked Sophroniska not to answer them and it hurt him to see her exhibiting her grief. He folded his away and hid it like a treasure.

It was certainly of him that Bronja was thinking when, a few days before her death, she said to her mother:

'Do tell me, Mamma. . . . What is meant exactly by an *idyll*?'

These words pierced Boris's heart and he would have liked to be the only one to hear them.

Madame Vedel offered her guest tea. There was some for Boris, too; he swallowed it hastily as recreation was finishing; then he said good-bye to Sophroniska, who was leaving next day for Poland on business.

The whole world seemed a desert to him. His mother was too far away and always absent; his grandfather too old; even Bernard, with whom he was beginning to feel at home, had gone away. . . . His was a tender soul; he had need of someone at whose feet he could lay his nobility, his purity, as an offering. He was not proud enough to take pleasure in pride. He had loved Bronja too much to be able to hope that he would ever again find that reason for loving which he had lost in her. Without her, how could he believe in the angels he longed to see? Heaven itself was emptied.

Boris went back to the schoolroom as one might cast oneself into hell. No doubt he might have made a friend of Gontran de Passavant; Gontran is a good, kind boy, and they are both exactly the same age; but nothing distracts him from his work. There is not much harm in Philippe Adamanti either; he would be quite willing to be fond of Boris; but he is under Ghéridanisol's thumb to such an extent that he does not dare have a single feeling of his own; he follows Ghéridanisol's lead, and Ghéridanisol is always quickening his pace; and Ghéridanisol cannot endure Boris. His musical voice, his grace, his girlish look – everything about him exasperates him. The very sight of Boris seems to inspire him with that instinctive aversion which, in a herd, makes the strong fall ruthlessly upon the weak. It may be that he has listened to his cousin's teaching and that his hatred is somewhat theoretical, for in his mind it assumes the shape of reprobation. He finds reasons for being proud of his hatred. He realizes and is amused by Boris's sensitiveness to this contempt of his, and pretends to be plotting with George and Phiphi, merely in order to see Boris's eyes grow wide with a kind of anxious interrogation.

'Oh, how inquisitive the fellow is!' says George then. 'Shall we tell him?'

'Not worth while. He wouldn't understand.'

'He wouldn't understand.' 'He wouldn't dare.' 'He wouldn't know how.' They are constantly casting these phrases at him. He suffers horribly from being kept out of things. He cannot understand, indeed, why they give him the humiliating nickname of 'Wanting'; and is indignant when he understands. What would he not give to be able to prove that he is not such a coward as they think.

'I cannot endure Boris,' said Ghéridanisol one day to Strouvilhou. 'Why did you tell me to let him alone? He doesn't want to be let alone as much as all that. He is always looking in my direction. . . . The other day he made us all split with laughter because he thought that a woman togged out in her bearskin meant wearing her furs. George jeered at him, and when at last Boris took it in I thought he was going to howl.'

Then Ghéridanisol pressed his cousin with questions and finally Strouvilhou gave him Boris's *talisman* and explained its use.

A few days later, when Boris went into the schoolroom, he saw this paper, whose existence he had almost forgotten, lying on his desk. He had put it out of his mind with everything else that related to the 'magic' of his early childhood, of which he was now ashamed. He did not at first recognize it, for Ghéridanisol had taken pains to frame the words of the incantation.

'GAS . . . TELEPHONE . . . ONE HUNDRED THOUSAND ROUBLES'

with a large red and black border adorned with obscene little imps, who, it must be owned, were not at all badly drawn. This decoration gave the paper a fantastic – an infernal appearance, thought Ghéridanisol – which he calculated would be likely to upset Boris.

Perhaps it was done in play, but it succeeded beyond all expectation. Boris blushed crimson, said nothing, looked right and left, and failed to see Ghéridanisol, who was watching him from behind the door. Boris had no reason to suspect him, and could not understand how the talisman came to be there; it was as though it had fallen from heaven – or rather, risen up from hell. Boris was old enough to shrug his shoulders, no doubt, at these schoolboy bedevilments; but they stirred troubled waters. Boris took the talisman and slipped it into his pocket. All the rest of the day, the recollection of his 'magic' practices haunted him. He struggled until evening with unholy solicitations and then, as there was no longer anything to support him in his struggle, he fell.

He felt that he was going to his ruin, sinking farther and

farther away from Heaven; but he took pleasure in so falling – found in his very fall itself the stuff of his enjoyment.

And yet, in spite of his misery, in the depths of his dereliction, he kept such stores of tenderness, his companions' contempt caused him suffering so keen, that he would have dared anything, however dangerous, however foolhardy, for the sake of a little consideration.

An opportunity soon offered.

After they had been obliged to give up their traffic in false coins, Ghéridanisol, George and Phiphi did not long remain unoccupied. The ridiculous pranks with which they amused themselves for the first few days were merely stop-gaps. Ghéridanisol's imagination soon invented something with more stuff to it.

The chief point about *The Brotherhood of Strong Men* at first consisted in the pleasure of keeping Boris out of it. But it soon occurred to Ghéridanisol that it would be far more perversely effective to let him in; he could be brought in this way to enter into engagements, by means of which he might gradually be led on to the performance of some monstrous act. From that moment Ghéridanisol was possessed by this idea; and as often happens in all kinds of enterprises, he thought much less of the object itself, than of how to bring it about; this seems trifling, but is perhaps the explanation of a considerable number of crimes. For that matter Ghéridanisol was ferocious; but he felt it prudent to hide his ferocity, at any rate from Phiphi. There was nothing cruel about Phiphi; he was convinced up to the last minute that the whole thing was nothing but a joke.

Every brotherhood must have its motto. Ghéridanisol, who had his idea, proposed: '*The strong man cares nothing for life.*' The motto was adopted and attributed to Cicero. George proposed that, as a sign of fellowship, they should tattoo it on their right arms; but Phiphi, who was afraid of being hurt, declared that good tattooers could only be found in seaports. Besides which, Ghéridanisol objected that tattooing would leave an indelible mark which might be inconvenient later on. After all, the sign of fellowship was not an absolute necessity; the members would content themselves with taking a solemn vow.

At the moment of starting the traffic in false coins, there had been talk of pledges, and it was on this occasion that George had produced his father's letters. But this idea had dropped. Such children as these, very fortunately, have not much consistency. As a matter of fact, they settled practically nothing, either as to 'conditions of membership' or as to 'necessary qualifications'. What was the use, when it was taken for granted that all three of them were 'in it', and that Boris was 'out of it'? On the other hand they decreed that 'the person who flinched should be considered as a traitor, and forever excluded from the brotherhood'. Ghéridanisol, who had determined to make Boris come in, laid great stress upon this point.

It had to be admitted that without Boris the game would have been dull and the virtue of the brotherhood without an object. George was better qualified to circumvent him than Ghéridanisol, who risked arousing his suspicions; as for Phiphi he was not artful enough and had a dislike to compromising himself.

And in all this abominable story, what perhaps seems to me the most monstrous, is this comedy of friendship which George went through. He pretended to be seized with a sudden affection for Boris; until then, he had seemed never so much as to have set eyes on him. And I even wonder whether he was not himself influenced by his own acting, and whether the feelings he feigned were not on the point of becoming sincere – whether they did not actually become sincere as soon as Boris responded to them. George drew near him with an appearance of tenderness; in obedience to Ghéridanisol, he began to talk to him.... And, at the first words, Boris, who was panting for a little esteem and love, was conquered.

Then Ghéridanisol elaborated his plan, and disclosed it to Phiphi and George. His idea was to invent a 'test' to which the member on whom the lot fell should be submitted; and in order to set Phiphi at ease, he let it be understood that things would be arranged in such a manner that the lot would be sure to fall on Boris. The object of the test would be to put his courage to the proof.

The exact nature of the test, Ghéridanisol did not at once

divulge. He was afraid that Phiphi would offer some resistance.

And, in fact, when Ghéridanisol a little later began to insinuate that old La Pérouse's pistol would come in handy, 'No, no!' he cried, 'I won't agree to that.'

'What an ass you are! It's only a joke,' retorted George, who was already persuaded.

'And then, you know,' added Ghéri, 'if you want to play the fool, you have only got to say so. Nobody wants you.'

Ghéridanisol knew that this argument always told with Phiphi; and as he had prepared the paper on which each member of the brotherhood was to sign his name, he went on: 'Only you must say so at once; because once you've signed, it'll be too late.'

'All right. Don't be in a rage,' said Phiphi. 'Pass me the paper.' And he signed.

'As for me, old chap, I'd be delighted,' said George, with his arm fondly wound round Boris's neck; 'it's Ghéridanisol who won't have you.'

'Why not?'

'Because he's afraid. He says you'll funk.'

'What does he know about it?'

'That you'll wriggle out of it at the first test.'

'We shall see.'

'Would you really dare to draw lots?'

'Wouldn't I!'

'But do you know what you're letting yourself in for?'

Boris didn't know, but he wanted to. Then George explained. '*The strong man cares nothing for life.*' It remained to be seen.

Boris felt a great swimming in his head; but he nerved himself and, hiding his agitation, 'Is it true you've signed?' he asked.

'Here! You can see for yourself.' And George held out the paper, so that Boris could read the three names on it.

'Have you . . .' he began timidly.

'Have we what? . . .' interrupted George, so brutally that Boris did not dare go on. What he wanted to ask, as George perfectly understood, was whether the others had bound themselves likewise, and whether one could be sure that they wouldn't funk either.

'No, nothing,' said he; but from that moment he began to doubt them; he began to suspect they were saving themselves and not playing fair. 'Well and good!' thought he then; 'what do I care if they funk? I'll show them that I've got more pluck than they have.' Then, looking George straight in the eyes: 'Tell Ghéri he can count on me.'

'Then you'll sign?'

Oh! there was no need now – he had given his word. He said simply: 'As you please.' And, in a large painstaking hand, he inscribed his name on the accursed paper, underneath the signatures of the three Strong Men.

George brought the paper back in triumph to the two others. They agreed that Boris had behaved very pluckily. They took counsel together.

Of course, the pistol wouldn't be loaded! For that matter there were no cartridges. Phiphi still had fears, because he had heard it said that sometimes a too violent emotion is sufficient in itself to cause death. His father, he declared, knew of a case when a pretence execution . . . But George shut him up:

'Your father's a dago!'

No, Ghéridanisol would not load the pistol. There was no need to. The cartridge which La Pérouse had one day put into it, La Pérouse had not taken out. This is what Ghéridanisol had made sure of, though he took good care not to tell the others.

They put the names in a hat; four little pieces of paper all alike, and folded in the same manner. Ghéridanisol, who was 'to draw', had taken care to write Boris's name a second time on a fifth, which he kept in his hand; and, as though by chance, his was the name to come out. Boris suspected they were cheating; but he said nothing. What was the use of protesting? He knew that he was lost. He would not have lifted a finger to defend himself; and even if the lot had fallen on one of the others, he would have offered to take his place – so great was his despair.

'Poor old boy! you've no luck,' George thought it his duty to say. The tone of his voice rang so false, that Boris looked at him sadly.

'It was bound to happen,' he said.

After that, it was agreed there should be a rehearsal. But as there was a risk of being caught, they settled not to make use of the pistol. They would only take it out of its case at the last moment, for the *real* performance. Every care must be taken not to give the alarm.

On that day, therefore, they contented themselves with fixing the hour, and the place, which they marked on the floor with a bit of chalk. It was in the classroom, on the right hand of the master's desk, in a recess, formed by a disused door, which had formerly opened on to the entrance hall. As for the hour, it was to be during preparation. It was to take place in front of all the other boys; it would make them sit up.

They went through the rehearsal when the room was empty, the three conspirators being the only witnesses. But in reality there was not much point in this rehearsal. They simply established the fact that, from Boris's seat to the spot marked with chalk, there were exactly twelve paces.

'If you aren't in a panic, you'll not take one more,' said George.

'I shan't be in a panic,' said Boris, who was outraged by this incessant doubt. The little boy's firmness began to impress the other three. Phiphi considered they ought to stop at that. But Ghéridanisol was determined to carry on the joke to the very end.

'Tomorrow!' he said, with a peculiar smile, which just curled the corner of his lip.

'Suppose we kissed him!' cried Phiphi, enthusiastically. He was thinking of the accolade of the knights of old; and he suddenly flung his arms round Boris's neck. It was all Boris could do to keep back his tears when Phiphi planted two hearty, childish kisses on his cheeks. Neither George nor Ghéri followed Phiphi's example; George thought his behaviour rather unmanly. As for Ghéri, what the devil did he care! . . .

19

BORIS

THE next afternoon, the bell assembled all the boys in the classroom.

Boris, Ghéridanisol, George and Philippe were seated on the same bench. Ghéridanisol pulled out his watch and put it down between Boris and him. The hands marked five thirty-five. Preparation began at five o'clock and lasted till six. Five minutes to six was the moment fixed upon for Boris to put an end to himself, just before the boys dispersed; it was better so; it would be easier to escape immediately after. And soon Ghéridanisol said to Boris, in a half whisper, and without looking at him, which gave his words, he considered, a more fatal ring:

'Old boy, you've only got a quarter of an hour more.'

Boris remembered a story-book he had read long ago, in which, when the robbers were on the point of putting a woman to death, they told her to say her prayers, so as to convince her she must get ready to die. As a foreigner who, on arriving at the frontier of the country he is leaving, prepares his papers, so Boris searched his heart and head for prayers, and could find none; but he was at once so tired and so over-strung, that he did not trouble much. He tried to think, but could not. The pistol weighed in his pocket; he had no need to put his hand on it to feel it there.

'Only ten minutes more.'

George, sitting on Ghéridanisol's left, watched the scene out of the corner of his eye, pretending all the while not to see. He was working feverishly. The class had never been so quiet. La Pérouse hardly knew his young rascals and for the first time was able to breathe. Philippe, however, was not at ease; Ghéridanisol frightened him; he was not very confident the game mightn't turn out badly; his heart was bursting; it hurt him, and every now and then he heard himself heave a deep sigh. At last, he could bear it no longer, and tearing a half sheet of paper out of his copy-book (he was preparing an examination, but the lines danced before his eyes, and the facts and dates in his head) scribbled on it very quickly: 'Are you quite sure the pistol isn't loaded?'; then gave the note to George, who passed it to Ghéri. But Ghéri, after he had read it, raised his shoulders, without even glancing at Phiphi; then, screwing the note up into a ball, sent it rolling with a flick of his finger till it landed on the very spot which had been marked with chalk. After which, satisfied with the excellence of his aim, he smiled. This smile, which began by being deliberate, remained fixed till the end of the scene; it seemed to have been imprinted on his features.

'Five minutes more.'

He said it almost aloud. Even Philippe heard. He was overwhelmed by a sickening and intolerable anxiety, and though the hour was just coming to an end, he feigned an urgent need to leave the room – or was perhaps seized with perfectly genuine colic. He raised his hand and snapped his fingers, as boys do when they want to ask permission from the master; then, without waiting for La Pérouse to answer, he darted from his bench. In order to reach the door he had to pass in front of the master's desk; he almost ran, tottering as he did so.

Almost immediately after Philippe had left the room, Boris rose in his turn. Young Passavant, who was sitting behind him, working diligently, raised his eyes. He told Séraphine afterwards that Boris was frightfully pale; but that is what is always said on these occasions. As a matter of fact, he stopped looking almost at once and plunged again into his work. He reproached himself for it bitterly later. If he had understood what was going on, he would certainly have been able to prevent it; so he said afterwards, weeping. But he had no suspicions.

So Boris stepped forward to the appointed place; he walked slowly, like an automaton – or rather like a somnambulist. He had grasped the pistol in his right hand, but still kept it in the pocket of his coat; he took it out only at the last moment. The fatal place was, as I have said, in the recess made by a disused door on the right of the master's desk, so that the master could only see it by leaning forward.

La Pérouse leant forward. And at first he did not understand what his grandson was doing, though the strange solemnity of his actions was of a nature to alarm him. Speaking as loudly and as authoritatively as he could, he began:

'Master Boris, kindly return at once to your...'

But he suddenly recognized the pistol: Boris had just raised it to his temple. La Pérouse understood and immediately turned icy cold as if the blood were freezing in his veins. He tried to rise and run towards Boris – stop him – call to him.... A kind of hoarse rattle came from his throat; he remained rooted to the spot, paralytic, shaken by a violent trembling.

The shot went off. Boris did not drop at once. The body stayed upright for a moment, as though caught in the corner of the recess; then the head, falling on to the shoulder, bore it down; it collapsed.

When the police made their inquiry a little later, they were astonished not to find the pistol near Boris's body – near the place, I mean, where he fell, for the little corpse was carried away almost immediately and laid upon a bed. In the confusion which followed, while Ghéridanisol had remained in his place, George had leapt over his bench and succeeded in making away with the weapon, without anyone's noticing him; while the others were bending over Boris, he had first of all pushed it backwards with his foot, seized it with a rapid movement, hidden it under his coat, and then surreptitiously passed it to Ghéridanisol. Everyone's attention being fixed on a single point, no one noticed Ghéridanisol either, and he was able to run unperceived to La Pérouse's room and put the pistol back in the place from which he had taken it. When, in the course of a later investigation, the police discovered the pistol in its case, it might have seemed doubtful whether it had ever left it, or whether Boris had used it, had Ghéridanisol only remembered to remove the empty cartridge. He certainly lost his head a little – a passing weakness, for which, I regret to say, he reproached himself far more than for the crime itself. And yet it was this weakness which saved him. For when he came down and mixed with the others, at the sight of Boris's dead body being carried away, he was seized with a fit of trembling, which was obvious to everyone – a kind of nervous attack – which Madame Vedel and Rachel, who had hurried to the spot, mistook for a sign of excessive emotion. One prefers to suppose anything, rather than the inhumanity of so young a creature; and when Ghéridanisol protested his innocence, he was believed. Phiphi's little note, which George had passed him and which he had flicked away with his finger, was found later under a bench and also contributed to help him. True, he remained guilty, as did George and Phiphi, of having lent himself to a cruel game, but he would not have done so, he declared, if he had thought the weapon was loaded. George was the only one who remained convinced of his entire responsibility.

George was not so corrupted but that his admiration for Ghéridanisol yielded at last to horror. When he reached home that evening, he flung himself into his mother's arms; and Pauline had a burst of gratitude to God, who by means of this dreadful tragedy had brought her son back to her.

20
EDOUARD'S JOURNAL

WITHOUT exactly pretending to explain anything, I shall not like to put forward any fact which was not accounted for by a sufficiency of motive. And for that reason I shall not make use of little Boris's suicide for my *Counterfeiters*; I have too much difficulty in understanding it. And then, I dislike police court items. There is something peremptory, irrefutable, brutal, outrageously real about them. . . . I accept reality coming as a proof in support of my thought, but not as preceding it. It displeases me to be surprised. Boris's suicide seems to me an *indecency*, for I was not expecting it.

A little cowardice enters into every suicide, notwithstanding La Pérouse, who no doubt thinks his grandson was more courageous than he. If the child could have foreseen the disaster which his dreadful action has brought upon the Vedels, there would be no excuse for him. Azaïs has been obliged to break up the school – for the time being, he says; but Rachel is afraid of ruin. Four families have already removed their children. I have not been able to dissuade Pauline from taking George away, so that she may keep him at home with her; especially as the boy has been profoundly shaken by his schoolfellow's death, and seems inclined to reform. What repercussions this calamity has had! Even Olivier is touched by it. Armand, notwithstanding his cynical airs, feels such anxiety at the ruin which is threatening his family, that he has offered to devote the time that Passavant leaves him, to working in the school, for old La Pérouse has become manifestly incapable of doing what is required of him.

I dreaded seeing him again. It was in his little bedroom on the second floor of the pension, that he received me. He took me by the arm at once, and with a mysterious, almost a smiling air, which greatly surprised me, for I was expecting tears:

'That noise,' he said, 'you know . . . the noise I told you about the other day . . .'

'Well?'

'It has stopped – finished. I don't hear it any more, however much I listen.'

As one humours a child, 'I wager,' said I, 'that now you regret it.'

'Oh! no; no. . . . It's such a rest. I am so much in need of silence. Do you know what I've been thinking? That in this life we can't know what real silence is. Even our blood makes a kind of continual noise; we don't notice it, because we have become accustomed to it ever since our childhood. . . . But I think there are things in life which we can't succeed in hearing – harmonies . . . because this noise drowns them. Yes, I think it's only after our death that we shall really be able to hear.'

'You told me you didn't believe . . .'

'In the immortality of the soul? Did I tell you that? . . . Yes; I suppose I did. But I don't believe the contrary either, you know.'

And as I was silent, he went on, nodding his head and with a sententious air:

'Have you noticed that in this world God always keeps silent? It's only the devil who speaks. Or at least, at least . . .' he went on, '. . . however carefully we listen, it's only the devil we can succeed in hearing. We have not the ears to hear the voice of God. The word of God! Have you ever wondered what it is like? . . . Oh! I don't mean the word that has been transferred into human language. . . . You remember the Gospel: "In the beginning was the Word." I have often thought that the word of God was the whole of creation. But the devil seized hold of it. His noise drowns the voice of God. Oh! tell me, don't you think that all the same it's God who will end by having the last word? . . . And if, after death, time no longer exists, if we enter at once into Eternity, do you think we shall be able to hear God then . . . directly?'

A kind of transport began to shake him, as if he were going to fall down in convulsions, and he was suddenly seized by a fit of sobbing.

'No, no!' he cried, confusedly; 'the devil and God are one and the same; they work together. We try to believe that everything bad on earth comes from the devil, but it's because, if we didn't, we should never find strength to forgive God. He plays with us like a cat, tormenting a mouse.... And then afterwards he wants us to be grateful to him as well. Grateful for what? for what?...'

Then, leaning towards me:

'Do you know the most horrible thing of all that he has done?... Sacrificed his own son to save us. His son! his son! ... Cruelty! that's the principal attribute of God.'

He flung himself on his bed and turned his face to the wall. For a few moments a spasmodic shudder ran through him; then, as he seemed to have fallen asleep, I left him.

He had not said a word to me about Boris; but I thought that in this mystical despair was to be seen the expression of a grief too blinding to be looked at steadfastly.

I hear from Olivier that Bernard has gone back to his father's; and, indeed, it was the best thing he could do. When he learnt, from a chance meeting with Caloub, that the old judge was not well, Bernard followed the impulse of his heart. We shall meet tomorrow evening, for Profitendieu has invited me to dinner with Molinier, Pauline and the two boys. I feel very curious to know Caloub.

Albert Camus

THE OUTSIDER

The Outsider, by Nobel Prizewinner Albert Camus, is considered to be one of the most important modern French novels, and is the forerunner of a great deal of contemporary writing.

Meursault is a young man who works as a clerk in Algiers. He lives in the usual manner of a French-Algerian, middle-class bachelor – cooking his evening meal for himself in his small flat, sleeping with his girl at the weekends, bathing, going to the pictures. But he has a glaring fault in the eyes of society – he seems to lack the basic emotions and reactions (including hypocrisy) that are required of him. He observes the facts of life, death, and sex from the outside. Even when he is involved in a personal tragedy which results in a frightening and unjust trial, he considers his own feelings and the actions of others with a calm and almost ironic truthfulness.

'A book so well written and profoundly disturbing that it is in a class by itself . . . Seldom have I read a work which says so much in so short a space' – John Betjeman

'Exciting, uncomfortable, and queerly impressive' – *Sunday Times*

and

EXILE AND THE KINGDOM

THE FALL

THE PLAGUE

A HAPPY DEATH

André Gide

THE IMMORALIST

This is the story of a man's rebellion against social and sexual conformity. The narrator is Michel – a rich, young, agnostic scholar who has just married and gone to stay with his wife in Algeria. Finding that he has tuberculosis, he gradually changes his life, abandoning the aspects of morality which restrict him, and following his own wants and needs.

This development is the author's theme, but it does not obscure the other characters in the novel: Michel's wife Marceline, various members of Parisian society, the youths on his estate in the country, and Arab boys.

The problems which are posed in *The Immoralist* are ones which exercised Gide himself in his own life – how deep is the protective veneer of civilization, and, to what extent should a man follow his own desires when they conflict with society?

André Gide

LA SYMPHONIE PASTORALE and ISABELLE

Though in length it is only a *nouvelle*, *La Symphonie Pastorale*, in which Gide showed profane love in conflict with Christian charity, is rated by some critics with *The Counterfeiters* or *The Immoralist*. This brief story is recounted in excerpts from the diary of a Protestant country priest who has removed a blind and seemingly deaf and dumb girl from a wretched home. Taught with care and patience in his own family the girl learns to speak, but in the meantime a subtle change has come over their relations. The priest's regard for his charge has deepened into feelings which are no longer merely paternal. When at length her sight is restored to her by an operation, she looks out on a world more beautiful than in blindness she had ever conceived, and straight into the eyes of a truth which forces the story to its tragic climax.

The notable strength and involvement which mark the story can be traced to the spiritual crisis through which the author was passing when he wrote it.

The atmosphere of a legendary romance lingers round the tale of *Isabelle*, in which a young scholar, set down among the eccentric inhabitants of an old Norman château, erects a dream on a glimpse of a lovely miniature and lives to see his dreams turn sour.

André Gide

STRAIT IS THE GATE

Strait is the Gate, a story of young love blighted and turned to tragedy by the sense of religious dedication in the beloved, is regarded by many as the most perfect piece of writing which Gide ever achieved. In its simplicity, its craftsmanship, its limpidity of style and its power to stimulate the mind and the emotions at one and the same time, it set a standard for the short novel which has not yet been excelled.

THE VATICAN CELLARS

The action of *The Vatican Cellars* takes place in the late nineteenth century, chiefly in Paris and Rome. This strange drama involves the alleged abduction of the Pope, a 'miraculous' conversion, swindling, adultery, bastardy, and murder. The characters are a motley crew of noblemen, saints, adventurers, and pickpockets, and – Lafcadio Wluiki. This picaresque Lafcadio, one of the most original creations in twentieth-century fiction, at once attracts and repels; he is the instrument through whom Gide works out his idea of the unmotivated crime, a theme which constantly occupied him, which in this book receives its fullest treatment.